Melissa
470-795

The triumphant return of
ROSEMARY ROGERS

Other Avon Books by
Rosemary Rogers

BOUND BY DESIRE
DARK FIRES
THE INSIDERS
LOST LOVE, LAST LOVE
SURRENDER TO LOVE
SWEET SAVAGE LOVE
THE WANTON
WICKED LOVING LIES
THE WILDEST HEART

ROSEMARY ROGERS

The TEA PLANTER'S BRIDE

AVON BOOKS ◆ NEW YORK

THE TEA PLANTER'S BRIDE is an original publication of Avon Books. This work has never before appeared in book form. This work is a novel. Any similarity to actual persons or events is purely coincidental.

AVON BOOKS
A division of
The Hearst Corporation
1350 Avenue of the Americas
New York, New York 10019

First Avon Books Printing: May 1995

One

England, 1892

She had been bending over, brushing her hair forward, and suddenly she straightened up and sent a tumbled cloud of night-black curls flying backward as she frowned challengingly at her reflection in the mirror.

The image of a Gypsy frowned back. In that one instant she forgot every stricture her aunt Gertrude had pounded into her head about smoothing out the frown lines that might cause wrinkles. In that one telling moment she looked, she felt, every bit as exotic as Aunt Gertrude constantly told her she was.

And Aunt Gertrude had been particularly virulent this afternoon as she had made conversation with her friends over tea in the rose garden below her niece's window, totally oblivious of the fact she might be able to hear every word.

Oh, she had heard. She had heard every blistering word that had once more ridiculed her resemblance to her mother, Marianna, the beautiful and passionate Spanish Gypsy who had lost her head and her heart to an English adventurer.

"I'm sure that in the end—with the right influences, of course—the child will turn out well enough," Aunt Gertrude had said with excruciating piety. "But it is a pity that with her *looks*—well, I suppose she cannot help the fact she has such—well—*singular* features. That mane of black hair—and those copper colored eyes . . . just like the eyes of that ugly black cat of ours who follows her everywhere. I can't help wishing she had taken more after Richard in looks rather than that *foreigner* mother of hers. Although one doesn't want to be uncharitable, does one?"

Dear, so-benevolent Aunt Gertrude, who never let anyone forget that she was a bishop's wife and a lady in her own right. Aunt Gertrude with her tall angular body, pinched face, gimlet eyes, and suspiciously dark hair, who excelled in Good Works.

Aunt Gertrude, who had decided that Celia must call her "aunt" as a courtesy, though Celia could never understand why, given Aunt Gertrude's antagonism toward her family.

Sometimes Celia Marianna Penmaris felt as if she had two selves—the outside self that everyone else saw, and a secret self that only she knew about and hid so well that she was able to play the role that was demanded of her by society even though she felt this powerful division within herself.

She understood very well that by bringing her to England to her home at the Grange, her aunt had done what she had determined was in her best interests to assure her future. She had had the right schooling and had come of age in the correct and cloistered atmosphere that ensured she would eventually make a good marriage.

But all of that meant she had had to subdue her much-deplored unusual looks—she couldn't help her olive complexion or the color of her eyes or the texture of her hair—nor her height, either, in a society where men doted on tiny doll-like women and she towered over them all at five foot eight.

And she wondered, so often, if her mother had felt like this when she had given up her glamorous life as a dancer and the toast of Europe to marry Celia's proper English father.

Had she been forced and betrayed just as her own daughter had been forced into leaving her beloved plantation home in the hills of Ceylon and brought here to cold confinement in England, where she had to learn to hide her real feelings under a kind of submissive civility?

When Marianna had looked in the mirror, had she seen the same flushed cheeks, the same glowing eyes, the same sensuous curve of the lips that were so *abominably* different from those of the stiff-necked, high-cheekboned girls Celia knew?

Did it really, really matter as much as Aunt Gertrude thought it did?

It didn't seem to matter to Ronald Winwood.

Celia smiled as her fingers lightly touched the framed photograph of him that stood close by on her dresser.

It seemed to her that she had always, for as long as she could remember, been in love with Ronald Winwood, whose father had owned the plantation adjoining her father's.

In the old days in Ceylon, he had treated her like a child, like a nuisance sometimes, because of her unabashed adoration of him.

But on that last occasion, when he had returned to England on leave, everything had changed.

He had come from Ceylon with a gift for a child, but he had found instead a self-possessed young woman with whom he'd instantly fallen in love.

They'd been walking in the rose garden at twilight. It had been as if the dream she had sustained all of her life had suddenly turned into blissful reality. Almost as if it were a page from the romantic novels she surreptitiously read.

"You're like a lovely little chrysalis, my Celia," he had whispered to her then. "And I want to be the lucky man who watches that delicate butterfly emerge from her cocoon."

How poetically he had put it. Ronald Winwood—who could have had any woman he wanted—loved *her* and swore he would wait for her as long as he had to. And the locket he had secretly given her that evening still hung warmly on a golden chain between her young breasts as a symbol of their betrothal.

What had Ronald seen in her that night?

Celia narrowed her eyes and attempted a mysterious half smile.

Perhaps her mother's wild Gypsy blood really did pulse in her veins just as Aunt Gertrude believed, and she was capable of enchanting and holding spellbound any man of her choice.

Or perhaps Ronald had merely felt the pull of destiny as strongly as she . . .

A timid knock on the door interrupted her reverie.

"I've come to arrange your hair, miss."

"Come, Alice." Celia moved to her dressing table in almost a trancelike state and settled herself before her mirror. "I think I'll wear it up this evening, Alice."

"Very good, miss," Alice said as she began vigorously brushing the heavy curls.

Yes, that was perfect. Just the way the lady of the house would speak to her servant. After all, it was her composure, her practical mind and her knowledge and understanding of the rigid standards of behavior expected of Englishwomen in the colonies that had prompted Ronald to be so precipitate.

And she would never let him down. She was already preparing herself for their future together. She had even kept up with her studies of Eastern languages, including the Sinhalese and Tamil she had spoken fluently as a child.

Ronald would not find her remiss in any way. And when the time came, he would claim her as his bride and take her back to Ceylon, to the wild and beautiful hill country that she remembered so vividly.

And there, maybe, she could at last feel free to be herself, and nothing Aunt Gertrude could say would ever touch her again.

The telegram that changed her life arrived at the Grange the very next morning, and she was the last to learn of its fateful contents.

A telegram in the country was an unusual event, and it was the butler, Mr. Morris, who carried it to the bishop, who was, fortunately, up early and working on Sunday's sermon in the study.

Having been in his Grace's service for some fifteen years already, Mr. Morris knew exactly how to approach him; he coughed discreetly, paused at the door, then entered and inquired, "If you'll excuse the presumption, your Grace . . . I hope it is not bad news—" as he tendered the envelope.

The bishop opened the telegram somewhat gingerly, perused its contents and uttered a vexed exclamation.

"No—no . . . thank you for your concern, Morris. It is just . . . well, it's going to be quite awkward, I'm afraid. Will you tell Wilson to give this to her ladyship and inform her that we should consult on . . . er . . . well, you might say it's rather an urgent matter."

The bishop was a scholarly man of some fifty years, slender and ascetic, with a smooth-planed face and gentle blue eyes that saw only the good in people. He preferred not to have to confront issues unless his wife insisted. And Gertrude had been horrified, he remembered, when they had visited Ceylon and seen the way his cousin

Richard's only legitimate offspring was being allowed to grow up on an isolated tea plantation far from anything that resembled civilization.

Even he had been quite perturbed when he learned that his unconventional cousin could not remember whether his daughter had been baptised or not. Certainly she had never been taken to church, although the child had been in the habit of visiting both the nearby Buddhist temple and the Hindu Kovil that the Tamil coolies attended.

That had been the final straw and the reason that the bishop, backed by his formidable spouse, had finally confronted Richard and forced him to see that he must think of his daughter's future and her prospects when she reached marriageable age; then the reverend bishop and Lady Gertrude had persuaded him to entrust Celia to their care.

The years slipped by and the monthly bank draft that covered all of Celia's expenses arrived without fail, even after Richard's untimely death; he had been careful and considerate enough to make sure that his daughter was provided for quite handsomely. And beyond that, the bishop, who was really not a very worldly man, had not thought.

Now he was saved from any further introspection as his wife swept into the room with the offending telegram clutched in one thin hand.

"I know he was your cousin, Theo, and did I not encourage you in every way to take the poor child away from that wicked, heathen environment? Was I not, in part, responsible for making poor, dear Richard realize he had a duty to the poor child he had fathered?"

Gertrude had been pacing around her husband's study, and now she turned to look at him, her mouth tightening before she spoke again. "I ask you, Theo—how could he *do* this? To us, to the poor child—just as she has started to grow, under our careful nurturing, into a young lady? And with prospects for a good marriage too, all things considered. So how could he have gone beyond our backs—from the grave, as it were—and consigned his daughter to the guardianship of—of—and *that* in spite of his depraved past!''

She paused, outraged and out of breath, which gave her husband just enough time to interpose mildly, ''But, dearest, his *sister*, after all, is a closer relative and more qualified, perhaps, since she is younger and moves in social circles that *we* do not—''

''Exactly!'' Lady Gertrude snapped. ''That is exactly my point. Since her husband died, Lady Wilhelmina seems to have lost all sense of propriety. She moves in the very fastest society, both here and in Europe as well as in America. I have this on the best authority, although I cannot tell you from *whom* I heard it. The point is that it is completely unsuitable and utterly out of the question, and when she arrives here, I am counting on you, my dear, to explain how damaging it would be to poor Celia to be removed from the stable and protected environment we have provided for her—''

She broke off abruptly because she could have gone on forever on the subject, and it all really boiled down to one thing: Richard Penmaris could not have been in his right mind when he had later sneakily and under-handedly drafted this codicil to his will that made his sister, Wilhelmina, the Dowager Duchess of Millhaven, legal guardian of Celia—and the considerable fortune he had left her when she reached her seventeenth birthday.

Such an addendum would never stand up in court, of course. Theo must naturally make this clear—along with the reminder that it had been *they* who had shown enough concern for Celia's welfare and her future to bring her to England and give her a suitable education and upbringing.

No one else had cared at the time—*no one*.

"I leave it to you, Theo, to be firm—and forceful. Do, please, quote as many times as you can from the Scriptures; you're so very good at that and it never fails to impress. And now, I suppose I should try to prepare Celia for the ordeal she will have to face. It will just kill me to have to offer that creature hospitality. I wish I could be so ill-mannered as to turn her out the moment this thing is settled. But that would reflect badly on *me*."

And with that Lady Gertrude swept out with a determined rustle of petticoats, leaving her husband in a worse quandary than before. Because, Scriptures or not, he had an overwhelming feeling that this was one battle that his formidable wife might not win.

Two

"I'm so nervous. I'm sure I don't know why I should be. Should I be, Mr. Pemberton?" The speaker was a fashionably dressed woman in her thirties, vivacious and attractive with light auburn hair and topaz eyes.

Her companion in the first-class railway compartment was a conservatively dressed older gentleman with graying hair and a carefully clipped beard that made him resemble the Prince of Wales, since he had the same rather portly build. Mr. Pemberton was a well-known London solicitor with a good reputation and expensive fees who was totally discreet.

"It is quite natural that you should be apprehensive about meeting your niece and ward for the first time, your—oh, beg pardon. Mrs. Hamilton, I think you said you preferred to be called? But I can assure you it is all quite cut-and-dried; your brother made quite sure that his wishes as to his daughter's future were made perfectly clear. *You* are the girl's guardian until she reaches her majority, and you—or whomever you might appoint— are in complete control of her inheritance until she is of age."

"Mr. Pemberton . . . I suppose this is a rather awkward

question, but . . . I'm sure you're aware that Richard and I had lost touch with each other for some years . . . but I wonder if he trusted you enough to tell you some of the circumstances of our past—oh, dear!'' She frowned as she realized how awkward this sounded, but before he could do more than raise a deprecating hand, she went on quickly. "I'm making a mess of it, aren't I? But never mind—that question was purely rhetorical, and what I really need to know, if you can tell me, is . . . why do you think Richard had any strong *reason* to feel that Celia might need a different guardian? Is it something to do with her inheritance and the possibility of fortune hunters who might be able to easily influence a child who has been brought up in such a . . . conventional and sheltered fashion?''

Mr. Pemberton shot his companion an approving look from beneath bushy brows. "Very astute, madam. Yes. Well, in the first place, Mr. Penmaris could see the advantages for the child having a proper kind of education here in England. But you are quite correct in thinking that he felt that her being overprotected and—the word *he* used to me was 'stifled'—wasn't in her best interests either. He told me, in fact, that you of all people would understand completely and that you were the only person he could trust to have her best interests at heart and to give her what he termed 'a real education in life.' He said that you would understand perfectly what he meant.''

"Yes,'' Wilhelmina murmured, and lapsed into a faraway silence, looking out of the window. Of course she understood. Dear, dear Richard, who had been her only friend, only ally and only confidant during those miserable childhood years that could never be wiped out of her memory. Years of torment and being *forced* into conforming, obeying without question or backtalk. Backtalk—that was what they said in America. She remembered her mother, Lilly, telling her that. But her damnably questioning and questing mind had always got her in trouble. How many times, before he finally ran away, had Richard taken a thrashing on her account? She could still hear his voice in her memory.

"I'm sorry, Willie—you know I hate to leave you, I'd take you with me if I could, but you're still far too young and—oh, God, Willie, can't you see that I can't stay? I can't be molded into what *he* wants me to be—everything foreordained. The Army or the Church—not to have a thought in my head that isn't his. No, I'd rather be dead! You understand, don't you, Willie? You're my best friend, you know. And when I come of age and have made my fortune, I'm going to come back and rescue you. I promise."

It hadn't been Richard's fault that he hadn't been able to keep his promise. He'd still been adventuring somewhere abroad when, at seventeen—Celia's age—she had been half starved and beaten into consenting to marry the man her father had chosen for her: her father's friend, a duke, a widower forty years her senior. He had lusted after her, admiring her tomboyish figure and wild ethereal beauty, from the day he'd first seen her when she was barely fourteen. And so he had purchased her—was there any other word that fit so well?

Purchased her, yes, perhaps. But he had never owned her, that old man who had been her husband. And she had made that clear to him from the very beginning— the sudden strength in her bubbling up from God knows what depths within herself.

"I will be your hostess; I will act in public as your shy and adoring young bride. And I am a virgin, as you very well know, since you insisted that I must be examined to prove it. Well, you have your proof, your Grace. But you will not have me against my will or try to force me, or I promise you such an ugly scandal that

you will not be able to show your face in society again.
I could send off letters to the *Times*—and to my mother's
family in America. And if you ever try to rape me or
mistreat me, I will kill you; and if I fail, I will kill myself—and most dramatically, I assure you. Do we understand each other, then, my husband?''

It had been Richard who had told her that the only
way not to become a victim was to face up to an adversary without ever showing fear. And, after all, what was
there left to fear? She was no longer under her father's
control, and now that she was married to this old man
who wanted above all things to appear still young enough
to have himself a nubile young wife—how had she ever
feared him? He was afraid of her, of gossip, of the specter
of senility, and most of all, of his two sons, who were
both older than his new wife. He had wanted her as a
symbol as well as a possession, and he could never bear
to have people laughing at him for his foolishness or to
be made to feel ridiculous. At his age, lusting was one
thing, but the act of fulfilling that lust was quite another.
After all, he had experienced mistresses who knew exactly how to arouse him and give him satisfaction—and
he could always imagine it was his little virgin wife doing all those things to him, couldn't he?

So the bargain had been struck, and she had played
her part as she had promised, with never a breath of scandal or anyone the wiser until, obligingly, her husband had
died of syphilis in Vienna, where he had gone to seek a
cure. They had been married for over ten years at the
time, and she was still a young woman, come into her
own at last.

Her current life pleased her and a secret smile curved
her lips upward, and Mr. Pemberton coughed warningly
to bring her out of her reverie. They were reaching their
destination, he noted, and there was still more business
to be discussed before they arrived.

Oh, yes, all those business matters, so many legalities to be taken care of. Language—just the right wording on a piece of paper that could make all the difference to someone's life.

And now, because of a legal document, because of old ties and yes, because Richard had been her champion, her friend and her beloved brother, Willie knew (as he must have known when he set all this in motion) that she would do as he wanted and accept the responsibility he had given her.

His daughter by Marianna.

"Well," Aunt Gertrude said brusquely as she hauled Celia up and away from her breakfast and into the library for a Talk. "*Well.* I have just had the most unnerving news. It defies all logic, all civility. After all we have done, after *all* this time . . . ! Well, read it and see for yourself, Celia, and I *know* you will agree with me that it is quite impossible."

She thrust the telegram into Celia's trembling hands.

Dear God, what *now?* Celia thought as she looked from her aunt's wrathful expression to the piece of paper she held in her hands.

She didn't want to read it. Whatever it was, it had put Aunt Gertrude in a fearful temper, and she herself always provoked her aunt so easily anyway.

"*Read it,*" Aunt Gertrude commanded, and Celia took a deep breath and forced her eyes down to the paper . . . the telegram . . . the words—she barely comprehended them as she leapt over them three at a time—

". . . by the terms of . . . Penmaris's will . . . guardianship remanded to his sister, the Duchess of Millhaven . . . who will assume . . . upon her arrival . . . full and complete responsibility for . . ."

Everything shifted; Celia felt as if she were walking on quicksand.

How could her father have done this to her? It wasn't fair! It wasn't right! Once again she was to be uprooted and taken away from all that had become familiar, taken perhaps even farther from Ronald. None of her uncle's sermons that were sure to follow could ever reconcile her to the fact that her life and her future were not her own to determine.

But Aunt Gertrude was waiting expectantly.

She swallowed hard. "I—I don't know what to say."

"Of course you do," Aunt Gertrude said. "You say, 'No, thank you,' and then we find a lawyer who can circumvent this odious codicil."

Oh, now what? Now what? She didn't know if she wanted to say *No, thank you;* she didn't know anything. How did she know what she wanted to do?

No, she knew: she wanted to run away to her room and pretend this awful telegram had never come. She *had* to get away from her aunt, who was hovering over her like some predatory bird.

Why couldn't she just stay and her father's sister stay with her?

Oh, God, *what* could she say to Aunt Gertrude to mollify her?

"I—I may not be old enough to have a say in this, Aunt Gertrude," she got out finally, her voice quavering a little at her daring.

Aunt Gertrude stopped her pacing. "No, you probably are not, more's the pity." She looked at her niece consideringly. "Of course this is a shock to you, especially after all the comforts we've given you and the genteel life to which we've introduced you. I've done my Duty and I will bow before no man. No one can censure my good intentions, not even your father's sister. Well, I'll deal with her when she arrives, Celia. What you need now is time to assimilate this news.

You're excused to your room. We'll talk more about this later.''

Wordlessly, Celia handed her the telegram and made a decorous exit.

And then she ran, positively raced up to her room and flung herself onto her bed, her tearless eyes gazing up at the rosette in the center of the ceiling.

Why? Why had her father allowed her to be taken away from everything she loved originally? Oh, she knew, she knew: he had said it was for her own good, to be sent from the warmth and love she had known into the cold frost of English society where feelings were always buried inside.

And she had learned her lessons, hadn't she? Just for him, she had done everything her aunt had wanted.

But he hadn't come to applaud her; he had died instead on one of his mysterious journeys, and all without even explaining to her that he had arranged the rest of her life and that she was to be handed over from one surrogate to another until she attained her majority.

Or would it stop when she became twenty-one? Perhaps there had been other arrangements made that she knew nothing of . . . ?

Oh, it was too much to bear thinking about—too much!

She turned over and pounded her fists against her pillows, biting down on her bottom lip to keep herself from screaming out loud.

She was not a horse or a cow. She was not a *thing!*

Oh, Ronald, Ronald, where are you? Why couldn't we have eloped the last time you were here? Then I would belong to you and not to whoever happens to be appointed my guardian . . .

But how could she rail against a system of rules and laws that had been in existence for centuries? Women *were* the property of men, and rarely did anyone rebel against that.

But sometimes—just sometimes—there were women who did reverse the pattern . . .

She sat up abruptly as that thought occurred to her, and wiped away her tears of frustration. Women like her aunt Wilhelmina, if what her aunt Gertrude had told her was true.

Her new guardian was a very proper lady, Aunt Gertrude had said. And yet—and yet—now that she was a widow, she enjoyed flaunting the rules.

Aunt Gertrude had made it sound like a vice, but to Celia it sounded like a virtue. Perhaps Aunt Wilhelmina was not such a bad choice of guardian after all.

And anyway, there was nothing she could do to prevent it except to keep her secret self and her secret dreams hidden until Ronald came for her.

For now, she would resign herself to the fact that she *had* no choice. This amendment to her father's will had made it for her, and she would do her *duty* as her father would have wanted.

As Ronald would want. Ronald, who understood "duty" so well, would surely appreciate her predicament.

The thought of Aunt Wilhelmina being just a little unconventional made her feel a lot better, and once she had washed her face and let Alice help her dress for dinner, she actually found herself looking forward to meeting her father's sister.

But nothing could have prepared her for the woman who was her aunt Wilhelmina. Nothing.

Aunt Wilhelmina was tall—almost unfashionably tall—but dressed in the height of fashion.

And she wasn't old. Celia had expected she would be very old, yet she could not have been much more than in her mid-thirties.

And she was beautiful, with her light auburn hair piled on top of her head, which only emphasized her glowing topaz eyes and her perfect profile.

She was like an illustration straight out of the magazines, all cool and calm and self-possessed, and not in the least harried or discomfited by Aunt Gertrude.

Celia couldn't stop staring. Her father's much-loved sister—and she seemed barely older than Celia herself.

And Aunt Gertrude, fussing and talking—talking too much because she was caught in between Aunt Wilhelmina's obvious disdain and her own notions of propriety and Duty.

But Aunt Wilhelmina was formidable; Aunt Gertrude could not make a dent in her composure, whereas Celia felt that *she* would have been reduced to tears practically the moment she walked into the room.

"Wilhelmina," Aunt Gertrude said, trying to infuse some warmth into her voice and holding out her hands.

Aunt Wilhelmina touched them coolly and said, "Call me Willie," and Aunt Gertrude dropped her hands and her jaw simultaneously.

Aunt Wilhelmina then turned to Celia and held out her hands to her niece. "You must be Celia. I'm Willie, and I've been *so* looking forward to meeting you."

Celia felt it instantly: the radiance, the warmth and caring that utterly enveloped her and made her feel *wanted*.

"I'm so glad you came," she blurted out before she realized how that might sound to Aunt Gertrude.

"Well, yes," Aunt Gertrude interposed. "We're *all* so glad you came. Of course, we need to talk about Celia's future now that she's in your charge."

"Oh, yes," Willie said. "I want to discuss most particularly my plans for my niece. I cannot tell you how seriously I am going to undertake my duty to my niece. My brother would have wanted it so."

She turned to Celia, who was just staring at her, trying to decide whether this collected creature *meant* what she said or whether she was mocking Aunt Gertrude and even Aunt Gertrude couldn't tell.

"I'm so happy to hear that," Aunt Gertrude said. "We'll just go into the parlor—no, not you, Celia. Your aunt and I have much to discuss, and when we're done I will be happy to inform you of our decisions."

Celia opened her mouth to protest and then, seeing the slight subtle shake of Aunt Willie's elegant head, closed it again.

"You'll go to your room," Aunt Gertrude instructed.

I will not! Celia thought rebelliously.

"And I'll send for you when we're done. Go on now, Celia." She stayed exactly where she was until Celia reluctantly moved away. "I need to see you go up those steps."

Celia thinned her lips and clenched her hands and mounted the steps.

And still Aunt Gertrude watched as she climbed them slowly, hoping her aunt would turn away so she could sneak back down and listen at the keyhole.

Not Aunt Gertrude; *she* had to make sure Celia was all the way *up* before she turned to Willie and gestured to the parlor door.

Willie politely entered the room, sat down on one of the stiff sofas beside the fireplace and waited for Aunt Gertrude to close the door and join her.

"Shall we have tea?" she asked, as if she were the hostess and not Gertrude.

Gertrude looked startled, and then she snapped, "I'll ring for it, of course." She grabbed the bellpull and yanked it furiously.

At least five minutes passed, during which Willie didn't prefer to speak to the matter at hand. This made Gertrude all the more annoyed.

And it was Willie who poured the tea when it was finally served and handed Gertrude a cup, then held her own cup delicately to her lips and took a long sip.

"Lovely, Gertrude. Beautiful china service. I can see that my niece has had all the advantages here." She then set down her cup. "Now, let me tell you exactly what my plans are. You will be delighted to learn, my dear Gertrude, that I am taking Celia to London."

She paused, waiting for Gertrude to utter one disparaging word, and when she saw that the older woman had thought the better of it, she continued in the same light, cool tone. "And I plan to bring her out into society."

She paused again—for effect—because she was certain that Celia was now listening at the door; certainly she had given her enough time to get back downstairs before she began her assault on the bishop's wife.

And Gertrude did not disappoint her. She slammed her delicate china cup down onto the table.

Wilhelmina waited, and when Gertrude still managed to hold her tongue, she said, "My beloved brother, Richard, whose most ardent desire this is—as set out in his will—has provided the wherewithal for me to outfit Celia like a princess."

Gertrude said not a word, and Wilhelmina, always sensitive to the delicate nuances of timing, concluded: "And we leave for London tomorrow—because we must accomplish so very much in a very short time."

Ah! Gertrude was enraged. She stood up abruptly, a tower of suppressed fury. "I cannot allow this."

"I beg your pardon?" Wilhelmina said politely, picking up her cup. "Oh, would you like some more tea, Gertrude?"

Gertrude looked rather as if she wanted to throw the teapot at Wilhelmina. The nerve of the woman, she thought—just taking over *her* ward, *her* house and *her*

duties as a hostess, *and* telling her what Celia would and
would not do.

"I will not allow this good Christian girl to be hauled
off to the fleshpots of London and shown off on the
whorish stage of London Society."

"Oh," Wilhelmina said, slightly taken aback by Gertrude's passion. "Well, that's quite all right, then, because I have no intention of doing that at all."

"I have done my best, mind you, to raise Celia with
propriety and humility. I rescued her from the heathenish
ways your brother had allowed her to fall into. I surely
expected more of Richard when he made this decision to
turn the rest of Celia's life over to . . . *you*."

. . . the likes of you . . .

Wilhelmina heard it as clearly as if Gertrude had said
it, and she put down her teacup gently. "But what more
could you expect, dear Gertrude?" she asked politely.
"Celia has a home and has been provided for and will
now have every advantage of a girl of her class. And the
advantages of marrying into your class are many, as I
can surely attest—not the least of which is that when
your husband dies, he leaves you pots of money and lots
of delicious freedom. I think Celia would like that very
well. Especially if, like me, she makes a wonderful second marriage."

Gertrude gasped at the appalling brazenness of this
statement and stood up once again, seeking to regain
some kind of control over this creature by the mere act
of standing over her and bullying her.

"I will *not* deal with your levity any further, and you
may be sure I will protest this action—this will—to my
dying day."

"Oh, please don't bother. We'll be leaving tomorrow
and we won't trouble you anymore."

"Trouble?" Gertrude stormed. "*Trouble?* Trouble is
where you are leading this child, among those blasphe-

mous heathens in London, *and* in spite of knowing her history and who her mother was. It won't surprise me one bit if she returns here in Disgrace. But I will be waiting—because I am a good Christian woman and I know my Duty."

She stalked to the door, oblivious of the faint scuffling sound beyond that indicated to Wilhelmina that Celia had run off to hide.

"You will forgive me if I do not join you for dinner. You have totally overset my appetite, and I really must allow myself some time to adjust."

The door slammed; the china rattled.

Wilhelmina sat calmly and waited and poured herself another cup of tea, mentally counting the minutes.

Three . . . four . . . five . . . Gertrude must be prostrate on her bed by now, she thought, and the vision of it gave her a great deal of pleasure.

Six . . . Possibly the Bishop was occupied elsewhere as well? Ministering to his dragon of a wife, she hoped. Eight—the tea was getting cold and she had to resist the impulse to ring for Gertrude's maid to freshen it.

Nine—stuffy old house, she thought, positively stultifying guardians.

Ten—the door behind her creaked open and shut again with just the faintest click of the lock.

And then she heard the light sound of Celia's hands clapping, and she turned and held out her own.

Celia rushed to her and knelt down beside her chair.

"Oh, that was *wonderful,* Aunt Willie. I don't know how you could stand up to her like that."

Willie reached down and stroked her luxurious hair.

"It was so easy, Celia, my dear. You can have no idea. And we will deal so very nicely together—and all because I do know your history. And I hate rules and strictures and propriety every bit as much as I suspect you do if you take after your parents at all!"

* * *

In the time that followed, Celia felt as if her whole world had turned topsy-turvy. She felt overwhelmed, torn between excitement and apprehension, wanting desperately to go with Aunt Willie, yet fearful that Aunt Gertrude would wrest her away at the last moment.

Aunt Gertrude had grudgingly joined them for dinner anyway; how could she not when her anger and manners got the better of her?

And Aunt Willie just as neatly got her off into a corner and said, very politely, "You will not protest my brother's action, Gertrude."

Gertrude drew herself up. "Why should I not? We are Celia's family; we have given her a home. We have seen her educated, morally and mentally, when Richard had given up all responsibility. And now—*this!*"

"There is no way you can break Richard's will. It will cost you time and money, a great deal of money, much more money than you have at your disposal and a lot less than I have at mine," Willie said pointedly. "You may very well wish to put yourself into debt over this, Gertrude, but I hope you will not. The documents are as tight-knit as they can be, and will just cause you a great deal of grief when you must back down anyway."

"I see," Aunt Gertrude said grimly, and Celia could almost visualize the light of battle banking behind her eyes into smoldering embers of hate.

And Uncle Theo didn't help by remaining obstinately silent.

It was merely a matter of getting through dinner and ignoring Aunt Gertrude's patent disapproval. Celia had become a princess in a fairy tale, and Aunt Gertrude would no longer be the wicked witch, and her opinions and strictures wouldn't matter anymore.

"There is the house in Town, of course," Aunt Willie said over soup. "Lovely house, Celia. Scads of servants. We'll have to get a lady's maid for you, of course. And a footman. We do not travel about without a maid and a footman," she added to Aunt Gertrude ever so politely.

"Your own carriage," she continued after the first course was served. "And you may redecorate your room as you will . . ."

"Blasphemy!" Aunt Gertrude muttered, waving her knife as if she would like to sink it right into Aunt Willie's toothsome descriptions.

"I'm sure your father would wish that," Aunt Willie said with a knowing little smile. "Church on Sundays, of course. We do not neglect the soul when we are in Town. We will arrive just in time to get ready for the Season. I've already given great thought to your wardrobe, Celia, and—"

"I feel faint," Aunt Gertrude interjected, rising abruptly from her chair so that it nearly fell backward. She couldn't bear to think about all that lovely money that she had minded so fiercely, frittered away on Celia's—room, maid—wardrobe . . . it was enough to make a decent woman swoon. All that profligate, heathenish waste! It would just turn Celia's head and she would forget everything Gertrude had ever taught her!

Well, she would see to that! Celia would not forget anything she had learned under her roof, Gertrude thought venomously as she forced herself to stay in place through the rest of the dinner, choking down her meal and *enduring* the twinkling, knowing looks that Willie exchanged with her niece.

And Celia could see very clearly that Aunt Gertrude was not done with her yet.

Not nearly.

The following morning Uncle Theo, as if to bring her

down to earth, presented her with a leather-bound Bible, suitably inscribed, with certain sections underlined. He also gave her a slim volume of some of his admonitory sermons that he had published privately.

"I will feel more secure about your leaving us if you can assure me you will turn to these books when you have problems or questions you cannot resolve," he told her, his voice gentle, his eyes sad.

How could she refuse him this last request? It wouldn't be a lie; she would read the Bible—she *would*.

And then came Aunt Gertrude, who just had to deliver a little sermon of her own, full of reminders that she, Celia, had been brought up and educated a young *lady*, and she must therefore not allow either temptation or sordid surroundings to influence her In Any Way.

Nor must she *push* herself forward or call attention to herself in any social situation whatsoever.

"But, Aunt—surely if I'm trained to make my formal curtsy to the queen, I should not fear that I am being *forward* . . . for example," Celia protested, hoping to divert her aunt from a long and laborious tirade that would only tire both of them.

"For heaven's sake, Celia, I think you should know very well what I mean. Do not be deliberately obtuse—it is not suitable for a girl your age. Of course I wasn't referring to your formal presentation to her Majesty, but to certain other environments to which you will no doubt be exposed. There are certain—well, rather *fast* elements in this so-called 'society' . . . the Marlborough House set, for instance, and that American, Jennie Churchill, who is such a close friend of the Prince of Wales—*and* of your new guardian. Well, I don't expect you to understand all the pitfalls and trials you might encounter, but I trust you will hold fast to the principles and self-discipline that the Bishop and I have, in duty bound, done our best to instill in you."

Her aunt paused for breath and then gave a disdainful sniff. "We shall pray for you, Celia—and I hope you remember that you can always call upon us for guidance and advice if you need help or counseling. And do not, I beg of you, let any of this nonsense go to your head. You will be under the most stringent scrutiny, particularly in view of . . . well, it doesn't matter. You have a fine and decent young man who is pledged to marry you, and I am sure you will keep his trust in you intact."

Aunt Gertrude paused again, looked as if she would say more, then closed her mouth firmly and waited for Celia to say something.

"Thank you, Aunt Gertrude," she finally managed, though her heart was pounding wildly.

Ronald! Oh, Lord, to think she had almost forgotten about him in all the excitement! She had to write to him at once and explain everything: the will and the reasons she had to go with Aunt Willie, her new address in London . . .

Oh, why must Aunt Gertrude look as if she were consigning her to the deepest recesses of hell?

If only she could be in control of her own life, her own future. Despite Aunt Willie's generosity, Celia already knew what she wanted, and it was so simple and it didn't involve London or society or rules of etiquette.

All she wanted was just to return to Ceylon to be Ronald's wife, the tea planter's bride.

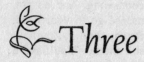 Three

Celia found that she had no time to herself, or *for* herself once they arrived in London and her "training" (as Aunt Willie apologetically termed it) began.

There was so much to be learned. There were different manners, different hours, a whole different social etiquette; and there were innumerable fittings for the most fashionable gowns for every conceivable occasion, from Ascot in the early spring to Cowes in late summer; there were morning gowns and ball gowns and afternoon dresses, and heaven forbid that she be seen wearing the same dress at more than one event.

And there were dancing lessons and instruction in almost every social grace—from the royal curtsy (which entailed dipping the knee and simultaneously swishing the inevitable train of her long gown out of the way nonchalantly, as Aunt Willie demonstrated one afternoon when they were having tea) to the art of flirting discreetly.

"Look—*this* is the way you get through it," Aunt Willie said with an understanding smile. "Try not to think about how ridiculous it all seems; just *do* it. That's how you get through it: practice it a few times in front of a mirror while you think of anything else, and you'll do fine. At least that's how I managed. I thought of it as a silly game, and I pictured myself above all the nonsense and rituals, and I determined that if I played the game the way *they* wanted, I would be free to do anything *I* wished to do.

"And, of course, you really don't want to be thought an oddity and have a miserable Season your first time out. There's time enough to learn just how to exercise your individuality. And I promise—you will.

"But right now, I feel I should carry out your father's express last wishes. He wanted you to experience something of the world—to have broader horizons. He felt so strongly about it, he even wrote to me."

Celia stopped in mid-motion. "He—wrote—to *you?*" She lowered her extended leg slowly from the point where she had been about to execute the blasé thrust of her make-believe court gown train. "He wrote to you and—and not to *me?*"

She felt an instant's grief and then a horrible feeling of resentment washed over her. Had he loved Willie more than he loved her? Why couldn't he have written to her and explained his wishes for her future happiness and well-being? Why did she always have thoughts and questions tormenting her about why her father had never shown his love for her? Was it because she reminded him too much of her mother? What had really happened between her parents to turn her father into the hard, distant stranger he had become?

"He wrote to me," Willie said finally after allowing Celia several minutes to assimilate this information. She was a little shocked at how upset Celia was by this revelation; she wanted desperately to ask questions, but instinctively she knew that Celia would not tell her anything. At least not yet.

Celia was thinking exactly the same thing as she

slowly moved to a chair opposite Aunt Willie and sat down. Aunt Willie had very kindly invited her to share her thoughts and her misgivings about all of this, but Celia still felt, in spite of Aunt Willie's obvious affection, a certain sense of reserve.

Aunt Willie was, after all, a complete stranger to her, and she was not used to sharing her feelings with anyone anyway. Even at school she had made no close friends. She had never, ever had a confidante to whisper and giggle with in private; what secrets did she have to confide?

And all her fears seemed to be channeled into strange occasional nightmares that she never remembered when she woke up, crying and drenched in sweat.

She had learned to hide her emotions very well, she thought as she faced Aunt Willie across the tea table and schooled her expression so that it did not reflect the turmoil she was feeling about her father's letter to her aunt.

She would just write all of this down in her diary; her diary was her best friend, her diary never betrayed her, and once the words were down in black and white, she would feel strengthened enough to face the next obstacle with some degree of self-possession and poise.

And eventually the searing disappointment would go away.

Celia was too quiet, Willie thought as she poured another useless cup of tea. Why hadn't she demanded to see her father's letter? She was too silent, too biddable and difficult to read. Not at all like the usual young women her age: silly, giggling little fools who blushed too often and were even a little clumsy at times.

Not Celia. Look at how gracefully she took her cup and sipped at it. So proper. So rigid. She couldn't begin to imagine the inflexible and overprotective environment in which she had been brought up by Gertrude and Theo.

But still, there was something missing. A lack of emotion, perhaps? Or something else as well—something hidden and tamped down inside her that was almost palpable . . . a sense of secrets locked away?

Willie understood this very well; she too had been a lonely and introverted child, and she wondered if she was seeing this same quality in Celia or if her imagination was overreacting.

She wanted everything to be exactly *right* for Celia, and for her to unbend and have fun and enjoy London.

But she wondered how much there had been to enjoy at the Grange. In point of fact, she and Celia probably shared a commonality of experience: she with her older husband, and Celia with the tyrannical Gertrude.

Despots, both of them, ruling by self-proclaimed edict.

And now vanquished forever.

A comforting thought. Particularly since she was now happily a dowager duchess *and* remarried to a wonderful American man who left her free as a bird to do as she would. And she wanted to make sure that Celia had every opportunity to stretch her wings as well.

She would start now, by voicing what Celia would not.

"Would you like to see your father's letter, my dear?"

Celia looked up at her, startled. It was the very last thing she expected Aunt Willie to say, and the very thing she desperately wanted to do. But she had the feeling she might be hurt even more by whatever was in the contents of that letter.

She lifted her chin and said, ever so politely—just as she had been taught, "No, thank you, Aunt Willie. I would rather be excused, if you don't mind."

Willie forced back an exasperated sigh and nodded, then watched as Celia gracefully levered herself out of the chair and made her way across the parlor and into the hallway.

She took that too, too quietly, Willie thought as she rang for a servant to take away the tea service.

It worried her; it was a moment when her great good common sense seemed to fail her, and she wished she had someone to turn to who had a better understanding of children.

She thought of her husband, who had not made this momentous journey with her from America; rather, when she had received the telegram from Richard's solicitor, he had encouraged her to go to England and take charge of her orphaned niece, whom her brother had been so concerned about.

How wise he was; how fortunate was she in this treasure of an unlooked-for second marriage.

And then there was her stepson, Grant, her blessing, the child she had never had. Her friend, her conspirator, her companion.

She had brought them both with her in a watercolor portrait that she had hung over the escritoire near the window, the two of them on horseback, looking awfully dashing and uncommonly like brothers.

She went to the portrait and stood thoughtfully before it.

Grant—he was in Paris now, and was soon to go on to Scotland for two weeks of shooting with Sir Thomas Lipton, who regarded him like his own son.

She wondered about Grant, and about the puzzle that was Celia . . . perhaps Grant could draw her out. She was about to be presented; she needed an escort, a handsome man to squire her around for a while, someone who would make her aware that she was actually a very lovely young woman.

Grant might be the perfect solution to her problem. Most assuredly he had a way about him that made women . . . well, even *she* was not immune to him.

Her smile became wicked. He owed her a favor too,

for that time she had covered up for him and pretended he'd been having dinner with *her* when all the while . . . It turned out that she had saved him from an ugly incident with a very jealous husband and he'd promised to repay her—somehow.

Well, now was the time, and she planned to make very sure that he did.

The cable from England was delivered along with the champagne and croissants he had ordered—nestled under the silver platter upon which reposed a cluster of chilled, freshly picked grapes that he had planned to put to a deliciously wicked use with his lovely young companion.

"Damn!" He hadn't realized he had sworn out loud until a warm, soft hand reached for him from under the tangled covers.

"*Chéri?* Something is wrong?" Gaby was half French, half Italian and all uninhibited passion, in bed as well as when she danced the cancan at Le Moulin Rouge. This was only his first night with her, and he'd been looking forward to a much more detailed exploration of her charms.

Why in hell had his stepmother summoned him to join her in London so urgently when she was perfectly aware that he had finished the onerous task of soliciting investors for his cattle syndicate and he was now enjoying a well-earned respite from business?

He scowled down at the thin sheet of yellow paper. Something had to have gone wrong with Willie's plan for this changeling niece of hers; she was already a nuisance both to him and to his kindhearted and far too generous stepmother.

He was inordinately fond of his father's second wife; his sister, Heather, had even teased him about being half in love with her.

Perhaps he was; Willie was the kind of woman a man

never forgot—witness his father, who had found his childhood love again after all those years and married her out of hand and taken her to his vast ranch in New Mexico, where they had been like perpetual honeymooners. Willie had been perfectly happy to live there and seemed never to long for London and the social life she had abandoned.

And then the letter had come . . . bringing trouble, just as he had predicted.

He was in a foul mood when he left Paris. Gaby had had no regrets and had probably gone on to the next willing man already—which thought did not improve his mood. After far too many hours of traveling, he finally arrived in London very much in need of a bath, a change of clothes and some decent refreshment.

He was not, however, angry with Willie. But as for this niece of hers, who had been brought up in a parsonage or some such place and was probably a plain, puritanical, pasty-faced little blonde with no idea how fortunate she was—well, he couldn't wait to deal with *her*. Her needs had ruined *his* vacation in Paris and he was quite prepared to dislike her on sight.

"Poor, quiet little . . . good God, *madrastra,* what kind of oddity are you trying to foist on me? And why should this mousy creature be frightened of *me?* Hasn't she ever seen a man before? Is there something wrong with her that you're not telling me? Because I promise you, I'm not going to have *my* reputation maligned by one of your lame ducks!"

Willie gazed at him in mock awe as he paced around her private parlor like a caged lion and lambasted her decision to summon him.

And when she said nothing in response to his tirade, he stopped and glared at her through narrowed and dangerously glinting green eyes. "I tell you, *madam,* there are limits beyond which—*dammit,* I don't like being laughed at, even though it will be clear to everyone that I'm only doing this to oblige *you.* What kind of female *is* she, this—whatever her name is?''

Willie hid her triumphant smile. ''Grant, darling, stop glowering. It's only a tiny little reception and dance to open this lovely house we were so fortunate to rent. Yes, all of our dear friends will be present, but I assure you, there's nothing really wrong with Celia. She has had a very sad and unnatural kind of upbringing and she is too quiet. She's obedient, knows her manners—she is most definitely *not* a little savage—and has been *trained* quite properly by these rigid, cold people who saw her as a duty and nothing else.

''It was a very strict household—her uncle is a bishop, did I tell you that?—so it's as if she'd been taught that enjoying herself is a sin.''

She watched his reaction to this, which bordered on boredom, and then she went on pointedly. ''I want her to be made to feel attractive and . . . womanly. I want her to *feel* like a success so that she will be successful. You do see, don't you? To have an escort like *you,* my dearest, scowling stepson, whom all the other young women will envy—not to mention their mamas and other sundry female relatives—will give Celia just the cachet she needs to attract all the other young men. Grant—?''

Grant swore feelingly under his breath in Spanish as he caught the twinkle in her eyes. ''A few centuries ago, *madrastra,* you would have been burned as a witch. I hope to hell I don't ever get myself tangled up with a woman like you.''

''Nonsense,'' Willie contradicted briskly, ''you need a woman who's a constant challenge, Grant Hamilton, or you'd be bored with her in no time—just like you are with all your other flights of fluff and fancy. Come on downstairs now. I want you to meet Celia.'' She tugged at his arm. "And be *nice*. She . . . well, I really do think she has possibilities, Grant, and I'm counting on you to make her popular."

As her aunt's maid arranged her thick dark hair in the coils and puffs decreed by the latest fashion, Celia sat at her dressing table deep in thought. She wished she were far away from this room with its gold mirror and its hothouse orchid in a vase.

Why, oh, why couldn't it have been Ronald who was coming tonight instead . . . ?

Instead of Aunt Willie's handsome and dashing (and, she was sure just from seeing his portrait, detestably arrogant) stepson.

Ronald would be so proud of her, and she would be in heaven instead of dreading the appearance of this—this American—who was being forced on her as her official escort and whose speech and manners she was quite sure she would find hard to understand or accept.

Couldn't Aunt Willie have foreseen what a disaster it was bound to be?

Celia stared at her rather wan appearance in the mirror. *Perhaps if this Mr. Hamilton decides I am quite hopeless, it would persuade my aunt that she would be wasting her time and money trying to launch me in smart society.*

And how was that possible, she wondered, when etiquette, rules, manners and mores had been pounded into her head until she had wanted to scream?

How did one simply relinquish the backbone of conduct with which one had been raised?

One acted like a fool, of course, going against everything one had ever been taught—

No, that wasn't right. She wasn't a fool. She was merely way out of her depth, immersed in the maelstrom of a London Season when she would much rather be in the colonies, tucked away on a tea estate with the only man she would ever love.

She would ever and always be more comfortable away from the chaos of the city . . .

A regular Gypsy, she thought, watching as the notion took hold and her eyes lit up and a plan suddenly formed, full-blown, right before her, and reflected back at her in the mirror.

Marianna, she thought, and her heart began pounding as that long-suppressed part of herself suddenly yearned for release.

She didn't need to be *herself* this evening. No one here knew her, except Aunt Willie. She could be anyone she wanted to be.

Did she dare?

Would Marianna have *dared?*

Marianna would have done anything. She would have danced and teased and played with them all, and made that man just despise her. And she wouldn't have given two farthings what anyone thought. She would have been herself, and she would not have let anyone dictate what she should be—

Her eyes widened at this rebellious and utterly alien thought.

She would try to be Marianna tonight—and she would embarrass that detestable man to death.

She hoped she had the nerve. To symbolize her resolve, she carefully plucked the orchid from the vase and placed it behind her ear.

Four

What her aunt had termed a tiny little reception and dance was actually a full-fledged party and ball, Celia discovered to her dismay when she finally made her way downstairs and joined the throng of people who had already assembled.

She felt a wave of panic and a need to run and hide someplace, anyplace, to get away from this perfumed, bejeweled crowd of endlessly chattering guests who represented the cream of society.

How *could* Aunt Willie have just thrown her to the lions like this her first time out?

There was not one familiar face, not one friendly greeting. But who knew who she was, after all?

She became aware of people looking at her as she moved with innate elegance through the crowd. She heard the covert whispers and thought instantly of Marianna, who would have loved the attention.

Why didn't *she?*

Of course she did; this was exactly the impression she wanted to make. She lifted her chin and sailed through the crowd—and was stopped short by a hand grasping at her gloved wrist.

She wheeled around to find Miss Anthea Langbourne, a casual acquaintance with whom she had had some conversation during visits to various of her aunt's friends.

Anthea was only one year away from attaining her majority, and she was *enduring* the Season only to pacify her family, after which she was determined to do exactly as *she* pleased—with the aid of a considerable annual income bequeathed to her by her grandmother, a kindred spirit.

She liked nothing better than to closet herself in the chaperones' corner, where she led Celia now so they could talk.

"I'm awaiting my *escort*," Celia told her acidly, "and I hope he has decided it is beneath him, after all, to act as the official *shepherd* to a simpering debutante. I am praying he has. I could not bear to be condescended to and . . . *humored* by a hypocritical *roué*. I still cannot understand what my aunt could have been thinking of."

"Of what *she* considers your own good, no doubt," Anthea commented dryly. "It's just something we females must *endure* the best we can until we attain that magic age of twenty-one and can be considered independent *spinsters*."

Celia had heard all of this before. Anthea was a strong believer in woman suffrage and woman's rights. Florence Nightingale was her idol, and Anthea, who was a young woman of strong principles and high ideals, had no doubts whatsoever about *her* future. She would train to be a nurse first, and then she would travel abroad to the remotest outposts of the British Empire as a missionary.

She had recognized in Celia a Cause and she had made a point of befriending her. The poor, bewildered girl needed Guidance and to learn how to believe in herself—

and this, at least, *she* could provide for her. In a way, it was her duty.

As it was to keep her company while Celia fretted about the unknown escort, and they waited while pretending they did not for some man, any man, to beg them for the honor of a dance.

"Barbaric custom," Anthea muttered angrily. "Savages, all of them, stuffed up with the knowledge that only *they* have the power to ask. Look at them strutting around and eyeing us like we were prize mares."

Celia was barely listening; her foot had been tapping in time with the waltz and she felt quite swept away by the music. A *Marianna* kind of swept away, which filled her with a yearning to dance and lose herself in the music and the motion for just a while—a short, secret while.

She came sharply back to awareness by the prod of Anthea's fan in her ribs.

"Quick, now—you're going to need all your wits about you, Celia. I see your aunt bearing down on us with that upstart American stepson of hers. Do keep to your resolve. Do *not,* I beg you, succumb—"

Celia froze and then she drew in a deep breath to prepare herself before she turned her head in the direction of Anthea's gaze.

And exhaled in a kind of helpless gasp.

Oh, no! Oh, no! It couldn't be, it *mustn't* be, the stepson! She had pictured him as much older, with lines of dissipation from the consequences of his loose living showing clearly on his face. She had pictured him with a villainous mustache—perhaps a full beard—and shifty eyes . . .

Be strong, Celia, be strong, she cautioned herself. This was just the result of reading too many novels and imagining the dark, brooding hero, like Mr. Rochester—or Heathcliff!

How dared he be so different from what she had imagined?

True, his hair was as black as any villain's, but there were glints of dark auburn when it caught the light. And he was clean-shaven—with what looked like and surely must be a saber scar worn like a badge of courage just under his left cheekbone.

Cleft chin, sharp green eyes . . . such a hard mouth and a very dangerous-looking face that could have belonged to a pirate or a highwayman. The kind with no scruples at all, the kind of man whom even *she* in her ignorance understood it was best to avoid.

No wonder Anthea had tried to warn her!

She hated the betraying flush that rose up in her cheeks. She wanted to cover her whole face with her fan.

And why did his eyes have to *rake* over her in quite that fashion? Why was there such a twist to his lips as if he despised what he saw?

And why did she *mind* so much?

Except—she had never before been looked over in such an assessing, appraising way. Nor made so sharply aware of the fact she was *female*.

Dear God, what was the brute doing? Stripping her bare with his gaze while with one knowing glance, he made sure she *knew* what he was doing.

She felt an involuntary shiver of pure terror run up her spine and she sat up straighter and made a giant effort to maintain her composure as she lowered her eyes and pretended she had seen nothing and felt nothing.

Even though her heart was pounding violently and she felt like nothing so much as a cornered doe.

"Courage," Anthea whispered as Celia grappled with the reason for this completely illogical feeling of panic and heard Willie sing out, "Oh, *there* she is! Grant, dear, could you please wipe that forbidding scowl off your face? You're going to frighten the poor child to death."

Grant tore his gaze away from the dark-haired beauty in the company of the long-jawed blonde he assumed was Celia. Those eyes—cougar eyes, by God. Copper, almost orange. Who *was* she?

And from what was she hiding—or *whom?*

"*Madrastra*, stop! You must tell me—who *is* she? Not your silly horse-faced Celia, but the other one—the Gypsy—"

Willie let loose a bubble of satisfied laughter as they approached the two young women. "Allow me to introduce these charming young ladies. Miss Anthea Langbourne, and, of course, my niece and ward—Miss Celia Penmaris."

Grant bowed over their hands, as formal and correct as the introduction warranted, his mind in a whirl. *This* was Celia? The dark Gypsy beauty trying to hide herself behind the shield of innocence and layers of restrictive clothing? With that luscious, full-lipped mouth that just begged to be kissed?

He hardly heard Willie's next words as he watched Celia toy with her fan and felt Willie relinquish his arm and give him a little push.

"They are playing my favorite waltz, and I claim my prerogative as hostess and insist that you and Celia dance. It is the perfect way to become acquainted, don't you agree, Miss Langbourne? After all, he is going to be Celia's escort for the next month or so. Well, *do* go along—Celia needs the practice."

But Celia didn't look as if she needed anything except to escape from her aunt's well-meaning machinations.

She allowed him to take her hand and followed him stiffly out onto the floor and waited for him to take her into his arms—

The wonder was she didn't just faint dead away.

But she couldn't, of course. She promised herself to-night she would act boldly, and she wanted so very badly to dance. The moment they began moving together, she could not have cared less who was leading her around the floor.

And she was a good dancer, light on her feet and responsive to every pressure of his hand on her waist. Somehow he was not surprised.

"You're very silent, Miss Penmaris. Surely you're not shy?"

She felt her insides seize up when he challenged her, but she just could not let this man best her. "I'm concentrating on my steps, Mr. Hamilton. Dancing is new to me—as all of *this* is."

"But you dance very well indeed, Miss Penmaris, for one unaccustomed to such worldly pursuits. You must be enjoying your debut into society; your aunt has put a lot of effort into it, and I know better than most that my stepmother is a very *caring* person. But you know that already, I'm sure."

How impossibly obnoxious he was! And how she hated the way he talked *down* to her! She controlled her rising temper. She would show him. She would bore him to death, not beat him to death with words, and so she said in a suitably *subdued* tone of voice, "Oh, I hope you do not think me ungrateful. I am only trying my very best to please my aunt—I would never want to embarrass her by my ignorance of worldly things."

She lifted her head and stared boldly into his glittering green eyes. Marianna would have done the same, and not been half as frightened as she at the arrogance she saw in them.

There was a dangerousness about him and a will that would bend to no other soul. She wasn't sure she could play at being Marianna.

It would be like playing with matches, and surely she would be burned in the conflagration.

The most she could hope to do was finish this dance

with her pride intact, and the only way she could do that was to concentrate on the small things—the firmness with which he held her—except that she might have wished he held her closer and tighter and with a loving warmth—forget that idea; she would focus instead on her steps and count the beat, which was underscored by her faintly swishing underskirts and the tight pitter-patter of her brand-new shoes as she followed every swoop and turn into which he guided her.

Better, much better.

His hand was so large, so warm, and his movements were so perfect and correct—but wasn't he holding her just a little bit too close? And was that one wide swirl around the floor just a little too brazen? And didn't he look just a little too forbidding in his severe black evening dress?

She didn't dare tangle with him; he would chew her up and spit her out.

Safer, much safer, to fix her gaze someplace beyond his and hope that this waltz would end soon and she could rejoin Anthea and hear her caustic, bracing comments about this "savage" who had been coerced into dancing with her.

But Grant didn't want the dance to end; he was enjoying himself enormously, which he would never admit to Willie. The kitten with the strange coppery eyes had raking little claws and more spirit than he had anticipated. And she was quite striking.

More than one couple had paused a step in the dance in order to stare at her.

She never noticed them. He wasn't sure if he liked that or not, because she wasn't paying attention to him either, and he certainly wasn't used to that.

He didn't know why he did it, but he said, he *growled* her name—"Celia . . ." and she turned her head to look at him. Just for an instant those exotic cat-eyes stared into his, and it was like a jolt of lightning right to his gut.

He let go of her almost involuntarily, and at that very moment the music ended, and he felt a most possessive regret that, according to propriety, he could not reclaim her again.

"Well?" Anthea demanded after Grant had escorted Celia back to her chair. "You are quite out of breath. You poor thing. Say not a word until you have had a chance to compose yourself. Use your fan. It will never do for *him* to see that he has succeeded in discomposing you. I must say," she added as Celia began to ply her fan vigorously, "I am shocked that your aunt would expose a young and innocent female like you to a man with her stepson's reputation. He could ruin your good name if you were seen too often in his company!"

"Nonsense. Mr. Hamilton is family, and they appear to be very fond of each other," Celia said sharply; she could not let Anthea discompose her. After all, that man had not really done or said anything that was in the least improper. And she could never explain to Anthea, who didn't understand *nuances,* that she *was* agitated.

She felt like a mouse, being played with by a predatory cat. *Toyed* with, in fact.

"As for me, I was merely uncomfortable because this was my first ever dance in public and I was afraid of making a misstep."

Yes, that sounded reasonable.

But unfortunately, it didn't deter Anthea. "Well, I'm not so sure that was exactly the case, my dear Celia. For even the most unworldly innocents among us are, I believe, protected by our senses, which can warn us of peril. I beg you to speak frankly to your aunt. I am sure she will not wish to force upon you anything or anyone who might be repugnant to you.

"Ah, look there—that is just what I have cautioned you about," she added with some satisfaction as she drew Celia's attention to the very intimate way Mr. Hamilton was bending his head to listen to something his lovely dance partner was saying.

"She is Lady Marvella Merrivale, one of those women they call Professional Beauties. Isn't that the height of vulgarity? She's married to Viscount Selwyn, but he's not here tonight, and rumor has it that they go their separate ways—the Marlborough House set, you know."

Celia didn't know, but she said nothing and watched their waltz keenly.

Grant Hamilton and the titian-haired Lady Marvella. What a wonderful time they seemed to be having too—quite oblivious of the other couples on the floor.

She felt a sharp stab of envy: if she had really been playing the Gypsy, that was the way she would have danced with him. Instead, she had done her best to persuade him never to ask her to dance again.

Which was exactly what she had set out to do, so why didn't that thought give her more pleasure?

"Don't look now," Anthea cautioned suddenly. "He's coming back this way again. Surely he cannot wish to compound his mistake."

Celia looked at her friend through a welter of conflicting emotions. *What would Marianna have done?*

But she knew, she *knew.* "Perhaps I really wish to dance with him again," she said pointedly, and she rose to meet Grant as Anthea's jaw dropped in dismay.

The Gypsy feels the rhythm, she adores dancing, she *adored dancing, and lessons could never have taught her the ease with which she swirled into Grant's arms. Her mother had bequeathed her that, and the breathless anticipation she felt being close to a man—*

No—only this *man . . .*

"You're nervous," he whispered in her ear as he

swung her into a polka, which always, regrettably, made her dizzy.

"*Never*," she swore as she leaned against him and tried to regain her equilibrium. Admit a weakness to *him?* She would *die* first. She smiled up at him, a Marianna smile. "My favorite dance, Mr. Hamilton," but she was beginning to think that the solid wall of his body was her favorite thing by far in this evening of new experiences.

Her smile was dazzling; her cat-eyes glowed with an incandescent enjoyment that was both rare and intoxicating.

The chit was bewitching and she didn't even know it.

Or—Grant's eyes narrowed imperceptibly—maybe she did. Look at how she snapped open her fan at exactly the moment when he chose to look deeper into those gorgeous eyes and read what it was she really wanted.

God, they all learned it by heart right from the cradle, even Gypsy enchantresses—and he was not going to be caught in her coils. Marvella was enough to deal with. One more dance and he would consider that he had done his duty—and that one would have to come later in the evening in order for it not to cause any comment.

And now he was protecting her as well. When would he ever goddamn learn?

Still, he counted the minutes; the pauses between dances; the number of other partners who, because of his lead, sought her out; the number of women who were not as beautiful as she; the number of mothers hovering around him, waving their hopes like egret feathers. He counted the number of steps in each waltz and gavotte until he could shake off Marvella's detaining hand and make his way back across the mausoleum of a ballroom to take Celia Penmaris in his arms again for the last waltz.

And she—she hung back for the barest moment beyond good taste, resenting him being *kind,* wanting to send his smug, mannered face crashing to the floor.

But Aunt Willie was watching, and ten dozen of her closest friends. Celia stiffened her spine and stepped into the circle of his arms, the Gypsy soul in her reigning once again, and gave herself up to the lure of the music, the sway of his body and the touch of his hand.

Celia paced the floor of her bedroom, walking back and forth from her small desk to the window overlooking the street.

She had been helped out of her stays and corsets and layers of petticoats, then helped into her lacy, beribboned nightgown. She had insisted upon brushing her own hair, and for the moment, it hung down her back in a dark cloud—so heavy sometimes that she longed to cut it all off. She would braid it before she extinguished the lamp and retired for the night, but now she felt too distracted.

Her aunt's idea about Grant Hamilton being her "official escort" was not going to go away: tomorrow they were all going to the opera—something by a Maestro Verdi which Anthea had already warned her was rather racy.

And *he* would be there, of course, doing his *duty* and hating every minute of it because his mind would naturally be dwelling on that Marvella creature, and so of course he would resent this whole escort business altogether.

As did she; surely this night she had proved that she didn't need him. Even though they had danced together, she had many other partners as well. Surely that proved there *were* some men in the whole city of London who might very well like to be invited to escort her someplace and would not consider it an obligation.

"Oh!" she exploded in frustration. It was the dance, only the dance, and the rhythm and the music, and the fact that he was such a marvelous dancer that had affected her and nothing else. *Nothing else.* Surely her Gypsy self should have brushed the whole thing off with a laugh and looked for the next-best man to entertain her.

She was sure of it.

She yanked out the drawer of the desk and removed her diary. She would finish her entry for this evening and then get some sleep, instead of letting her imagination run away with her.

And tomorrow she would finish her lengthy letter to her poor, darling Ronald and make sure it got posted.

She didn't need to go into detail about the reception. She didn't want to make him jealous, but there was nothing, really, for him to be jealous about.

But if he knew about it, perhaps, just perhaps, he might decide to cast all other considerations aside to come after her and carry her off with him.

It was her dearest wish, her only dream.

But that night her uneasy dreams were the exact opposite of her romantic wishes—disconnected and disoriented.

She was Marianna, a Spanish Gypsy dancer on a stage—her dancing uninhibited and inviting, tempting every man and any man to fall under her spell. She was so sure of herself; she was so powerful.

She could have any man she wanted . . . she *saw* them all there, yearning for her behind the footlights. But it was Ronald, with his glinting gold hair, to whom she threw her rose.

And when the door to her dressing room opened and she turned around from the mirror, it was another man, a dark and dangerous stranger, who stood there instead of her love, and he was holding her rose all bruised and crushed in one hand, while in the other he held a revolver that was pointed right at her heart.

She wept in anguish. Why must she make a choice?

Ronald was safety and security; the Dark One was danger and uncertainty . . .

She tried to run from both of them, and suddenly she was running on yellow sand, by the ocean, and the tide was coming in, and with each step she felt her feet slowing and sinking deeper into the wet, sucking sands until she had to stop and turn—to face her relentless pursuer. And she was sinking, sinking, and holding her arms out to him, begging him to save her from suffocating and drowning—

And he stood there smiling, a dark satyr in the moonlight, and the nemesis of her dreams.

Five

"*My dearest Celia* . . . yes, it's a beginning at least—but can't you write a passionate love letter that will stir your little fiancée's maiden heart, Ronnie, dear? Do you want her *and* her fortune stolen out from under your nose while you hesitate and look for the right words? Shall *I* dictate this letter? Pay attention, or I shall be very cross with you—and you know what *that* means, don't you, lover?"

Ronald Winwood, naked and sweating from the heat, was lying on his stomach in bed with his writing tablet poised promisingly in front of him between his propped-up arms.

His mistress straddled his body and was watching his every move over his shoulder, and as she ordered him and he did not do as she wished, she gave him a stinging slap on his buttock that made him jump.

God—Adriana was such a tiger! He could just picture her riding him, her glistening auburn hair falling over her face that never showed emotion, and her cognac eyes glittering with triumph. He could feel her knees and thighs gripping his hips, he could imagine the long line of her body and her naked breasts swinging over his back, barely touching, just enough so he knew she was there.

How could he be expected to write to his self-effacing little fiancée when Adriana kept teasing and tempting and tormenting him, making him crave her domination?

She slapped his flinching flesh a second time, and he groaned with a mixture of pleasure and pain.

"Ronnie! I told you—write! *Con passione—capisce?* We need her here, your betrothed, do we not? Now *write!* And if you cannot compose a billet-doux by yourself, then I will help you find the right words, even if they hurt you—each one—as you write them out. You have to stir this dull little creature into a feeling of longing for you, of desire for she knows not what— only that she is becoming excited by feelings that are unfamiliar to her. So now—I'll give you the words. I am in the mood, I think, to seduce a little virgin with words that will rouse her senses and make her curious to discover more."

She began to dictate the words and Ronald wrote and it was unlike anything he had written to his fiancée previously. It was a love poem, couched in veiled terms of how much he missed her and longed for her to be there with him as his wife, as his own true love.

"*'Carissima,'* Adriana? Really? To that simpering little virgin?"

She slapped him again. "*Write!* Men are cretins—they know nothing about what is in a woman's heart. Say, *mi dolce amore*. Tell her you long to caress her—"

"I ache to caress you—"

She pinched him and he yelped. "Now you understand, Ronnie, dearest. You fondle your fiancée with words first—and then, if you have done a good job and properly convinced her to come to you, I will allow you to fondle me . . ."

* * *

Grant turned lazily in bed, stretching, his one arm grazing the soft, bare skin of Marvella Merrivale, who lay beside him.

Dear Marvella, convenient, beautiful, practiced and practical. A man was fortunate to have a Marvella in his life, someone he could turn to for the physical necessities, and walk away from at the drop of a diamond necklace.

Even in sleep she looked as though she had arranged herself for the best effect. So beautiful, so businesslike.

Such an alien concept to someone as naive as his stepmother's gorgeous Gypsy . . .

Damn, he hadn't wanted to give a moment's thought to *her* this morning, especially when there were more interesting things at hand.

He had just begun his assault on Marvella's very willing body when he heard the discreet knock at his bedroom door.

Blast! He ignored it . . . and the second time, it came even more insistently.

"*What?* What is it?" he demanded testily as Marvella stirred beneath his hand, wakened by both his silken touch and his uncharacteristic bellow.

His valet appeared in the doorway.

"What *is* it, for God's sake?"

"It's—it's—"

"What? Am I late for a funeral? Or a lady?"

Marvella giggled and his valet moved aside and in marched the tornado he called his stepmother.

Marvella shrieked and dove under the covers while he stared grimly at Willie, not moving.

"You've gone too far *this* time, *madrastra*. Damn it! You are an impossibly overbearing female, and I am *not* sixteen years old. Christ! Don't you have any tact?"

She ignored him and *that*, and bent over the bed to the lump that was Marvella's shaking body. "How *are* you, Marvella, darling? No, you don't have to reply this minute. To expect *that* would be the height of bad manners. Perhaps I should wait in the anteroom while you two collect yourselves and your various garments.''

"*Willie!*'' Grant growled through gritted teeth.

"Well, don't blame poor Turner—I forced my way in here. We were supposed to go riding this morning, but I see you've already exercised *your* mount . . . Grant, I must talk to you, and I think Marvella should be aware that her husband is on his way home to surprise her, so she'd better hurry along. Go ahead, dear— I'll just turn my head. It will be as if I never saw you . . .''

And Willie turned her back to the bed, and heard the rustling of the covers as Marvella eased herself out of bed with an intimate whisper to Grant and disappeared into the anteroom.

"Well, thank God she's gone. Really, Grant, you could do better than Marvella. Or have you reached the point where you dislike a challenge?''

He rolled over and pulled the sheet with him to cover his body. "I think I am not going to answer that most impertinent question. Marvella is none of your business, *madrastra,* and I think your manners leave a lot to be desired. Now tell me what is so urgent that you had to invade my bedroom this morning. I just know it had nothing to do with—*riding.*''

He folded his arms behind his head and waited.

She watched him, craftily, cagily, trying to gauge exactly how he felt. Finding Marvella in his bed was both a hopeful sign and a disappointment; she didn't like Marvella in the least, but the fact he had sought her out could indicate he meant to stay in London long enough to help with Celia.

But at that moment, in the dusky light of the late morning, with his temper about one degree from exploding at her high-handedness, she could not tell whose side he was on—and she couldn't have stood waiting another moment to find out.

"I need your help, Grant. And you *did* promise, didn't you? For no more than a month or two, until we instill Celia with some self-confidence and she can go out on her own? I want to make absolutely sure you are with me on this—and then you will be able to feel that you have done at least one good deed in your life," she added lightly. "Isn't there a line in a play or a poem that goes like that?"

There was long, edgy silence during which she forced herself not to say another word, and it was so very, very hard. But Grant was as loyal to her and as affectionate as a son; he wouldn't let her down, she was almost positive.

And finally, she felt a palpable release of pressure in the air and he threw up his hands.

"Very well, dear Stepmama, but I'm warning you right now—there are limits to my endurance, *and* to my sense of humor. And I think it's only fair that I know about Celia's background. You had better spell it out for me, Willie, or I might end up seducing your prim and proper Gypsy, just to make sure she comes out of her shell. Or was that what you had in mind?"

"Don't be ridiculous, Grant," she said dampingly, and then she looked at him sharply. There was a tone in his voice as if something else were underlying his words, but her sense of it was gone like the snap of her fingers, and she thought she must have imagined it.

"No, this is what I want you to do. Start by teaching her how to *flirt*—how to do it, just how far to go before pulling back, just how far a man will let her go. You know the sort of thing—you do it all the time without even thinking."

"So I'm to put myself in a virginal female's place? And I'm to teach her to tease and provoke while she remains chaste? Are you *crazy?* I'm to play traitor to the male sex—not to mention acting as if I were a eunuch and not following through?'' He shook his head as if he couldn't believe what he was hearing.

But it was Willie, and she was looking at him with that provoking look she had that was all her own and just dared him to make some excuse and back down.

"Christ, I'll tell you what—you've laid down your ground rules; now I've got some of my own. I'm not interested in seducing your little virgin while I'm teaching her to flirt and tease—but I promise you, Willie, if *she* tries to seduce *me,* then I'm not making any promises that I won't let the wench have her way with me. So watch out—you're opening a Pandora's box, and not even you know what you could be unleashing.''

Willie heaved a sigh of relief. ''Oh, nonsense, Grant. You're a gentleman, which is more than I think Celia's betrothed is. Ronald someone-thing, his name is, and supposedly he's known her from her childhood in Ceylon, so of course she's infatuated with him. But it's also possible he's only after her because she's an heiress now. So we need to educate Celia to be a little more worldly, and perhaps see through the posturing of some . . . *interested parties?*''

She left him with that thought and he simmered for an hour over how neatly she had turned his affection—and curiosity—to her advantage.

What in hell difference did it make to *him* whether the Gypsy had a mind in her pretty little head or not? He had all but decided to present Willie with some urgent excuse to escape the situation—but leave it to her to turn the tables. He really had to admire her; it was almost as if she were a mind reader. He hoped to hell she was reading his mind right now—

Or maybe he was reading hers. What in hell was that business about a *fiancé?* She had slipped it right by him with the ease of a knife slicing through mutton. The Gypsy had a *fiancé?*

He levered himself up into a sitting position. A baby she was, taking baby steps into a world she knew nothing of, and she had someone somewhere *waiting?* Waiting for what? For Willie to polish her up with the veneer of a debutante—and then what? He would come riding through the streets of London, ready to claim his prize?

Who the hell was he?

There was something about the whole story that just didn't mesh, and Grant didn't think it was coincidental that Willie hadn't given him one detail about the Gypsy's history.

Well, he was committed one way or another, so he was going to do some research into the background and antecedents of Willie's niece—and the fiancé, Ronald someone-thing. If Celia had known him from childhood, then he quite obviously came from Ceylon and he might even be involved with growing tea—which was not such a lucky guess: it was a place to start, and it might prove interesting.

In any event, he might find himself in the position of needing to protect dear Willie all around—even from her precious deceased brother, Richard.

Six

Celia awakened the next morning swamped with a feeling that she was nothing more than a little wooden puppet and that someone else always seemed to be pulling the strings.

The dream had crushed her.

She was no Gypsy; she longed for simplicity and an ordinary life as Ronald's cherished wife. It was a waste of time and money, having a Season. All those silly rituals she had had to learn—and why was a lady always required to be polite, under any circumstances, no matter what the provocation? And why had none of her tutors ever told her how to respond to a man who said one thing on the surface with his smooth serpent voice and quite another with his *eyes?*

Or were her moral fiber and spiritual strength actually being tested, as Anthea had suggested?

And now this business of attending the opera tonight.

She wondered what she was afraid of; it wasn't as if she were going to be alone with anyone. All she had to do was remember her training, act as she was supposed to and pretend to be just what she was supposed to be; then all would be well.

All she needed to do was play the part of a debutante and fade into the scenery, colorless, expressionless and without an opinion of her own. And she must not let her imagination run away with her.

And if she felt an unnatural excitement at the possibility of catching a glimpse of the Prince of Wales and Princess Alexandra, she wouldn't show it; she would act as if it were the most common thing in the world, like those stiff-jawed aristocrats who were her aunt's friends.

She made a face, squaring her jaw and tilting her chin up in the air. Like that—what *must* she look like? She climbed out of bed and posed in front of the mirror. She would clench her teeth and talk in muted syllables—like this: "My deah, it's ounleh the prin-*cess*. Whot a bore. We had tea ounleh an houah ago, and I can think of nothing else to say to *her!*" she told her reflection quite haughtily.

She giggled as she watched her mouth contort around the words and she thought how out of place they sounded coming from her full-lipped mouth. She could never carry off that degree of nonchalance—not with her face, not with her body.

Slowly, she slipped out of her modest, high-collared peignoir and stood daringly in her chemise in front of the mirror.

What did other people see when they saw her? Her looks were *so* different, so striking, so much like her mother's. Celia had a precious photograph of her when she was dressed for the stage, a beautiful Gypsy woman in a low-cut peasant blouse and long, tiered skirt. There had been bangles on her graceful, sinuous arms, and her hair had been a waterfall of ebony over her shoulders.

But it was the eyes—the light eyes against the darker skin, the knowing look in those eyes—that she remembered most and which she always saw staring back at her in the mirror.

It was Marianna who had had men falling all over themselves chasing her, throwing bouquets onto the stage, sending her gifts, offering her everything.

How did Marianna *know?*

What had Celia's father sacrificed when he fell in love at first sight with Marianna?

And for what? What had her knowledge and his love gained them both?

Only she was left, a reminder of someone's folly, and about to commit her own.

London was *her* stage—she had felt it last night, acted on it last night in spite of all her misgivings. She was not an outcast in this world: she had the support and the sponsorship of Aunt Willie and the sure hand on her arm of Grant Hamilton, *escorting* her, guiding her.

Aunt Willie would never let anything happen to her; in the proscribed circle of her friends, these things did not happen. Grant was safe, and she was acting like an utter fool.

All she needed to do was dress for the evening and let events take their course.

And if the Gypsy within her surfaced for the occasion, so be it. If her mother's spirit was protecting her, she might even come away from this blighted ritual of the Season relatively unscathed.

Willie, however, was having second thoughts. Celia's success the previous night was unprecedented for a stranger newly introduced to the rigors of the Season, and even Grant's stamp of approval couldn't quite account for the rather sophisticated face that Celia had presented to her aunt's guests.

And tonight she seemed to have come to life again, a different person entirely from the rather obedient and colorless young girl who had sat across from Willie at the breakfast table.

She wondered if she was beginning to regret having pulled Grant into her scheme to initiate Celia into the particular world of the aristocracy. What if the child became infatuated with him? Why hadn't she thought of that? Of course, he had made it plain he wasn't interested in Celia—but men never said what they meant anyway. She would have to talk to him again, and keep a keen eye on him when they were together socially.

It was really all she could do, especially since Celia the aspiring debutante was such a different creature from the Celia whom she had brought to London from the Grange.

But she let none of this show as she dressed Celia for this next occasion in a gown of ivory peau de soie, caught up on one side of the skirt by pink and red silk roses. There were roses and pearls threaded into her high-piled tresses, and elbow-length ivory silk gloves to match.

"Oh, Celia, look at you! Don't ever forget how beautiful you look tonight. And I have here just the finishing touch—"

She held up the most beautiful pearl-and-diamond necklace and motioned to Celia to bend her head so that she could fasten it around her neck.

"And the earrings." Willie handed them to Celia and stood back as she put them on. "There!"

Celia turned toward the mirror and back again to Willie. "Are you sure there isn't just a little too much skin showing?"

"Oh, no, not at all. You look absolutely perfect. And the color of the gown is marvelous with your eyes and hair. You can't imagine how lovely you are to me," Willie added, hugging Celia lightly and impulsively.

Celia turned to the mirror again. She saw something, a recklessness perhaps that went with an elegant gown and a backbone of steel stays and a resentment that all things must be as others dictated, even her pleasure for the evening.

She felt dangerous, as only a beautiful woman can. She felt as if she could command some measure of control, but that she would have to give herself over to the secret self within her.

She turned and looked at her reflection once again. It was not her; it was yet another part of the equation of selves that she was discovering.

Very well, then. She would enjoy this night as well as this other self, and let the consequences fall where they might—tomorrow.

"It's called a stirrup cup, my dear, and it's perfectly permissible to have a few sips before we leave for the opera. You didn't eat too much, did you?"

"Oh, half a sandwich, a pastry, nothing that would spoil my appetite for dinner."

"Very wise, Celia. It's a long evening, to be sure, but one does want to take the edge off without filling up. Well? Do you like champagne?"

Oh, she did, she did; the bubbles tickled her nose, and the dry, fizzy taste positively went to her head. "It's lovely, Aunt Willie."

"Yes, it makes things so much brighter and bearable," Willie said, motioning to the footman to bring their wraps. "Here's the carriage, Celia—watch your step."

She did feel somewhat light-headed as the carriage moved forward, and she stared out the window at all the other passing carriages and hackneys and the people standing on the pavements and staring.

All of London seemed to be lit up with electric lights, which made the gaslight fade into flickering eclipse by contrast.

She drank in everything greedily. This was London, the London of plagues and fires and rebirth, hustling and bustling and never quiet. And *she,* Celia Penmaris, was on her way to the Covent Garden Opera House to see a performance of Verdi's *La Traviata,* the story of a girl who strayed but who regained her soul in the end. A biblical kind of story, almost, which had somehow been set to music.

And then they arrived, and she could not believe the crowds of people all around that seemed to press closer every time a carriage stopped and its occupants alighted.

As they waited their turn, she heard the sound of voices rising and falling, almost a nerve-racking roar. Her hands, encased in those elegant gloves that fit like a second skin, suddenly felt clammy.

She squeezed her eyes shut so she wouldn't have to see the people. She could not do this—she was an impostor, and everyone who saw her would know it in a minute.

She felt Willie grasp her hands warmly and firmly and hold them comfortingly for a few minutes, and then she opened her eyes and looked at her aunt.

"Celia, dear, I know just how you feel, believe me. I ran this gauntlet once too; everyone has a first time. The crowds out there, they love this. It's their only free entertainment, to watch all of us and make up stories about us. Your mother would not have been afraid of them, I'm certain. She would have thrown kisses at them—"

Yes, yes, that was exactly what Marianna would have done, Celia thought as she smiled gratefully at Willie.

"I wish I had known her," Willie added with regret tingeing her voice.

"Me too," Celia whispered as she squared her shoulders and tried to imagine Marianna debarking from the carriage and looking over all the strange and curious faces.

She knew she glittered like a fairy princess as she stepped out of the carriage. Glittering diamonds at her throat, at her ears, in her dark, dark hair; the glitter of her knowing amber eyes . . .

She heard none of the comments or the cheers that went up, but Willie did and she felt the same discomfiting sensation she had experienced earlier.

" 'Oo's *she?* Bloody beauty *she* is!"

"You watch out fer 'is 'Ighnness, luv! Now, 'e's got an eye fer the pretty ones, 'e 'as!"

Watch out, watch out! She had gone and done it again, Willie thought—placed Celia in a situation that could well spin out of her control. Of course the Prince of Wales would notice her—who wouldn't?—but what if he started to make discreet inquiries and that led to— She refused to think about that right at this moment. It was enough just to let the thought float around the edges of her consciousness.

She would make it a point to be more conscientious about chaperoning Celia this evening and to be thankful that they were to see the opera from the elegant private box that her friend Jennie Churchill had lent her.

To make things worse, Grant was late. He should have been there before them, and his disregard of her wishes was just too much, Willie thought furiously even as she smiled and whispered apologies to the friends she had invited to join them.

Fortunately, the lights dimmed soon after they had arranged themselves in their seats, and the overture began. It would give Celia time to get used to things— and it would give *her* time to think about what she'd do to her stepson if he didn't turn up before Act One began.

Seven

Celia felt as though she was floating on the surface of a glistening champagne bubble: the music was magical, the opera heart-wrenching.

But she hadn't cried at the end—although her eyes were huge and shiny with unshed tears—and she had managed quite well to maintain her composure, even when so many people, mostly men, simply crowded around them as they left their box.

"This is unbelievable," Willie muttered exasperatedly. "We'll just go to the Ladies' Retiring Room and freshen up until everyone leaves."

"How long do you think it will take?" Celia asked, but she wasn't sure she really wanted to know. What she didn't want was to face Grant Hamilton again so soon. *He* was too much, with his wicked eyes and that devilish expression on his face. *He* made her feel as if she were still a child, and she hated him for it.

Willie, meantime, was pacing back and forth between the sitting room and the hallway door, and starting to feel extremely anxious about Celia. Her niece was flushed and glowing—too flushed and much too glowing—and her voice was a little too bright, almost as if she had had too much champagne.

And Grant hadn't helped matters any the way he had kept gazing at her with that very dark and dangerous look.

She didn't know what to think. To all intents and purposes, Celia was still a child and playing at being the sophisticated debutante, but there was something very unnerving about the fact that she did not look or act like a child tonight.

"Celia, dear, this hasn't all been too much for you, has it?" she asked worriedly.

Celia smiled, a mysterious, knowing smile that instantly set Willie's hackles up. "Oh, no, Aunt Willie. I feel wonderful. I feel so—how I should love to dance tonight! And didn't you think I handled those rash young men very well? Do you think I'm learning to flirt—just a little?"

"Just a *very* little," Willie said grimly, feeling suddenly as if she had no control over her charge whatsoever. How silly, she told herself, when she was the one who had set these events in motion.

But her unease escalated as the rest of the evening progressed. They left the safety and quiet of the Retiring Room to find Grant waiting for them, and then they had to walk what seemed like miles of red Chinese carpet from the upper floors to the lobby, their voices echoing eerily off the ornate molded ceilings now that most of the crowd had dispersed.

And at that, there wasn't much to say: Celia seemed giddy and full of herself, and Grant looked every bit as displeased as Willie felt.

It didn't help matters that they had hardly been seated at Grant's usual table at Romano's before they were interrupted by other diners, all angling for an introduction to the latest beauty.

Willie's appetite vanished. This was too much too soon. Celia had barely been formally presented anywhere and already they were clamoring to meet her. Willie didn't know quite how to react to the demand. Celia wasn't ready, that was all there was to it—look at her now, Willie thought; the girl was still as sparkling and effervescent as the champagne she had begun to sip.

And Grant was impossible, with that inscrutable way he kept looking at Celia, as if he were assessing her as a woman—as prey.

She hated that she had to trust him to behave himself and remember Celia's age and her innocence.

Although she didn't look terribly innocent at this very moment.

Grant caught her eye just then and she frowned loweringly at him. He raised one eyebrow and gave her an impudent grin, and she wished she were close enough to kick his shins good and hard under the table.

Damn him, what did he think he was doing?

But it was quite obvious: Grant was damned well enjoying himself at the sight of the virgin Gypsy turned temptress.

It suited her, he thought, to have a personality that matched her looks. She was a spitfire under the guise of submissive innocent, and this dinner was proving much more interesting than he could have imagined.

He wondered, as he leaned back in his chair to get a clear view of her deliberately turned, golden-hued shoulder, how this Celia would meet the challenges that would now surely come her way. And how would Willie handle this changed—and charged—situation?

Of course, *he* was just an observer, the escort who blended in with the woodwork, and besides, his taste didn't run to virgins.

Their waiter approached the table and handed Grant an engraved card inviting the Dowager Duchess of Millhaven and her party to a late supper, with dancing afterward, at the home of an old friend, Countess Remoyne; she had written a little note to the effect that this small gathering was an extremely spur-of-the-moment affair suggested by the Prince of Wales, who felt in need of some further entertainment this evening among friends.

Willie's spirits sank even lower. Celia did not need this, not the way she was acting this evening, and neither did Willie, but how could she say no to this express invitation from the prince?

Obviously she couldn't; she would just have to stay as close to Celia as a duenna, and not let one man get within ten feet of her.

Celia, meanwhile, was nibbling at her food and relishing the secret power that seemed to bubble up from some place inside her. It was *easy* to talk to men; one merely had to say the right thing at the right moment, and one discovered what that was just by listening raptly to whatever they chose to talk about.

And she wasn't going to let the obnoxious Mr. Hamilton spoil her evening at all; she did think her reminding him earlier of the great difference in their ages had really put him in his place. And she had made it a point to call him "sir" at every turn and to refuse to meet his dangerous eyes head-on, while she gazed attentively into the eyes of whichever man had been introduced to her at the moment.

So much for escorts.

The young man on her left could do just as well as Mr. Grant "Rude" Hamilton, even if he was rather callow. At least the Honorable Jack Swinnerton had political ambitions and knew a great deal about India, where he hoped to go soon as an aide to the new viceroy.

And he seemed very gratified to find a young lady who was intelligent and versed in several languages and who was fascinated by the knowledge and wisdom that he could impart to her.

She didn't need Grant Hamilton at all, she thought rebelliously. She was a success without his patronizing help.

Still, Mr. Swinnerton was leaning rather close to her—and then she felt a not-too-gentle nudge at her ankle. Swiftly, she moved her feet beneath her chair.

He pretended not to notice her rebuff and he dared, the unutterable boor, he had the *gall,* to pinch her thigh under the cover of the tablecloth.

She never could have imagined the outrage she felt; it overset even her irritation with Grant Hamilton as she swiveled around to face him, her fingers clenched around her fan as if she would use it as a weapon.

"Mr. Hamilton!"

"Miss Penmaris, I apologize for nudging your ankle. It was a crude way to get your attention, I'm afraid, but you must allow me the privileges of my advanced years. My apologies, Swinnerton, but Miss Penmaris's aunt has been trying to catch her attention for some time now. You'll forgive me?"

Celia's gaze shifted over toward Willie, and she immediately rose and went to her side. "Oh, dear, Aunt Willie, have I done something wrong? I'm so sorry! Must we leave?"

"I need to talk to you at once, and in private," Willie said succinctly. Celia had learned a lesson tonight, and it was one that neither she nor Grant could have taught her.

"Come, accompany me to the Retiring Room; you've done nothing wrong, but I need to speak to you for a moment in private. Watch out for the waiters over there, now. It is crowded tonight. Doesn't that dessert look delicious? Well, one can dream, can't one? Here we are—you can fix your hair later, my dear, and I daresay you will want to."

She handed Celia the invitation to read for herself.

Her mouth fell open. "The Prince of Wales? Dancing? But—*me*, Aunt Willie?"

"Well, I've known the countess this age. And the prince admires youth and beauty; of course he noticed you tonight, but he is a gentleman. So all you have to do is be yourself, and—well, who knows what might happen? You might even be presented to Princess Alexandra, which would well and truly launch you into society. You would be accepted everywhere without question, but of course, this is putting the cart before the horse. We will naturally accept the invitation and see what happens from there."

And there it was again, that look in Celia's eyes, that other self coming to the fore. Celia liked the idea of meeting the Prince of Wales—who wouldn't?—but more than that, this once in her life, Celia wanted to feel like Cinderella at the ball.

Eight

They waded into the fawning crowd of eligible gentlemen to get their wraps, and waited an exhaustive fifteen minutes until their carriage crept up to the door.

"And look at the traffic," Willie moaned. "It will take at least an hour to travel five city blocks to get to the countess's town house."

"One could send one's regrets," Grant suggested, his tone faintly tinged with acid as he looked at Celia's flushed face.

"I wish," Willie murmured. "But I cannot cry off Sylvia's express invitation. Very likely she wants all the company possible to deal with *him*. I never could understand why people fall all over themselves to brush up against royalty, but there it is. Even Celia is overcome at the thought of it."

"That is because of your egalitarian American ways, dear Stepmama, and Celia is looking more *come over* than overcome. We know better than to trust the prince within inches of any woman under the age of twenty-five, no matter what the gossip says about him."

Celia looked from one to the other, feeling resentful that they were ordering things about for her as if she weren't there. Willie had no right spoiling the event for her before they had even arrived.

And Grant—she had no words for him at all; she wished she could just ignore him with his cynicism and his mocking tone of voice. He made her feel gauche and callow when she had begun the evening by feeling sophisticated and reckless.

The incident with Mr. Swinnerton made her feel stupid, and the fact that *he* had not been the one nudging her ankle embarrassed her.

So she was very much in a mood to be contrary *and* bold, if only to show both her aunt and Mr. Grant "Rude" Hamilton that she wasn't some imbecilic little chit who couldn't handle herself amongst the high and mighty.

How different could it be, after all, from dealing with the swarming men who had surrounded her at the opera and in Romano's? One was polite, murmured agreement, wasn't too forward and curtsied when being presented to the prince. She could not hope for more than that, she thought. She would meet him and he would never remember who she was by the very next hour.

Which was a very lowering thought that would definitely keep her from getting carried away.

But the sight of the town house of Countess Remoyne bowled her over. It was the sole residence on a small crescent off Hyde Park Lane, it overlooked the park and it was lit up like a veritable Christmas tree.

The front stoop looked to be at least a quarter of a block long, with wide, shallow marble steps that led up to an imposing ten-foot-high, polished mahogany door which was thrown open and attended by the butler.

A footman stood at the bottom of the steps, greeting guests as they alighted from their carriages.

"Well," Willie said repressively, watching the line of

elegantly attired visitors who had arrived before them, "here we are . . ."

Their carriage lurched to a stop and the footman punctiliously opened the door.

"The countess bids you welcome."

"Thank you," Willie said, extending her hand so he could help her out. "The former Duchess of Millhaven, Mrs. Hamilton; my ward, Miss Celia Penmaris; and my stepson, Mr. Grant Hamilton."

"Very good," the footman said as he took Celia's hand and guided her safely out of the carriage. He waited for Grant before he preceded them up the stairs, whispered their credentials to the butler and left them in his hands.

Celia stopped stone-still on the threshold of the reception hall, utterly dazzled by the magnificence beyond the door.

It was an entrance two stories high, with the walls painted a pale peach and moldings picked out in creamy white. On the walls there were lush landscapes framed in gilt, and there was a jewel-toned Turkish runner leading from the front entrance to an anteroom which was recessed beyond a graceful arch, its doorway hidden in the shadows.

The sheer simplicity and elegance of this small reception area was breathtaking. Celia felt as if she could just drink it in for the remainder of the night. What must the rest of the house be like?

Yet another footman appeared from some other hidden anteroom to help Willie remove her wrap, then waited patiently for Celia to enter the room so he could take hers.

It was Grant who pulled her over the threshold, his expression amused and—did she dare expect it?—even a little kind.

She surreptitiously looked up as she shrugged out of

her cloak. The ceiling soared, outlined in thick criss-crossed moldings and centered with a rosette from which hung a Waterford chandelier.

An ancient tapestry was suspended from a balcony fifteen feet above Celia's head, its colors as vibrant as if the cloth had been woven this past year. And a marble bust of the queen sat in a small niche in the right side wall between two unobtrusive doors which were closed.

The footman reappeared through one of them and motioned for the threesome to follow the butler, who paused at the formidable doors beyond the arch before he thrust them open and announced their presence in stentorian tones.

Celia stood behind Grant, so she could not immediately see inside the room, but she had the impression it was immense, bigger even than Aunt Willie's ballroom. Gaslights flared everywhere from elegant sconces evenly spaced along the walls and from the six fixtures that hung from the ceiling.

She heard music and the murmur of voices, neither loud nor overwhelming, but just as she might expect the sounds to be in the house of a countess who entertained royalty.

And then she heard Aunt Willie: "Sylvia, my darling—"

And a low, mellifluous voice in return: "Wilhelmina, my dear—!"

And then Grant moved aside and Celia caught her first glimpse of Countess Remoyne and the pageant she enacted at the whim and will of royalty.

The room was crowded, but not uncomfortably so, and the sweet scents of mingled perfumes pervaded the air with what Celia imagined was artful conversation.

It was as if the participants were dancing a quadrille—

an exchange of pleasantries and change partners for the next go-round, and this against a backdrop of the utmost elegance: the glow of the gaslight, fragile brocade-covered chairs grouped together for conversation nearby the ten-foot-high French doors, which were swagged with matching brocade curtains.

They moved over a polished parquet floor, mingling one group to the next, a groundswell of guests invariably hewing toward one side of the room where the Prince of Wales must be holding court.

On a balcony above, a string quartet played the soothing airs of Mozart and Vivaldi; below, footmen walked amongst the guests, offering tidbits to tide them over until a midnight supper would be served.

"Just a little spontaneous get-together for two hundred of the prince's most interesting friends," Countess Sylvia Remoyne said in her fluty voice, and it was impossible to tell if she was being serious or sarcastic.

She was tall, almost as tall as Grant, and she positively towered over Aunt Willie, and she was slender, almost angular, and sharp, too sharp, in both her look and her words. But she was dressed in the height of fashion and she obviously knew everyone and everything, and by her frankness and her station in society, she was probably considered an original who set styles and determined celebrity.

And she obviously approved of Celia, from her unusual looks and fashionable dress right down to her stature.

"And, of course, the moment he saw this little dove, he would not rest until I issued you an invitation," she added, moving on to Celia and tilting her face upward toward the lights so she could see her face, her eyes. "You are breathtaking, my dear. No wonder he noticed you. Celia, is it not?"

She would not be tongue-tied, she *wouldn't*—but *how*

did one address a countess? "Yes, ma'am," she murmured, and hoped frantically it would do.

"And Grant," Sylvia went on, extending her hand. "You are most welcome, especially because you are Willie's beloved stepson. I know every detail, my boy. We have kept in sporadic touch. Your father is a magician—he has made Willie very happy, even though he has taken her so far away. I see her happiness in her eyes and in her smile. Willie, dear, we have much to talk about. These two youngsters will find their way by themselves. Come—"

Celia wanted to protest, but Sylvia led Willie away without a further word, and she suddenly felt as if she were adrift without an anchor. And the women were already clustering around Grant—*of course*—so she would get no help there.

She squared her shoulders and turned away from the fawning crowd of pastel dresses that had corraled him in their midst and started to walk resolutely around the perimeter of the gathering.

What would the Gypsy do?

The thought insinuated itself in her mind like a twisty little snake.

She would get up and dance and make sure everyone was watching her.

Which would surely be a social gaffe that would destroy any chance Celia might have of success.

More than that, she would hold her head high, and never think that because she was not an aristocrat these fluttery, fluty people were any better than she.

"Well, hello—"

"Have we been introduced?"

"You came with—"

"Of course. Millhaven—"

"I saw her arrive—"

"She is gorgeous—"

"Those eyes—"

She heard the polite excuses for an introduction and the whispers as she made her way through the crowd.

She didn't even know where she intended to go, but as she got closer to the knot of people surrounding the prince and her heart began pounding wildly, she thought perhaps that she had intended to just catch a *glimpse* of him.

And that she wasn't madly flattered by the fact he had specifically asked for her to attend this evening's party.

And besides, he was so enveloped by the crowd, he would never notice her.

She was shocked that everyone else did, and that a path seemed to open just for her as she skirted the edge of those congregated around him. Suddenly he could see her and she could see him.

She froze as he turned away from his intimates and walked slowly toward her.

"Well, well, here she is," he murmured, so that only the closest surrounding him could hear.

She could hear, and she couldn't have moved a muscle if her life depended on it. This was *not* the way she had envisioned this moment.

And he was not nearly the way she had envisioned *him*, and the most stunning surprise was how *old* he was.

Nor was he tall—not much taller than she—but not discomfited by it either as he came to her and stopped a step or two in front of her.

She felt like a living statue—like an intruder, a fool, an impostor.

"Here you are," he said in a faintly starchy accent as if he had been expecting her all along, and she wondered dazedly how that could have been unless he was actually *looking* for her.

She licked her lips and tried to calm her shaking hands. *What now? What should she do? Should she curtsy?*

Should she even respond without a formal invitation?
Dear God, every stricture flew out of her mind and the
quelling voice of Aunt Gertrude echoed deep in her con-
sciousness: ''—fast elements in this so-called society—
hold fast to the principles—hold fast—hold—''

She couldn't think of a thing to do but sketch a curtsy
and murmur, ''Your Highness,'' and she was convinced
that the countess would come thundering down on her
for even that breach of royal etiquette.

''My dear, we are among friends,'' he said kindly, and
she thought he sounded like the wise old uncle that Theo
had never been. ''Quite informal here—''

''Do go on, Bertie. You are scaring the poor thing to
death,'' a new voice interposed, and Celia recognized it
as Sylvia's. She had come, thank heaven, to rescue her
from committing a faux pas. ''I will make the necessary
introductions. May I present the Dowager Duchess of
Millhaven, Mrs. Wilhelmina Hamilton . . .''

Willie curtsied and extended her hand.

''And this extravagant creature is her ward, Miss Celia
Penmaris.''

''Ceee-lia,'' he mouthed, lengthening the syllable into
a caress. ''Miss Penmaris.''

''Your Highness,'' she said again, and followed Aunt
Willie's lead and curtsied again.

''There, now,'' Sylvia said. ''Formalities and ameni-
ties have been observed and you may commence a conversation, Bertie. But remember that Celia is new to
London society, and do not go shocking her with your
libertine opinions.''

''I?'' his Highness said with an expression of pure
deviltry on his face. ''Surely not I, Sylvia. I only wish
to talk to Miss Penmaris and perhaps claim a dance if
you can arrange it.''

''A capital idea, Bertie; less talk, less trouble. I'll just advise the musicians, and you may by all means have your dance."

As Sylvia floated off, with Aunt Willie in tow, the prince turned to Celia.

"So you are new to Town, my dear. What a breath of fresh air you bring with you. And you are so beautiful. And so nervous. Ah, my dear, do not be afraid of *me*."

"I think perhaps I am not," Celia murmured shyly.

"Ah, that is good. Tell me, where is your home? How is it you come to London now, and why have we never seen you before?"

His interest seemed genuine, but even so, Celia meant to keep her answers short and to the point. But the dewy expression in his eyes, all concern and focused solely on her, and the encouraging nods he gave when she paused in her narrative, made her reveal more than she had intended to, including how grateful she was for his interest, rather like that of the uncle she wished she had had.

"Ah, my dear, what a sweet compliment, how flattering, but I daresay my wife is better suited to advising a young woman about the ways of society. I must arrange for you to meet. She will be entranced. My only hope is that you can keep your freshness and your delightful outlook on life in this rather jaded milieu. It will serve you well." He paused as the quartet struck a long attention-getting chord. "Ah! The music begins. Do you waltz? Perfection. Permit me to lead you to the floor, Miss Penmaris."

Permit? *Permit?* One didn't *permit* the prince. One followed blindly and felt his experienced arm encircle her waist and his hand take hers, and one tumbled headlong into the sway of the music and the total excitement of the moment.

All eyes were on them as they glided and swirled in great loping circles around the room.

And if she felt just a frisson of disapproval undermining her moment of triumph—well, she would simply ignore it and pretend she hadn't seen Mr. Grant "Spoilsport" Hamilton in the crowd with his mockingly lifted eyebrow and his icy green eyes cutting her to ribbons.

Tonight she was a princess, whirling into her future on the arms of a prince, and nothing Grant Hamilton said or did could ruin it for her.

This was a night, she thought, when dreams could come true.

By the time they returned to Carlton House Terrace, it was past five o'clock in the morning; the prince did like to keep late hours, particularly when he was enjoying himself.

Willie, who had lost the tenseness and edginess she had felt earlier in the evening, sighed from sheer weariness as she contemplated the joy of getting out of her corsets and sinking into her own soft bed.

"Would you mind very much if I sent up one of the chambermaids to unhook you and see you to bed? Emily—have you seen her? She's new, but she seems to admire you tremendously. Tomorrow"—and Willie could not help yawning the word—"tomorrow we'll have to see about finding you a personal maid of your own. And, my dear, let me congratulate you on how you seemed to have conquered all of society—including his Highness. I'm not going to ask you now how you performed such magic; we're both too tired. Tomorrow we'll talk."

And with an affectionate hug and an impulsive goodnight kiss, Willie swept out of the room.

Celia waited until the door closed behind her aunt, then swung her gaze to the mirror. Strangely, she didn't feel the least bit tired. She felt exhilarated and just a little irritated.

She *looked* rather like a gorgeous animal, with her cheeks all flushed and her eyes large and glowing with a kind of feral light in them, almost like . . . well, like a cat's—

"Miss!" And there was Emily peeking in the doorway. The maid didn't look much older than Celia, and her dark eyes sparkled and her heart-shaped face was alive with curiosity even though she had probably been roused out of a well-deserved sleep.

Still, she was neat and trim in her uniform and her dark hair was tucked up under her cap, and she looked as fresh as if it were morning.

"Come in, Emily."

"Yes, miss. If you would just turn around, miss." Which Celia did, and she felt Emily's inexperienced fingers begin the torturous job of unhooking her gown.

She could hardly bear to stand still, she was filled with so much triumph and so much vexation; she felt like pacing the floor to expend her energy.

"Please, miss." Emily's tone of voice sounded as if she were wringing her hands, as if she would be punished if Miss Celia made it impossible for her to perform this incredibly tedious task in the dead of the morning.

Celia willed her frenetic body to be still. "Is that better?"

"Oh, yes, much better, miss. Thank you, miss. And if you'll just step out of your pretty gown now, I'll get you out of those stays and petticoats as quick as I can."

She knew, of course, where Celia had been this night, but she didn't understand the suppressed emotion in her, and she wondered if she had the nerve to ask.

In the end, her curiosity overcame her fear of prying into the lives of her betters and she blurted: "Did you have a good evening of it, then, miss? Was it very grand and all at the opera?''

"Very grand," Celia murmured as she felt the constricting stays and corset and weighty petticoats fall from her body to the floor. "And exciting," she added, almost to herself. "I met the Prince of Wales. He danced with me *twice*—" And who cared if that nasty Grant Hamilton had made some lowering comment about innocents and randy old roués?

"—and he talked to me for quite a time. He really is most kind and dear and an absolute gentleman—"

"As if gentlemen don't have genitals," Grant had said snidely.

"I can believe that you are unbelievably ill-bred and ill-mannered to say such a thing to me," she had interrupted heatedly.

"On the heels of your royal triumph? My dear innocent, the man's a satyr—he would have eaten you alive if you had been alone with him."

"As opposed to your more toplofty instincts, I suppose," she had retorted rashly. "You, of course, never touch a woman when you are alone with her—of course not. How could I mistake this? You are always with women who are pure as the driven snow."

He had choked back an answer; he had to stop himself from choking her. She had seen the look in his icy green eyes, the look compounded of annoyance, exasperation and pure male righteousness.

The look that said, *I am allowed to do whatever I want—and you're not.*

The very look that aroused the hot blood in her and made her want to run the course directly opposite to his wishes—and anyone else's . . .

And so she had—

But she didn't want to think about that. She wanted to think about the warmth of the little fire burning merrily in the grate, and the feel of the nightgown slipping over her head and down her body until its hem settled at the tips of her bare feet.

She heard Emily's sigh of envy: "Oh, *miss*," as she seated herself at her dressing table so that Emily could thoroughly brush her hair, and she abstractedly admired the embroidered sleeves of her high-necked gown as she watched the rhythmic movement of Emily's arm.

She felt different tonight—this morning—in some subtle, undefinable way, but she still felt raw and untried, and maybe just a little unsure of herself, even if she looked the part of a finished debutante.

There were situations she still couldn't handle, and they had nothing to do with royalty and everything to do with the mercurial Grant.

She hadn't known what to make of his sudden reversal not a half hour after they had had that searing exchange. He had stalked off and she had pointedly turned in the opposite direction until they had met again on the other side of the room.

"I will, of course, accompany you to the riding school tomorrow, and you'll have to bear my company in the park."

Her Gypsy blood surged in resentment. "You don't have to do anything of the sort. There must be some innocent somewhere else on whom you can *force* your company."

"But I'm obliged to *escort* you, Miss Penmaris, and I always fulfill my obligations."

He could not have said anything worse.

"Oh?" she replied silkily. "I am a Duty, am I? A burden? A commission? A chore? An *assignment*? Look behind you, Mr. Hamilton. I have all the *escort* I could possibly ever want, and I now excuse you from Duty and absolve you from Responsibility."

The ice in his eyes thawed to a hot emerald green. "Scared, are you, Miss Penmaris?"

"Of you? My dear Mr. Hamilton, you are a disinterested observer, nothing more, nothing less. Or at least that is how I see you—"

But she didn't see him that way at all, and she couldn't see any way to cry off either, because it probably wouldn't do her any good if she did. He did not scare her—not now, after he had made it abundantly clear what he thought of her—and she would put up with his company for the ride even if he would criticize her inexperience and make her lesson more nerve-racking than it already was.

She didn't even know why she was devoting so much energy to thinking about him. She should be writing in her diary, and completing that long-overdue letter to Ronald. Dear Ronald, so safe, so gentlemanly. How could she even think about Grant when Ronald was waiting for her so patiently.

The diary first, perhaps.

She drew it out and opened it to the succeeding blank page. So much to tell; so smart of her to create a shorthand comprised of a mixture of Greek, Sanskrit and Sinhalese which no one else could read so that she could confide all her inmost secrets.

What inmost secrets this night?

That she had waltzed with a prince—and matched wits with a frog—and wished he did not have the capacity to *annoy* her so . . .

Perhaps she could persuade Aunt Willie to accompany her to her riding lesson, and then it wouldn't be quite so bad . . .

She yawned, stared at the several words she had written and snapped the diary shut determinedly.

She had to get some sleep. And she really would finish

her letter to Ronald later; then she could feel less guilty about succumbing, even briefly, to the glitter and glamour of a London Season—and to a pair of glittering, gloating green eyes.

Nine

Emily brought her breakfast—too soon, Celia thought as she yawned and stretched and fought against her drowsiness. Her eyes felt so heavy she was sure they were swollen and puffed. Her head ached slightly too— the effect of a very late party or all that champagne she had consumed just as easily as if it had been lemonade?

She sat up and rubbed at her eyes and decided she simply wasn't going to think about the previous night— at least not until she had had some tea and toast—and then she ducked her head back into the pillows as Emily drew open the curtains and the blinding sun streamed into the room.

Too early for sun, she thought as Emily began pulling at the bedcovers.

"Well, miss . . . 'er Grace said as you was to be allowed to sleep late, even though she herself is up and about and Mr. Hamilton is already downstairs taking breakfast with her. He thought you might like to get used to drinking coffee like the French and Americans do."

She set the tray in front of Celia, along with a pile of newspapers, and Celia looked up at her blindly, not having heard the half of what she had said.

"Go on, miss. It's coffee—'er Grace did say she 'oped you wouldn't mind trying something different, and then too—she said that *she* had found that a cuppa coffee woke her up faster than anything else."

Celia looked at the black brew warily. Coffee instead of the usual comforting cup of tea? Croissants instead of the usual triangles of brown toast?

She took a cautious sip of the scalding-hot liquid—and almost choked on the bitter, unfamiliar taste.

"*Whose* idea was this?" she muttered, but now she remembered clearly exactly what Emily had said. How *dared* that man dictate to her what kind of breakfast she should have?

She took a bite of the croissant, which she found she liked very much. Of course, Aunt Willie had recommended she try this breakfast. She took another tentative sip of coffee, and she supposed that one hot liquid in the morning would do just as well as another. Then she looked up at Emily and signaled her approval.

Emily bobbed a quick curtsy, all smiles. "Please ring as soon as you're done, miss, and I'll come right up to draw your bath. Oh, and, miss—you must be sure to take a look at the newspapers. I went out special myself to get extra copies for you."

The newspapers? Oh, yes, the newspapers. Celia fortified herself with another cup of coffee and reached for them.

But not the staid and respectable *Times;* these papers were the ones devoted to gossip and . . . *photographs* of the wealthy and titled.

Her fingers shook as she drew in a deep breath and opened the first one.

AN ENGLISH BEAUTY ROSE MAKES HER DEBUT, one

headline screamed, directly comparing her with the American heiress, Miss Jeannie Chamberlain, whom the press had dubbed "the American Beauty Rose."

She felt the heat rising in her face as she read the rest of the story, which was accompanied by a rather blurred picture and a great deal of detail about her personal life outlined in the most flamboyant and melodramatic prose.

She had been protected and carefully nurtured in obscurity, although she too was an heiress, the article said, and it made much of the difference in upbringing between a young English girl and an American girl of the same age.

But more than that, the reporter had delved into her past and turned up things that even *she* had not known—things about her background and her parentage that she had never been told.

How was it possible, she thought despairingly, that the press had uncovered her mother's maiden name—which had been Rivera—and knew that "Marianna" had been her stage name, and had unearthed the fact her mother had had brothers—and a mother and stepfather too—who had formed a whole troupe, along with dancers and performers who had provided a background for Marianna's talent and beauty?

She had been called the Magnificent Marianna, the article went on, who had had so many offers—from kings and princes, from titled gentlemen of only slightly lower rank. Yet Marianna had chosen to give up everything for love, and had eloped with a penniless English adventurer.

Celia closed her eyes and leaned back against the pillows in a futile rage. Her whole past life, her whole family history, paraded in print for the titillation of the public.

She barely heard the knock at the door, and then Willie burst into the room in a swirl of lace and perfume to take

Celia directly into her arms to hug and rock and soothe her.

"Celia . . . Celia—as soon as I heard that Emily had brought the newspapers up to you . . . Oh, my dear, you mustn't be upset. I should have prepared you—"

But she herself was not prepared for the tears streaming down Celia's beautiful face.

"My dear girl, my dear, dear girl—*nothing* is your fault—it's mine for thrusting you into these shark-infested waters. Celia, dear, don't cry . . . don't cry . . ."

"But you don't understand, Aunt Willie. It was *me— me;* I let myself be tempted by my own vanity. I wanted to be *noticed* and I thought all I had to do was playact. I pretended to be *her*. When I think about her, I feel strong and confident—*she* was strong and confident—but I never, ever thought to carry it so far, and now . . ." she sobbed, "now it's all public and I am *ruined*—"

Willie hugged her tighter. "Will you *stop* that talk? You're beginning to sound like your insufferable aunt Gertrude. Your mother was a very beautiful young woman—your father loved her and she loved him. They loved each other enough to escape together from this stifling society that would have condemned them. They got free, my dear, and they were very happy."

Willie lifted her hand and wiped away Celia's tears. "The past *doesn't* matter—only you. You, and not your parents and the mistakes they might have made. Believe me, nobody who *matters* really cares."

She took Celia back into her embrace again. "And do you know what, my dear? There are invitations piling up downstairs from the most distinguished hostesses. And one from the Prince of Wales as well. So you see? All that scurrillous gossip has come to nothing, and *you* have nothing to be ashamed of."

She released her then and rummaged in her pocket for her lace-edged handkerchief and handed it to Celia.

Celia wiped her eyes and choked back a sob. "It's really all right?"

Willie patted her hand. "It's really all right, and you are going to have such fun, I promise. Besides which, you should have heard what they said about me when I rushed off to America to marry Mr. Hamilton so soon after Millhaven died. But you see, dearest, what they didn't understand was, I had conformed and done what was expected of me, and it was my turn to live my own life. And I'm very happy now. Hamish loves and understands me and gives me a great deal of freedom, as you can see. So what I want to say to you, Celia, is that before *you* settle down and marry someone you truly love and cannot live without, enjoy yourself. And I intend to help you do just that. So dry your tears. Emily is waiting to pour your bath, and when you're dressed, come right downstairs. No nasty horseback-riding lessons today. We have other things to do!"

Aunt Willie hugged her again and left her to wash her face and submit to Emily's ministrations as a line of servants marched in with the steaming, scented water for her bath.

She sank into it gratefully and waved off Emily's offer of help. She wanted only to give herself up to the heat and the scent and forget about the embarrassment of the article.

And it was awfully nice to be pampered and spoiled. She could not ever remember having been coddled before, nor could she recall anyone who had hugged and petted and made her feel loved.

Aunt Gertrude had considered any kind of open demonstration of emotion or affection in bad taste. How many lectures and sermons Celia remembered that exhorted her to develop strength of character—which meant denial of all things pertaining to the flesh and fleshly comforts.

Aunt Gertrude would have considered her soaking naked in a luxuriously large bathtub with hot and cold water the height of decadence. And the full-length mirror, in which she could see herself climbing out of the tub—Aunt Gertrude surely would have made some allusion to Sodom and Gomorrah or Pompeii.

And, in fact, she had ingrained the notion of sin so deeply into Celia that even without her presence, Celia always turned her back to the mirror when she stepped out of the tub.

She wondered why. What was so wicked about a woman's body? Her mother hadn't been ashamed of her body. Aunt Willie surely did not deny herself the pleasures of the flesh. So why should *she* follow the strictures of Aunt Gertrude, who was nowhere around to censure her?

Normally, she would automatically reach for one of the large, fluffy towels that were always at hand on the towel rack, and she would wrap it around herself before she could fully catch a glimpse of herself in the mirror.

But this time she stopped herself and forced herself to lift her eyes and look at her naked reflection.

The mirror was foggy from the steam, and the image that looked back at her was all misty and obscure.

She stared with undisguised curiosity at the naked nymph as if what she saw were something else—a painting or a blurred photograph—and it wasn't her.

The nymph had a triangular kind of face—all eyes and cheekbones and too-full lips. And she had breasts that were well defined and tipped with crimson nipples that seemed to point upward in invitation. A small enough waist, not too large hips and—legs that seemed shapely enough, down to passably slim ankles.

Her critical gaze skimmed past the dark triangle of hair between her thighs, although a sudden undefinable feel-

ing that was almost panic made her catch her breath and
snatch the towel around herself with a shiver.

Who was she?

What was she?

She tossed back her wet hair and stared at her towel-
wrapped figure.

She was a woman and she suddenly understood what
it was she felt when she looked in the mirror.

She felt no shame.

Celia heard the clock downstairs chime warningly and,
holding her skirts, she dashed out of her room to Aunt
Willie's suite, where she was to have her hair dressed by
Willie's maid, Hilda, while Emily watched and tried to
learn.

Willie had a chair already positioned for her by the
mirror. "Right there, my dear girl. That sea green is just
gorgeous on you; I don't believe you've worn any color
like it in the past two weeks. And that dress is perfect
for dancing. I can remember when gowns didn't have *any*
flare whatsoever, and about all you could achieve was a
mincing little step. Don't you love that lace dripping off
the bodice and sleeves? Hilda, make sure you fasten
those poufs tightly."

Celia closed her eyes as Willie went on with her soothing chatter and Hilda's deft fingers went to work arranging her long, abundant hair with strategically placed
hairpins.

Daydreaming, her aunt Gertrude would have said. And
how horrified she would be, on top of being scandalized
about the bathroom, to hear how Celia had been occupied
these past fourteen days.

Dancing with the Prince of Wales; having been given
his official and public seal of approval by his invitation
to take tea with his gracious and lovely wife, Princess
Alexandra; staying up all night almost every night; re-

ceiving flowers daily from admirers she couldn't even remember half the time; and learning to drive her aunt Willie's phaeton in the park.

A glorious two weeks that had been thankfully devoid of any sign of Mr. Grant Hamilton because he had been off hunting with friends somewhere.

Celia bit her lip in annoyance. She didn't miss his abrasive presence in the least. He was merely a rather annoying and patronizing man, and she didn't know why the thought of him crossed her mind at all right now.

"Oh, miss, you do look like a princess, you do!" Emily exclaimed, and Celia opened her eyes, startled, to see Hilda twining a rope of pearls into the clever arrangement of her high-piled curls.

"You are a magician, Hilda," she murmured as Hilda placed a pearl and diamond-encrusted comb at the back to anchor everything in place.

"Another minute, miss," Hilda said, flushing with pleasure at the compliment as she began pulling out artful tendrils of hair to curl teasingly at the nape of Celia's neck and her temples. "There you are . . ."

There she was indeed; she stood up just as Willie bustled back into the room, having gone to make sure the carriage would be ready.

"Hilda is a genius at arranging hair," she said with great satisfaction as she surveyed Celia. "Are you ready? Oh, dear, my fan—there it is. Do you have yours? Very well, then, let's be off."

Tonight it was a return to Covent Garden, and just in time for the prelude to *Tristan and Isolde*. This time Celia hardly noticed the staring crowds, the loud, admiring comments or the photographers who seemed to spring up out of nowhere.

Tonight Anthea Langbourne was one of their party— escorted by a serious-looking gentleman who had been introduced as Mr. George Maitland, a student of theology and an American from New England whom Anthea had met at a prayer meeting.

"You poor dear," Anthea whispered by her side. "How can you bear it? Or are you already becoming blasé about being called a Beauty?"

The question brought Celia up short for a moment; she would have thought it sounded curiously like envy, except that Anthea did not have a jealous bone in her independent body. And she certainly would never Seek Attention.

"Why, I try to imagine I'm a horse—with blinkers—so I can see only what is directly in front of me," Celia said lightly, but there was something about that thought that vexed her even as she said it.

Anthea raised an eyebrow. This was a much more self-possessed Celia. Surely she had not allowed all the adulation to go to her head. Of course, since she herself had met George, she had neglected her friends, and it was obvious she was going to have to remedy that. Celia needed some level-headed, mature advice. And perhaps a word or two from George might prove helpful as well.

But Celia's attention was turned to another of their party, the oldest son of the present Duke of Millhaven—Albert Vernon, Viscount Harville—accompanied by his rather shy young American bride, who was the daughter of a newly rich railroad magnate.

Celia was rather charmed by his easy manner and the way he kissed Willie's cheek fondly; obviously he at least considered his step-grandmother a friend and ally, and he seemed delighted to make Celia's acquaintance.

"So you are my uncle Richard's daughter. Well, well! Now that we've met, cousin, you must come visit us. Eulalie doesn't know very many people in London yet—we met in America, you know. At Newport."

"How charming," Celia murmured, wondering why he was looking at her so intently. Of course he was curious about her and her black-sheep father who had married a Spanish dancer and disappeared from civilization. But still, his interest seemed to go just a step beyond the ordinary.

The orchestra struck the first notes of the prelude and she was saved from having to engage in any further conversation.

She had read the libretto, so she knew the story of the opera with its doomed, predestined lovers—but the *music!* It spoke to the senses, it stroked and teased and caressed until one almost could forget the grim, recurring threat beneath it of a price that must be paid.

It was the devil's music, but she didn't care, and she gave herself up to the haunting melodies that seemed to reach in and touch her mind and her body.

The first act was long; there were the usual discreet coughs and rustles of skirts; a sudden gleam of light as some gentleman left his box to smoke or to quench his thirst; and then when some gentleman returned with champagne for the ladies . . .

The viscount, of course, so newly married and so thoughtful. Celia felt his shoulder brush against her arm as he leaned forward to whisper in his wife's ear and hand her a glass of champagne just before, with a light touch to her wrist, he did the same for Celia.

"You didn't have to drink the *whole* glass," Anthea whispered on her other side as the curtain fell on Act One and they got up to make their way to the Ladies' Retiring Room. "And you surely are not obligated to accept a second. You are so inexperienced, Celia. You cannot know the effect spirits have on those who are unused to imbibing. Don't look so cross with me, please. If I did not consider myself your *friend,* I would never even mention it."

Celia's lips tightened. Anthea was talking down to her

and she hated it, even if Anthea meant well. And surely she wasn't acting giddy or flighty.

Even so, she was much more subdued when she returned to her seat for the beginning of the second act, and she decided it might be more prudent to sit next to Aunt Willie, who never criticized.

"Of course you may sit with me, my love. But is anything wrong? Are you feeling well?" Willie murmured anxiously as she settled Celia in the seat beside her. All the vivacity had gone out of Celia, and there was this tiny worried frown which she could not entirely smooth out when she caught her aunt's questioning look.

Willie's back straightened and she glanced around the box.

Anthea! she thought angrily. Who else?

She leaned back and smiled and patted Celia's hand reassuringly. She would make sure that her niece enjoyed the rest of the evening, with or without Miss Langbourne's approval.

Oh, but at times like this she missed Hamish so. He could cut through hypocrisy and layers of lies and convention with a few well-chosen and blunt words. He would have known exactly what to say to Anthea to put an end to her well-meaning but smugly self-righteous criticism.

But by the time the orchestra struck the opening notes of the second act, Celia was again caught up in the spell of the music and the haunting love-death theme underlying everything else.

The ill-fated lovers, bound by a magic spell, rushed toward each other and doom, victims of the inescapable force of a forbidden, predestined love, a love so powerful and all-consuming that even the agony of knowing it could never end in anything but death and disaster could not keep them apart.

Celia didn't realize that she had been clutching Wil-

lie's gloved hand so tightly or that there were tears in
her aunt's eyes as well.

"I brought extra handkerchiefs," Willie whispered. "I
always cry when I see *Tristan and Isolde*—I can't help
it."

In the midst of the second act, the viscount offered
more champagne, accompanied by tiny canapés adorned
with caviar and egg to stave off everyone's hunger until
supper.

"How thoughtful," Willie murmured, passing a flute
of champagne to Celia, who drank it rather recklessly,
almost as if she thought she could quell the emotion of
the story by drowning it.

And she ate her fill of the canapés and dainty sandwiches and smoked pheasant and truffles that followed,
then sniffed happily into her aunt's store of handkerchiefs
until the end of the second act.

Afterward their box was besieged by gentlemen seeking an introduction to Lord Harville's pretty wife—oh,
and Miss Penmaris as well.

"Aren't you all the rage, cousin!" the viscount whispered teasingly and far too closely into her ear as he
leaned over the back of her chair. "And how is it that
you've been kept from us all until now? Where have you
been hiding?"

Celia turned slightly so that she could just meet his
penetrating blue eyes. Friend or foe? She could not tell
from his whispered comment, but she felt wary of him—
enough to square her shoulders and respond.

"In a high-walled convent for my own protection, of
course. And I am not sure we are really cousins, you
know, so perhaps you should stop saying so."

"Hmmm—but perhaps you would be safer if we
were."

And before she had time to digest the implications of
that statement, he turned back to his wife.

Thankfully, the warning bell rang in the foyer, signifying the beginning of Act Three, and Celia directed her attention to the stage.

Tristan, now wounded and sick to the heart, waiting for his beloved Isolde. The music, like a love potion itself, captured Celia's emotions and tore at her soul.

She cried; Aunt Willie had not come prepared with enough handkerchiefs, and she had to wipe away the tears with the back of her hand like a schoolgirl.

And then a hand came from behind her, offering her a large male handkerchief which she seized with gratitude. It was of the softest, finest linen and it smelled faintly of tobacco, and it was ample enough to contain her tears at Isolde's keening lament over her lover's body.

Under the cover of the thunderous applause that met the falling curtain, Celia blew her nose very quietly, then allowed Aunt Willie to shepherd her to the Retiring Room, along with the other ladies, while the cast was taking curtain calls and bouquets were being thrown onto the stage.

It was a relief to see that the other women had puffy eyes too and wanted to splash cold water and cologne on their faces and rearrange their hair before they returned to the box.

Aunt Willie had come prepared with tiny vials containing witch hazel scented with rose water—so soothing to dab under the eyes and against the temples.

Celia liberally drenched one corner of her gallant's handkerchief with the cool solution and almost dropped it when she noticed the initials embroidered in the corner.

GH—Grant Hamilton!

He had slipped into the box late, of course, and then left. Typical of him—rude and mannerless as usual, coming back to Town without any warning or prior notice.

The wonder was the way Aunt Willie doted on him.

Only she and Anthea Langbourne seemed to be able to see through the wretch to his savage masquerading as a gentleman.

But since he was gone, his presence was of no moment. And besides, there was scarcely time to think about anything else after they left the opera house. They had to go back to the town house and change and adjust their clothing and hair before they went on to their next engagement.

There would be supper and dancing, and Celia was feeling just that little twinge of irritation that made her eyes flash dangerously and her Gypsy cheekbones stain with color.

She would be a cat on the prowl tonight, seeking to scratch the veneer of a gentleman savage.

She was angry enough with the viscount and Grant Hamilton's offhand treatment to claw them both.

And just maybe she would have the chance tonight, in the jungle of yet another society party.

Ten

Grant Hamilton prowled the room like a caged tiger: hungry, edgy, angry, spoiling for a fight—and he did not know why.

He wished he had stayed in Scotland, where royalty, relatives and rambunctious Gypsies couldn't complicate matters.

He didn't know what annoyed him more—the telegram from the detective he had almost fired before he'd gone off shooting, or the fact that the only thing he had seemed able to sight on the whole trip was those glowing, knowing Gypsy eyes.

Or maybe he had been looking for an excuse to come back early, even though he had been loath to leave on the heels of Celia's little social triumph and the subsequent revelations in the scandal sheets.

But he and Willie had gone over that the following morning, and she had been quite unfazed.

"Of course you must keep your engagement, Grant, dear. I hope you don't think we need a *man* to help fend off the gossipmongers? Celia is fine; we will manage perfectly fine. Who knows, perhaps Sir Thomas may be of service someday."

He hadn't liked her cavalier attitude one little bit either, and the tittle-tattle in the papers bothered him still more because the detective he had hired weeks before hadn't come up with information nearly as detailed as the gossip columns. He should have hired a reporter.

"Leave it to us—we was just one step behind them tattlers," Detective Macy had sworn, "and we're onto somethin' they ain't got a clue about."

"There had better be *something,* or you'll forfeit your fee," Grant had threatened, even though at that point he hadn't expected any results at all.

Two weeks later, Detective Macy put it in his hands.

"Ain't nobody knows about that, guv'nor. And nobody will, if you get my meanin'."

Oh, he got it. Enough money changed hands to build Buckingham Palace all over again, and he made the detective sign some official-looking papers full of promises not to resell the item or reveal where he had gotten it on pain of legal suit and criminal proceedings.

Grant wasn't even sure how much of a deterrent all the threats were. Or if the end result was worth the money and the risks.

The story the detective had uncovered was much the same as Grant had read in the tabloids; the difference was, he held in his hands a picture of Marianna—and her daughter looked so much like her, she could have been her twin.

The Gypsy was dancing the flamenco, her arms arched over her thrown-back head, her slender fingers clicking castanets above a face that seemed caught up in some ecstatic dream, and she looked so alive and so vital that it was no wonder no man had been able to resist her.

No wonder Richard Penmaris had been so fiercely possessive and so jealous. But he had been no saint either, and by all accounts he had allowed that jealousy to consume their powerful love.

Grant wondered how much Celia knew of that legacy, and whether she was even aware of how much like her mother she was with her exotic face and her lithe dancer's body . . .

And he wondered why in hell Willie hadn't told him the whole goddamned Shakespearean tragedy in the first place—and he wondered what he would have done differently had he known.

He wouldn't be here, he thought savagely as he pushed his way through the usual crowd of après-opera partygoers who were arriving in spurts to this private party to celebrate tragedy and triumph and to dance till dawn.

And why was he here?

He was here to escort the daughter of a wild Gypsy queen.

He shook off that fancy; certainly she didn't need his escort for educational purposes any longer, and they were as mismatched as night and day.

And the minute he thought that—the minute he was ready to walk out the door and leave his stepmother to all the nonsense attendant upon the Season—he felt her light touch at his elbow and he couldn't move another step.

"Well, I thought that was you during the last act," Willie said complacently, reaching up to bestow a cool kiss on his cheek. "You're back early. Did you see Celia? Didn't she look ravishing?"

"Her eyes were blotchy and her nose was running," he said tonelessly.

"Nonsense. Everyone was in tears—I'd daresay even *you*," Willie said feelingly. "Oh, look, there's Celia now."

He didn't want to look—he knew what he would see if he looked—that wild Gypsy face with the body, grace and manners of a lady, the irresistible contradiction that made him want to stay.

"Oh, I certainly gave up another four days' shooting just so Miss Penmaris could impale me with that hostile look. Why the hell is she mad at me?"

"Go ask her," Willie said.

"I'd rather go to any lengths *not* to," Grant hissed as Celia slowly approached them with Anthea in tow.

"Why, Grant," she said, feigning surprise, "I didn't expect to see you here. Or is this your next *assignment?* Did you forsake pleasure for duty? You need not have, I assure you. Aunt Willie will tell you—everything is going along swimmingly. You remember Miss Langbourne?"

He bowed stiffly, feeling as if he wanted to throttle Celia, and then watching helplessly as she accepted a flute of champagne from an admirer who had stopped for a moment to greet her.

Obviously Willie was not about to stop her; and obviously that censuring look in Miss Langbourne's eyes counted for absolutely nothing.

Grant reached out and lifted the champagne glass from Celia's hand. "You shouldn't drink too much champagne before supper."

"Yet I expect you have had a glass or two already," Celia said resentfully. He was treating her like a child, and that after he had gone and abandoned her—and Aunt Willie—with not so much as a fare-thee-well.

"*I* can handle it."

"And I can handle *you,*" she retorted, ignoring Anthea's horrified expression and Aunt Willie's edgy little laugh.

"Really—I can see you've had *so* much experience dealing with men these last two weeks," he whipped out angrily, sarcastically, as the orchestra sounded the opening notes of a waltz. "I believe this is my dance."

"No! I—"

"Don't make a scene—or was that also part of your curriculum while I was gone?"

"You can't teach me *anything*, Grant Hamilton," she whispered fiercely as he clasped her hand and dragged her onto the dance floor.

"Maybe I can teach you how to behave in public," he growled, pulling her into his arms so tightly she could barely breathe. She felt like slapping his hard, arrogant face; she felt like swearing.

"Smile, Celia," he said roughly as he swung her into the swirling movement of the dance. "Appearances are everything, as I'm sure you've learned very well."

"And things aren't always what they seem," she countered through gritted teeth while he expertly whirled her into a great looping circle around the other dancers. "And I'm certain you understand *that* very well."

Oh, she was a piece of work, he thought; this was no innocent child in a woman's body, for all that she was unschooled in the ways of the world. She was learning too quickly, and he had the grim feeling that Celia Penmaris operated on pure instinct, which was honed fine and true.

He did not feel like being careful with her or kind to her. He wanted to shake her and make her look at him with those glowing coppery cat-eyes—and he had the most unholy urge to crush her in his arms and taste that tempting virginal mouth.

Willie would kill him . . .

The waltz was ending, the tempo speeding up into a crescendo of movement, and Celia felt as if she were being swept away in a tidal wave of emotion. Her anger evaporated, and for one glistening moment, life became a swirling, swooping dance with no beginning, no ending, no meaning but the pure, shimmering beauty of the music that penetrated her soul.

It was so simple—the rhythm, the man, the certainty of his sure touch guiding her, the knowledge she would follow him wherever he led.

It was the music, really, and her own volatile emotions. She knew instinctively he was mesmerized by her enchantment with the motion of the dance.

And she understood somehow deep within her that he thought it could have been anyone holding her and moving her through the dance and that he wanted her to be very aware that it was *him*.

And that was the difference between them, because she knew that she could only have responded to the dance this way because she was with him.

The thought both exhilarated her and frightened her. It was like a living thing, secret inside her, that she did not want to acknowledge to anyone, least of all herself.

It was a wild thing, the notion that she, Celia, could make even this arrogant, hard-edged man just a little unsure of himself.

She could not allow herself to believe she had such power—not *her* . . .

And yet . . .

And yet—

As the final strains of the waltz echoed through the room, she felt herself being whirled into a final turn and out an open pair of French windows onto a terrace overlooking the garden.

She had a sense of things ending and something beginning; she stood in that moment still enclosed in his arms and somewhere between darkness and light and Marianna and madness.

This was no game she was playing. Grant Hamilton was a man who was beyond such things.

He had brought her out here deliberately and she had followed, she hadn't protested or pulled away from him, and now—and now . . .

He held her so firmly against him, and the hand that had grasped hers so tightly in the dance relinquished it and moved ever so slowly to cup her cheek, and his blazing eyes looked deeply into the shadowed wonder in hers.

Her lips parted at his touch and she tilted her head—or he gently and subtly lifted her chin; she didn't know which. She only knew her breathing became ragged as he lowered his head and slanted his mouth over hers, hovered above her lips for a tantalizing, breath-stopping instant, waiting, waiting, scenting her fear and her excitement both . . .

He's too experienced, she thought frantically in that breath of an instant, and then his lips touched hers. Touched and pressured and probed with a kind of suppressed energy as if he were holding himself back because . . . because . . . she knew too little, she realized in a wave of humiliation; because she did not know what to do.

How could she have known what to do? Not even Ronald had ever kissed her like this, with such force, and with the sleek tip of his tongue seeking, seeking—what?

The Gypsy within her should have known.

Oh, yes, her Gypsy self would have been so knowledgeable in the ways of men; a kiss would have meant nothing to her except that she had another man in her power.

I want the arrogant Grant Hamilton in my power.

The forbidden thought made her knees weak; her fingers clutched his shoulders and she could feel the tense straining movement of the muscles of his arms as he pulled her still more tightly against him.

Seeking . . .

Pushing tightly and insistently against all the barriers that she had raised. All she had to do was surrender to his passion—but never give up her soul.

Even so, her excitement was building as she warily allowed him to breach her resistance. What did it mean after all but his lush possession of her tongue?

But still, she wasn't prepared for the sensations that swamped her; she wanted to wrench away from him and run, and she wanted to explore all the possibilities of the pleasure she felt.

Such contradictory feelings: she felt helpless and strong, weak and powerful, innocent and knowing—and ripe and ready—all at the same time.

This was how, this was what . . . a man could be enslaved by a kiss, she thought; she could be enthralled just like this forever.

Enslaved. Controlled.

She pulled away violently as another little dart of pleasure attacked her vitals.

Dear Lord . . .

It was too addicting, his mouth and the pleasure.

And she wasn't sophisticated enough to know how to enslave *anyone*.

But still he held her and the taut silence stretched between them, elastic, pliant, almost at the breaking point.

Her lips were swollen and her eyes shimmered with all the knowledge of Eve. The virgin had metamorphosed into a courtesan in the space of two weeks, and wasn't that an interesting turn of events?

Nevertheless, he should not have kissed her, nor should he have discovered the world of knowledge in that tempting mouth, or even want to possess it again.

Nor should she have known the things she knew, virgin temptress that she was.

Damn her, damn Willie . . .

"How right you were, Miss Penmaris," he said coldly, releasing her so abruptly her knees almost gave out from under her. "No one can teach you anything. Least of all me."

She wanted to kill him right there, right then; she had nothing to hold onto but her burgeoning fury—and her pride.

What a supremely arrogant man!

She lifted her chin, Marianna to the core. "Another duty you can cross off your list, Mr. Hamilton? I feel quite contrite that your boyish groping came to naught. But after all, two weeks can seem almost a lifetime, can it not? Well, surely Aunt Willie must be looking for me by now. I won't mention this embarrassing little interlude—and I expect neither will you."

And at that, she turned on her heel and marched back into the house, her shoulders stiff and her eyes swimming with tears that he never saw.

But Anthea did. She was so quick to leap on the fact something was wrong, it almost seemed as if she had an extra sense about it.

"Dear Celia, what conclusion can one draw but that you are entirely out of your depth here?" she asked chidingly.

Oh, not anymore, not anymore.

She would just drown her folly in the brightness of the party, ignore Anthea and dance with anyone who asked her.

The thought gave her a heady, independent and willful feeling. She could and would do anything she wanted tonight.

And she would utterly ignore Grant Hamilton standing

by the French doors, his arms crossed and his face scowling with a narrow-eyed, dangerous look that did not bode well for anyone who crossed his path.

Especially her.

Eleven

"This won't do! This simply won't do! Theo! Will you please put aside that musty old book and pay attention to me? I *must* insist you take the time to glance through these newspapers I have just received in the post. Just look at these photographs—*and* what is written beneath. The Prince of Wales has been paying our poor, dear Celia *marked* attention. Well, we all know what *that* means! And to be escorted in public almost everywhere by Wilhelmina's stepson—that Grant Hamilton, who, besides being so much older than Celia, has a none-too-savory reputation— Theo!"

The bishop sighed, took off his pince-nez to massage the bridge of his nose, then put it on again.

"Well, my dear," he said soothingly, "you really must not allow yourself to become so agitated. Remember what Dr. Reynolds told you. Just calm yourself while I peruse these . . . specimens. What are they after all but gossip sheets meant for the titillation of the masses? They will surely be ignored by those of our set. So do sit down, Gertrude, because you're distracting me."

The tone of his voice brooked no argument and subdued her into a rare silence. She sat down, with a rustle of skirts, in the comfortable wing chair across from him and compressed her lips.

Theo picked up the newspapers she had flung on his desk and read them so slowly and carefully that she thought she was going to scream with impatience.

"Well, my dear," he said finally, "I hardly know what to say. Of course, when one moves in certain circles, it is not possible to prevent certain persons from indulging in gossip and speculation. So it seems to me the best course is to just ignore such scurrilous scandal sheets. Celia *is* being carefully chaperoned at all times, I'm sure of that, and in any case, I cannot quite see what either you or I could possibly do at this point—"

"Oh, really, Theo! Can she not be saved from gossip even at this late stage? Surely it is our duty to try to repair whatever damage has already been done to her reputation. We must rescue the poor child from that unsuitable environment and bring her back to the reality of her situation!"

"Now, Gertrude, my dear," he began, a frown knitting his forehead as he directed what he hoped was a quelling look at her over his glasses. "You must really make an effort not to work yourself into such a state about things over which neither you nor I have any control. Celia is no longer our charge or our responsibility, and all we can do is pray that whatever situation she finds herself in, she will have been strengthened by the years she spent in our care. And there, of course, I give you *all* the credit," he added handsomely. "Faith, my dear—we must have faith."

Lady Gertrude sniffed. "I can plainly see you are in one of your difficult moods, Theo, and not in the least inclined to listen to anything I might be concerned about. I will therefore leave you to your studies while I busy myself with more practical matters."

She stood up abruptly and swept the newspapers off her husband's desk and then sailed majestically out of the room, pausing at the door to glare at him and take one more parting shot.

"I should perhaps inform you that I have written to Ronald Winwood to apprise him of the change in Celia's situation. After all, we do not know if the poor child has even been allowed to let him know what has been happening. *And,* on the chance that a visit with us and a serious talk with *you* might strengthen her character and resolve, I have written to Celia and Mrs. Hamilton, inviting them—or just Celia and her maid—for a weekend. You do not object to *that,* I hope?"

She did not wait for a reply; she swept through the doorway, letting the heavy door slam behind her emphatically.

Later, when Theo was in a more reasonable frame of mind, she would remind him of the saying about casting one's bread upon the waters, which was exactly what she had done, instead of doing nothing at all.

Willie reluctantly unfolded the note that Gertrude had sent to her. The last thing she wanted to do was accept an invitation to the Grange, but undoubtedly Gertrude had heard some of the gossip and read some of the newspapers and had let her sense of duty to her niece get the better of her.

But, of course, Celia must make this decision herself, and the conflicting emotions chasing one another across Celia's face made it all too clear she was not at all eager to accept this invitation.

"They certainly seem to miss you," Willie said finally, noncommittally.

"I wonder just what they miss," Celia murmured, and then wished she could have caught back the words. She had never questioned Gertrude's motives before, and Gertrude certainly had not been happy to remand her to Aunt Willie's care. Of course her aunt and uncle missed her. She was being uncharitable.

"My dear," Willie said quickly to cover her niece's too-candid comment, "there's no need to make up your mind right away. We are committed to Harville this weekend, and after that, well, there's nothing we cannot get out of if you feel you do want to visit the bishop and your aunt. I will come with you if you want me to, of course, but if not, you can always travel with Emily—or ask Anthea to accompany you. I believe I heard her say that her friend Mr. Maitland admires your uncle Theo's sermons excessively."

Willie could not keep a rather mischievous tone out of her voice as she added the last.

Celia smiled ruefully. "You are so patient with me, Aunt Willie. I always was a little frightened of Aunt Gertrude, I suppose. She was never especially unkind to me, or even unfair, but . . . she was never as easy to talk to as you are."

"She is rather overwhelming," Willie said encouragingly, "but you have grown and become very strong during our visit. You are so much more sure of yourself, and now that you have met and conversed with the Prince of Wales, how much more intimidating could it be to deal with your aunt?"

And she had handled Grant Hamilton too, Celia thought with some satisfaction, and they hadn't seen his face at Carlton House Terrace since that last party—and their kiss—and as far as she was concerned, never was too soon to see him again.

She looked up at her aunt. "A visit to Aunt Gertrude will be a tea party compared to that," she agreed with amusement lacing her voice. "But I would much prefer that you go too—"

"To protect you?" Willie murmured, unable to help herself.

To save me from my habitual rash behavior, Celia thought, but she could not admit that, even to Willie.

"To help me face things I would prefer to avoid," she said instead, but in her heart of hearts she wasn't too sure that her aunt hadn't hit exactly on the truth.

It was a source of irritation to Grant Hamilton that, try as he might, he could not stop thinking about Celia Penmaris.

And that it was obvious to one person at least, and the one person he would have preferred not to know about it at all: Lady Marvella Merrivale.

"Grant, my dear! It's really quite unlike you to be so very puritan about your male impulses. The girl is quite exotic-looking *and,* we presume, a virgin. Isn't that what every red-blooded man desires? A passionate virgin?"

"You have it quite wrong, Marvella," he said stiffly.

Marvella ignored him. "And she is quite the Cinderella, isn't she? Just waiting for her prince to sweep her off her feet and into— But the sequel hardly matters, does it? Even Cinderella must discover what life is all about. So what difference does it make whether it is you or this invisible fiancé of hers who is waiting for her to grow up?"

He quelled an exasperated sigh. "A fairy tale, Marvella. You have no idea what you are talking about."

"Pooh, Grant; this is the first time in weeks you have talked to me, and all the gossip is about how you are being led by your nose around Town by the beauteous Miss Penmaris—"

"With Willie in tow. Now tell me I make a practice of seducing virgins in the presence of my stepmother."

"My dear, she had no compunction at all about breaking into your room when you were otherwise . . . occupied. Who knows what kind of libertine life she leads in America—''

She broke off as Grant's expression darkened. She had made a mistake obviously, impugning both his beloved Willie and his father. But then, she was desperate. This business with Celia Penmaris was disheartening. He acted as though he couldn't stand the chit, but he hadn't been to see *her* in weeks, and the last time she had tried to contact him, she had been told he was in Scotland.

Yet here he was, at an intimate dinner of a mutual friend, and among the select guest list, which included herself, of those who would be traveling down to Harville for the weekend.

No doubt the Celia chit would be there too, after her screaming success in London. It was too much! How Grant could put up with her for more than thirty seconds was more than she could understand.

However, her talking about Celia seemed to get under his skin, and she wanted most of all to make him uncomfortable and very aware of the differences between an experienced Beauty and a virginal debutante.

"It's amazing to me that you even have scruples about the whole thing," she went on, ignoring the dangerous look in his eyes. "She seems so eager to find out about life and all it has to offer. They tell me men are just falling all over themselves to get to know her—especially after the prince put his stamp of approval on her. That kind of thing can turn a girl's head. You can't tell me she hasn't wanted to . . . experiment a little."

He gritted his teeth and bit back an answer. This was so close to what he had been thinking since that abortive kiss that it was eerie.

"Always the bitch, aren't you, Marvella? No sympathy at all for an innocent in the throes of her first Season."

"Men!" Marvella spit. "*Innocent!* I was innocent

once too, and too eager to find out about everything I dreamed of and knew nothing about. But once something is lost, it's over and done with. And one has to go on and become stronger and wiser or be ruined forever.''

He looked at her closely for a moment. This was an odd confession for someone who was the very epitome of the Professional Beauty who knew everything, had done everything and was forgiven everything because she was so lovely and so very discreet.

She was daring and dashing, and when she wanted something—or someone—she went after it, and the thing that was the most attractive to the men who had been her lovers was the fact she never had any regrets.

Or perhaps she did, and he was the first ever to get a peek into her icy soul.

No matter. Ice burned every bit as much as fire; his passion for her had been doused weeks before, and he had no time or energy to sift through the embers to try to fan some flickering flame.

"And do you go to Harville?" she asked, breaking into a lengthy and, for her, uncomfortable silence. "And does your little virgin?" she could not resist adding.

He hated her then. "Isn't everyone?" he asked noncommittally.

But not everyone was Lady Marvella Merrivale, whose husband invariably skipped these long, boring social weekends, and who had enough position and influence to make certain the room assigned to her would be conveniently adjoined to that of Mr. Grant Hamilton.

He wouldn't get away from her *that* easily, and with that thought, as dinner was announced and Grant remained obstinately silent, she had to be content.

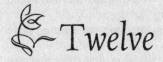

Twelve

They went down to Harville by train early Friday morning in a compartment stacked with luggage and with the comfort of knowing that the viscount had arranged to have carriages waiting to meet every train.

"What lovely weather for a weekend away," Willie said comfortably as the train whisked them from Victoria Station and London's teeming streets into the bucolic countryside. "And thankfully, Harville isn't so far from Town. Three hours at the most, I think; such an easy accommodation for most of the guests. I do hope," she added wistfully, "that Grant will be able to make it. I haven't seen him or heard from him in days."

Celia felt a wave of heat wash her cheeks and she turned her face to the window. "Oh, really? I hadn't noticed."

Willie looked at her suspiciously. "Well, of course; you've been so busy," she said lightly with just a touch of irony. What *was* going on between Celia and Grant? They had been like sharks at that party several nights before, circling and snapping, with the one looking to absolutely devour the other. And Grant wasn't usually like that about anything—or anyone.

But still, it was passing strange that he had not stopped by in the succeeding days, or confirmed that he would be coming down to Harville.

And Celia did look a touch uncomfortable sitting there and staring out the window.

Willie made a conscious decision that the important thing was Celia and her exposure to the right kind of people and the best of situations; nothing could polish up a beautiful debutante more than a closely confined weekend at a peer's country home, where she would mingle with the crème de la crème of society and meet awkward social moments head-on.

It was almost like throwing a child in the water to teach him to swim, and none of the social gatherings or theater parties—or even her great success with the Prince of Wales—could have prepared Celia for a situation from which she could not politely excuse herself and leave the premises if things became awkward.

Of course, if Grant were there, things might become distinctly discomforting. Or it might just be that Willie was totally imagining the whole thing, which was her next thought as she watched Celia's expression perceptibly brighten. The train was passing through a quaint village and nearby farms, and then the scenery gave way to wide swaths of rolling hills and fields dotted with long views of lakes and terraced gardens and great sprawling houses just on the horizon.

This was the setting in which Celia belonged.

"Who do you suppose will be there?" Celia asked after a while.

"Do you know, I am not so well acquainted with Albert and his new wife that I could predict," Willie said thoughtfully. "But still, Millhaven traveled in the best circles, so it wouldn't surprise me if the countess showed up, or even the prince, who, like each of his predecessors, gets notoriously bored notoriously quickly. But probably Albert would not wish to thrust his new wife into such fast company so soon. We will just have to see.''

''And Harville—what is it like?''

''Sad to say, this will be my first visit,'' Willie said slowly, wondering how she could make Celia understand her first husband's reluctance to take herself, his young, bought bride anywhere—including his son's home— where there might be some handsome young man to turn her head. ''They tell me it's a beautiful and quite manageable house. And I expect we'll shortly find that out for ourselves.''

But it was another half hour before the train pulled into the station, which, as far from Town as it was, still reflected the affluence of the aristocracy who resided there.

The platform was concrete and was shielded from the elements by a roof that mimicked the steel-supported archway of Victoria Station and the classical columns in between which were the exit doors to the station and the main street toward town.

A porter appeared instantly with a wagon to take care of their luggage, and they needed to do nothing but proceed onto the platform and into the station.

There, several drivers were waiting, each with an elegantly printed little sign, one of which said HARVILLE.

The carriage was commodious as well, and the driver efficiently loaded the trunks and boxes in the time it took the two women to settle themselves in their seats. Then they were unceremoniously on their way.

They passed very few houses; it was almost as if the track from Harville ran directly to the station. There were miles of fields and grass and trees, and a curious silence between them that Willie did not want to breach because she herself was feeling a little strange.

She would be stepping into a world that was a component of her past, and although she would not have thought it, the memories of her marriage to Millhaven were not so deeply buried beneath her skin.

She consciously shook off her discomfiting thoughts. The only thing that was important was Celia, and she could see from the expression on her niece's face how seductive she found the country.

And then the carriage topped a small rise and stopped for an instant, and they caught their first glimpse of Harville in the distance.

It was two and a half stories of mellow yellowed brick, the main section with its broad, shallow, balustraded steps flanked by two ells, the arms of the letter H, the elegant shape of the house.

It stood shimmering in that golden haze that was late summer in the country—a mixture of heat and the smell of crushed flowers and grasses cooled by the greenness of old gnarled trees overhead and redolent with the scent of ripe apples.

They could almost imagine the sound of water rippling over the sun-bleached stones of some hidden stream deep in a magical forest behind the house.

But that was fanciful, even though Harville itself looked like the perfect invention of the imagination.

They came back to reality as the carriage lurched forward to pass between two stone columns and onto the long sloping track that wound its way through the lush fields and gardens and around the centuries-old trees that dotted the lawns of Harville.

As they came closer and closer to the house, the driver sounded a horn, and when the carriage finally stopped, a whole phalanx of servants awaited their arrival.

And at the top of the steps, in front of the etched-glass double doors of the entry, Viscount Harville stood, waving and eager to greet his guests.

*   *   *

The reception hall of Harville was both overwhelming and comfortable, the scale and quality of the decorations exactly what one would have expected, and yet the house had a homey feel as well.

"Well, it is someone's home," Willie said in response to Celia's observation as they stood in the middle of the marble-tiled hallway and watched the servants scurry with their trunks into the reception room to their right and up the massive staircase to the bedroom floor.

"This paneling is exquisite," she added, moving closer to examine it, "but the secret is that the walls are not overpowered with family portraits or landscapes. Just those two gilt-framed paintings, and that swirl of gilt over the fireplace. And nowhere to sit, just in case the host wishes his guest to effect a speedy exit, which I hope is not so in our case—"

She broke off as Harville reentered the hallway, his hands outstretched toward her, but his cool, appraising gaze on Celia.

"Everything is in your rooms and you now must decide, Wilhelmina—do you wish to freshen up or have something to eat?"

Willie grasped his hands as she followed his eyes. *Now, what is this?*

"I think I want to freshen up. Do you suppose we might have a tray up in the room, Albert? Tea and biscuits would do nicely."

"I'll tell Marden," he said, squeezing her hands, "and let Lally know that you will be with her shortly."

He turned and snapped his fingers and a servant immediately appeared.

"Fellows will attend to you. Come to us soon."

He stepped aside so Willie could pass, but she had the uneasy feeling that his eyes still rested on Celia as she led the way out of the reception hall.

The walls of the staircase hall were paneled in ivory picked out in gilt, and the stairway itself was laid over with the same thick wine-colored carpet as the hallway above.

The bedroom allotted to them faced the rear of the house, at the end of the near ell, and even Willie was impressed with its sumptuousness. It was laid over with the same quality carpet as in the hallway, but this time in green, and it was papered in a floral pattern to match that echoed the ivory wainscoting beneath and picked up the colors in the curtains and bedspreads.

There was a lovely marble fireplace, a huge closet next to a second door in which a maid was already hanging their clothes, a pretty bench at the foot of the two twin beds against the wall, a desk in the corner and two wing chairs and a table by the window.

But above all, there was a spectacular view of the terraced gardens of Harville, which were in full bloom, and of the rear piazza, where even now a few guests were gathered for an outdoor repast.

"Lovely," Willie murmured as she stood by the window and stroked the material of the curtains and watched the scene below. "Albert has done well for himself. I wouldn't have thought so, but—"

She broke off as a knock sounded at the door.

"Celia, my dear—"

Celia opened the door to admit a footman who carried a tray into the room and set in on the table near the window.

"Thank you. And you," Willie said to the maid as she withdrew with the footman, and then she motioned for Celia to join her at the table.

"Well, here we are," she said with a sigh, lifting the fat porcelain teapot and pouring. "Celia? You've been so quiet."

Celia nodded and took the cup and sipped gingerly at

the hot, affirming tea. "I hardly know what to say. It's different than going about in Town, which isn't to say that the countess's house, for example, isn't as spectacular. But it's different. I feel like there must be another etiquette or a new set of rules to learn for this situation. Everything is so vast, even out there."

"Yes, different and vast, and common to those who take these weekends and these beautiful houses for granted. There's hardly anything like this where I live. Not to say there aren't such grand houses—Mr. Hamilton and I often visit—but even in America, it *is* different . . ."

Her voice trailed off and she retreated into a private thought. Celia looked out the window and marveled at the gardens and how the late-morning summer sun haloed everything and everyone in an incandescent light.

She wanted to step out into it and be enveloped in the light—she already felt as if this part of their world were hers; she wanted to race into it with her arms outstretched and take everything that it offered, *everything*.

And then Willie said, "Oh, look, there's Grant!" with such a joyous, heart-stopping note in her voice that Celia did not even have to look where she was pointing.

She had seen him too, cloaked in sunlight, looking like the lord of everything and the master of every desire she wanted desperately to suppress.

They were greeted by the sound of raised voices as they made their way down the great staircase, and Willie automatically pulled back as she recognized one of them.

"Marvella!"

Celia's heart sank. The beautiful, sophisticated Marvella, who had danced so beautifully, so sensually, with Grant, was now prowling the lavish gardens of Harville—waiting for what? Waiting for *her?*

That ugly voice so shrill and demanding, so strident

and distinct that they could hear every word even in the next room?

"Just what do you mean, Albert, *dear?* You know exactly the arrangement I requested; there could not be any mistake."

"Dear Marvella, circumstances . . . Wilhelmina . . . and then the telegram from Lord Merrivale. You couldn't expect—"

"The old fool never would have known . . ."

". . . it could not be done, not in the face of his stepmother's invitation. Any other time, Marvella—happy to accommodate—but Lord Merrivale . . ."

"You make the change nonetheless, Albert. You *will,* or I will know why!"

"Too late, my dear. They're here already, and Eulalia—"

"Eulalia! For God's sake, Eulalia—that sniveling little nitwit that nobody understands why you married—and you gave over your guest accommodations to *her?* What can that simp know about *arrangements?*"

"*Enough,* Marvella. It is what it is and I will not tolerate slurs against my wife."

"Don't worry, Albert; I'll behave."

"That is the last thing I would expect you to do."

She must have moved then, away from the warnings and innuendos in Harville's voice, because in the next moment she exclaimed: "Why, there's Mrs. Hamilton . . . and *Celia,* whom I have heard so much about!" with every appearance of delight. Still, Celia hated the note of mockery that underlay what on the surface seemed like a very enthusiastic greeting.

How well schooled these people were in hiding their feelings; they were absolutely skilled at donning masks and then discarding them at will.

It amazed her that not so long ago she had been with her aunt and uncle and living in an imaginary world of lords and ladies, and now she moved among them with the ease of a born aristocrat and they were nothing like she had imagined.

And it *was* a world of wickedness and vice, just as she had been warned; before her now, smiling her smile of false welcome, was a woman who was the personification of those very things and the antithesis of everything Celia believed.

But in spite of that, she could not subdue the fury of envy she felt while looking into Marvella's maliciously glittering eyes.

She was evil disguised as perfection, and Celia was positive her sole purpose in accepting the weekend invitation to Harville was to pursue Grant Hamilton.

And there was nothing she or Willie could do about it.

But what would I want to do about it?

She quelled the insinuating little voice within. Grant Hamilton's romantic liaisons were none of her business.

"Lady Merrivale," she murmured, touching Marvella's cool hand with a mere brush of her fingers.

"Is Grant here?" Marvella asked ingenuously, turning to Willie, who gave her a baleful look.

"I'm sure you know that better than I," she said tartly.

"No, how could I?"

"Will my Lord Merrivale be in attendance?" Willie returned, her tone just as sugar-sweet as Marvella's.

"Why, I'm sure I don't know," Marvella answered flutily. "Oh! I see someone I must talk to—excuse me, won't you?"

She floated off toward the steps, which several other guests were descending to the hallway, and Celia stared after her, utterly stupefied by her effrontery.

"She is a bitch," Willie said succinctly.

"How can Grant have anything to do with her?"

"That," Willie said grimly, "is something you must ask *him*."

She wasn't even going to stoop to ask *him* for the time of day; she wasn't going to talk to him at all if she could possibly help it.

But nothing ever went the way she wanted it to.

She and Willie had no sooner greeted Eulalia, who seemed distracted, than Grant strolled into the Red Parlor, where Eulalia was receiving her guests.

"Dear boy," Willie exclaimed, instantly abandoning polite conversation with Eulalia to greet him.

"Willie," Grant murmured, taking her hands. "I had no idea . . ."

"Neither did Marvella—you should have heard her. *We* did, I assure you. Something about the usual *arrangements . . . ?*"

Grant shrugged, his gazed fixed on Celia, who was straining to make conversation with Eulalia and not finding it very easy.

"Marvella has an overactive imagination."

"Then I must have imagined the last place *I* saw her," Willie said acidly, "and you have been no help whatsoever."

"I promise, I am at your disposal now," Grant swore. "And how *is* Celia getting on?"

"She is perfection. Whereas you are the very devil, Grant; how can you have ignored us like that?"

The plaintive note in her voice caught him and he looked down at her. Oh, she was a sly fox, his stepmother. She knew exactly what he was about, but he wondered if she had even guessed that he had kissed Celia and just how devastating that kiss had been.

A man would have to be a saint to put himself in the realm of temptation again—and he was no martyr. He was, in fact, a fool, but he would never admit that to Willie.

Celia was here and he would have to deal with that—and Marvella's nonsense to boot.

It would be easy, in these first hours, when the influx of guests would keep everyone occupied with settling in, making introductions, taking tea and gossip in equal measures.

But after, when the games began . . .

"Celia—"

Her chin went up as he turned toward her.

"Grant," she said coolly, holding out her hand (well, she had to give him her hand or it would have looked as if she were snubbing him); his touch sent a shock wave up her arm.

But worse, he bent toward her, his green eyes glowing with unholy amusement, and he brushed his lips mockingly against her cheek.

The feelings engulfed her, the opposing, luxuriant, fury-making feelings; she hesitated for a moment, and then, as she caught sight of Marvella out of the corner of her eye, she murmured, "Ah, another item to cross off your list of things to do, Grant. Be nice to Celia before you are devoured by that whale, Lady Marvella."

Grant crushed her fingers in his meaningfully. "Bitch. And no one had to teach you *that,* I'd wager."

"*You'll* never know," Celia retorted under her breath and was instantly rewarded by the temper-containing flex of his jaw muscle.

"*Grant!*"

"Lady Marvella—I'd better get out of her way, Grant, or she'll pull me down in her undertow."

"*You* are not going anywhere."

"*Grant!*" Lady Marvella said insistently as she bore down on them, her flawless face and benign expression concealing perfectly the rage she felt at seeing Grant with his stepmother's little millstone.

"Marvella," he said neutrally.

She waited, but he didn't take her hand, because he was still forcefully holding onto Celia's.

"Celia doesn't need an anchor, do you, dear?" she asked sweetly.

Celia despised her; she had donned yet another mask, that of the patronizing, experienced Beauty, and she was looking at Grant expectantly as she spewed her venom.

"I rather think it's the other way around, Lady Merrivale. It is Grant who needs security, not I." She smiled up at Grant as she wrested her fingers from his viselike grip. "However, as you can see, I have slipped my moorings and he is now vulnerable to all predators."

Oh, she didn't like the glint in Grant's eyes, nor the fury in Lady Marvella's. But she loved slinging those barbs and having them hit home.

And he deserved it—for kissing her, for ignoring her, for treating her like a child and, above all, for flaunting Lady Marvella in front of her.

Damn him and damn him again. Her fingers curled like the claws of a cat. She felt like sinking her teeth into him.

And it didn't matter one bit that he stood there stiffly, trying to converse with Lady Marvella, who was making more than enough small talk for the two of them.

He had to look polite, when probably all he really wanted to do was—

Oh, but she wouldn't think about that . . . that forceful mouth taking the perfectly sculpted lips of Lady Marvella—

She moaned, unaware she had even made a sound.

"Well, well, well—and who have we here?" an insinuating voice said behind her.

Dear Lord, what now? Whatever now? She wheeled around and almost fell into the arms of a somewhat portly older man with a mane of thick white hair and icy blue eyes.

"My dear child," he murmured, catching at her hand. "Lord Henry Merrivale at your service."

"Oh," she said faintly, snatching her hand back. *No, no—I have got to get in control of myself. This must be Lady Marvella's husband. I can handle this. I can.*

She cleared her throat. "Lord Merrivale." She looked into his eyes and felt herself tumbling into that glinting, knowing blue ice.

She extended her hand. "How do you do? I am Celia Penmaris."

"What you are is beautiful, my dear," he murmured, bowing over her hand. "Did the very astute Albert invite you here just for me?"

She stiffened slightly. Surely he couldn't mean what she thought he meant.

Best to play naive with him. "I'm here with my aunt, the former Lady Millhaven. Do you know her?"

"I'm sure I do," he said lightly. "But I would much rather know you."

"But you do—now," Celia said. "And I have just met Lady Marvella, who is right there with my aunt's stepson. She is charming."

"She is a viper," Lord Merrivale said. "And you are an angel."

"You are too kind, Merrivale." A new voice entered the equation. Grant, interfering as usual.

"Ah, the knight-errant. Amazing how he hops from amorous to avuncular at the drop of a hat. Grant, did you say something?"

"I said Celia's aunt was looking for her," Grant said tightly.

"Ah. The dear Wilhelmina." Lord Merrivale looked down at Celia. "Of course I know your aunt, my dear. Every bit as well as Grant knows my wife, I daresay. And so I am delighted to make your acquaintance. Perhaps we can talk without any precipitate interruptions tomorrow?"

"I'd like that," Celia said as he bowed over her hand. And she liked the blistering green glare of Grant's eyes too.

"Pompous ass," he muttered as Merrivale sauntered off in the direction of his wife. "And whatever the hell he is doing here, you keep out of his way."

"Excuse me?" Celia said, infusing her voice with a tone of deliberate disbelief. "Are *you* telling *me* . . . ?"

"I am damned well telling you. Keep away from that lecher."

She feigned horror. "Are you telling me—"

"Goddammit, Celia!"

"Well, I'll tell you, Grant Hamilton. I'll keep away from that handsome, courtly man as long as you keep away from his wife. Because if he is a rake, then Lady Marvella must be a wh—"

"Celia."

There was no mistaking the warning tone in his voice.

Wasn't it just like a man: he would treat her like a fragile flower that needed protection while he went sniffing after another man's wife.

But he didn't know her, and she hardly knew herself or the white-hot fury that engulfed her.

She was not a child, and he could not dictate to her, and she would go where she wanted and see whom she wished to see.

"I didn't think you would agree to that arrangement,"

she said coolly. "And I would wager you have probably made a different one for tonight."

God, it was like turning a knife to say those words; but how could they not be true? Marvella had as good as insinuated it, and the appearance of her husband would make no difference to her.

"I could throttle you," Grant growled.

"And I hope you choke on your intentions," she hissed, wheeling away from him, secure in the knowledge that he wouldn't make a commotion or call attention to her and that—gentleman that he was—he would just let her go.

⚮ Thirteen

But there was nowhere to run to; it was still so early, and guests were arriving in pairs and threes and swarming into the parlor and greeting old friends and new acquaintances.

Too many people, and not so many that she could get lost in the crowd.

She felt as if she had to escape.

There was something about the cloying atmosphere surrounding Lady Marvella—and then Grant, with his insufferable condescension—!

Even Aunt Willie could not soothe away her resentment and Celia didn't even mean to let her try. She evaded Willie and slipped through the crowded parlor and out into the hallway.

Here, at least, one could breathe air that was not fogged by the odor of thick perfume and rank duplicity.

She felt like sinking right into the floor and disappearing.

Why on earth had Aunt Willie thought that coming here for the weekend would be a good idea?

The only good idea *she* could think of at the moment

was a strategic retreat to her room and a cold compress across her aching forehead.

She mounted the grand staircase slowly and made her way up to the landing amidst the bustle of still-arriving guests.

But all that noise diminished as she stepped into the second-floor hallway.

Here it was like an oasis of calm.

Except she could hear the faint rasp of angry voices around the corner and down the hall near her and Willie's bedroom, and without thinking, she moved closer to the wall to make herself less conspicuous—and put herself in the unfortunate position of being able to hear the conversation clearly.

". . . knew I would find you here."

"Oh, really? The real question is, what are *you* doing here?"

"Following the trail of your underclothes, of course, and it has led me exactly where I expected. Fellows tells me this is Grant Hamilton's room."

"Oh, nonsense. This is *my* room."

"Nice try, my dear. *Our* room is on the other side— same location, of course. It's no wonder you got confused."

"Our?" Marvella's voice dripped with disdain.

"Harville is overbooked, my dear. Albert had no idea how popular a weekend in the country would seem after all the roiling and toiling of the last several weeks of the Season. Oh, yes, endless people, most of whom neither of us would wish to meet under any other circumstances."

"Under any other circumstances, you would be in Paris. Why here? Why now?"

"Why not, my lady? I seek amusement, as does every other jaded silk stocking in England. Paris is dull—no new faces—whereas here, here I have found what I live for: the discovery of the gorgeously unexpected. And what keeps me going is that one chance in a thousand of finding her . . ."

"You leave Celia Penmaris alone." The threat in Marvella's voice was palpable.

"Oh, ho-ho, my dear—jealous? Tell me how jealous . . ."

"I hate you . . ."

The voices were coming closer, almost as if he had taken her arm and were steering her back toward the room they were unexpectedly going to share.

Which meant they were going to pass *her*—and Celia felt a moment of unreasoning panic, as if she were doing something wrong and had to hide.

Dear Lord, she had to do *something*. She didn't want either of them to see her, and she couldn't go forward, and she couldn't run down the opposite hall without them seeing her.

She turned and raced back down the stairs, almost tripping on her dress in her haste.

They were coming, they were coming—what if they were coming downstairs instead of going to their room? She ducked her head as she rounded the newel-post and stepped into the reception hall and made herself disappear into a crowd of milling guests.

There was an appointed time for everything, and the women had to keep changing their dresses to suit each event.

There was tea taken outdoors, there was lawn tennis; and there were parlor games indoors if one did not want to stroll through the maze or the rose garden, or admire the fountains, or be a spectator at the little stream where the fishing was said to be so good.

Celia could not bear to sit in the house and take part in the inane conversations of the women, and she wanted to avoid Grant, so she walked aimlessly around the grounds by herself.

And, of course, the first person she saw was Grant, casting his lines—literally and figuratively—at the little stream with a half-dozen other men who stood patiently waiting.

"But what do you do while you're waiting for the fish to bite?" Celia asked the group in general. "Look for other small and helpless game?"

Grant shot her a sharp look while the others tumbled over themselves to provide an explanation of the romance of fishing.

"You must feel so powerful after you've baited and trapped some poor, unsuspecting fish and pulled it around this way and that before you lift it out of its element and devour it at your table," Celia murmured, unable to stop her runaway mouth as Grant's chipped green gaze positively skewered her.

Not that she cared.

"And what about the laws of nature? Pursue or be pursued?" he asked silkily. "There is always a creature in nature who is made to be preyed upon."

"Truly?" Celia asked artlessly, wide-eyed and utterly shaking with anger. "Then it can only be the gender susceptible to the seduction of the lure—both out of doors and in. Gentlemen, I bid you good day."

Oh! The fury she felt—it was like a steam engine propelling her, except that she wasn't on track and she had no destination whatsoever, only the goal of getting through the weekend without committing some awful faux pas.

And Willie was uncharacteristically silent, leaving her to her own devices and spending her time with several pigeon-breasted older ladies who were dripping with jewels and high, penetrating voices that carried.

"Oh, is that your niece? She's positively extraordinary!"

Celia turned on her heel and walked away from them. If she heard one more word about her unusual looks—

Dinner was a disaster; there was no way to sit apart from the two dozen guests, and she was seated toward the middle of the table, next to Willie and opposite Lady Marvella and her husband.

There was no way anyone could avoid looking at her, even if a guest only wished to make a casual comment to someone on either side of him.

And she could not avoid seeing Grant's hard-set face and she made it a point to avoid his implacable eyes.

Which meant if she even looked across the table, she would meet the encouraging smile of Lord Merrivale, who was enjoying all the silent byplay, including the simmering temper of his wife beside him.

It was easy to smile back at him. There was something about him—he was probably a cad, but he was as charming as light, and his knowing eyes seemed to say *I understand all, and they are all wretched boors.*

Later, after the gentlemen had returned from taking cognac and a smoke, Lord Merrivale came to speak with her.

"It is a trial, isn't it—to behave the way *they* think you should behave."

"Or to have tea if one had really wanted a sip of whiskey. Oh, yes," Celia murmured. "Why is it always one way for men and another for the ladies?"

"They are swimming in envy over how beautiful you are and the fact that all the men cannot keep their eyes off you," Lord Merrivale said with some appearance of sincerity, and when she reacted, he held up his hand placatingly. "It is a fact, my dear. You must get used to it. You are beautiful and out of the common way, and people will always stare. If I were you, I would enjoy it—

and when you are ready, you will know how to exploit it.''

The thought was both appalling and tantalizing.

She felt Grant's disapproving eyes on her and she lifted her chin and turned to look at him with all the disdain she could muster.

Grant got to her first the next day on the pretext of wanting to choose a suitable docile mount for her, but really, she suspected, to dress her down for encouraging Lord Merrivale's attention.

"Just stay away from that man."

"You smell of fish," Celia said. "And this horse will do fine. I did have lessons, I am not a child and I can take care of myself."

"The most you can take care of is getting yourself out of bed in the morning," Grant snapped. "And you're being foolish beyond permission."

"And who asked you to sanction what I do or whom I speak with? Do I have the same privileges with you? Do I get to censure the very *obvious* way Lady Marvella's bosom was hanging over your arm last night? Is *that* her only mode of conversation? At least Lord Merrivale and I had some common interest in horses. And since by your expression I can see that *she* is none of my business, I fail to see how *he* is any of yours."

She pushed by him. "Now excuse me, Grant."

He pulled her back to him, closely, tightly, his large hand severing any feeling in her upper arm where he grasped her.

He was so angry. "The man adores seducing virgins."

"And you adore ravishing aristocratic whores. So we are even. My body, my life, my decision."

He almost bit and made excuses—but he could see in her eyes that was exactly what she wanted.

On some level, he wanted it too. Who could have

dreamed that one little kiss would throw them both into such turmoil?

And him especially, because he should have known better. But to kowtow to her need for him to grovel was something else altogether.

"Your folly," he growled and relinquished his hold on her so abruptly she staggered backward.

"I'm glad we understand each other," she said stiffly. "You are absolved of all obligations to either me or your stepmother. You are relieved of all charge, care, burden and responsibility, and you are free to pursue whichever cocotte claims your attention."

"You little witch. You still don't get it, and, by God, I'm not going to stand by while you emasculate me until you do."

He held up his hands. "Gone. Over. Good luck." And he turned on his heel and stalked away.

Later, she wasn't sure that Lord Merrivale hadn't been privy to the whole scene and then happened upon her to take advantage of the situation.

The funny thing was, she felt that in spite of his reputation, he still had a vulnerability that attracted her.

And he was there, almost the moment Grant disappeared from the stables, with a handkerchief in his hand and a comforting word about clods with the sensitivity of manure.

Oh, yes; at that moment she thought that exactly described Grant Hamilton.

"It's early," Lord Merrivale said comfortingly. "You don't want to return to the house with tearstains on your face. Rather, let's go for a walk so we can get the roses blooming in your cheeks. There's the girl. Now, have you seen the maze? Do you know about mazes? They're the most fascinating things, almost like a toy for grown-ups. The object is to get lost in them and then find your way out. And, of course, it's never easy. You take one wrong turn after another, and paths that seem to make sense often don't and lead you nowhere.

"And sometimes, just when you think one way is closed off to you, it opens up and reveals a whole new way to proceed. My dear, you could spend hours shifting around through the thing, but I do have the key, and so we shall be there only long enough for you to appreciate the intricacies of it.

"Come—"

And she went, intrigued by his description and fascinated to be in his company.

He was devilishly entertaining, but, of course, that kind of man would be, she thought, which was the only little stirring of conscience that she felt.

The heat had not risen yet, and the overhung paths were cool with a faint morning breeze which was overlaid by his light and amusing comments about the house, the guests, society in general, his life in particular.

The maze was located well beyond the house and adjacent to the terraced gardens and was entered by means of an ornate iron gate into a corridor lined with boxwood hedges that seemed to go on forever.

And it was such a game, trying to find the right path. She could see how it could take hours, and how much amusement it could afford both adults and children.

"And you," Merrivale said, "you are the best combination of both. You are enchanting."

"The puzzle is enchanting," Celia said, feeling not a frisson of fear in his sole company alone in the maze. "And I am determined to discover the secret."

"Oh, my dear," Merrivale murmured achingly, "you already have."

"You saw her *when?*" Willie demanded, horrified. "My God, Grant, where can she be?"

He had searched already, every place possible. And he didn't want to admit to Willie how he had left her—reckless enough to do anything.

Everyone was down to breakfast by then, and Marvella was already hanging all over him, but it was curious her husband was nowhere in sight.

"Oh, dear Henry is still asleep," Marvella cooed. "Isn't that convenient?"

Grant extricated himself from her seeking hands.

No one had seen Celia.

Except—the stableboy said that a gentleman had joined her and they'd gone off together after Grant had left her with the horses.

The information put him in a complete panic. The "gentleman" was obviously Marvella's husband—and they could be anywhere.

Harville provided the welcome information that there was an observation deck in the cupola.

Grant raced up the steps and scooted up the narrow ladder to the one place from which he would be able to see all around the grounds.

It was the only hope, unless they were hiding someplace unsavory or Merrivale had already taken her beneath the bushes and left her crying.

Grant wriggled up into the small housing which was framed by multipaned floor-to-ceiling windows on six sides, one of which could be opened like a door.

Damn—and damn—and damn.

Nothing, nothing, nothing—rolling fields and flowers and a gentle breeze lifting the leaves of the trees.

The sun blazed overhead as if to provide the maximum light.

Celia was the maximum light. He felt his fear for her squeeze his very vitals. Whatever happened, it could not, would not, be Merrivale who first made love to her.

No, he could not be thinking that way—

Wait—a movement in the distance . . .

He almost put a fist through a window. How perfect. The maze.

Harville had the key, and Grant went alone.

It wasn't even that difficult to find them. The hard part was maintaining a light tone so as not to scare Celia, who looked as if she were having a perfectly fine time and resented his interruption anyway, damn her.

"I've been sent to look for you two," he said with just the faintest undertone of mockery in his voice. God, how he had to restrain himself from throwing Merrivale into the bushes.

"Indeed?" Lord Merrivale murmured. "How thoughtful. I suppose we lingered longer than we should, dear Celia, and it is time to return to the real world. Shall we? And how can we ever thank the inestimable Mr. Hamilton for bringing it to our attention?"

Insufferable bastard, Grant thought furiously.

And isn't that the difference between a gentleman and a cow-handed provincial, Celia mused smugly as they trudged their way back to the house.

When they paused outside the piazza door, Merrivale took her hand and assured her of his pleasure in her company, then bowed to Grant and disappeared into the house.

"Jesus!" Grant exploded.

"Excuse me?"

He turned on her. "You stupid fool, do you realize you could have ruined your reputation? A few more minutes and he'd have had your skirts up and your virginity in his hands, and make no mistake about it—he would not have been kind. Or did the thought of playing with fire excite you?"

She slapped him. And it felt so good, so satisfying, to ram those awful words back into his mouth.

"I've had just about enough of you, Grant Hamilton. Did you really think I would be Merrivale's willing victim? I would have killed him if he had even tried to so much as kiss me. Merrivale is a gentleman; he knows his place, and I would wager he knows when to make his move and when to proceed with caution—and that is the difference between him and you."

"Don't try that again, Celia; your spitting-cat routine doesn't impress me, and you've got about the strength of a kitten, which would hardly be enough to fight off a flea, let alone a determined man. You know nothing of that kind of man, and your survival instincts are nonexistent, as proven by the fact you even went somewhere alone with the bastard."

"Exactly. Men may go and women may wait, and never the twain shall share the same reputation. Who would have run after you if you had gone off with Lady Marvella? No one, I fancy. They would have envied your daring and your imagination, always assuming you could have boxed her in—so to speak—among the hedges."

He lifted his hand, almost as if he would have slapped her in turn, but he forcefully held back from doing anything. "God, God, dear God, give me patience . . ."

But she wasn't done; again she felt as if she were on a speeding train, out of control, and she wanted to push him to his limit.

"And what about my reputation now that I am alone with you?" she went on recklessly. "Why doesn't that matter? You're every bit as much a libertine as Lord Merrivale, are you not?"

"Oh, Jesus, shut up—just *shut up!*"

"Oh! I'm sorry—am I not properly grateful to you for rescuing me from social disaster? Let me think . . . I know . . . I promise to be much more careful in the future so you do not have to come after me again."

"*Celia . . .*"

He began walking toward her and she began backing away.

"You cannot be my warden one moment and my counselor the next. And I won't let you be my—my—"

He had backed her against the side of the house. "Your what? Your keeper? Your custodian? Your watch-dog?"

"My . . . tutor."

"A tutor is a teacher, Celia," he murmured, imprisoning her between his arms.

"Yes," she whispered. "And haven't you been one? Haven't you?"

"What? Taught you the ways of a Merrivale? Not hardly."

"Taught me to—flirt."

"You were born to . . ."

She could hardly breathe. She wanted—she wanted—

His lips tentatively touching hers on the scouring tide of their mutual anger felt like a balm.

She could never have wanted Merrivale—because of this, because she remembered and she didn't want to, and because she wanted it now and she didn't want to want it.

His mouth settled on hers, delicate as a moth, savoring the sweet nectar she offered, and then lifted, poised to taste again.

The sun was bright and hot upon them and something else hung in the gold-flecked air between them, something that shut out everything but her awareness of him and his straining resistance to her.

Not again, not again . . .

They were caught in the heat of his anger, her resentment, her burgeoning passion, his volatile emotions . . .

It wasn't right, and it was as right as it could be.

Her body moved against his restively, instinctively,

and he pulled her more tightly against his thrusting need and delved into the honeyed taste of her again.

And again. And again. Lightly, sweetly, in sensuous opposition to the coiled tautness of his body, as if he were holding himself in check, pulling back, straining against the seductive hot wet taste of her.

She could never have imagined how delicate her body would feel against the inflexible hardness of him, or how much she would want to give herself up to it.

She felt older than Eve, following her every inclination, challenging him, playing with him, answering his every foray into the intimacy of her mouth with a demand of her own.

This could never have happened with someone like Merrivale. She knew it, deep inside she knew it. She would not have wanted anyone else to kiss her like that; she would not have ached to have anyone other than Grant touch her the way she wanted him to touch her—now.

He knew it too. There was something in the way she moved against him and into his featherlike kisses that aroused him unbearably and made his body lock with utter resistance.

She felt it and hated it, and the moment he realized it, he deliberately moved away from her, and the magic, the feeling, the moment evaporated as if she had imagined them too.

She caught her breath as a mask dropped over his expression and wiped away all the passion she had seen there.

"I am no better than Merrivale," he said stonily. "That will not happen again."

She wanted to protest, but his damnable green eyes were shuttered against her as he uttered those conventional words that had nothing to do with his feelings.

And that was the difference between men and women: he could blithely and unconcernedly walk away, and she—she would be marked by his touch forever.

⬙ Fourteen

He was so good at it. The kiss was as if it had never been, and it lingered, butterfly-wet, on her lips to remind her of her folly and her innocence.

She ought never, ever to have tried to match wits with Grant Hamilton. She felt like a fool.

And now it was time for her to don a mask; but how did one do that, how, on the heels of such a crushing rejection?

No, she wouldn't—she *couldn't*—let one disturbing moment with Grant Hamilton destroy her weekend. She was stronger than that, and it was becoming clearer and clearer that these people treated the nuances of love as lightly as air.

A kiss was as fragile as a butterfly's wing, broken in a moment by the merest threat of a breeze.

Puff—and gone.

She squared her shoulders and moved slowly toward the piazza doors just as they swung open and her hostess and half a dozen female guests swarmed out.

"Celia, dear, we're going riding," the viscountess hailed her. "You *must* join us; go change—we'll wait."

The last thing she wanted to do was sit astride a horse for several hours; she started to make some excuse, and then she caught sight of Grant and several of the men with their fishing gear.

She cast aside the enticing idea of pushing him into the stream and thought, Why not keep out of sight and so busy that the memory of that stupid kiss would never intrude for the rest of her stay at Harville?

And so she smiled and waved at Eulalia and called to her: "I'd love to; you're so kind. I'll be as fast as I can." And she dashed into the house and up to her room before anyone else could waylay her.

After that, it was cards in the library, tea in the solarium, a walk to whet the appetite for the next meal, a grand, formal, sit-down dinner and dancing afterward.

Between each activity and changing into the proper dress and maintaining her mask of cool disdain, Celia hardly had time to think about anything.

And Willie did not have a moment to catch up with her until they were all finally gathered in the grand hall, waiting for the musicians to tune up and the evening's festivities to begin.

"You've been a busy girl," Willie commented lightly. "I've hardly seen you all day. Grant came back, said you were fine and just outside in the garden, but we never saw you at all."

"We went riding," Celia said coolly. "Did you know Albert's wife is a most accomplished horsewoman? She was so helpful and patient with me. She may not do well at cards or tea, but she knows her horses, and that seems to count for a lot here."

"She is finding her way, of course. This is vastly different from what she is used to, and, of course, her accent seems to grate on some people's nerves, as does her lack of experience. But even so, they reach out with both hands to accept her hospitality. Ah, listen, the music—'' Willie's slender body moved subtly to the rhythm. "I wish . . . I wish . . .''

She wished Hamish were with her at this moment, and then she would have swirled onto the floor and into heaven.

But her wishes were not paramount here. She would dance, if asked, with Grant and with her host. But she was a little dismayed when Albert came directly to Celia's side, bowed and requested the first dance—which he ought to have asked his wife for.

Of course, the difference between the two was as palpable as night and day. Celia was a creature of ineffable mystery, while Eulalia was as plain as pudding, and as wholehearted and filling too.

Even Celia hesitated for a fraction of a second—which Willie was pleased to note—before she gave him her hand; but she looked so stiff and uncomfortable that Willie could only hope the dance would end sooner than later so that Celia could be spared.

The first problem was, Albert could not dance. But worse than that, he seemed to want to look only at Celia rather than concentrating on his steps, and Willie did not like that one bit.

What *was* it about Celia?

In this situation she looked purely miserable, with none of the pulse and fire that usually characterized her. And yet Albert was mesmerized—*not*, Willie thought, a good sign.

"I would call him out in a second if he weren't related to you," Grant murmured in her ear.

Dear boy, how had he fathomed her distress?

"Hamish would shoot him for his flagrant disregard of his wife," Willie said. "And I just don't know what to do."

"We can waltz," Grant suggested, his glittering gaze pinned on the offensive Albert.

"I *hate* the way he's looking at her."

You aren't the only one, dear Stepmama.

He said nothing and merely held out his arms to Willie and swung her neatly out among the waltzers.

He hadn't intended to be anywhere near Miss Celia Penmaris and her gorgeously seductive mouth if he could help it . . .

God, but that clod was making him crazy the way he was looking at Celia—as if he wanted to devour her right on the dance floor. And that snake, Merrivale, was slithering around the dance floor, just looking for the moment to strike.

Grant felt murderous and he also felt like running for cover, because his feelings about Celia were slipping fast and furiously out of control.

And he was absolutely sure that Merrivale, especially, was very much aware of it.

Willie was aware of nothing as she moved blissfully in his arms, and he maneuvered them close by Albert and Celia until they could actually exchange a couple of words.

Or rather, Willie did. "Albert, dear, do let's change partners. I was hoping for a go-round with you before I went up to bed."

Albert stopped, faltered and then relinquished Celia, who was frozen in horror at her aunt's suggestion. He took Willie's hand and began pushing and pumping her away.

"We don't need to," she whispered as Grant moved to take her in his arms.

I need to.

No, he didn't need to; she was too young, too beautiful, too unaware of her own exotic power, and he needed—he needed—

He needed to hold her just one more time before—

The music, mingling scent, the low hum of conversation, the buoyant feeling of Celia in his arms—*where she belonged*—

The last thing in the world Willie would want him to be thinking; the last thing in the world he wanted—to be captivated by an unworldly innocent who would *expect* things.

God, he was crazy; and, crazier still, he wanted to kiss her until she was dizzy with desire—for him, and only him.

He could do it too; he could waltz her right out the door and seduce her in the hedgerows and then perhaps— perhaps he could get her out of his mind and out from under his skin.

He did none of that, of course; she held herself just as rigidly with him as she had with Lord Harville, her face a mask of pure contempt, discouraging intimacy, inviting him to leave her in the middle of the floor if he so chose. so as not to prolong the agony for either of them.

And he almost did it. He felt so twisted around by his contradictory feelings, he almost left her there.

But in the end, always the gentleman, he finished the dance and handed her over to Willie, then stood on the sidelines and watched her enchant Lord Merrivale all over again while he fended off Marvella's persistence, which over the course of the evening became both obvious and offensive.

And then he couldn't even begin to count the sundry other buffoons who made their way into Celia's bewitching orbit and seemed not to want to leave.

He had had enough. In the midst of the merriment and the full swing of the party, he found it very easy to depart Harville in the middle of the night.

* * *

And that was that. Everything afterward became an anticlimax.

He was a coward and she was a fool, and she could not wait to get back to London because she was sick of the country and especially the venomous Marvella and the too-charming Lord Merrivale.

The breakfast, the hunt, the packing, all took way too long; she slept on the train while Willie read, and she was brought up short by Willie's reminder of their succeeding week's itinerary.

"When do we rest?"

"Are you serious, my dear? I thought that was what we had been doing at Harville."

And she didn't know if Willie was being sarcastic or serious.

The evening after they returned to London, they were off to the opera again—*Rigoletto* this time—and another lavish supper and ball following at the Bellinghams'.

She really was too tired for all this, Celia thought wearily as she and Willie freshened themselves in the retiring room of the Bellinghams' town mansion.

And, dear Lord, the last person she wanted to see was Anthea the moment she walked into the ballroom—but there Anthea was, rushing eagerly to greet her in her usual way, with that touch of disapproval before she demanded details.

"Celia! How *are* you? You look as if you have been in the sun, although with your complexion, that flush of color can only be becoming. You *do* look well. Did you enjoy your weekend? Did you do much riding? Harville is said to keep an excellent stable."

"It was most entertaining," Celia answered noncommittally, thinking perhaps she was being a touch uncharitable toward Anthea, who was at least genuine and had a kind heart.

She tempered her impatience and went on to describe

the guests and what they had done; she left out anything to do with Lord Merrivale or the damnable Grant Hamilton.

"Well, it sounds as if you enjoyed yourself enormously, and it is obvious that I didn't spoil your weekend with all my dire warnings. George—Mr. Maitland—has been telling me that I need to strengthen my *faith* and to trust in Providence and prayer."

Here Anthea's expression took on a dreamy kind of look. "Oh, Celia, you cannot imagine how different my life has become! And how much strength and sense of purpose I have found from within. I am so happy"—she gave Celia's hand a little squeeze—"and I can only hope and pray that you too someday will find the same kind of happiness."

"Then you must tell me what has happened," Celia said encouragingly, although she was fairly certain what Anthea would reveal to her. "You sound positively evangelical."

"You know me too well. But that is just the half of it, and I hardly realized it until George helped me to find the truth. We have become committed to each other, Celia—and to God. As soon as this charade of a Season is over, we plan to be married. We will go to America first—I must meet George's family and friends—and then there will be a period of training and testing to prepare us for the trials and hardships that lie ahead before we leave on our holy Mission."

Her voice lowered. "We have been praying, George and I, that the Lord's will might take us to Ceylon."

Celia was absolutely nonplussed; she could think of nothing to say for a full two minutes.

"You mean—you are engaged to be married?"

"Oh, yes," Anthea whispered; she seemed transfixed. Her cheeks were glowing and she looked almost beautiful. "We understand each other and we think alike on almost everything. It is *so* important to be *friends* with one's future partner in life and to have mutual trust in each other . . . just as, I hope and pray, you and *your* betrothed have in each other.''

She paused for a moment to gauge Celia's reaction, and when she saw none, she went on suggestively. ''You have been writing to him regularly, I trust? And he does understand the difficult position you are in at this time? He obviously has the same faith in you that you have in him.''

What on earth was Anthea talking about? And why was she expecting her to respond?

Ronald. Oh, dear Lord, Ronald—who had been the last thing on her mind for days—weeks even.

Wasn't Anthea right—she was enjoying herself too much—but still, it seemed as if Anthea took particular pleasure in reminding her of her obligation to Ronald and making her feel guilty.

Except she felt no remorse whatsoever; she had come so far since she had last seen or heard from Ronald that anything she did or learned could only be an asset to her as his wife.

And yet Anthea seemed to be looking for some reaction from her. How curious. It reminded her of Aunt Gertrude: always seeing or imagining the worst and almost *relishing* it.

Which prompted Celia to remember that she was slated to visit Gertrude and Theo this very coming weekend.

That on top of everything else.

Wouldn't it be wonderful if she could provide someone as virtuous as Anthea to distract her aunt so she could have the semblance of an enjoyable weekend?

I could come with you . . . or ask Anthea to accompany you . . . She could almost hear Aunt Willie's mischievous voice. . . . *her friend Mr. Maitland admires your uncle Theo's sermons excessively . . .*

No—

Could she?

She gathered her wits; she hadn't even offered congratulations on Anthea's engagement.

"I'm so very happy for you, Anthea! And Mr. Maitland, of course. I'll be sure to tell *Ronald* about you both and how very romantic it was. Right from your first meeting!" She shook her head in wonderment while Anthea preened just the tiniest bit. And then she took a deep breath and gave in to her impulse.

"I wonder . . . you know, I've been racing about so much that I decided to spend the next weekend with my aunt and uncle. I was going to travel alone—well, with Emily, my maid, of course—but I wonder if you would like to come with me. I'm sure Aunt Gertrude and Uncle Theo would dearly enjoy meeting both you *and* Mr. Maitland—and *you* could do me the very great favor of persuading them that I am not leading a dissolute life in London."

She could see immediately that Anthea was torn in two ways: she could not pass up an opportunity to introduce Mr. Maitland to Uncle Theo, but she also felt she would be sheering past the truth to say that life in London was nowhere near as unrestrained as Celia's aunt and uncle imagined.

On the other hand, she was living proof that one need not be tempted; she was just not so sure about Celia.

However, virtue won.

"I would be delighted," Anthea said with unfeigned sincerity. "Of course you ought not to go alone." And she had now put herself in the position of savior so that Celia must feel indebted to her.

But she was curious, above all, about what she might find out about Celia and her strange disregard of her loving fiancé, who had obviously stayed too long away in Ceylon.

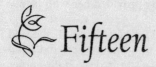

Fifteen

They arrived at the Grange just in time for tea, a carriage having been sent to the station to pick them up. Unfortunately, it wasn't meant to accommodate either an entourage or an excessive amount of luggage, so Anthea wound up practically sitting in Mr. Maitland's lap, and Celia and Emily both held suitcases precariously perched on their knees for the whole trip.

And, of course, Aunt Gertrude didn't make things better. No one disapproved of extravagance more than she, and Emily and a half-dozen suitcases and trunks all piled helter-skelter certainly qualified as that.

So Aunt Gertrude's gimlet-eyed look as they spilled out of the carriage did not bode well. Neither did her first words to Celia.

"How nice of you to fit us into your busy schedule, Celia."

How nice of you to try to make me feel like a disgraced child in front of my friends, Celia thought rebelliously, but that was so like Aunt Gertrude. She almost felt as if her aunt were going to make her stand in a corner again, just like she used to whenever Celia displayed the slightest sign of willfulness.

But she supposed she had learned something from all of that, even if it was only to preserve appearances and not talk back to her aunt in front of company.

And Aunt Gertrude certainly provided her with plenty of provocation.

"I see there is an invitation for you already," she said as she led them into the parlor. "Now, where did I put it? Ah, yes." She went over to a sturdy desk in the corner of the room and removed an envelope from one of the drawers. "There you are. Someone has had the supreme ill grace to tender an invitation solely to you. Well, it's all of a piece with *some* people. You have my permission to open it," she added as she handed the envelope to Celia.

However, Celia did not want to read the invitation in front of her aunt, but she could not escape the expectant look on the women's faces, or the benign encouragement on her uncle's, and so she slowly tore open the flap and took out the thick sheet of creamy paper within.

"How nice!" she murmured as she read the contents. "The Templecombes have invited me to spend an afternoon riding with them. They are dear friends of Aunt Willie's—"

She caught herself suddenly, disengaging herself from the pure pleasure she felt that Aunt Willie was obviously looking after her from afar. Aunt Gertrude and Uncle Theo did not mingle with the Templecombes' set, even though they lived barely a few miles apart, and the resentful expression on her aunt's face said as much.

"Oh . . . the Templecombes," Aunt Gertrude said witheringly, as if *that* explained everything, including their bad manners at leaving her and Theo out. "I quite understand; it wouldn't do at *all* to *cut* the Templecombes at this stage in your London career. You will have to tell me the details later, Celia."

She turned to Anthea, her fiancé and her husband with a bright—a too-bright, Celia thought—smile. "Come, everyone. You must be perishing to have some tea."

Celia followed them slowly into the small parlor, where a young betweenmaid had laid out the tea service, but was just in time to hear her aunt's further diatribe on the subject.

"I must say," Aunt Gertrude commented as she directed where everyone should sit, "the manners of the nobility—thinking a young girl like Celia could just hop in a carriage and take herself off for an afternoon with them. Is it so impossible to conceive of someone being raised with morals and manners these days? I shudder to think what influences poor Celia has come under during the time she has been away from us. Oh—my dear Celia! Come have a seat. Have a cup of tea."

What she wanted was a bromide, preferably one that would silence Aunt Gertrude once and for all.

But she hardly needed to say a word during the whole excruciating ceremony of taking tea, because Aunt Gertrude and Anthea seemed to hit it off. And she could see that the bishop was extremely flattered to hear that Mr. Maitland not only had read all of his published sermons, but greatly admired his grasp of theology and modern science, and was eager to learn more from one he considered a master and a mentor.

She sat listening politely to Mr. Maitland fawn all over her uncle and watching Aunt Gertrude and Anthea chatter away; she said hardly anything. Anthea was talking enough for both of them, and the odd thought occurred to her that Anthea would have made a much more tractable niece than she had ever been.

But then, her mother could never have borne such a *righteous* daughter as Anthea. A woman who had captured hearts all over the world, who had been used to hardness and harshness, who had triumphed and conquered—a woman like that could never have given birth to such a constricted and opinionated person.

And it was obvious that Aunt Gertrude wished that she had.

Celia was probably being fanciful and making more of it than it was—a courtesy call on her relatives. She could even say she was happy to see Uncle Theo, for whom she had a great deal of affection, but not under the trying circumstances of his discussing protocols of the Church with Mr. Maitland.

She stood up abruptly in the midst of one of his lengthy dissertations.

"You must excuse me. I find I am tired and I would like to go to my room and lie down."

"Well, of course," Aunt Gertrude said. "Everyone understands how wearing it must be running around London with princes and viscounts. I don't doubt you're tired, my dear. Anyone would be. Do take your rest. I'm sure you'll find time to visit with us after you dispense with your social obligations."

She turned and patted Anthea on the hand. "We're having such a delightful conversation. I'm sure we won't miss you at all."

Celia bit back a retort. There was no point in antagonizing Aunt Gertrude. Aunt Gertrude was the epitome of moral rectitude, and Celia had always been too young to know what was in her best interests.

But she knew now. A month with Aunt Willie had opened her eyes. And it was just like Willie had said. She had debuted in society and danced with a prince; how could Aunt Gertrude hurt her now?

And how strange it seemed now to be back in this house, mounting the steps to the room she had slept in for all those years.

The house appeared smaller somehow, the steps narrower, the room itself positively claustrophobic—and sterile.

And as she stood there, mesmerized by the changes, she suddenly understood why: Aunt Gertrude had wiped away every trace of her the moment she had left the house.

She had a headache by then, although she never would have admitted it to Aunt Gertrude, and so she felt relieved when, after a restless hour of tossing and turning, she heard a sharp knock and Emily came in, her eyes rolling upward, her hands clasped dramatically over her breast.

"Oh, miss! I swear I never felt like I was too much of a sinner before—'specially 'cos I just 'appened to be born in London! I am so sorry, Miss Celia, but if I couldn't laugh inside meself, I wouldn't 'ave been able to keep from laughin' in their faces!"

Celia levered herself into a sitting position on the narrow bed that had once been her own, her lips twitching in response to Emily's clowning. "What do you mean, Emily? What on earth happened downstairs? What did they say to you?"

But she could almost imagine the scene: Emily being subjected to a barrage of sly and nasty questions all couched in conjecture—all due, no doubt, to her dear aunt Gertrude's malicious influence.

She ought to have insisted that Aunt Willie come with her. Aunt Willie would have known exactly how to rout them all.

"Oh, this is too much! You must prepare me before I have to go downstairs and face them all again."

"I didn't mean for you to get upset, miss—but Lor', I swear I never did see such a bunch o' hypocrites, pretending all the while they was just good God-fearing people. Asking me all kinds of questions about *you*, miss, *and* her Grace too, which ain't none of their bloody business— Oooh! I'm sorry *that* slipped out, miss, but it's 'ard to stop it! They got their set, nasty ideas about anyone who lives in London and likes to enjoy life, or,'' she added as she began unpacking Celia's trunk and shaking out the first gown, ''wear beautiful clothes.

''And I think some of 'em—the butler, for sure—'ave been readin' all the London papers that her ladyship's been gettin' all upset over. The ones that 'ave your picture in 'em, I warrant, and all that gossip—you know, about the Prince of Wales, and about where you been and what you been wearing and all that.

''So I said to them—nice as you please, even though I was fair boilin' underneath—I said that when you're in high society you can't help if or when they take your photograph, and that the prince and princess *both* had taken a likin' to you. And anyway, the only evil is in the bad thoughts of bad people—which is what you told me once.

''And that's what I told them, miss—bunch of old carrion crows they reminded me of—ugh!''

She scowled as she laid the last of the gowns across the narrow bed for Celia's approval.

''A nice, elegant and daring gown, I think—don't you?'' Celia said angrily, picking one up and holding it against her body to measure the degree of décolletage. ''How *dare* they call themselves Christians and then presume to *judge!*''

''But that's exactly what they *want* to do, miss, and it don't matter none what you be wearin'. So why give them more fodder to chew?'' Emily said sensibly. ''Here, now, miss, this dress is country proper.''

What an ally she had in Emily, Celia thought as she allowed the maid to remove her traveling clothes. And Emily was eminently right about her aunt and the way

Celia should dress this evening, because Aunt Gertrude would undoubtedly be on the attack.

Perhaps she even invited you here for just that very purpose.

Dear Lord, where had that unbelievable thought come from?

She lifted her arms so that Emily could slide the dress over her head and begin the endless pulling and patting to make sure every line and ruffle was exactly right.

The gown was cut exquisitely and simply to mold to her naturally slender figure; it had layers of silk over tulle that shaded from pale yellow into gold, and matching ribbon trim on each frothy layer of flounces on the skirt and edging the tinier ruffles that cascaded off her shoulders.

It wasn't too low in front either, just enough to give the discreet impression of the crease between her breasts.

And as the final touch, Emily threaded more gold ribbons into her high-piled hair and around her neck and placed pearls set in gold in her ears.

"Oh, miss, you look just beautiful! Now, don't you let any of 'em downstairs scare you. If they look sour, it'll only be because they're all jealous!"

Celia bit her lips and pinched her cheeks to put some color into them. She was a little bit scared of her aunt's reaction and she didn't fully understand why.

Slowly and reluctantly, she made her way downstairs to the drawing room, and as she paused at the door, dismayed by the number of people who would be joining them for dinner, she heard Aunt Gertrude's voice slicing through the genteel murmur of conversation.

"Well, Celia—at last! You're ten minutes late. I can only suppose that the weeks you've spent in *Town*, where quite obviously they keep different hours, have made you forgetful. However, you are here now. Do come and stand beside me so that I may present you to everyone."

It was the last thing she wanted to do, and only Uncle Theo seemed to fully appreciate how she felt. She caught his apologetic look before she moved warily to her aunt's side, her head held high, wondering why her aunt would want to introduce her to people she already knew or had met casually at some church function.

There was Colonel Dartwood and Mrs. Dartwood, who was *such* a close friend of Lady Gertrude. And their horsey daughter, Veronica, who had always looked down her long nose at the bishop's unfortunate niece, and her brother, Algernon, who was as plain as she was.

And the self-effacing vicar and his equally self-effacing wife; the round-faced, purse-lipped young curate, Mr. Denby, who was destined, of course, to be her dinner partner; and Lord and Lady Snelgrove, who were distantly related to Aunt Gertrude and had a country estate nearby.

Dorinda Snelgrove was one of the ladies who had been taking tea with Gertrude in the rose garden the day Celia's aunt had maligned her one time too many.

She felt the old, painful anger shoot through her; her back stiffened and her eyes flashed.

She wasn't imagining it; it wasn't pushing that old hurt too far to believe that her aunt meant to try to humiliate her in front of her friends.

But Aunt Gertrude had no power to make her feel foolish anymore. All she had to do was keep control of her temper and a civil tongue in her head.

But even that was difficult when she was bombarded with questions from all directions. She felt like a criminal under interrogation.

And the first on the attack was Lady Snelgrove, who leaned forward as she snapped out her questions, the better to watch her face. Or to make her feel uncomfortable.

"Do tell me, dear—I'm simply *dying* to know—how did you happen to become acquainted with the Prince of

Wales? Is your aunt Wilhelmina among his circle of close friends—that Marlborough House set? Does she know Jennie Churchill? I am *so* out of touch with the latest London gossip that I feel quite woefully *provincial!*''

She tried to ignore their barbed words and honeyed insinuations. But it took all the good grace she possessed to answer with equanimity.

''I was introduced to his Royal Highness at a late supper after the opera, and he was so kind as to invite me to tea to meet Princess Alexandra. She, of course, is exceptionally kind and generous in every way. She has quite become my idol. She even offered to be my mentor. She never thinks ill of anyone and she never listens to gossip. She prefers to make up her own mind about the people she meets.''

At this point, Celia shot a meaningful look at Lady Snelgrove. ''She told me so herself. Such an example to us all, who are far too quick to jump to conclusions or to condemn, don't you think? I try to conduct myself using the princess's example. I am sure I could not have any better model. Do you not agree, Aunt Gertrude?''

Gertrude was caught up short by Celia's question. The last thing she expected was that bold baggage turning to her for corroboration of her tasteless set of new values!

She hated being placed at a disadvantage, and the unbecoming flush that mottled her cheeks betrayed her true feelings. She was seething at the way the minx had managed to turn the tables when it was *she* who was supposed to have been taught a lesson in manners and deportment.

So now Gertrude had no choice but to give a grudging nod in response to her niece's brazen question, or else everyone would perceive that she was maligning the princess.

It was clear, she thought grimly, that all her worst fears had been realized, and that Celia was acting more and more like her poor, unfortunate mother.

Even her *looks,* enhanced now by her new, daringly fashionable wardrobe—and her hair, styled to make her appear sophisticated and much older than her years—this was what loose living had brought her to, and all in the space of a month.

Truly, it *was* her Christian Duty to save the poor child from the baser side of her nature before it was too late.

But Celia had effectively silenced them all; not a one of them was brazen enough to gainsay the example of Princess Alexandra.

So the only thing they could do was whisper amongst themselves.

She watched them surreptitiously, just waiting for someone to make a snide remark about her life in London, because she knew it couldn't quite be over yet. Not yet.

The get-together was already a disaster. Her initial gratitude and even fondness for Anthea Langbourne were diminishing by the moment, and it wasn't because of the cozy way she and Aunt Gertrude conducted their dinner conversation.

And whatever emotion she had felt about her aunt was fast turning into active dislike.

Had they always been such mealy-mouthed hypocrites?

She wished she were rude enough to tell them so, especially after the ladies retired after dinner, with Aunt Gertrude leading the way.

Matters got worse when the ladies were closeted without their husbands.

Mrs. Dartwood began, with every evidence of friendship and exchanging confidences. "Well! It's perfectly understandable that you might be reluctant to speak in front of the gentlemen, dear Celia—especially your uncle, the bishop. But we are away from them now, so perhaps you will tell us, such fearful provincials that we

are, how it really feels to move in the very highest levels
of society. I'm sure my own dear Veronica would like to
know, wouldn't you, love?"

She cast a short speaking glance at her daughter, who
sat staring at Celia as if she were a visitor from another
world. Then Veronica leaned forward, her bright, beady
brown eyes making her seem like a plump, inquisitive
little partridge.

They all waited.

And Celia waited. She was going to prove she was
better than all of them, and that she alone had the good
manners to exercise self-control. When she spoke, she
made sure her voice was calm and controlled.

"You must forgive me if I find myself at a loss
to understand exactly what everyone wishes to know. I
am only a novice and just beginning to learn what
is expected of me and how to comport myself in society."

That sounded humble enough and didn't satisfy the
vultures in the least. What now? She looked around at
their rapacious faces.

They wanted details, gossip, something to besmirch
the image that for them was totally unobtainable. How
else could they humiliate *her?*

And why should she let them?

She flashed a sudden, brilliant smile as a perfectly
wicked idea occurred to her.

"I'm sure my friend, Miss Langbourne, would be so
much better suited to describe a London Season with all
its proscribed rituals than I—she has been through the
ordeal once before. Perhaps she would talk about her experiences."

Anthea looked shocked and a rush of color flushed her
cheeks. She stood up awkwardly. Perhaps Celia was embarrassed because of the attention and all the questions
and in desperation had looked to Anthea to rescue her.

It had to be that. It was the only charitable way to think.

"Celia is being overly modest," Anthea finally said when she was able to collect her wits. "She has been—well, quite a success, and of course I am happy for her—even if it wouldn't suit *me* to be in the limelight. But you must really ask her about the rest, because even though we have become close friends, we do not live in each other's pockets."

It was a wonderfully delicious awkward moment; no one knew quite how to follow up Anthea's disingenuous statement, and no one wanted to take up the vicious questioning.

Once again she had put paid to their malice, Celia thought triumphantly, and now all she had to do was get through another hour, when they would rejoin the gentlemen and everyone would go home.

"Do you ride?"

Veronica Dartwood's blunt question took everyone by surprise; Veronica seldom spoke and was deemed to be unutterably shy except when it came to horses.

She was speaking to Celia, and she seemed quite unaware of the previous conversation with its many and varied nuances while she had sat there as quietly and unobtrusively as she always did.

She did not really know Celia either, although their paths had crossed on several occasions in the past, but she suddenly felt that she wanted to find out something about this strange and rather exotic creature who seemed very different from all of *them,* quite unlike the way she remembered her, *and* awfully nice.

But she could only relate this to what she cared the most about—horses and riding.

And Celia felt distinctly grateful for her unintentional interference.

"Do I—? Oh, yes. I enjoy riding very much, although

I still have much to learn. I have a friend, you might be interested to know, who rode a horse bareback and astride—in California. She married and came to England, and I met her last weekend—''

She paused, suddenly aware of faces avidly listening to her words. So it wasn't over.

"Anyway," she went on, "she was kind enough to give me some instruction to make me feel much more comfortable and confident on a horse, especially once I was able to understand and even talk to the horse I was riding—or do you think that sounds silly?"

"Far from it!" Veronica exclaimed eagerly. "No, your friend is quite right. Horses *do* understand and respond. I wish I had known before that you might have enjoyed riding—"

And why hadn't she, Celia wondered, *or had Aunt Gertrude decided it for her?*

"—I would have asked you."

Of course she would have; Veronica Dartwood didn't have a mean bone in her body. She was as sincere as the sun and happy to have found someone with whom she could discuss horses.

Celia could see the disdain on Mrs. Dartwood's face; she could almost hear her dismissing her daughter's unfeminine and *dirty* pastime. The woman had probably given up all hope of Veronica's attracting a husband.

She was really too nice to be used the way Celia intended to use her.

"Well, I have been invited to ride tomorrow at the Templecombes'. You probably know them—"

She could just hear the ladies lapping up every word, because none of *them* had *ever* been invited to the Templecombes' in all the years they had lived cheek by jowl in the country.

Celia gritted her teeth and went on. "I'm told the Templecombes breed the very finest bloodstock, and I feel

rather overwhelmed by the responsibility. I wonder . . .
I'm sure you could teach me so much, but there really
isn't any time. So . . . if you would accompany me, Miss
Dartwood, I wouldn't be nearly half as scared of riding
one of their horses.''

Anthea, who had not moved an inch from Celia's side,
drew in her breath sharply. Celia was actually manipu-
lating poor Veronica Dartwood—and everyone else present, including *her*. And Veronica was completely taken
in.

But she, Anthea, was *not,* and she meant to tell Celia
when they had a moment alone.

''I would be happy to,'' Veronica said, her face flushing with pleasure at the invitation. ''It will be lovely; the
horses are . . .'' And she went off into a long dissertation
about the way the Templecombes bred their stock, which
made the older women with the more delicate sensibilities want to cover their ears.

So insensitive, they told each other with silent, meaningful looks. So gauche. So single-minded, not caring for
a moment who was listening and whether anyone even
cared.

And poor Gertrude, they were thinking; she could do
nothing to stem the flood of descriptives and she was
obviously having a hard time controlling her temper.

And Gertrude simmered, too well aware of the movement of her friends' eyes and heads. And Celia! She was
just an ungrateful, wicked little chit who had been transformed in just a short month into a forward and manip-
ulative creature, and obviously nothing remained of the
quiet young girl Gertrude had done her best to bring up
God-fearing and respectful toward her elders and her betters.

Look at her flaunting her newly acquired Town polish
and her new clothes and impertinent manners in front of
her old friends.

Accepting invitations from comparative strangers! And never having the courtesy to ask the permission of her host and hostess—or even to insist that they accompany her!

And choosing that hayseed daughter of the Dartwoods over her own flesh and blood to be the one to go with her!

Her behavior defied everything that was proper and right, and it cemented Gertrude's impression that Celia must be rescued before it was too late.

And, by heaven, she was the one who was going to do something—and soon!

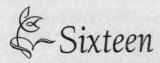

Sixteen

When Lady Gertrude came downstairs to breakfast the following morning, she discovered to her annoyance that Celia had obviously been up before her and was now closeted with her husband in his library.

And after she had patently made it clear the previous night that something had to be done.

"Think, Theo!" she had begun, quelling her simmering anger and approaching the matter in a way that would appeal to him.

"What is that poor, young Mr. Winwood going to think of *us* and the way we have brought Celia up if he ever happens to see those scandal sheets with those photographs and scurrilous innuendos? You do remember how carefully he stressed his complete disregard of her mother's past and the unfortunate circumstances of her death. And you are very well aware that, given her doubtful background, it would be very hard for the poor child to have such an offer come her way again—unless it is not the *right* kind of offer. There's no need for you to shrug, Theo, as if you could slough off your responsibility for her future."

"But we did do our duty by Celia. And now the responsibility has been taken out of our hands—according to her father's own wishes, don't forget. We should just *accept* the Lord's will and continue to pray for Celia's happiness. One must have faith, after all, in the Almighty's complete plan for all of us."

She had felt like snorting at his insufferable preaching. She had turned it into a cough. "Thank you, Theo, but I have no need of a homily at the moment. I for one have always found that God's will requires some effort of one's own."

Well, he hadn't liked *that* comment, but there was no way she could or would have tempered it. "I wish you would not keep trying to evade me every time I broach an issue that is important. It is an unfortunate flaw in your character."

"Well," Theo said mildly, ignoring that last deprecating remark and letting his irritation show by some uncommon plainspeaking, "perhaps you would be good enough to come to the point and tell me what you expect me to do about this situation with Celia that has you so upset that even *you* cannot deal with whatever you think needs to be dealt with."

And, of course, that had stopped her, as he had known it would, because the truth of the matter was that her anxiety over Celia was unfounded and unnecessary, and her interference, now that Celia was Wilhelmina's responsibility, was totally unwarranted.

But he had also known she would never see it that way and that all she wanted was his tacit approval to proceed with whatever imprudent plan she had already conceived.

And he hadn't been willing to humor her this time.

She understood as clearly as if he had said it out loud that in trying to trap her, he had ended the discussion— leaving everything up to her as usual.

She wished she had been born a man—privileged and in charge of everything—and not like Theo, who always had his head in the clouds, except when he put up that barricade of male superiority and forced her to back down.

She hated him for it, but it was all of a piece: it had always been up to her to salvage what was left of Celia's innocence and honor, and just because Celia and Theo both looked like conspirators when she stalked in through the library door was no reason for her to feel so betrayed.

"Do you have any idea what time it is? Or that there are *other* guests who might want to avail themselves of your company? Truly, Theo, you are *never* there when I need you."

That was enough—it had to be enough—even though she dearly wanted to say more, which was obvious to both of them.

But neither of them said a word as she turned to leave—and then Celia spoke up, mainly to save Uncle Theo from further scorn.

"You must forgive me," she said placatingly. "It is all my fault. There is so little time during this visit for me to have a chance to talk to Uncle Theo."

But Gertrude had to find fault anyway. "Indeed, you've crowded your weekend very nicely with social events that will keep you very busy and away from the Grange," she snapped ungraciously.

Celia drew in a tight breath; time to mollify Aunt Gertrude, and she hated doing it even though it was obviously very necessary. "After all," she went on as if Gertrude hadn't spoken, "to whom else can I speak frankly and receive loving guidance and advice?"

Me, Gertrude fumed, instantly in a rage that Theo would be the receptor of all those delicate confessions that a young girl ought to impart to a *female* mentor.

"I see. Yes, I can see that your time in London would precipitate a need to *talk*. I admit it's not usual in the Church of England, but since your mother was Catholic and your uncle has High Church leanings . . ." She felt as if she were babbling in order to contain her anger. "Well, it doesn't surprise *me*. I shall endeavor to keep our guests entertained while Celia unburdens herself to you, Theo. But breakfast *is* served and—"

"We'll be there shortly," the bishop promised, and Lady Gertrude had no choice but to withdraw, closing the door behind her with a definitive slam.

They looked at each other in mutual commiseration.

"I'm sorry, my dear, but as you know, your aunt has her moods. She does not mean—"

"Yes, she does," Celia said composedly. How easy it was to say once the truth was acknowledged. "She has never liked me; she has only tolerated me, and now it is worse because she doesn't approve of anything about me. And why does she speak of my mother in that certain tone of voice, tell me? Why does no one ever speak of my mother—or my father, for that matter? All I hear are hints and innuendos, but no one ever says anything, and all of it seems entwined somehow with who I am and how Aunt Gertrude feels about me."

She felt him withdrawing even before she finished her gentle plea.

"Please, Uncle Theo—you are a bishop and I know you're a good person; please tell me about my mother and why Aunt Gertrude dislikes me so."

Oh, dear, Theo thought. Oh, dear! She deserved answers, she did, but he was a scholar, not a pastor; he hadn't the faintest idea of how to tell her what she wanted to know without hurting her.

All he had was platitudes, and the overweaning shame that he was protecting Gertrude once again.

"You misunderstand, my dear," he murmured. "Your mother—your aunt—they have nothing to do with each other . . ."

And quite obviously he was not going to say a word about her past, Celia realized, listening to his almost incoherent protests. How could he speak against Aunt Gertrude, after all?

"Well, then, perhaps I have misunderstood," she said gently, going over to give him a hug and a kiss. "And perhaps I haven't. What I do know, and what I have always known, is that I will have to find out the truth for myself when the time comes. And meantime, you must not worry about me. I am very happy and content with my new life, and Aunt Willie is everything you could wish in a guardian, Uncle, I promise you."

She tugged at his hand. "Now come. Breakfast is served, the others are waiting and surely Mr. Maitland has yet another question to ask you."

They found Anthea already downstairs and deep in conversation with Lady Gertrude. Mr. Maitland was seated nearby, doggedly eating and listening without comment.

At the sight of Mr. Maitland's cheerful, open countenance, the bishop heaved a sigh of relief. He really did like this young man; he was a scholar and a theologian and tremendously interesting to talk with. And he was not quite thirty years of age yet!

The bishop filled his plate, took his tea and settled gratefully down beside him, looking forward to a morning's discussion of abstract theory.

Celia, meanwhile, stared at the array of food before her. She really did not feel like eating anything, everything seemed too rich and heavy compared with the Continental breakfasts she had become used to.

And she was not unaware of Aunt Gertrude's icy stare as she picked her way through the offerings on the sideboard.

In the end, she settled for toast, marmalade and tea before taking a seat next to Anthea, who turned to her animatedly.

"Isn't it a beautiful morning? Lady Gertrude has promised to take me around to see the countryside and the ruined abbey. I do wish you would come with us. The bishop and George will be engaged in discussion all day—I believe they started on *this* topic yesterday."

She reached over to put her hand on Celia's arm. "I cannot ever express how grateful we are for this invitation, dearest Celia. And now I can see why you were so quiet and shy when I first met you. Your sensibilities must have been shocked after the peace and tranquility you experienced here. Forgive me for my lack of understanding, I beg you."

Celia looked at her, mystified, and Anthea leaned closer. "Is anything the matter? I know Lady Gertrude is concerned about you, and I could not help but notice a kind of tension in you since we have been here. Something that is not quite *you*. Dear Celia, can you not confide in me?"

Celia felt a flash of pure anger as Anthea went on confidently. "Sometimes a man—well, even though your uncle is a bishop, perhaps he was not able to advise you . . ."

"What can you be talking about?" Celia said stiffly, aware suddenly that Aunt Gertrude was avidly listening to this exchange. It was too clear: Anthea was the spy, assigned to ferret out just what she and Uncle Theo had talked about.

"Dear Celia, surely after all we have been through together in London, it is not presumptuous of me to offer my help now."

"No help is needed, Anthea. Nothing is wrong, except that if I do not attend to breakfast and change, I will be late for my appointment with Veronica Dartwood."

She felt the tension shift again. In the uncomfortable pause, Uncle Theo excused himself and Mr. Maitland to retire to the library to continue their conversation, and Aunt Gertrude, having heard that last exchange, waited with her usual disapproving frown for Celia to remove herself as well.

Celia looked from her aunt to Anthea Langbourne. How alike they were, and how eager Aunt Gertrude was to make a confidante of Anthea, she thought angrily, shoving in her chair forcefully as a measure of her feelings.

How perfect—and how fortuitous it was that she had brought Anthea with her to distract her aunt. She was very well aware of her aunt's displeasure as she exited the room.

"I can hardly keep silent," Gertrude fumed when Celia was out of sight. "You will forgive me, Miss Langbourne, when you realize the depth of as well as the reasons for my concern about Celia. Especially since—and thankfully, I might say—you have been kind enough to befriend her. It has become more and more clear to me that the poor, misguided child needs the right kind of friends—and a great deal of spiritual guidance. I give you credit for trying to advise her and moderate her behavior.

"You cannot imagine how concerned we are, the bishop and I. This is quite a different girl altogether from the carefully nurtured and protected creature we were forced to release into the custody of this aunt she had never seen or heard of before. Can you imagine the shock? And the effect on a hitherto innocent child of being thrust into the most licentious society without having any idea of how to deal with the temptations thrown in her path?

"I shudder to think of it. And, of course, I still feel a sense of responsibility for a child I had nurtured as if she were my own. You cannot have any idea of what we rescued the poor child from . . ."

Anthea leaned forward as if to encourage Lady Gertrude. "You may be assured of my discretion and my fondness for Celia."

"Yes, yes, poor Celia." Lady Gertrude shook her head. "Out of one horrible circumstance and thrust into another. Her father had allowed the poor thing to grow up *jungli,* as they say in India—wild, like a native among natives, can you imagine? She had never had a pair of shoes; she had always run around barefoot and wearing the skimpiest excuse for garments. It was the saddest, most shocking thing I have ever seen, Miss Langbourne."

"Terrible," Anthea murmured. "She has adapted so well."

"My dear," Gertrude said stringently, "she has gone *jungli* in London, living a life every bit as shocking as the way she ran around in her childhood. I beg you, Miss Langbourne—exert your good influence; help me convince her that she has chosen the wrong path and that she must keep herself pure and untouched for the man she will marry."

It was a call to battle for which Anthea was willing to martyr herself. "I will help in any way I can," she swore with evangelical zeal. "I will begin at the instant." And she left Lady Gertrude, as the older woman had hoped she would, to immediately seek out Celia.

But when she went to Celia's room, she found only Emily. The maid informed her that Miss Celia had gone out with the other young lady, and Emily was

absolutely sure she did not know when her mistress
would be back.

That news undercut the ardor of her mission, and
Anthea had no choice but to back down, regroup and
spend the day planning one of several possible scenar-
ios with which she would confront Celia when she returned.

ℰ Seventeen

Veronica Dartwood's riding habit was several years out of fashion, but she cared only that it was still serviceable.

She was a superb horsewoman. On horseback, she was transformed into a totally different person, confident and sure of herself—and patient with Celia, giving her helpful pointers without seeming at all arrogant or patronizing.

A slight breeze had come up as they rode toward the Templecombes' that morning that put color in her cheeks and made her plain face look more animated than usual.

"When you get a bit more steady on your mount, you could take the track through the woods or skirt around the pond a half mile in that direction. And you're not doing too badly at all, Celia. I do wish I had thought to ask if you would have enjoyed riding when you were living at the Grange. I just always had the impression from your aunt that you were too busy with your studies to indulge in any trivial pursuits."

"Yes, I was always busy, wasn't I?" Celia said dryly.

"And then, of course, when Lady Gertrude announced

that you were betrothed to Mr. Winwood—well, one would never have time for riding if one were the mistress of a huge tea plantation. I can't even conceive how you are going to cope with it all. I mean,'' Veronica added awkwardly as she began to trip over her words, ''I'm sure that *I* would never know what to say or how to act or cope with any situation that might crop up unexpectedly—even if I am a few years older than you are . . .''

Thank heaven Veronica was all tangled up in her thoughts, Celia thought; the mention of Ronald's name had positively frozen her in place. Thank heaven her mount was gentle and slow. Thank heaven Veronica couldn't hear her pulse pounding, because she couldn't remember if she had ever sent him a note telling him she had gone to live in London with Aunt Willie.

Dear Lord, it should not be so easy to forget about Ronald Winwood when her every action, thought and feeling should be centered on him as the beacon of her future. When she should be begging her aunt every day to be sent off to him.

''I see two riders in the distance,'' Veronica called out. ''Who do you suppose . . . ?'' She shaded her eyes with her hand. ''They're coming at quite a fast clip too. Quick, Celia, move over—I make out Mr. Templecombe, but the other gentleman . . . ?''

But Celia hesitated a moment too long as both horsemen came barreling toward them along the narrow bridle path and started reining in too late to avoid colliding with them.

''For God's sake,'' Celia muttered as both Veronica and the stranger grabbed hold of her reins to control her skittery mount.

''Well, well, well—two wood nymphs,'' Grant Hamilton said wickedly as Celia's horse subsided into an edgy foot-stomping stillness that mirrored her feelings exactly.

"What are *you* doing here?" she demanded ungraciously.

"Why, Tom and I were on our way to visit you—which I thought was only polite after he told me that you were the guest of your aunt and uncle this weekend. I'm sure Willie would have wanted me to."

"Oh, and you are ever the mannerly gentleman," she snapped, devoid of all patience with his sudden appearances and disappearances. "Yet you found not a moment to bid your stepmother good-bye this weekend last."

"Of course not," he replied reasonably. "I only say hello to my stepmother, as you very well know. She has only to ask for me and I am at her service."

He sounded so very devil-may-care and a lot calmer than he felt. He had made it clear to Willie that he had not wanted to spend another weekend in the country, yet somehow, some way, she had convinced him to go to the Templecombes' in her stead, because it would have looked quite fishy indeed if she had shown up and had not visited the Grange.

And he was, against his conscience, his wishes and his desires, wet-nursing Celia, who did not look in the least grateful, and feeling as if he wanted to throttle her and Willie both.

"Ah," she said caustically, "yet another commission for you to execute. *Now* I understand."

"My dear child, you understand nothing, least of all manners. I expect I must introduce myself to your friend—"

Who was staring at them openmouthed and looking a little stunned, while Mr. Templecombe merely looked amused.

"Miss Veronica Dartwood," Celia said grudgingly, "may I present Mr. Grant Hamilton, who is my aunt Wilhelmina's American stepson."

"How do you do," Veronica murmured, still rather appalled by their public sparring. "And, of course," she added quickly, "this is Mr. Thomas Templecombe, to whose home we were just on our way."

"Well, isn't that a coincidence," Grant said lightly, because he instantly read Veronica's gentleness in her expression and wanted to do nothing else to upset her.

Celia, of course, was another matter.

He put a staying hand on her horse's neck. "Let them get a little ahead of us."

"Dear Grant, it would take nothing at all to get a little ahead of you." Lord, she was angry, and she didn't know why. Yes, she did. She was furious because he was here and her fiancé was not, and he acted as if he had forgotten everything—and she had not.

She would have to.

"I never expected to see *you* here," she said edgily as she nudged her mount forward, following his lead. "My impression was you had had quite enough of the country and cloistered innocence."

"My dear Celia, you were hardly acting like a nun the last time *I* saw you."

She gritted her teeth. "You were no saint yourself, Grant Hamilton."

"But your friend Veronica is, so let us just cease hostilities for this afternoon and enjoy her company and the *virginal* countryside, shall we?"

He was too much, too much for *her;* she felt like attacking him—but that would shock Veronica still more, and she seemed to be getting along so comfortably with Thomas Templecombe as they rode along, companionably engaged in conversation.

Celia wondered what it would feel like to be *companionable* with a man.

And then she just stared in wonderment as Templecombe House came into view.

It was a brick-and-stone structure set low to the ground, almost as if it had grown there, and it meandered off into wings and ells with huge floor-to-ceiling, sun-flooded windows. There was such an air of comfort and tidiness about it that she felt instantly at home.

As did, apparently, Veronica, who seemed completely at ease with the Templecombes and shed even more of her formality once they entered the house.

Almost immediately they were accosted by Tom's sister, Jennifer, a freckled redhead with an open and friendly manner who wanted above all things to be a veterinarian, which she announced to them all as she was pouring tea outdoors in the garden.

"How wonderful," Veronica said wistfully. "I wish I were brave enough to follow such a course. I love animals—just *love* them."

It was almost like a picnic; they sat on the sun-drenched terrace right by the kitchen garden with its fragrant herbs growing in wild profusion in between orderly rows of vegetables—tomatoes, beans, cucumber, rhubarb, peas, carrots, several different kinds of lettuce and onions—all surrounded the herbs and flowering shrubs that were meant to keep insects away.

"Mrs. Evans—that's our housekeeper—really has a green thumb," Jennifer told them.

"Don't be modest," Grant interjected. "You have quite a knack yourself with herbal remedies."

"Ye-e-e-s," Jennifer said shyly, looking at Grant flirtatiously from under her lashes, "it's true—I've had some success with both my family and animals . . ."

And wasn't *this* little postulant fascinated by Grant, Celia thought trenchantly. She looked as if she couldn't mouth an opinion without seeking his approval first. Poor girl. She obviously had no idea what he was like, and it would be hell for her if she even imagined herself in love with him.

Celia found she didn't like that idea at all—and she hated the idea she was stooping so low as to *think* about it.

His voice, close to her ear, startled her.

"So, Celia, are you enjoying your weekend with the bishop and Lady Gertrude, or are you ready to be rescued?"

She looked up slowly and met his smoldering green gaze.

"I'm sure I have no idea what you are talking about."

"Little liar. Your face gives away your every feeling and emotion. This is the last place on earth you want to be and why you feel you must sacrifice yourself to your Aunt Gertrude's ridiculous sense of what is due to her is beyond comprehension."

"It's beyond your business too," Celia said tartly. "If Willie sent you to be some kind of watchdog, she has made a grave mistake. All is as it should be with my aunt and uncle, so you need not poke your nose where it does not belong. And anyway, it is quite obvious you have your hands full here with yet another cloistered innocent."

He caught the waspish note in her voice. "But she is not nearly ready to take any vows, while *you*—you're the antithesis of innocent with that face and the mouth and eyes of a woman. You're right—I ought to stay the hell away from you. I should just stand on the sidelines and let all the other men pursue you, and not worry about whether you're going to be able to save your precious virginity for this patient fiancé of yours."

She shuddered at his words. *Ronald again*—almost as if Grant were deliberately trying to make her feel guilty for forgetting for days and nights on end that she was formally affianced.

And dire predictions about her future . . . at his hands? Not bloody likely; not after their parting at the viscount's country house; not after that kiss which he, like all men, was pretending never happened.

She folded her napkin and pushed aside the food that she had hardly tasted. "You may rest assured that my—innocence"—she almost tripped over the word—"will be no concern of yours, Mr. Hamilton. I have all good faith in Mr. Winwood's skill and ability, when the time comes."

Oh, was that a telling flash in the depths of those glittering green eyes? Did he not like the thought that she was saving herself for Ronald? Or was it that she was the biggest hypocrite in the whole of England for kissing him and then preaching the virtues of restraint?

She didn't know the meaning of that word these days, but she would die before she would admit it to *him*.

She wanted so badly to slap him.

Tom Templecombe suddenly looked over at them and queried mildly, "I say, are you two quarreling? Should the rest of us clear out and leave you to it, or shall we all take sides and play?"

"I certainly don't wish to be left alone with Mr. Hamilton so that he can continue to try and quarrel with *me*," Celia said calmly.

"Was that what I was doing?" Grant retorted as he uncoiled his long length from where he had been lounging with his back against a gnarled old apple tree.

He bowed deeply in her direction, and only Celia caught the mockery in his eyes. "Well, then, you have my sincerest apologies and my promise that I will not say another word to you for the whole of this visit."

Now they were all looking at *her,* as if she were a child who had been caught throwing a tantrum.

"What a pleasant thought to contemplate," she murmured, "though it would seem unlikely you could keep such a farfetched promise."

"But so easy if only I remove myself far away from you."

"By far the best suggestion I have heard all day, Mr. Hamilton," she retorted, sending him a simmering glance with those golden catamount eyes of hers.

Goddamn. What a piece of work she was—a vulnerable girl one moment and worldly woman the next. She was like sun and shadow, constantly changing, always in motion and evolving interesting new angles. A touch-me-not seventeen-year-old with whom he had already taken one too many liberties.

The difference in their ages and experience was like a chasm just waiting for him to make the first misstep into a fall from grace.

And why did the thought of her handsome tea planter—who had staked his claim when she was a mere child—drive him crazy?

She never talked about Winwood; she always looked stricken whenever he was mentioned. It made Grant want to take her in his arms and kiss her until she was senseless and could think of nothing else but him; and then he wanted to tear her clothes off layer by layer until he could look and touch and explore every inch of her lithe young body to find out what really lay behind the promise in her glorious golden cat-eyes.

Hell—damn—

"Let's stop this farce," he said tightly. What he needed to do was exorcise all those thoughts from his mind before he made himself look ridiculous lusting after a green girl. A *child.* Who needed a tight rein. Who probably needed only this tea-planter fiancé of hers and marriage and children to keep her busy.

Let her sail away to her betrothed in Ceylon—and oblivion. She would not haunt his nights. He could go back to living his own life and Willie could go back to his father—where she belonged.

"Excuse me?" Celia said politely, and just a little maliciously. It was not a game they were playing. She, at least, was deadly serious and she meant to kill him with words, if nothing else, because he was treating her like a child and she did not like feeling so defenseless. "Were you speaking to *me?*"

She should have swooned with pleasure when Grant turned on his heel and stalked off in a rage. Instead she felt desolated, as if she had committed some faux pas.

Veronica appeared distressed; Thomas shrugged and took off after Grant, and Jennifer looked at Celia and said, just as if nothing had happened, "I hope you will call me Jenny."

Or did she look too pleased that Celia had angered Grant beyond anything publicly permissible?

Was she being too nice?

"I didn't want to admit it when Grant was here," Jennifer continued, "but I really love riding western-American style—and wearing breeches."

Veronica, whose attention swung back to them the moment she heard the word "riding," now looked horrified.

"Oh, no, no—under a slit skirt, of course," Jennifer amended quickly. "Wonderful ease of movement. I can't tell you. A most comfortable and practical costume."

"I quite agree," Veronica responded enthusiastically, stunning the other two into silence. "I have often wished that *I* had had the courage to do so. I knew some young ladies in India whose parents had more liberal ideas than mine—although, of course, Daddy had a *position* to keep up—and they would ride in those riding breeches that were made popular by the Maharaja of Jodhpur—for playing polo, I believe. It made a lot of sense to me."

"Well," Jennifer said, "why don't we go look at my horses and perhaps go for a ride? I have several American-style riding habits, and I know just the place we can have some privacy so we can practice riding *astride.*"

Celia felt like an outsider as Jennifer and Veronica chattered on about horses and animals and found they had many common bonds that made it seem as if they had been friends forever. She was the one who had the least to contribute to the reminiscences they exchanged.

And that was further borne out by the pace they had to ride to accommodate her inexperience. But it gave Jenny a chance to elaborate on her history.

It turned out that she had traveled a great deal with her brother. They had lived in America for a while, in New Mexico, and had bought Appaloosa horses there. In fact, Thomas and Albert, Viscount Harville, had been partners in a horse ranch in New Mexico, which was how they had met Grant Hamilton.

"It was a bad and troubled time for anyone British—or *foreign*—who wanted to put down roots there. But at least we learned a lot, Tom and I, and we did manage to bring back some magnificent horses which became the start of our stable. And I am glad we are in England, where men don't wear guns and pick quarrels just to find out which one is the faster draw."

Veronica's eyes had grown huge as she listened, but Jenny's gaze rested meaningfully on Celia as she continued. "Grant—Mr. Hamilton—saved Tom's life once. We'll always be grateful to him. You can't imagine . . ." And then she caught back the rest of her speech as they emerged from an overgrown thicket of trees into a meadow that sloped down toward a fast-running stream that glinted silver and gold in the morning sun.

And around that stream were scattered a dozen colorful wagons which looked bizarre and out of place in such a bucolic setting.

"Gypsies!" Veronica breathed. "Oh, dear! Should we ride back, do you think, before they see us? But isn't this *your* land, Jennifer?"

"Oh, yes, according to the books, but it's been their

camping place from the time before there were any books. Gypsies have camped here for as long as I can remember, and I *think* there was an ancestor who married a Gypsy—or who *was* one. Tom would know all the details.'' Jennifer nudged her mount forward confidently and left Veronica and Celia to trail rather hesitantly behind her.

There were wagons and horses and children running everywhere, and more women in evidence than men, none of whom seemed discomposed by the presence of strangers.

''Hello,'' Jenny said brightly, and they acknowledged her with a brief nod and continued whatever they had been doing. ''Is Alzena—''

She broke off as the most powerful-looking woman Celia had ever seen stepped down from her wagon with all the majesty of a queen, shaking out her bright-colored skirts as she came toward them.

She acted as if she had been expecting them.

''Alzena is here, of course. Where else would I be but with my people? I knew you were coming—with others. And I saw too that one of the two young women who ride with you here today is one of *us*—whether she knows it yet or not.'' And looking so much like her mother that any of her people would have known instantly who she was and why she was there.

Celia felt those bright black eyes concentrating solely on her, looking *into* her through her slowly dilating pupils and pulling her out of herself. She felt helpless, immobilized, during the infinitesimal space of time it took Alzena to see all the way inside her, into all her fears and apprehensions, into the depth of all the hidden and forgotten memories that lay buried somewhere so deep in her unconscious mind that she no longer knew they were there.

She felt drawn to the woman—no, *pulled* toward her as if by a strong current.

"Come, come! You must rest your horses—and look at ours, eh? We have some brought over from Spain you might be interested to see. And perhaps I will read the cards for you young ladies? For nothing. Because my feelings tell me that it is necessary on this occasion to give guidance to whoever needs it most. And who is it? That remains to be seen. I will tell as much as needs to be told—enough to warn and advise all of you. Yes, all three of you ladies who have come here to the Romany camp today. Come!"

It was obvious that Alzena was the matriarch of the tribe; she had such an air of command, Celia didn't see how they could refuse her.

"We have to accept," Jennifer whispered in awe. "This is an honor."

"I don't think I really *want* to know what my future might hold," Celia protested faintly. "I think I would much rather it be a surprise, really!"

But Alzena was determined. "You are one of us, you are Romany. High time you discovered what is in your past cannot be changed. Come with me, girl. I have been waiting for you to come. There is a destiny you cannot change—let the cards tell you, if you do not choose to listen to me."

Celia felt mesmerized—and frightened—almost as if she had stepped into another time and place and she was no longer herself. She had absolutely no will to disobey Alzena nor to question her vague prophecies.

She could only obey.

"Come," Alzena said again, and Celia followed her to her caravan, which was larger than the others and reminded her, once she was inside, of a cool, dark cave.

But it was surprisingly spacious and almost luxuriously Oriental in its furnishings. Heaped pillows—a section curtained off for sleeping—and thick, colorful rugs, obviously handmade, to cushion every tread. A hammered brass-and-copper lamp hung overhead, and just beneath it was a low circular table with a crystal ball set in its center on a stand of rosewood bound with silver.

There was a faint trace of incense in the air, a scent that was both foreign and familiar to Celia, and she could not imagine why.

The sudden contrast between the brightness of the sun and this shadowed space into which she had been led made her feel confused and disoriented.

"Sit, child, sit! There, across from me where I can see you."

There was only one overstuffed cushion and Celia sank into it cross-legged, almost as if she had been doing this all her life.

"That's good. Now, has anyone told you that you resemble your mother? I wonder how much you have inherited from her and how much from your poor, misguided father, who understood so much about so many things—and so little about her. Ah, well—in any case, we shall see.

"For you, I am going to read the Gypsy tarot cards—there is nothing to be afraid of, little one! You are one of us, and you are safe—never forget that."

Celia was gripped by the passion in Alzena's words. She leaned forward urgently.

"But I don't *understand*. There is so much I can't remember, and I was never told anything about my mother; my aunt Gertrude always said wicked, spiteful things about her, so please . . . I don't want to know my future. All I want to know about is my mother, what she was really like . . ."

Her fierce eyes met Alzena's carefully hooded gaze and did not glance away in fear or trepidation.

And so the old one, the Phuri Dai, knew what she must

do: she must protect and nurture this young creature who was so like and yet so unlike Marianna, who had given up everything and gambled on love and one particular man—only to lose everything, even her life.

Yes—and it must not happen again. Not with this one, as young and untried as she was. This one, with the power lying coiled up and asleep within her that she did not know about and could not use properly unless she was led to understand *how* this knowledge was to be used.

And why it could never be misused without invoking the most painful consequences. How did she tell a mere child all of this?

"So you want to know *everything,* and all at once too? Ah, I think not. That would be too much for your mind to digest. And life does not yield its secrets easily, especially not to pounding on doors or tables to the cry of 'Now! I must have all my answers and my solutions immediately!' For the answers for *now* might not be the solution for the problems of tomorrow. And what the cards might indicate for your future is merely an omen of what very well might *be,* taking into account all the events of your present circumstances."

Alzena sighed, then took a deep indrawn breath that began in her abdomen and pushed all the way up into her mind and her mystical third eye before she exhaled. This was Yoga, practiced in India, where the Rom had had their beginnings, and she had always practiced this way of breathing and concentrating, which gave her inner strength to be detached when she most needed to be.

"I see you don't understand. But it is not necessary for you to understand, only to *hear.*"

But why, *why?* Celia felt so frustrated that Alzena was not answering her questions.

She had not realized she had been testing her strength and her anger against the older woman until their eyes clashed; she was breathing quickly, her fists were clenched and she had to consciously unclasp her hands and straighten her back and her body in order to release the tension she felt.

"My mother—Marianna," she said finally with some semblance of control. "What *can* you tell me? Why did you bring me here if you only meant to tease and play with my feelings? And why would you do that unless you had some reason to hate me, or my mother? Everyone seems to have hated her. Why? *Why?*"

"Why, you ask?" Alzena's eyes flashed like lightning. "Only because they were all so jealous of her—especially those cold *gadje* women who could not understand why their men were drawn to someone so warm and natural and without guile. *That* is why women like your Lady Gertrude hated your mother and tried to drive her spirit out of you and make you feel ashamed of her. Your bloodlines go back so much further in time than *hers*. And they are afraid—the *gadje* have always been afraid of us because we are different from them and they do not understand our ways or our ancient heritage. It is so much easier for them to think of the Rom as bad—as thieves or criminals or cheap entertainers and fortune-tellers with loose morals. They do not see us as a People and accept the differences between us. Child, there are things that none of us, however wise, can quite understand."

Celia's eyes flared with a look of angry impatience. Such nonsense—and all to avoid answering her questions! Obviously she was wasting her time and Alzena had nothing to tell her—nothing at all.

She started to rise, and Alzena leaned forward and placed a bony yet surprisingly strong hand over hers to keep her in place.

"First I will read the cards for you—this is most important. Only then will I know how I can help you. Now

sit quietly and stop trying to fight me with your mind. I
am infinitely stronger and wiser, and that is why I am
the Phuri Dai of this tribe. You would do better to listen
if you truly want to learn. Well? Do you want to run
away and rejoin your *gadje* friends now? Or are you
ready to face the truth?''

Celia could not move her eyes from Alzena's dark,
steady gaze; she felt as if every thought in her mind had
been picked up and blown around in a whirlwind and she
knew nothing, she could be sure of nothing anymore.

"I'm sorry," she whispered. "I will be patient."

"Hah!" Alzena snorted disbelievingly, producing a
well-worn pack of cards from a small chest beside her.
"Never seen the true Gypsy tarot cards before? Well,
these are the cards I use only for *our* people—the Rom—
not for those who come to have their fortunes told so
they can laugh about it afterward.

"These are the true cards. And in order for them to
read true, you must empty your mind of all doubt and all
fear. Listen to me! You are a seeker of knowledge and
strength, a seeker of the truth—whether it be painful or
not. Therefore, concentrate only on what I am saying and
on what it is you wish most of all to learn.

"Here—touch the cards. Yes, feel them with your fin-
gertips before you shuffle them in any way that *you*
choose. Think only of your question and the answers and
solutions that you seek."

Her voice had modulated into a singsong chant that
made Celia feel drowsy.

"You are of the Rom—there are things you already
know that are hidden deep within you. But if there is
anything you are not ready to know or that would be too
painful for you, I will guide you past those dangers.

"But for now, we are on a journey together into *knowing,* you and I. The cards—and the way they fall—will
lead us."

Was the old woman speaking in different languages, even Sanskrit—and it seemed as if . . . was it really so? . . . that somehow she was able to understand?

The smell of incense appeared to grow stronger, and she—who had never held a deck of cards in her hand—seemed to know, suddenly, exactly how to manipulate them.

Her card was the one in the middle—she sensed it.

She shuffled the deck and cut it, following the Phuri Dai's instructions.

And now, as the old woman laid out the cards, with the one that was *hers* in the center, she was seized with a feeling of fatalism that was totally alien to everything she had ever been taught.

What is to be . . .

But I can change it, she thought fiercely as Alzena arranged the cards. I can change anything, everything, if I believe that I can, no matter what is foretold in the cards.

And so what was she most curious about?

Ceylon . . . yes, Ceylon, the place of her birth.

She concentrated. Will I go back there to claim my inheritance?

Will I marry Ronald and will we be happy and content together?

Will I be able to forget Grant?

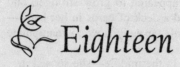# Eighteen

So much darkness—so much danger . . .

Alzena could feel the perspiration begin to drip down her temples, between her breasts, and down her sides.

How could Celia be warned? Especially when she was so wary, so inquisitive, so untried . . .

Ah, but this was going to be so much more difficult than Alzena had anticipated.

And Celia was looking at her so expectantly and impatiently, waiting to hear what she was not yet ready to be told.

Almost the same as when she, so much younger then, had read the cards for Celia's mother, Marianna. Only Marianna had chosen to ignore the warning signs because *she* would control her own fate and her future.

And so the question was, how much should Marianna's daughter be told?

"What do the cards say? They say something about my mother, don't they? You knew my mother, didn't you?"

Alzena let a long moment of silence go by; then she sighed. "Yes, I did know your mother. It was long ago.

In Spain. I read the cards for her and I warned her not to be so . . . impulsive. But she was stubborn and determined to follow her own will.''

''And?''

''And she ended up unhappy and isolated from her own people,'' Alzena said sharply. ''*You* know that well enough. But how well did you know your own mother?''

More evasions. Celia's expression turned stony. ''I didn't. I can remember some things, but then everything gets all blurred. I seem to remember being left alone a great deal with the servants. My mother used to go away with my father quite often, and then that stopped, and I think she was very lonely. But I don't know what she was really like. All I was told was that she was a Gypsy dancer before she married my father and that she was quite famous and applauded on the stages of Europe. I used to wish that I were able to dance the way she did— and be admired and sought after.''

''Yes, and be despised by people like that wicked Aunt Gertrude of yours. Be careful what you wish for, little gitana. Perhaps you *are* better off hiding as a *gadje* in the *gadje* world.''

Celia flushed. ''Why did you bring me here and insist on reading the tarot for me? What do you really mean by all this?''

''The naked truth can cut just as deeply as a naked sword—have you considered that? But you're still a child, and at your age, your mother was not. It's not your fault and neither was it hers. I will tell you as much as I can.

''But what you must know and always remember is that the ultimate power to rise above every situation lies within yourself. If you remember nothing else, remember *that*.''

Celia felt a simmering anger erupt. This woman was intent on doing nothing but circumventing all her questions about her mother, and her torrent of words and her emotions were frightening her; she wanted to make some sense out of this somehow.

"You insisted that you must read the cards for me. If you see something negative, why won't you tell me about it so I can be prepared? You said you had been waiting for me to come, and now all you are doing is confusing me. Where is the justice of the Rom—your people—and now, as you tell me, *my* people?"

Alzena remained silent, impassive, scrutinizing Celia's face, weighing, judging and finding . . . what?

"Is my future to be as dark and miserable as my mother's?"

Alzena's expression changed slightly, and if Celia had not been so intent on watching her, she would have missed it altogether. This secrecy was positively scary, and she sensed that Alzena was warring with herself whether or not to tell her anything.

This gave her just the slightest advantage and she pressed it relentlessly. "What did the cards say? I demand to know. It is my right."

"Hah! And now it's talk of your rights? What *are* you anyhow—Rom or *gadje?* Do you know *who* you are yet, little child who knows everything?"

Alzena's eyes glittered dangerously as she deliberately scattered the cards and then gathered them up with marvelous one-handed dexterity.

She began shuffling them, never once removing her gaze from Celia's.

She knew very well it was a woman who looked out at her through this child's eyes.

Poor, lonely Gypsy child, who had been taken away from heat and sunlight and running barefoot on her familiar earth to live with cold people who despised her because of her mother.

She had seen that much in Celia's cards, but there was

something else that was dark and hidden away in the child's own memory—something too terrible to be recalled and therefore mercifully shut away.

Something to do with poor, willful Marianna? Her sudden death?

She had to read the cards for herself—and for Marianna.

"So, young one," she said sharply as she cut the deck left-handedly the required number of times and began to lay the cards out once again with incredible swiftness. "What is it you want to know about yourself? Let's see . . . you are of an age to be interested in young men—do you want to know which one you will choose, or which one will choose *you?*

"Ah! There are two of them whose influence is very strong. One fair, one dark. Both dangerous in one way or the other. Does this satisfy you, or would you know more? You will travel—you will have to go back in order to be able to move forward in your life. You will have to solve a mystery—this is typical Gypsy nonsense, you are thinking.

"But if you believe in it, it is true. Most true is that you have to be careful—very careful in whom you put your trust.

"And now, be still for a while and very quiet. Cease your questions until I have read the answers to *my* questions."

Something in those glittering black eyes made Celia draw in a very deep breath to quiet the tumult of emotions inside her.

She looked down at the arrangement of the cards that Alzena had dealt herself. The old woman was muttering under her breath in some kind of dialect that sounded vaguely familiar, like a word or phrase that lingered on the tip of the tongue, known but inexpressible.

"Ahhh!"

Celia blinked her eyes, bringing them back into focus. She felt as if she had actually nodded off to sleep—or had she allowed herself to become hypnotized by the swinging lamp overhead, the cloying scent of incense and the droning chant of Alzena's voice?

The Gypsy woman's hooded eyes gave nothing away as she looked intently at Celia.

"So—is there anything else you *have* to know for yourself, rash one, or have my warnings been enough? Time is passing. Soon you must rejoin your friends or they will think the Gypsies have stolen you!

"Here! Give me your hand, then—no, the other one. There." Alzena's gnarled hand took hold of Celia's and turned it over so that it was palm to palm between her own.

Celia felt a mild shock pass through her body; she felt Alzena trace her fingers over the lines in her palm, seizing the other hand to study it before concentrating on her right hand.

And then she abruptly let go of both hands and sat back with her eyes closed in thought.

The girl was surrounded by darkness that seemed to press in closer and closer to the bright light—her soul-light—which had kept her safe, so far. There *were* certain indications that were good—the cards had said so too. But would this woman-child have the strength to endure and to surmount all the perils that lay before her?

Again Alzena's silence was unnerving. Celia wanted to shake her to force her into revealing something, anything, that would give a clue to what her garbled warnings meant.

"Was this what happened with my mother, old woman? Did you read her tarot cards and foretell her death? Did you tell her your magic couldn't save her? Where *were* you when she was most in need of help? What was she running from?"

"Hush! Hush!" Alzena interrupted her tirade. "Now look at me and listen, or you will be able to hear nothing but the angry beating of your heart clashing with all the questions muddled in your mind. Yes, listen! I will tell you as much as I can and as much as I dare.

"I can tell you only of signs—of indications. What transpires ultimately is for *you* to make happen. You have this power already, lying dormant within you. It's a matter of knocking at the right door after you have stilled every thought, every fear within yourself in order to listen *to* yourself.

"No, you do not understand what I am saying yet, but perhaps someday you will, and it will save you. Do you hear what I am saying? I am not your enemy, child of the Rom. I want to help you. But I can go only so far, and then you must take the next few steps forward."

"But—"

Alzena reached forward to cover Celia's clenched fists with her warm, papery hand.

"Yes, you are impatient to know everything, and why not? You haven't learned patience yet, but you will."

Once again she turned Celia's hand palm up on the table. "This hand, your right hand—since you are right-handed—shows what you have done so far and what you are capable of doing. Put this together with the cards and . . ."

"And I think once again you are putting off telling me the truth," Celia finished for her, just barely concealing her irritation.

"Of course—you are right," Alzena said on the heels of a deep sigh. "And this is *my* weakness. Ask me your questions—not too many, mind, for I am old and all this saps my energy."

Celia's eyes blurred with sudden, unwanted tears. She had been too harsh, too demanding. And Alzena was old; she would die too, and then who would help her?

"I feel like my mother must have felt," she began tentatively, "unsure of who I am, what I am; caught between two worlds . . ."

The harsh lines in Alzena's face softened as she caught sight of the tears that Celia strained to keep back. "And between two men as well? Oh, I saw all of it in the cards and in the lines of your palm. I cannot tell you which man will be the right one for you. All I can say is that if the wrong one threatens your life or your well-being, you must turn without hesitation or false pride to the other—and he will save you."

Alzena grasped Celia's cold hands within the warm, strong grip of her own. "Child, I can neither see nor know everything. I am given only hints, indications, as if through a dark, swirling mist. All I can do is warn you to be careful—very careful. There are clouds, black, threatening clouds all around you. Do not trust easily! Just tell yourself always, little child of the Rom, that you can and will survive—as our people have always managed to do."

"But my mother—will I ever know . . . ?"

"One day you will discover the truth. And the lies. But you're not ready yet. Try, try to learn patience!"

Alzena picked up a small clay pipe and proceeded to light it and draw deeply on it. The sweetish acrid smoke immediately permeated the room, rising and pluming in a spiral in the tightly enclosed space.

Celia's head began to spin; she coughed. She could hear Alzena's voice coming into her mind as though she were talking from the length of a long tunnel, and she was saying things that were barely comprehensible but that seemed nonetheless to take root deep down inside her, along with the smell of the smoke that penetrated her lungs and her brain.

"Listen to me . . . listen to me! When the time comes, you will remember, and what you must do will be clear to you. You will go back to the land of your birth and your mother's death because you must—it is the only way to unlock the darkness that will oppress you for all of your life. You must fight it. Your people are everywhere and in every country of the world, even in this Ceylon.

"Call for them—you know the language of the Rom. Look for them when you need them and they will come. You will not remember any of this or be tormented by the pain that is hiding very deep inside your soul. That too will be cleansed—later . . . later . . ."

Her voice receded. ". . . later . . ."

Celia had been coughing and she thought she must have blacked out, but suddenly she found that she had stopped, and Alzena was insisting that she take very small sips of some bitter tea that made her mouth twist and pucker in protest.

The pipe was no longer in evidence and there was nothing but the faintest trace of smokiness in the air.

Celia shook her head to clear it, but the smokiness seemed to have pervaded her throat, her voice even. "What happened? The smell . . ."

"Yes, Gypsy tobacco. Now, take just a few more sips of tisane, eh? This will make you strong again and ready to face anything, even your treacherous aunt. Are you going to tell this dragon that you have been visiting with the Gypsies and found someone who knew your mother? Better not—she won't like it. This is your first lesson, girl: learn to keep your own counsel. And don't trust a man too far, not unless you know him from the inside out and he has nothing to hide from you.

"There, that's enough Romany wisdom for one af-

ternoon. I think your friends are growing impatient and
a trifle apprehensive. Come, we will go to them.''

Celia followed Alzena outside, feeling as if she were
stepping into a frighteningly alien world. The sun assaulted her senses and she almost stumbled down the
wooden steps; Alzena steadied her, murmuring under
her breath in the Rom language: "You must be
strong—call on the strength within you. Keep your
head up and smile. Never let anyone else see the weakness in you, or you will be devoured by that person.''

Celia hesitated on the bottom step, thoroughly confused by Alzena's words, which she somehow seemed to
understand, and by the smiles and clapping that greeted
her.

A small child with a large gap-toothed smile offered
Celia a garland of wildflowers, and as she bent her head
so the little girl could put the wreath around her neck,
she felt the stirring of a memory . . . sweetly scented gar-
lands, in Ceylon . . .

Behind her, Alzena intoned, "Your grandfather, your
mother's father, was the Voivode—the king or chieftain—of our *vitsa*, our band. Your uncle Beltran, your
mother's brother, is now our Voivode. So among us,
you are considered a princess, just as your mother
was.''

But even as she recited Celia's history, she felt a
growing uneasiness coil and knot in her stomach. She
knew very well what was happening—but why? And
how?

Was it Marianna herself, coming back through her
child to cry for vengeance—or was this something else?
The child's only way of protecting herself? The things
that Celia's unconscious mind had revealed while she
was in the smoke-induced trance were black and frightening . . . and dangerous to Celia herself if she ever remembered them.

She must not be allowed to remember until it was safe—until *she* was safe. The girl had to be protected first, and then came the matter of revenge. No small thing when it pertained to Gypsy honor and Gypsy law.

In this matter, Alzena decided, she herself needed guidance before a true and meaningful decision could be made, which meant consultation with the *Voivode*, who had once danced with Marianna on stages all over Europe.

How he had loved that sister of his, before the *gadje* adventurer had stolen her away, kidnapping her in the Gypsy fashion and pretending to adopt Gypsy ways himself.

But he had not been able to protect his bride from the evil that had driven her to her destruction. And now something had to be done to save Marianna's daughter from the same evil forces that had smothered her mother's life.

Celia . . . the wild card in the deck . . . still unaware of the power she could wield . . .

So like her mother—and not. Her mother had given up everything for love of her English adventurer and had followed him all over the world. And she had lost him and the game they had both been playing when she had become filled and fulfilled with a child.

Then she had become prey to all those others. Easy prey. Poor, trapped, exotic bird of paradise, so used to adulation and admiration.

Alzena toyed with the idea of abducting Celia, taking her away to Spain, teaching her the Gypsy ways—and how to defend herself against *them*. But that would never work. Celia was stronger inside than Marianna had ever been.

Celia had experienced deprivation and degradation at far too early an age. And Celia was a survivor.

The old woman watched them all as they crowded

around Celia—her people, Celia's friends with their round, awed eyes; everyone laughing, talking, asking questions, and Celia, slightly disoriented, responding with her innate warmth and interest.

Someone started strumming a guitar—one of the wilder young men, seeking to draw everyone into the sobbing flamenco that several couples were already dancing to.

She should put a stop to all this, Alzena thought, and then, as she looked over the heads of the crowd, she encountered a certain pair of eyes that made her catch her breath.

He was a *gadje*—or was he?

His eyes were as changeable as a chameleon. And he did not try to avoid her incisive look. He seemed instead to want to seek her out.

Oh . . . he had to be part Gypsy, this one, whether he knew it or not.

His eyes crinkled and creased at the corners as he smiled and lifted one hand in a casual salute, almost as if he could read her mind.

If she had been younger, Alzena thought fleetingly, if she had only been younger . . . She liked the way he looked, the way he dressed. He was not an Englishman, so what was he doing here?

Ahh! this was the other one Celia had mentioned, the dangerous one—yes, and that he was.

Celia would be no match for him if he decided he wanted her.

Did he?

She had to find out.

And as she made that decision, he began to make his way through the crowd, slowly and purposefully, toward *her*.

Lord, but he was handsome. How was it that he had not yet swallowed her poor little Celia up whole?

But still, Celia almost bristled as he passed her and spoke a few words to her.

So what was this? Backbone? Antipathy?

Intriguing . . .

What was he saying to make the girl's face drain of color? And why was she looking so speakingly at *her* as the *gadje* spoke so urgently for her ears only?

The wicked one—Alzena felt it in her bones. Celia's first test, of her strength and her power—

But Celia wasn't feeling particularly strong. Grant's appearance startled her, and his glowering expression only put her hackles up.

His first words were hardly reassuring either.

"No more games," he said, his voice pitched just so she could hear. "Listen to me and keep your mouth shut. Gertrude is on the warpath. She is expecting you back at the Grange immediately and you go. I'll be back at the Templecombes' within the next hour. You must promise me to come there if she makes it impossible for you to remain at the Grange. Do you hear me, Celia? She had blood in her eye when I encountered her a short while ago and she means to take it out on you."

Celia could hardly grasp the sense of what he was saying. She looked beyond him, toward Alzena, and wondered distractedly how he knew her. Or if he knew her.

But he was heading right for her now that he had delivered his worrisome message, and she wanted to know why.

She turned to follow him, to seek Alzena's counsel, and found herself face-to-face with both Jenny Templecombe and Veronica Dartwood, who had overheard.

"Do hurry, Celia. We'll go back to the house first. I'm sure my brother will ride back to your aunt's with us to explain why we've been gone so long. After all, our little outing *was* quite innocent, wasn't it?''

"It was," Veronica responded stoutly. "And when I think of those wonderful horses we were allowed to ride . . . but I shan't even mention a word about that, no matter how I long to come back here again, I promise."

"We have done nothing wrong," Celia said.

"But are you really a Gypsy princess? It's so romantic!"

But it wasn't romantic at all. It was a stunning revelation, coming on the heels of Alzena's telling her of some of her history and all of her odd warnings.

And she had the disturbing thought that perhaps her isolation and feeling of apartness while she had lived here had been all Lady Gertrude's doing—because *she* had not wanted the Gypsy child she had saddled herself with to be accepted, even in the small social circle that *she,* as an earl's daughter and a bishop's wife, ruled with an iron glove.

"Well! A few weeks in Town and associating with the most licentious set in society and you obviously think yourself above censure or criticism. Have you forgotten your obligations, your manners, your vows? I can only hope your behavior will not reflect on *me,* my dear. I have always tried to guide you in the right direction and away from your natural inclinations, given your unfortunate bloodlines. Gypsies! Pagans! What were you thinking of?''

Celia's expression turned to stone. "I don't understand. What are you accusing me of? Meeting with my mother's people? Surely it would have been unmannerly not to, for you have reminded me often enough of my Gypsy heritage."

She watched in dismay as Aunt Gertrude's lips pressed together in mean-spirited disapproval.

"Have you no sense of gratitude—of decency? And what about Mr. Winwood, that fine, upstanding young gentleman who is looking after your inheritance for you while you are engaged in an endless round of carousing and the amusements of a London Season—and God knows what else! I'm even surprised that Miss Langbourne has continued to stand up for you. If not for her persuasive words, I would not have hesitated for a moment before I informed Mr. Winwood—as a matter of Christian Duty—of your behavior and your reputation, which is fast becoming a matter of some question, I can tell you."

Celia felt her face drain of color, and for several murderous moments she could not catch her breath. She had to grab the back of a chair to steady herself.

They seemed frozen in time, like a tableau—Lady Gertrude unable to look away from Celia's eyes, which almost licked fire at her. She had never encountered such strength of emotion in Celia, and it positively immobilized her.

Celia became aware of the ticking of the clock on the mantel—and of the sharp-eyed look on her aunt's face in response to the fury in her own.

"Perhaps you are suffering from a touch of the sun, Celia. It might be a good idea for you to go upstairs and lie down in a darkened room with a compress on your head. We can continue our discussion later, when you are more ... composed and ready to listen to reason."

Her mild-mannered tone made Celia explode.

"*Reason?* Is that what you call all those wicked, ugly, *smearing* words that you've been pouring on me from the moment you called me in here? Wicked and vile. And you call yourself a good Christian! I wonder

if you have ever actually read the Bible—especially the
New Testament. Who appointed you judge and jury of
other people's behavior? Where's *your* Christian char-
ity? If you had lived in biblical times, you would have
been one of the first to cast stones even on hearsay.

"*You* are a hypocrite, dear Aunt, just like those Phar-
isees whom Christ spoke of. All you can see in anyone
is the very worst. You look for it. You revel in it. No
wonder Uncle Theo is always shutting himself away from
you."

Lady Gertrude's breath hissed between her clenched
teeth as she fought for control.

"And you have learned to be insolent too, I see—
along with other deplorable habits your new guardian
seems to have encouraged in you. Indeed, I pity your
fiancé, who seems to imagine you are still the young
innocent he chose as his bride. You should consider yourself fortunate that a decent young man, knowing your
background, would still offer you an honorable marriage.
And if you even thought that anyone in Wilhelmina's
circle—particularly that disgraceful stepson of hers—
would offer you anything but a dishonorable arrangement—especially if the whole truth were known—well,
my poor, deluded child, you are sadly mistaken.

"I have done my Duty; I have warned you. And
now—here is Mr. Winwood's last letter to you, pleading
for a reply, for some word from the fiancée he chose to
idolize. You had better answer it, while I must try to
compose a temperate and honest response to the letter he
sent *me,* begging for news."

From one of the deep pockets of her gown, Lady Gertrude produced a letter covered with exotic-looking
stamps and thrust it at Celia.

She took it, her numb fingers closing over the envelope
as she said in a detached voice, "But this letter has been

opened . . . and read. By *you*, I suppose. And yet it *was* addressed to me.''

''And so it was,'' Lady Gertrude snapped. ''But what did you expect? Of course a young girl's correspondence should be inspected by those in charge of her, whether she's engaged or not. And I'm sure you would have written to Mr. Winwood yourself, informing him of your changed circumstances and giving him your direction— if you could have spared some time between your many social engagements!''

Here it was, the evil, the test—and Celia found herself surprisingly calm. She should have seen it before—it had been right before her eyes. Or maybe Alzena had opened her eyes.

''What a wicked person you are,'' she said softly. ''I wonder why I never realized it before.''

She turned on her heel and all but fled the room, and Lady Gertrude's insidious presence, slamming the door behind her.

The sound brought the servants out of nowhere, and Anthea popped her head out of her room to stare as Celia caught her skirts and ran upstairs.

''Emily! Em—quick! Help me pack. We're leaving— *now*. As soon as possible. Emily!'' She tugged at the bell cord in her agitation, but by then Emily was already there, commiserating under her breath as she edged her mistress aside and out of the way while she hauled out trunks and began pulling gowns out of the armoire.

''Now, Miss Celia, why don't you just sit down and try to calm yourself. I knew this wasn't going to be no good. Do you want a glass of water?''

''That—won't—be—necessary,'' Celia managed between clenched teeth. She did sit down, still clutching Ronald's letter, unable to override her fury with her aunt.

Private words, private thoughts—intercepted and no doubt interpreted in the worst way by Lady Gertrude.

How dared she!

"Oh, Celia! What on earth has happened? Oh, my dear—what is it?"

Anthea, knocking at the door softly just twice before slipping in, her pale eyes wide with concern.

"Why are you packing to leave when the weekend has just begun? You cannot mean to humiliate your uncle and aunt by running away so precipitately. It will cause all kinds of gossip and speculation. Oh, my dear friend, please think carefully of all the consequences, I implore you. Your aunt means well, for all that her manner might be a trifle brusque and forthright—and if she appears cross with you, I'm sure it is only because she cares about your future well-being."

Really, it seemed as if Celia weren't even listening to her! She tried again.

"Celia, *do* be reasonable and give yourself time to *think* before you act. You will upset your uncle terribly, you know—and he *does* care about you! Won't you at least go downstairs and talk to him about whatever is troubling you? He is such a dear and saintly man, such a source of comfort, as both George and I have discovered."

Anthea bit her lip as Celia did not respond.

"Celia?"

Celia rose abruptly. "Emily, you may keep packing. And yes, Anthea, I *do* agree with you that I should talk to Uncle Theo before I leave. And would you in turn be kind enough to send a message to the Templecombes'— to Mr. Hamilton? Tell him I will be needing his escort back to Town."

"But—"

"Anthea," Celia said patiently, "if you will not send a message for me, you will force Emily and me to walk, and I think that will cause more of a stir. Or perhaps my Gypsy relatives will give me shelter for the night if no

one else will. What do you think? While you are decid-
ing, I will try to find my uncle.''

Anthea stared at the door as Celia closed it behind her.

What on earth had gotten into Celia?

Oh, if she could only summon dear George to give her
some sane and sensible advice! She was not used to being
at a loss for words or unsure of which action to take.
Nor did she enjoy this feeling of helplessness.

She just didn't know what to do: send for Mr. Hamilton and incur the wrath of her hostess, or—or—surely
Celia did not really mean to create a little scandal?

The bishop would certainly be able to talk some sense
into her.

Anthea devoutly hoped so. Ignoring Emily, who was
making grunting noises under her breath, she left the
room.

Had she been Catholic, Anthea would have crossed
herself.

ℰ⁓Nineteen

It was a wildly growing, old-fashioned kind of garden that caught the sun from all directions, and, because of the ancient stone walls that surrounded it and soaked up the heat, it was always warm and comforting somehow.

It was here Celia finally found her uncle at the time of day she usually expected to find him locked in his private study, working on his sermons.

He was pottering around happily, dressed in his shabbiest old clothes, oblivious of everything, and she stood watching him for a moment, reluctant to invade his only private place.

But with the unerring divinatory perception that someone was in need, he sensed her standing there, and he straightened up, trowel in hand.

"Celia? My dear child—no, you're not intruding—" He stopped abruptly, studying her face, her eyes. "What is wrong? Is it your aunt Gertrude again? Has she said something to upset you?"

How dear he was, how kind—how did he know? Suddenly the tears she had repressed for so long—tears of anger, frustration and hurt—just streamed down her cheeks and she shook with deep, gasping sobs.

The bishop dropped his muddy trowel and caught her in his arms as she collapsed against him, weeping uncontrollably against his shoulder.

She clung to him fiercely as if she were seeking his protection, and he felt a surge of guilt and humility. She was his niece, after all, and she had been his responsibility in the first place. He had removed her from an unsuitable environment and an unsuitable life, and what had he offered her instead?

An occasional pat on the shoulder? Access to his library?

But had he ever shown her real affection? Or a feeling of being loved, for that matter? St. Paul, Corinthians II, Chapter 13, on love—he had quoted it so often in sermons, but he had never practiced what he had preached.

He kept patting Celia's back, murmuring soothing words that seemed hollow even to his own ears. Was this a sign of how far he had withdrawn and removed himself from his real duties as minister to his congregation?

"Ah, Celia, Celia. Forgive me for not seeing, for not understanding long ago how intolerable life has been for you here with us. Ah, don't weep, child. Never stop believing in your God just because your old uncle has been such a poor example of His servant on earth.

"Come, come—no one can hurt you now. Can't you tell me what happened? Let me get you something to drink from that little fountain you used to love so much as a child. Remember the old pewter cup I used to hide under the willow branches? It's still there, you know. Will you share a cup of water with your old uncle Theo? And can you ever forgive me for being so neglectful of you? Could you do that, my dear?"

As he talked, he guided her to the rough stone seat that she remembered from her childhood, and he retrieved the pewter cup and dipped it in the fountain and gave it to her.

By then, her sobs had given way to hiccups, which she was trying vainly to suppress, and she was hating herself for losing her hard-won control.

She sipped the ice-cold water slowly, letting it ease over her raw throat and letting her uncle's real concern ease her heart.

"I have to go," she said slowly. "I cannot bear to stay here another moment—and it's nothing to do with you, darling Uncle Theo. I love you. But my aunt has made it impossible, and so I've asked Anthea to send for Mr. Hamilton, if he will come—if she even has the courage to defy Aunt Gertrude. In any case, please understand, Uncle Theo. I didn't intend to make you unhappy or upset."

"My dearest child, I have been so blind to your needs. I see that now. Of course, your father saw—even in his anguish—what would be best for you. Willie! Yes, she has always been the one to help you. But do you see— your coming here to seek me out was what God intended to save us both. Do you know," Theo continued, his eyes shining with enthusiasm, "that in my most secret heart I have wished—and prayed—for a . . . well, a Revelation of sorts. A sign, a direction. And now I do believe I have received it."

He squeezed her hand reassuringly. "Don't worry, I am quite compos mentis. Leave everything to me. Come along with your old uncle and we shall face and slay all the dragons."

It was Emily who sent for Grant Hamilton while Anthea dithered over choosing between her duty to Gertrude and her friendship for Celia.

And if she had been any kind of a friend, Emily thought dourly as she wrote out her simple note, Anthea would have gone to the Templecombes herself and brought back Mr. Grant without questioning what or why.

But Miss Anthea was a coward, and she, Emily, was not; it was simply a matter of sneaking down to the stable and finding the boy who was a little sweet on her, then convincing him of the nobility of this course of action—and swearing he wouldn't get punished for it.

The things in the world that could be accomplished with a silly little kiss!

It was nothing less than an invasion and Lady Gertrude was royally not pleased. She was outflanked on both sides—her own husband conspiring against her, siding with Celia of all things—and then, before she could gird herself to do battle with him, she had to face a veritable army in the form of the Templecombe brother and sister (who had never had the decency to call or leave a card before this!) and that officious and arrogant Grant Hamilton, demanding to know where Celia was.

If she were a lesser woman, she would have collapsed with smelling salts, but this was a matter of honor—and appearances—and she found herself grateful that Anthea Langbourne, at least, sided with her.

"Mr. Hamilton," she said stiffly, holding out her hand. "So nice to meet you at long last."

He brushed aside the niceties. "Where is Celia?"

She bristled, enormously disliking his foreign accent. "Where should she be, Mr. Hamilton? She is with her family, resting before dinner. Miss Langbourne has just come from her room—have you not, Anthea, dear?"

"Yes," Anthea said staunchly. "Resting."

Grant shot her a withering glance and then turned his

attention to Gertrude. What a righteous witch she was! "Tell her she has visitors, then."

"This is exactly the kind of bad manners you would expect from people from *away*," Gertrude said, aiming her comment at Anthea, while her eyes maliciously raked over Grant. "My dear sir, you are obviously not aware of the customs of the country. One sends a card, a note, and one is *invited* before one appears making demands."

"I make no demands at all," Grant said coolly. "Celia is leaving this house at the instant. That is not a demand, that is a fact. And if you will not call her, I will go and find her. And that is a fact. So how will you have it, Lady Gertrude? Your evasions or my facts?"

Gertrude drew herself up, well aware of the two avidly listening Templecombe siblings. She could not afford to be put into a bad light over this. "My dear Mr. Hamilton, this is a hospitable place, the home of a bishop of the Church. You should be ashamed of your behavior. Of course you may see Celia, but there can be no question of her leaving today. She promised us a long visit and it is not yet nearly over."

"But it is," Grant said succinctly.

"This is out of all bounds of good manners—and you may tell your stepmother I said so," Gertrude snapped. "No, I shall write her myself. Obviously you have the manners of a rag-tailed cowboy and would never see fit to relay any message of mine."

"Exactly," Grant said.

"She is not the child whom I commended to Wilhelmina's care."

"I should hope not."

"You are impossible and arrogant."

"Yes, ma'am," Grant agreed calmly. "Now call Celia and tell her to get ready."

Their eyes clashed; Gertrude's chin lifted just another

notch, her indefatigable sense of rectitude shoring her up once more.

"We will call Celia," she decreed as regally as any queen.

She really was something to watch, Grant thought as she stalked across the room, yanked the bellpull and told the maid who appeared to summon Miss Celia.

But Celia was already hovering on the stairs, having heard every blessed word between her aunt and Grant Hamilton. He was like a wall and Aunt Gertrude could not even start to chip away at his rock-hard exterior, and if she weren't so put out with him—and dreading the still-unread letter crumpled in her hand—she might have cheered.

As it was, she nearly scared Aunt Gertrude's rabbity little maid half to death when she rounded the corner of the staircase and bumped into her.

"Oh! Miss—oh—I—"

"I'm here," she said dryly, brushing by the maid and pausing just one breath-catching moment before she entered the parlor.

Grant's angry, glittering gaze pinned her to the spot.

"Ah, Celia," Aunt Gertrude said, her voice too bright and her anger too obvious. "You have visitors. I believe these are the Templecombes, although, of course, we have never met before or even been formally introduced. And Mr. Hamilton, who keeps rudely insisting that you are leaving with him tonight. I do not see how that is possible when you have come to us for the entire weekend."

She looked expectantly at Celia, having now put her in the position of having to deny one or the other. Celia swung her gaze back to Grant, who nodded almost imperceptibly.

"Celia *is* leaving us tonight." A new voice was heard from, and Aunt Gertrude froze.

"Really, Theo, what can you be thinking?"

Theo smiled at Celia. "Yes, indeed—thinking. I most certainly am thinking, but I don't believe you are." He strode into the room, his hand outstretched toward Grant. "How do you do, young man. I am Celia's uncle Theo, and of course she will be leaving with you"—he turned and shot a speaking glance at his wife—"*as arranged*. We know how delighted you were to have Celia with us for even this long, my dear wife. But Wilhelmina was quite specific that she must return by tomorrow, and I do believe you had forgotten that."

Celia had never seen her aunt look so nonplussed. Her jaw dropped slightly, and her mouth began working to refute her husband's neat and mannerly glossing over the situation.

Uncle Theo preempted the oncoming hurricane of words by asking, "Are you packed, my dear?"

Celia smiled tremulously. "I am, Uncle Theo."

"That's good, my dear, very good. Your carriage is outside, my boy? And this, of course, is Thomas Templecombe. Very nice to meet you, son. And your sister? Jennifer, is it? Welcome to the Grange, my children. Now let us look to Celia's belongings. And even though Gertrude and I will be so sorry to see you leave, I promise that the Lord has a plan and that I may see you soon again."

Celia hugged him, near to tears once more. "Thank you, Uncle Theo."

"Be well, my child."

She turned to her aunt. "Aunt Gertrude."

Gertrude drew herself up stiffly. "*I* cannot countenance your going off with Mr. Hamilton, who is not one of *us*, in spite of what your so-called guardian thinks is proper. You will see, my dear; things are done a certain way, and when they are not, the innocent will reap the consequences, as indeed I believe you eventually must do. Well, you have made your choices and you will have to live with them. I have done my best—I have tried to educate you in a good Christian and moral way. I have done my Duty, and in the end, the forces of evil have won out yet again. It is ever so. Good-bye, Celia. I can only hope you do not suffer too much the repercussions of your actions.''

And she turned her back on her niece and stalked out of the hallway.

''She hopes I burn in hell so that she will be right,'' Celia whispered, her eyes shimmering with tears. Aunt Gertrude had proved consistent to the end, wishing her everything negative and nothing good.

''Perhaps it is time for your aunt to learn to see things in a different light,'' Theo said thoughtfully, staring after his wife, rather confounded by her virulent parting speech. Worse than he had thought, and as if he had never really *heard* what she was always saying before. And all heaped on the slender shoulders of the poor, innocent child whom they had thought they were saving from the unrestricted life of a heathen.

Perhaps they were the heathens, and she was the one who was blessed.

He hugged her once again. ''Godspeed, my dear. I hope you can find it in your heart to write to me once in a while.''

''I will,'' she promised fervently. ''I love you, Uncle Theo.''

''I love you,'' he murmured, holding her for a moment more before he relinquished her into the strong hands of Grant Hamilton, who had watched the whole scene with a cynical lift of his brow.

The Templecombes were already in the carriage as Grant helped Celia and then Emily inside.

''Sir.''

Uncle Theo smiled and offered his hand. Grant shook it with great solemnity.

"Take care of her, my boy," Uncle Theo said.

"My stepmother has made that my mission in life," Grant said dryly.

"Or perhaps," Theo said, "you have made it your own."

It was the most beautifully appointed bedroom, even nicer than her room at Carlton House Terrace, a fit place to hide away from the embarrassment of the way she had had to leave the Grange and her aunt's nettling words.

Dear Aunt Gertrude. Celia could hear her talking to her friends now about the disgraceful, disrespectful and indecorous way she had been treated by one who had every reason to be inhumanly grateful to her for her kindness and her sacrifices all these years.

Oh, yes, Aunt Gertrude wanted to make Celia feel obligated and indebted—but for the life of her, Celia could not understand why.

And I don't want to, she thought in a flare of rebellion. She had had enough—of Aunt Gertrude, of restrictions, of Gypsy prophecies that haunted her thoughts, of Grant Hamilton and his grazing green eyes that made her feel heated and *wanting.*

She didn't want anything from him. She wanted what she had: a London Season with her beloved aunt Willie, and at the end, she wanted to journey to Ceylon and fulfill her vow to Ronald.

And only that.

But then, why had she not yet read his letter?

What was she afraid of?

Nonsense! It was all the emotional turmoil—from meeting her Gypsy family and the confrontation with Aunt Gertrude.

How could she have read her fiancé's letter in the midst of such chaos?

And knowing that Aunt Gertrude had perused it first? That was the most galling thing of all.

But perhaps it was time. Grant was slated to return her to Aunt Willie the next morning, giving up the rest of his own weekend basking in the admiring gaze and the simpering simplicity of Jennifer Templecombe.

And he was intemperately annoyed about it too. And especially irritated with her.

"Your aunt is a world-class bitch," he had exploded once they were in the carriage and not a hundred yards away from the Grange. "Why the hell did you ever accept an invitation to return there? And why the hell did you go alone?"

She had no answers for him. She felt the gratitude— more to Uncle Theo than to her aunt, certainly—and the burden of reciprocation for all they—he—had done for her.

But why? Even she did not know, and Grant's irritation and anger only set her hackles up.

"I suppose," she had snapped, "if Willie had been a ... bitch ... you would never have returned to visit your father after their marriage? That you would have been strong, so righteous, that you could have denied your family ties? Or is it easier to pass judgment where you have no experience by poking your opinions where they are not wanted?"

That shut him up for about one minute. And then:

"Goddammit, she was ripping you to shreds and she didn't care who the hell heard it."

"She was surely hoping that we would spread the gossip," Thomas Templecombe interpolated, "but we don't betray our friends."

"She is a nasty person," Jennifer pronounced, "and Grant stood up to her like a fortress. You were so strong;

she couldn't get any slings and arrows past you.''

''I could have wrung her skinny, righteous neck,'' Grant said feelingly.

''Nevertheless, she is my aunt and she did raise me,'' Celia had said rebukingly, hating to have to defend Gertrude and wanting to put an end to Grant's blunt assessment of her, ''and she did the best that she was capable of.''

But oh, what she had been capable of—demeaning her, degrading her ancestry, dishonoring her mother and her father—and deluding *her* that Ronald Winwood's nobility would be the saving of her heathen soul.

And her aunt had relished every moment of it.

And perhaps, just perhaps, that was why Celia could not bring herself to read Ronald's letter.

I am not the same person I was when I consented to marry him.

The thought shot through her mind like a bullet.

And then she knew: she was scared of what she would find in that letter, and how she would respond to it when she had hardly thought about Ronald at all since she had left the Grange.

But when Aunt Willie had swept her up and away from everything she had known, she had still been certain that, just as Aunt Gertrude had prophesied, her only option was to marry the man who had been her childhood idol.

And that a Season in London would be a useless frivolity that would turn her head and make her hope for more and better.

I have to read the letter.

She didn't want to read the letter; she knew better now. Aunt Willie had opened her eyes. She had no stain upon her soul. She was not a freak of nature, or a mistake that could be rectified only through the outside good offices of a savior.

She wanted things to go on just the way they had been; she wanted to return to London and continue enjoying the unabated social rounds.

And she didn't want to think about getting married at all.

I have to read this letter.

It was her conscience talking, her guilt at relegating the man who should have been the most important thing in her life to some unused shelf space in her mind, to be taken out only when it was convenient for her.

Well, now it was convenient for him. She had wanted to marry him, and now he was asking for answers from her. Simple things like, Why haven't you written? What have you been doing? That was all; nothing more demanding, surely. Especially if he had the faintest inkling Aunt Gertrude might read the letter. And he had to know she still wasn't ready . . .

She took the letter out of her skirt pocket with trembling fingers. It was almost irredeemably crumpled— perhaps, she thought hopefully, unreadable. Then she could just write back a light and airy letter full of inconsequentials and not have to address any of *his* concerns.

She took the letter out of the envelope. It was closely written and just a little smudged by all the manhandling.

She could barely read the salutation: Celia, *carissima*—

Her heart started pounding and she moved stiffly to a small slipper rocker by a corner window and sank into it.

This was worse than she had imagined. She smoothed out the page with shaking hands and angled it into the late-afternoon light so that she could see it more clearly.

Celia, *carissima,*

It has been so long—too long. As I sit here in the evening twilight, I am thinking of all the months, all the years that have separated us, and I long for you as never before.

You have finally grown up, *cara mia,* and the time has come for us to be reunited. I yearn for you as a lover does for his beloved; I want to be able to hold you in my arms, to whisper to you of my love and devotion, to kiss your sweet, innocent lips, to claim you as my own for once and forever.

Come to me, darling Celia, and let me make you my wife as it has always been intended. The days grow long now—you are always on my mind as I imagine how beautiful you have become, how ripe and ready for our nuptials, and I want nothing more than to fulfill our mutual dreams with a lifetime of pleasure.

I need you now, *cara;* put aside your hesitations in the name of all we have meant to each other. You will find everything you want and need within the environs of your native home; you will never want for anything, ever—I swear.

Come to me and be my wife, my darling, and let us conquer the world.

Never forget, it was ordained by your father and mine, and I hold sacred your father's trust in me to see to your future.

But it is more than that, beloved Celia—I have wanted you for such a very long time and I can suppress my hunger to possess you no longer.

You must honor your commitment to me as I intend to honor mine to you. You have only to say the word, and I will drop everything and come for you if that is your heart's desire.

Write to me, my soul, after this long, unbearable drought of no word from you whatsoever, and tell me when I can expect to hold you in my arms again.

Your ever-faithful
Ronald

Disaster.

She wasn't even aware of the letter falling from her hands.

She felt an overwhelming sense of doom.

It was time to pay the piper.

Twenty

"That woman is a positive dragon," Jennifer Templecombe was saying feelingly the next morning at breakfast just as Celia entered the room. "It is no wonder Mama and Papa have never had anything to do with her. Oh, hello, Celia, dear. I beg your pardon. But—surely you cannot disagree?"

"I beg yours, for obviously interrupting what must be a private conversation," Celia said tartly, her tired gaze sweeping over Thomas Templecombe and settling on Grant's rock-hard features. "Because surely you wouldn't be mean-spirited enough to criticize my aunt to my face."

"Oh! But—!" Jennifer looked around wildly, seeking some kind of guidance from Grant, which immediately fueled Celia's temper still more. Nor did she like the fact of Grant's instantly putting one of his large hands reassuringly over Jennifer's and then snapping at *her* as if she were the offender.

"Sit down, Celia, and stop it. Your aunt is a hypocrite and we all know it. It is enough to make anyone lose his appetite. Therefore, the subject is now closed so we all can digest our breakfasts."

And he smiled sweetly at that baby, Jennifer Temple-combe, and Celia felt like throwing the boiled kidneys across the table at her.

"Sit down," he said impatiently, breaking into her thoughts. "And eat something. You look like hell."

I'd like to take a bite out of you, she thought virulently as she allowed the Templecombe maid to pour her a cup of tea.

"How nice of you to notice," she said acidly, lifting the cup to her lips and savoring its warmth in her hands and the soothing scent of lemon emanating from it.

"I sent word to Willie that you will be remaining here for a few days," Grant went on, his gaze still fastened on Jennifer as if she were the most fascinating creature in the world.

"Did you?" Celia murmured, pushing her plate toward the maid, who was serving biscuits and eggs hot from the oven. "I wonder why you did not consult me; *I* wish to return to London as soon as possible."

"And so we will—in a few days."

"But I think not, Mr. Hamilton. I wish to go today."

"We cannot."

"We will see."

"We will see nothing. I am charged to accompany you and I will be ready to leave in three days' time."

"Yes, I see that you will. I can quite understand how discommoding it is to have *duty* interfere with your plans. Take heart. You need not put yourself out for me. I am content to travel with Emily, and we will leave today."

"We will discuss this later."

"Oh, undoubtedly," Celia said, casting a covert glance at Thomas Templecombe, who once again looked utterly bewildered by the abrasiveness of their inter-change. "But I do not see the need to alter my plans."

And if Grant would not see her back to London, she thought, perhaps she could prevail upon Mr. Templecombe's good nature, and that surely would please Grant: he would have so many more hours to enjoy Jennifer's naive country charms.

Which was only what he had wanted in the first place.

And that idea only made her anger seem more futile. Why on earth should she fight with him? It was but one short step from the simple life in the English countryside to the even simpler life on a tea plantation in Ceylon.

It was as if she were there already; she could not deny Ronald Winwood his rights—they had been set in stone years before she had understood she could ever change her mind.

And every step she had taken had led to this moment when he would demand that she join him as his wife—forever.

She did not know why she felt so distraught.

This was what she had dreamed of, had wanted with every fiber of her being not four months ago.

How fickle was she, fearing the end of the story and resenting the time and attention given by another man to a child he was perfectly free to fall in love with?

If she stayed in this room another moment, she might find out.

She stood up abruptly. "You'll excuse me. I'm going to pack."

"Celia—"

She barely heard Grant's imperious voice behind her as she fled the room.

"Celia—"

Oh, God, how could he already be right behind her as she mounted the stairs?

But she felt him, felt the heat of his hand grasping her arm, felt the strength of him stopping her in her tracks.

Felt the blazing fury of his glittering green gaze as it bored into her.

"You're acting like a spoiled brat."

"And you're acting as if I'm spoiling your fun, Mr. Hamilton."

"I ought to turn you over my knee and give you the spanking you deserve."

"Ah, yet another burden to be borne. How long-suffering you have been on my behalf. It is no wonder you itch to exercise some discipline. But even you, Mr. Hamilton, must come to terms with the fact that some things are just beyond your control. Like my returning to London today."

"Damn it, Celia—don't flaunt your bad manners in front of me or my stepmother's friends. It is bad enough we have to cover your leaving your aunt's home in the midst of your visit. You can't go alone up to London today."

"It breaks my heart to have to disturb your country idyll, Mr. Hamilton. Quite obviously you had other things on your mind during this visit to your friends. You need not abandon your intentions to attend to me."

He all but choked on his anger. "Goddamn—abandon my intentions! You ungrateful wretch—my only *intention* was to see to your safety and comfort, for Christ's sake. Why the hell else would I choose to immure myself in this godforsaken place for a weekend?"

"I see," she murmured, awash in a feeling of bitterness. "Willie. And your everlasting sense of responsibility. Yet another commission. Just another dirty little task: mind Celia, in case her aunt upsets her. Yes, I quite see . . ."

And her feeling of humiliation was crushing.

How could she, now that she knew she was a child of the Rom, have thought she could escape her fate?

"Well, Mr. Hamilton, let me assure you, this will be the last time I will be a millstone around your neck. So you must do me this one last service. I will return to

London today, with you or without you, because I have
received a long-overdue letter from my fiancé, reminding
me that it is time for me to honor my promises to him.
So''—surely her voice wasn't breaking?—''I must prepare to go to him—''

Her words were like a kick in the gut. He moved one
step up so that he was face-to-face with her; he could
smell her fear and feel her agitation.

''Who said? Who said?'' His voice was rough, his
hands prickling with the urge to touch her, to confine
her, to keep her. ''Who said you had to go to him?
You're not going to him. *I* won't let you go to him—''

He broke off abruptly as he saw the stunned look in
her expressive cat-eyes.

''What did you think? Willie was just going to let
you sail off into oblivion after all this? That any bar-
gains or unholy alliances your aunt Gertrude made
would have any kind of validity once Willie took over?
God, you have no faith. Why the hell did you think
your father arranged for you to leave Gertrude when he
did?''

''Ronald is managing my affairs until we are
married,'' she said stiffly. ''I am indebted to him; I owe
him . . . it is arranged.''

''Then your father committed folly upon folly if he
both gave you over to Gertrude and put your affairs
into the hands of a man you barely knew. What manner of man was this, Celia, that he could just sell you
like that?''

''No—*no!*'' She pushed away from him and he pulled
her back so that she was so close, she could see his eyes
dilating with fury.

''Yes—yes—what kind of fairy tale have you been
living, little girl? Let me tell you. Gertrude was the
wicked witch, but your fiancé is no Prince Charming—
and Willie is truly your fairy godmother.''

"I won't listen to this. It is what it is. Ronald will marry me—who else, knowing my history, would ever offer for me? Tell me, Prince of Critics, tell me—who?"

Me.

Did he think it—did he say it? Was she even ready to hear it? Hell, was he ready to commit to it?

"Anyone," he growled. "Any damned one of a hundred men you've met over the last month or two would fall on his knees begging you to marry him—"

"Except you. . . ." she whispered.

He felt like throttling her. He wasn't supposed to want her. He pushed closer, so that she could almost read the words as they formed on his lips.

"I'm your goddamned nursemaid; I'm your houseboy." He moved closer to her still. "I'm your drudge; I'm your conscience." His lips slanted across hers, and he was a breath away from kissing her. "I'm your cousin, and, by God, the last damned thing . . ." His mouth settled on hers forcibly, his body shifting against hers so that he encompassed her, all of her, between his mouth, his hands and his fulminating anger. ". . . the last damned thing I want . . ."

Her mouth was willing, so willing, her lips pliant, her body melting against his in timeless invitation. ". . . I want—"

He sought her mouth again with no remorse. He didn't want—except at this very moment he *needed* to hold her, to taste her, to fathom the mystery of those haunted golden eyes.

She opened to him like a flower, her heat enveloping him, inviting him to explore the tender recesses of her mouth, meeting him touch for touch, tongue to tongue, as if they had been lovers forever.

Forever. He was drowning in the lush, wet taste of her—he could live there . . . forever.

This was insanity—to take from her, to kiss her, to

want her and to want to relinquish her to her destiny all
at the same time. It was crazy and he was out of his
mind, not thinking of consequences and ramifications—

And Willie.

Goddamn—Willie would kill him!

The thought doused his ardor like cold water. He
pulled away from her slowly, gently, easing the pressure
on her mouth with such reluctance that she reached for
him as he lifted his head.

"No, Celia."

"But—"

"No."

She froze. "I see."

He thought she probably did. "You see nothing," he
said impassively, stepping away from her. "But you're
right; it *is* time to return to London. Go finish packing
your bags. We'll catch the eleven o'clock train."

Just like that. Just because *he* wanted it this time.
Everything got arranged with the most amazing effi-
ciency: her luggage was attended to, a carriage was
procured to take them to the station, he managed his
good-byes to the Templecombes with a minimum of
fuss, ignoring the shimmery sheen of tears in Jennifer's
eyes.

"Why do you have to go with her?" she demanded
angrily. "Why can't my brother go? Or why can't she
just travel with her maid the way she planned?"

"Because she can't," Grant said brusquely. "And that
will be that, Jennifer. There are other considerations, not
the least of which is that your brother is not a relative."

"Promise you'll come back soon."

"Either that, or you will come up to London and set
the Town on its ear."

"When?" She leapt on the suggestion eagerly.

"Let me send word."

"You never will."

"Then Thomas will remind me, won't you, Tom?"

"She won't let me forget, you can be sure."

They said their good-byes, with Grant's assurances that Willie was deeply in their debt for their kindness to her niece in her hour of need, and then he settled Celia and Emily in the carriage, gave Jennifer and Thomas his hand and signaled to the driver to be off.

Easy, when you were in control and in command.

When you were a damned statue, refusing to give in to the feelings and emotions of mortal men.

She hated him. She hated his strength and his resilience and the fact that he was so indomitably male, which made it so easy for him to take what he wanted and not even care about the aftermath.

And she hated how easily he handled everything, from buying their tickets to choosing the car in which they would travel to stowing their luggage.

Men had it all their own way.

And women were always left waiting.

They made the trip in a simmering silence. She couldn't think of one thing she wanted to say to him that didn't start out with Please kiss me again.

How on earth was she going to live without those kisses? Or with the knowledge that she must commit her own to a man who had become a virtual stranger to her?

And Grant didn't even care. His face was like stone, and he spent too much time staring out the window, almost as if he wanted to avoid looking at her.

As well he should, after the way he had treated her.

After the way he had kissed her.

He had kissed her like a lover . . .

Except how would she know what that felt like?

She knew what it felt like: it felt like her heart was being torn in two between her feelings of duty to Ronald and her intense desire to get back at Grant Hamilton for the way he made her feel.

His chore . . .

His liability . . .

She couldn't see any way around it. No matter what anyone thought, she was honor-bound to marry Ronald Winwood, for whom she now knew she had no depth of feelings whatsoever.

Twenty-one

And then Willie was not at home when they finally arrived at Carlton House Terrace.

"This is where your responsibility ends," Celia said primly, offering Grant her hand.

"Don't be a little fool," he said curtly and stalked up the steps ahead of her.

She followed him wearily, totally worn out by the emotions she had to summon up to deal with him—or even to sit in silence with him during a two-hour railroad trip.

It was too much on top of Ronald's letter and all the stupid attention Grant had paid to that rustic simp, Jennifer.

And her having to tell Willie that all their plans must be changed.

She dreaded having to tell Willie anything because she knew that Willie could reasonably talk her out of anything, and that Willie wouldn't understand the serious portent of this letter.

Or her wretchedly intrusive feelings for Grant Hamilton.

He turned to her in the reception hall, waving away

the butler and the footmen who were struggling in with her luggage.

She looked as white as the marble floor.

"You are a fool," he said abruptly. "Why don't you go upstairs to rest until Willie returns, and then we'll thrash the whole thing out."

I'd like to thrash you, she thought furiously, futilely. He was still treating her like a child. Go to your room. Don't bother your pretty little head. Your parents will take care of everything.

She let out a deep, angry breath, all her hostility showing in her golden eyes. "Yes, Father. . . ."

It was lighting a match to tinder: his eyes flared with green fire, and he took an explosive step toward her.

"No, father confessor," he corrected tightly. He took another step. "You ungrateful wretch." Another step. "You have absolutely no conception of what you're saying . . . you just know you love to play with fire. . . ."

He had her back up against the front door now and all she could see was the burning light in his eyes and the dark, sculpted planes of his face.

And his mouth . . . his voluptuously unerring mouth—

She couldn't let . . . she didn't want to let . . . but how could she stop a force of nature?

No—the force of her nature.

She tilted her head . . .

She invited his kiss . . .

She had been longing for this kiss all day—

All her life . . .

No, no—just this once more—just this once—

His mouth slanted across hers, and in an instant, in his anger, he took her, fully, forcefully, a hot, bittersweet taste of sin and seduction.

His arms surrounding her now, his hard arrogant body

pinning her against the door, his mouth possessing hers as if he owned it—

She melted against him, into him, around him. Her body felt boneless, weightless, suffused with a languid yearning that made her feel both defenseless and powerful.

It would take next to nothing for her to succumb to him. She was too innocent, and every time she was in his arms, she felt it, she knew it, and it did not matter.

She clung to him, enslaved by the heat of his mouth, his pulsating body, his strength, his delicacy, the way he savored her and touched her by skimming his hands lightly over her body and her breasts, and then waiting with a fine sensuous patience for her to deny him what he wanted.

She wanted everything. In the heat of the moment, she could not get enough of him seeking her nakedness beneath the awful impeding layers of her clothes.

She felt her nipples harden under his touch, she felt a swirling pleasure as he stroked them, even through her blouse and corset, and she felt it settle tellingly in that forbidden place between her legs.

She felt like she wanted to strip away every piece of clothing that hindered his expert fingers, and she pressed herself more tightly against him as if the heat of their bodies would melt away any obstruction.

She felt the pleasure point thickening, demanding some kind of pressure to make it explode.

She whimpered with frustration that she did not know what to do or how to ask for what she wanted.

She didn't know what she wanted except that he be her lover forever and then she would never have to give up his hard hot body, his caresses, or the thrill of his kisses.

She did not know how she could live without his kisses . . .

Not Ronald's kisses . . .

Oh, God!

She pulled away from him violently. He pulled her back just as violently, and held her tightly against him.

"Remember this moment, Celia; remember my kisses. Remember how you gave yourself to them—and to me."

"No!"

She wrenched away from him, pushing at him wildly, catching him off-balance.

"Celia!"

"Don't you ever, ever touch me again."

"Until the next time," he warned. "You're every bit as much a hypocrite as your inestimable aunt. Maybe you and that pretentious fiancé of yours deserve each other."

She slapped him then—just hauled off with all her weight and rounded on him.

"I hope you and the country mouse choke on weeds," she lashed back, stunned at what she had done and the fury behind it. "You're no different from every other man in the whole of England. You want someone flashy in Town, and a country mouse to keep your house."

He hated that; she saw it in his eyes, and in the flexing of the muscle in his jaw. And in his reddening cheeks.

And she wanted to push the knife in further and further until he bled.

"Well, I think it is obvious you've baited the mouse-trap for the one. And you may even be lucky enough to offer cheese to the other. So how can you possibly set yourself as the standard for my fiancé? You're the impostor, not he."

"And you're the biggest liar of them all," he said, his voice deadly.

And then he wheeled around and walked away from her.

* * *

Willie found him, an hour later, wearing a path into her parlor carpet.

He leapt on her the moment he saw her.

"You are *not* going to let her marry that money-grubbing son of a bitch just because that foul woman made a contract—"

"Grant, dear, sit down. You're roaring like a lion and I can hardly *think*," Willie said calmly as she entered the room and took a seat.

She watched him thoughtfully as he edgily eased himself down into a chair opposite her.

"Well?" he demanded.

"Well, what? I have no idea what you're talking about. I thought Celia was due back in London tomorrow."

"Plans changed."

"And now what? She is not to be permitted to marry Ronald Winwood? My dear, that goes without saying. You don't hare off in the middle of a Season to marry some provincial tea planter in Ceylon. Everyone knows that."

"Well, Celia doesn't, and neither does that plowboy. And the only thing he wants to plow is her."

"Grant!" Willie said reprovingly. "This is all a bunch of nonsense. She is going nowhere except to Scotland next weekend, as you well know."

"Thank you, I've done my time."

"And you'll do some more; I certainly expect you to be there and I don't want to hear a word about other plans."

He looked uncomfortable, and she regarded him closely. "Grant?"

"I've been invited."

"I'm so relieved. And you will accept. Now, tell me exactly what is going on with Celia."

"All of it? About the Gypsies and the way Gertrude was treating her? Or do you just want to know about the letter from the plowboy which made her feel so guilty, she needed to come home immediately to prepare to sail to Ceylon at the instant?"

"Oh, my," Willie murmured, "it was an eventful weekend. Well—tell me first about Mr. Winwood; I'm not sure I'm quite up to the Gypsies just yet."

He hadn't expected the Gypsies either, until some more information had come trickling in to him from the investigator whom he had hired. He had thought he had seen the end of it, the picture, Marianna's history—the tabloid nonsense—but then, out of the blue, he had been handed one small, inconceivable supposition, one additional little fact, and everything had turned topsy-turvy.

"Where else would I go but the Gypsy camp?" he murmured in answer to Willie's question about the Gypsies. "After Thomas told me their location, of course. Jennifer has never been able to resist them—why should she? But it was that old woman, Alzena. Celia was with her. And Celia looked dazed and unfocused. Especially when they began calling her 'princess' . . . Willie?"

"Yes, dear, I know," Willie said, looking a little distracted. "They told her?"

"They told her. She has a family now. And who knows whether it's for good or ill? But the old woman—a witch . . . it was like she was reading my mind. There was no way to avoid her. She knew—even before I stepped foot in the camp, she knew. I went to her straight as a magnet, as if I had no choice whatsoever. She read the cards for me and looked in her crystal ball—the one she used only for herself and her family."

"And?"

"In typical Gypsy fashion, she answered no questions, she told me no lies and she couched everything in fog and illusion, so I can't tell which way is up. Suffice it to say that she has concerns about Celia—as do we—''

He couldn't bring himself to tell Willie just what Alzena had told him he had to do. It was just a lot of mumbo jumbo. It was crazy; it made no sense, and there was no way he could possibly do what she had suggested.

His use of the plural was not lost on Willie, and neither was his evasive answer about Alzena's prophecies. There was something else there, either something that was so bizarre as to be unbelievable or something Grant was not prepared to tell her.

Either way, she had other things to contend with, not the least of which was making sure that Celia went to Scotland and that Ronald Winwood stayed where he belonged—in Ceylon.

Celia sat listlessly at her desk, a half-written letter in her hand and her one picture of Ronald directly in front of her, looking at her, she thought now, with supreme disapproval.

Dear Ronald,

I earnestly beg your forgiveness for not having written sooner. There have been such changes in the past several months that I have not had time to come to terms with them.

For one thing, I am no longer living with Aunt Gertrude and Uncle Theo. The reasons for this are complicated; however, you need to know that my father's will entrusted me to the care of my aunt Wilhelmina, his only sister, who was charged with

The letter broke off there, and continued a little way farther down the page:

> None of this, of course, has affected my feelings or my loyalty to you. Indeed, of late I have felt guilty that I am enjoying the fruits of a London Season while you are toiling on my behalf, utterly unaware of all these changes and denied all reasonable assurances of my . . . of my . . .

Her pen tripped on the word "affection."

> I have trusted you implicitly as I hope you trust me.

Her golden knight—she had buried him with the rest of her past life when she had come to London; Ronald, the man she had worshipped and adored since she was a child. She had folded him away with her dowdy clothes and her aunt's strictures, and had utterly forgotten about him as she pursued her frivolous course.

And now—and now—

Did he look different to her now? She had always been so proud of how handsome he was, how gallant, how faithful.

So why did she seem to see another face, dark and saturnine, superimposed over his?

She shook herself. It was the letter, and the sense of urgency she suddenly felt to get the thing over with. She could not argue with anything Ronald had written.

She couldn't find one reason to delay.

The knock at the door startled her. And then Willie's sweet face peered around the door.

"May I come in?"

But she was in even as she said the words and reading

the threads of Celia's letter over her shoulder without asking permission.

"I must go to him," Celia said dispiritedly.

"No, you must not," Willie countered firmly. "You must write him, certainly. But until you attain your eighteenth birthday, you are my responsibility by your father's terms. And I mean to honor his wishes. You will have your Season, Ronald or no Ronald, and when the time comes, we will proceed with prudence and caution because your intended must first pass muster with me. And whatever agreement Mr. Winwood may have had with Gertrude—well, she was never empowered to act in your behalf.

"Only you will decide whom you will wed, and I will not allow you to leap feet first into a marriage with someone about whom I know nothing.

"So take my advice—blame it all on me. If Mr. Winwood is in such a hurry, he will surely seek to curry favor, and then we will test his mettle and see whether he is indeed the man for you."

How she loved Willie! Kind, practical, ever-looking-out-for-her-best-interests Willie!

"And, of course," her aunt added, as if this were the most important thing, "we cannot back out of social obligations in the midst of a Season. It is simply Not Done." She spread her hands. "So, you see, there is no problem."

Celia forebore to say there was a letter, but that traitorous Grant must have said something, because Willie began stroking her hair and then asked softly, "I don't suppose you would care to show me the letter."

Celia opened the drawer of the desk and withdrew it.

The pages crackled as Willie unfolded them and began to read.

Celia stared at Ronald's picture so that she wouldn't sneak a look at Willie's expression.

But it was almost as if the expression of the picture changed, as if Ronald were reaching out to her in some mesmerizing way, as if she were drawn and repelled all at the same time.

"I see," Willie murmured as she folded the letter up and returned it to the drawer. "He is most anxious for your return; I cannot fault him for that. So it seems that I must write to him as well. He cannot gainsay your legal guardian or demand you do anything of which I can't approve."

She stroked Celia's hair once again, a light reassuring touch that conveyed affection and support. "It could be that your father was very wrong to have encouraged this liaison, you know. So rest easy, my dear. I will never allow anyone to force you to do anything you don't want to."

And then they were traveling to Scotland and suddenly Celia was in a room in one of the smaller turrets of a castle that overlooked a loch, and she was looking out of the turret window and feeling as if she were the ill-fated Lady of Shallot yearning for a glimpse of Sir Lancelot, even if it might cost her her life.

And who was *her* Lancelot?

And who would exact the price of her life?

The dark thought startled her. It was almost like the continuation of the disturbing dream she had had the previous night, a dream wherein she had turned and started running just as Ronald was reaching out his arms for her; a dream that made her toss and turn restlessly, trying to escape the darkening sky and a strange dark man.

Dreams—heretofore she had not believed in dreams. But the Rom believed in dreams and portents, and she was a child of the Rom.

In a castle in Scotland and thinking about dark lovers and wild dreams.

Emily's down-to-earth, Cockney common sense brought her back to reality.

"Fer Gawd's sake, miss, you lean any further out that window and you could fall. And it'd be a long way down too. There ought to be bars or glass or something safer than just them old, broken wooden shutters. Would you please come away now an' tell me where I'm to put everything?"

It was perfectly obvious that Emily did not approve of the room allotted to them. There were only two armoires standing against the tapestry-draped stone walls, and they were small and old fashioned, from another century when women dressed more simply. There were also two deep chests that would hold most of Celia's clothes, except the evening gowns, which needed to be hung carefully.

Celia watched as Emily unpacked several riding habits and walking suits with divided skirts; tennis dresses and even a hunting outfit, and she felt a swirling feeling of dismay.

All those clothes to eventually go with her when she returned to Ceylon, but what was fashionable in London would doubtless not matter very much on an isolated tea plantation.

For one aching moment she longed for the freedom of her childhood, which had had no constrictions and allowed her, she was sure, to run free.

She leaned out the window again and inhaled the fragrant air. "Doesn't it smell wonderful?"

And then, as if to underscore her feelings and her words, she heard the skirling sound of a bagpipe in the distance, unearthly and heavenly at the same time.

It beckoned to her, it spoke to her soul in a language she had known for an eternity.

She had never heard anything like it. She wanted to leap out the window and follow it.

She turned abruptly to Emily. "I'm going outside to explore."

"But—but—please don't go. Pay no mind to that unnatural music; I've been hearin' it ever since we got here and it's scared the daylights out of me."

"But it's only the bagpipes."

"But the sound of 'em is like nothing I've heard yet on earth. I'm begging you—don't run off after the sound of the pipes. It's like one of them stories I heard tell— you could be followin' the devil's call . . .''

"Nonsense, Emily."

"But what if there's some kind of monster lurkin' out there in the water? I've heard tell of such things. And, miss, I'm supposed to unpack for you first thing; that's what I was told to do. I could get in trouble for lettin' you run off by yourself."

"You're talking superstition, Emily. I'm not afraid of anything. I am going to follow the sound of the pipes; all you have to do is tell them I'm sleeping and can't be disturbed. I'll come back safe, don't worry."

But she wondered—she wondered about the sound that seemed to draw her along with it and toward it. It was instinct that propelled her, and the keening sound of the pipes that seemed so akin to the sobbing sound of the flamenco.

Somewhere along the way, she lost her thin slippers; somewhere along the way, her decorously coiled hair came undone until it streamed behind her in the rising wind.

Her blood pounded in her veins, driving her, pulling her forward; the music was like an elusive phantom— always just out of reach.

But the haunting reedy melody beckoned her, almost as if she were on the brink of finding whatever it was prophesied she was meant to discover.

Leaves swirled around her and against her face and eyes, blinding her.

And then she tripped over a willow root and into a headlong fall forward—and then she was caught up and lifted off her feet in a harsh grip that held her so tightly that she almost lost her breath.

And she found herself suddenly and unpleasantly held captive against a bare male chest.

A hairy, sweaty male chest. Belonging to someone whose face she could not see.

And when his stroking, caressing hand slipped below her waist and cupped her bottom, Celia bit him as hard and as fiercely as she could.

And then she brought up her knee, with all the strength and anger she could muster, and took an absurdly primitive satisfaction in hearing the man's cry of anguish as he doubled over and released his grip on her.

She could hardly catch her breath, she was so furious. She barely heard the laughter and the admiring masculine comments—until she suddenly realized that the men who surrounded them were speaking Spanish.

She tilted her chin defiantly and narrowed her golden eyes as a man stepped forward to confront her.

She was stunned to see that he was an older man— and a Gypsy. He had a gold ring in one ear, silver in his dark, curly hair, and eyes that looked exactly like hers.

He grinned down at her, his teeth flashing white against a fierce-looking mustache and his sun-browned skin.

"So! Here is the daughter of my favorite sister! And you have her wildness and her stubbornness too. At your feet, still squirming in well-deserved pain, is your cousin Cosimo. And I—I am your mother's brother, your uncle Beltran, the Voivode of our tribe. We have come here to find you, and to find out about you. Oh? You looked shocked. I have spoken with Alzena, and now I have to know you for myself, daughter of my most beloved sister."

He grinned, his eyes crinkling at the corners. "You have Marianna's spirit and her hot temper as well—I have already seen that for myself. Come, our camp is some distance away, on the other side of this pretty lake."

With some kind monster lurking . . .

She could hardly comprehend it: her uncle Beltran with the same eyes, the same hair, the same high cheekbones. He looked like her mother; he looked like her; how could she not go with him?

She took a deep breath and accepted her uncle's outstretched hand and felt his rough, warm fingers close over hers.

And when they sat across from each other in his caravan, Beltran said gently, "Do you not remember your mother?"

"No—yes. I remember her perfume, I feel her presence, I know I look just like her . . . and sometimes I feel as if I am her—" She broke off at something she saw in her uncle's expression. Pain? Loss? Regret? Resentment, perhaps, that she looked so much like the sister he had so loved? What was he seeing? What was he remembering?

"*Why?*" she demanded. "*Why?*"

He knew she could see his anguish. His beautiful sister, alive in her tempestuous daughter—how could he not remember them dancing together?

They had been the toast of Europe—brother and sister: partners in the intricate pattern of the flamenco—and what else?—until Marianna had fallen in love with the scapegrace Englishman and had run off with him.

And here was Celia—Marianna come back to life, still innocent and untried—and already in the hands of a fate that Alzena had warned him he must not meddle in.

But how could he not interfere? He had failed to protect Marianna and Marianna had died—no, she had been murdered; he had always been certain of it.

How could he not try to redeem himself by safeguarding her daughter?

And she was someone he could be proud of too, with the Gypsy blood running strongly in her veins; she was a fighter; but her emotions would rule her heart.

She would have to make her own choices, just as the Phuri Dai had said.

And he would make his own choices too—and one of them was that he would watch over her and protect her, even if it was only from her own passionate nature.

And unfortunately, by doing so, he would have to make Celia an instrument of revenge.

But that would come so much farther in the future. First, she had to understand more about her own people.

Twenty-two

Time seemed suspended in a haze of sun and shade, and the soft breeze from the loch made the leaves dance on ripples of air.

It was possible for Celia to believe she might see the pale white arm of the Lady of the Lake rising from the shadowy depths of the water, holding the sacred sword of Excalibur, as she sat with her uncle and watched the swell of the silvery lake and involuntarily inhaled the sweet, curling smoke from the pipe he had lit.

"All Gypsy women smoke the pipe—you must try it."

"Did my mother?"

"Not often. But when she wanted to go inside herself, then she did. Take it." He put the ornately carved wooden pipe into her hand, pressing it insistently against her palm, so that her fingers curled around the bowl.

"Now, don't inhale too deeply. Just very gently, a very short breath, and that will be enough for the first time. Trust me, I will look after you."

Had she only imagined that he added under his breath, "And I will teach you to dance and I will gift you with the castanets that once belonged to your mother, and your instincts will teach you how to use them''?

There was a small clearing where the colorful Gypsy wagons formed a semicircle, and now one of her new-found cousins, an exotic beauty called Pilar, stood poised in the center, her eyes fixed encouragingly on Celia as the guitars began to throb and cry.

And then, as if she had heard a signal, Pilar threw her head back, her castanets suddenly snapping fiercely in a counterpoint rhythm to the wailing song that emerged from her arched throat.

From all around her as the Gypsies gathered, Celia heard a sudden sharp clapping and cries of encouragement as Pilar began to stamp her feet disdainfully before she began the dance—now lifting her tiered skirts and petticoats, whose bright colors caught the light with her every teasing movement, and then moving backward with a deliberate challenge.

Celia's breath caught in her throat, and she moved restively. Her uncle put his hand on her arm, whispering, "Watch!" when a young man leapt into the center of the ring to confront Pilar and dance with his own arrogant masculinity that dared and defied her.

He teased her as he threatened her with his body, his stamping feet and the male desire she had ignited.

And Celia was so absorbed in the interplay and the music that she was barely aware of Beltran slipping the castanets over the thumb and forefinger of each of her hands and whispering to her encouragingly, "Feel the music, become the feeling. Come—let's dance!"

Instantly she felt it—the change in her—as she succumbed to the music, the clapping, the exhortations of the onlookers.

It was as if she had come back finally to what she was:

a Spanish Gypsy, wild and abandoned to the pulse of the music.

The castanets felt like extensions of her slender fingers. And she had always known the coquettish movements of the dance, the stamping of her bare feet against the hard-packed earth as if she meant to trample the nearest man into the dust beneath her toes.

It was a contest of wills between a woman and a man; it was ageless, stretching back for centuries, and the knowledge and the feeling of every sensuous movement ran in her blood and pulsed in her veins and came from someplace else beyond her, possessing her, while the sobbing sound of Pilar's song of unrequited love soared over the Gypsy guitars and took her up above the trees and into the heavens.

"By God!" Albert, Viscount Harville, exclaimed. "That cannot be Celia Penmaris, can it? Can it? No, I can't believe it!"

Grant Hamilton froze, clenching his rifle in a murderous grasp.

"Perhaps we had better retreat tactfully, what do you say, Grant? I mean, that can't possibly be Celia. Not dancing among the Gypsies . . ."

Grant swore under his breath. They had been drawn by the unfamiliar sound of the flamenco and the rhythmic clapping—a contradiction that was so out of place in a Scottish glen, it had demanded investigation.

Who would have thought they would find Celia, making a spectacle of herself—

"But, damn it—look at her!" Harville whispered. "How did she ever learn to dance that way?" He shifted uncomfortably under Grant's skewering look. "Oh, for God's sake, Hamilton, so there are certain things I can't help—nor you either, my friend. It's quite obvious you want her too."

Damn, damn and damn . . . damn her and her irresponsibility; damn him for being pulled by her innocence and her latent sensuality and for being so careless about it that even Harville could see it . . .

Damn, goddamn everyone and everything—she had every man panting with desire and had no conception of what desire was.

He felt on the very edge of a raging fury. He wanted to jump into the dance, and he wanted to catch her up and carry her off to some secret and private place where he could unleash all her true virgin passion.

He felt explosive with anger; his finger twitched on the trigger. The telltale muscle flexed in his jaw as he watched her thrusting her hips, stamping her feet, snapping her skirts.

She was ripe for plucking, ready for the right man. Alzena had already warned him—

He squeezed the trigger. The rifle shot sounded like a cannon echoing in the glen.

Everything stopped abruptly as Grant and Harville emerged from the shadows.

"Ah, *perdóneme;* I did not mean to put an end to your festivities," Grant said smoothly, tightly, in fluent Spanish. "Where I come from, it is the custom to warn others of your approach. You understand, the young lady is the ward of my *madrastra,* so it is natural that I was concerned."

Beltran came forward slowly, perceiving very well the underlying threat in those uninflected and precisely uttered words.

"She is my niece as well," he said softly, feeling his way, feeling the words. This was the one, the one Alzena had deemed either the savior or the destroyer. This was pure danger; it was just as well the dance had been interrupted. This was a man who could take only so much, and Beltran did not want to sin and be cursed yet another time.

For this man knew who he was and knew Celia's story; there was nothing he needed to tell this man that he did not already know.

"I do not want the same fate as my sister's for her child. I failed to protect my sister, and I will not let the same thing happen again. Can you swear she will be protected and kept safe? And tell me, stranger, what do you want of her—and with her, eh?"

"Perhaps," Grant countered coldly, "it is you who have some explaining to do."

They stared at each other for a long, unforgiving moment, and then Beltran nodded. "You trust the *gadje?*" he asked.

"He is of my family, related by marriage to Celia's guardian, who is her father's sister."

"That one," Beltran muttered. "Oh, very well, then. Tell the *gadje* to take my niece back to the castle. We will talk."

Celia was half dazed and did not comprehend at all what was happening. Grant saw this and his fury rose again as Harville gently took her arm and led her away, murmuring something comforting and consoling.

And then he and the Gypsy chieftain strode toward the tree-shaded loch, unheeding of the subdued whispers that arose behind them.

And what had he learned after all that? Grant wondered in disgust. That Celia had been possessed by duende—the power of song and dance?

Yes, and by whatever power was in the sweet smoke that clogged the air.

And moreover, Beltran was besotted with the memory of Marianna.

"She possessed the power of enchantment, and Celia, for all her protective upbringing among the *gadje,* is Marianna to the life—in looks, in her soul, in her spirit. It is all in the blood—all in the blood."

And? Grant demanded impatiently, silently.

"The *gadje* destroyed my sister. She went off with the brother of your stepmother. He stole her away from her people, and then he abandoned her to a life that stifled her spirit and took away her will to live. It is a debt that must be repaid in full. Revenge . . . an eye for an eye . . .

"My sister thought she could change because she imagined herself in love, but she could not bury the restless spirit of the Gypsy. When they were roaming everywhere, she and her husband, she was happy. But when the child came, he wanted her to stay in Ceylon . . . and he pinned her butterfly soul."

Marianna—she still seemed impossibly alive—to her brother, to Celia's relations, to Celia herself.

All because of Marianna, Grant thought trenchantly, with everyone overlooking the one salient point.

"Celia is *not* Marianna." He tried to keep his suppressed rage out of his voice.

Beltran heard it nonetheless and shrugged. "So there is nothing to be told, Mr. Hamilton, and everything rests on you. Celia's destiny was written long before she was born. A child of fate she is, and the path she will choose has been ordained from the beginning. It remains only to be seen whether you are the instrument of her redemption and whether Gypsy vengeance shall be served. But that is in the future, is it not? And whether you understand it or not, I have said all I have come to say, and you have in hand all that you need to know."

All because of Marianna—

And so he was back at the beginning, and now, with Beltran's blessing, designated once again Celia's savior with the impossible task of protecting her—and keeping his pounding fury and his racing desire in some kind of reasonable check.

* * *

Celia awoke as thunder echoed through her turret chamber; lightning flashed and the thunder rolled again ominously as she eased herself out of bed and around Emily, who was fast asleep on a pallet beside the bed.

She felt as if she were moving in a dream—the thunder and lightning sending a shimmering, unearthly radiance over the room as she moved, barefoot and clad only in a thin lawn nightgown, to the door.

She was going—she had to go. The storm called to her every bit as powerfully as the music of her people. She pulled open the door . . .

To be with her people, to be herself among those who would love her and care for her, and never have to pretend again . . .

She had felt it in the music, in the drifting, dazzling dream where she danced with the freedom of the wanderer to the music that claimed her soul—

There did not need to be anything else. She would go to them, and she would be free—

Free of her dreams, free of the past, free of the ghost of her mother that haunted everyone who had ever known her.

Free . . .

She ran, down the stairs lightly to the booming of the thunder that seemed to shake the castle to its very stones; she ran, across the backstairs domain of the servants to the door through which she would claim her freedom.

She ran, as lightning split the sky in a jagged, incandescent counterpoint to the fury of the storm.

She ran.

Such freedom. The rain slashed against her body with a corresponding urgency.

She ran, her arms outstretched to embrace her freedom and her future.

She ran . . . straight into a hard male body, blindly wrapping herself around it and feeling—feeling far too much against her quivering, rain-wet flesh.

She wasn't supposed to know what male desire was like, yet the feeling of him pressed hard along her thigh as he held her and kissed her open mouth hungrily was as familiar as the feeling of the rain.

He seemed to draw her very soul from her—and she was lost; she didn't know who she was, she didn't care who he was.

He was the embodiment of the lightning-streaked, thunder-dark night—and he desired her—and the raging of the storm only intensified her own wild and uncontrollable feelings.

She felt both inside and outside herself; she was Celia, she was Gypsy, she was Marianna and he knew it—he felt it and he damned her and he damned himself for feeling this hunger and this need for her.

He pushed her roughly backward and down against the rain-soaked grass; he felt her legs part under him, sensed her pulsing readiness for him.

There was nothing between them but the thin, drenched material of her nightgown, fragile as a tissue and as easily ripped away.

She was waiting for him, she wanted him—her hands reached for him and pulled at him, commanding, demanding, tormenting him.

She had no fear of his body now; she knew him, she had always known him, and she sought his flesh eagerly, tearing at his sodden shirt to dig her fingers into his taut, rain-slicked skin.

"Yes, yes"—she murmured the words against his mouth, against the ravishing tide of her need—and she was certain he could feel her form the words against his lips.

Yes to his ferocious kisses, yes to his voracious hands feeling her everywhere, cradling her, holding her, loving her.

She had waited so long for him to love her.

And he sank down against her restless body and surrendered to her yielding mouth as the rain soaked them both and hot, brilliant flashes of lightning illuminated the fine bones of her face and the black sheen of her hair.

Her arms wound around his neck and her body arched up under his; her kisses were fierce, wanton—and dangerous.

He could feel the line of her taut young breasts under his roving hands, and she murmured incoherently against his mouth, her body undulating against the hard thrust of his.

She didn't know what she wanted, but he did. It was like a hurricane inside him, this wanting her. It threatened to sweep him up, and toss him around; it gained strength with every touch, every kiss, furious and almost out of control, and if he succumbed, it would consume them both.

And then he felt her reaching for his engorged manhood; he felt her hand seeking, delicately prying apart his soaked clothing, her fingers splaying out against the taut thrust of him, and then slowly, hesitantly, closing around him and grasping him with all her strength.

He was a heartbeat away from mounting her.

It would be so dangerous, so seductively dangerous, to take her now. In one part of his mind he knew it—but he simply couldn't keep his hands off her wet, writhing body any more than he could resist her hot, passionate kisses.

How did a man tame a temptress?

When did a man pull back from leaping over the edge into oblivion?

Or did the forces of nature ordain it for him?

A crack of lightning shocked them both as it flashed close by over their heads and split a tree directly across from where they lay—as inevitably as he would have rended her maidenhead.

Nature had spoken, or destiny, or fate—he didn't know which—but it was enough to shake him up and bring him back to his senses.

And the last thing he wanted to do was seduce a Gypsy virgin on a storm-dark night . . . in spite of what his body told him and in spite of how much he had needed her heated, innocent kisses.

He would never admit it.

It was enough, and he knew it.

He pulled her to her feet and lifted her into his arms, swearing under his breath at the fury of the storm.

"Let me go," she whispered, pushing away from him futilely.

He held her more tightly. "This is no time for games."

"Was that what we were playing?"

"I rather think it was Russian roulette, and I was just about to pull the trigger."

His flat-out fury silenced her; she stopped struggling in his arms and wanted to become invisible altogether.

The rain came down like a curtain before them, chilling her heated body and washing the imprint of sin from it.

He was angry at her? She was furious with herself and appalled at how easy it was to succumb to a woman's need and a man's touch. She felt like nothing so much as a harlot, ashamed and degraded because of the way she had almost let him take her in the rain and the mud.

"You can leave me at the servants' door," she said imperiously.

"Oh, no, your Highness must be deposited right in front of her bedroom door. A chivalrous man can do no less."

"A chivalrous man could have done more," she murmured nastily, hating the killing disappointment she felt.

He set her down so abruptly and so roughly, her bones shook.

"And a less-than-chivalrous man would have ravished you and damned the consequences . . . but that is not what I want from you, your precious Highness. What I want from you is some discretion, damn it, and a modicum of control. And I want you to keep your virgin body to yourself, and your damned kisses for your husband"—he grabbed her arms in his fury—"whoever the unlucky son of a bitch will be, and I want—damn you—damn you—"

He pushed her away again. "Damn you."

"You want what?" she whispered, rubbing her bruised arms as they faced each other in a tumult of anger and feelings.

He drew in his breath—a harsh hissing sound that made her think of the pent-up moment before a snake strikes.

"And I want—I want not to want you."

The moment was etched indelibly in her mind: the sultry darkness, the wet of her nightgown, his heaving rage, her crackling resentment that he would not give in to his desire for her.

How could she ever be free? She was as much a slave to her passion for him as her mother had ever been to her love for her father.

Now she knew—now she understood: the freedom was in the loving and not in her Gypsy blood.

And now that he did not want her, she could never be free.

She had come this far, over all this unfamiliar terrain, to find a family and lose a love. Where was the justice in that?

The futility of loving—was that all her beloved mother had discovered after everything? Or had she found some redemption in following her heart, no matter what the end of the adventure had been?

~ Twenty-three

"So at last she's coming, your little bride-to-be. Is she still the innocent you think she is since she's been taken up by the Marlborough House set? What do you think, Ronnie, darling? Is she still a virgin?"

"I don't think . . . you stupid bitch—you've got me by the balls! Don't—! It hurts! Please, Adriana, we have to plan what we're going to do when she gets here. I have to remind her . . ."

"Remind her of *what*, Ronnie? Well, it's quite obvious you've never told me the whole story about poor, innocent little Celia, have you? Consider this. If you want my help, don't you think you had better tell me everything? Otherwise . . ."

Ronald Winwood groaned, his body arching. "Please, *principessa*, don't hurt me anymore! I've been good, haven't I? Haven't I? I swear, I'll tell you all about Celia—I'll *show* you, in fact—"

He almost screamed with the pain as his tormentor's grip tightened. Here they were, out in the open on the sun terrace overlooking a steep gorge with a waterfall spilling into it, and he was naked, controlled by her hard little hands and his own lust—

He—the master, the Periya Dorai of this whole verdant expanse of tea estate. Until he had met Adriana di Alberti and her husband, Eddie, he had been in charge of his life, his future, his feeling of superiority.

Until Adriana had introduced him to new experiences—being dominated by a strong mistress, and loving it; even groveling before her, when in the past it had always been he who'd been the one in control.

And now he was Adriana's willing love-slave—even when her husband was present, which he often was.

"Tell me more, Ronald, darling," Adriana cooed as she tightened her grip on his most tender parts and contrived simultaneously to straddle his body. "Is she anything like her mother? And do you think you will be able to control her once she gets here, Ronnie, darling? Stop groaning and answer me, or I'm going to have to take my riding crop to your plump backside, and you'll be too sore to ride around the estate tomorrow. And what will you tell your mistress, hmmm? Have you told her *anything* yet?"

"No! No . . . aagh, Domina! But she knows—she's English-educated, and I'm positive she has read the letters—ahhh—please—!"

Men! Adriana thought coldly and viciously as she looked down at her struggling victim. She despised them all. Strutting roosters, thinking they were the lords of the universe and masters of their wives and any other stupid females who believed their lies and who allowed themselves to be taken in by their attitude of superiority.

Well, who was the superior one *now?* And who was the strongest?

"How old was she when you first began to play with her, Ronnie, hmmm?" Her voice was a low, husky whisper that almost drove him into losing control.

She leaned over him and he felt her full breasts brush tantalizingly against his skin. He was going to lose control. Oh, God, he couldn't lose control; if he dared to climax without her permission, she would punish him.

He started to talk, very fast, licking his lips now and then as the memories flooded back—and the feeling of power.

He remembered his father—big, bluff, laughing— and all the man-to-man talks they had had. His father had known many women, and how to handle them too. Even that Gypsy bitch, Celia's mother—but that was *his* secret.

Celia—the big-eyed little brat who always kept following him around and staring at him so worshipfully— so willing to do anything he wanted her to do just to gain his approval . . .

He could talk to Adriana about *that* part; it was just the sort of thing that would excite her.

She was like a drug to him, a sweet addiction of the senses he never wanted to give up.

"I can't remember how old she was—maybe six or seven—but she was her mother's daughter, all right. My father told me—it was in the blood, that pulsing Gypsy blood . . ."

His voice trailed off as he remembered: a seductive and knowing smile; a young, nubile body arranging itself just for his delectation, inviting his eager hands to explore, to arouse, to erupt—

He couldn't stop the memories—he couldn't suppress the pleasure—he spewed uncontrollably all over Adriana's hand and his body. What he had tried to avoid he could not—the pleasure and the punishment; the two went inextricably hand in hand.

"You stupid, weak bastard!" she shrieked. "To defy me that way! Ohhh, you are brazen and you must be punished! Do you hear me? Punished to an inch of your life.'' She raised her crop so that he could see it clearly, and then she lowered it and ran the harsh leather tip down the length of his body until she nudged his still-erect member. ''An inch of your life,'' she whispered, raising the crop again.

''So that next time you will remember only what *I* want you to remember.'' And she brought it down within an inch of his genitals once, twice, again and again and again, until he was almost senseless with the pain of it and falling over the edge into a swoon of pleasure in which he thought he would remember nothing else ever again.

Celia felt as if she were sleepwalking through the remainder of their social engagements.

Scotland seemed like a dream, a Gypsy dream, now mixed and meshed with the rest of her dark and elusive nightmares.

What more was there after the man you discovered you wanted pulled you and himself back from the brink of folly and then abandoned you?

In all the dizzying round of social events that followed—the dinners, the balls, the card parties, the theater performances—she couldn't remember one incident or one man who attracted her.

I don't want to want you.

Folly, folly—who wanted to want anything?

The thing was what it was: magnetic, intense . . .

Inevitable.

It wiped everything away and it made nothing possible because *he* had decided, in his typically *male* way, that nothing was possible.

It made two things totally impossible: she could not marry Ronald and she could not stay in London, and once she had decided, she would not even let Willie try to dissuade her from her course.

"You want to what?" Willie shrieked, losing her composure for the first time since Celia had known her.

"I want to return to Ceylon and take over the management of my affairs," Celia said clearly, outwardly calm because she had thought it all through and it made perfect sense and it didn't matter that her hands were freezing and her heart was broken.

Besides, it was the right thing to do. "And I need to tell Ronald personally that I cannot marry him."

Willie looked at her sharply. She knew her niece. There had to be something more. "Nonsense," she said briskly, forcibly suppressing every emotion to deal precisely with the problem at hand. "*I* will tell him, and you need do nothing but continue as you are."

"And should he continue as he is?" Celia asked delicately. "Having total control and say-so over my property and my inheritance? Dear Aunt Willie, think it through; it would be unconscionable for me to cry off from this engagement from England. It has been set in stone forever—"

"More reason, then," Willie interrupted.

Celia shook her head and went on inexorably. "In any event, since he has written, I have felt nothing but guilt at how badly I have used him—"

"Let us say instead," Willie interposed once again, "how badly both your father and your aunt Gertrude have used him. And, in fact, I think it is extremely suspicious that he has seemingly been so constant all this time. It is just not in the nature of men. And tell me, please, why has he not come for you? And why has there been but one letter from him in all this time? I will tell you why, my dear—and here is your first lesson in Real Life. Mr. Ronald Winwood does not want to crush the delicate egg with which he will feather his nest."

Celia turned away from her; Willie was making it too easy for her, but her aunt just did not understand. "I cannot believe that of Ronald. I have idolized him all my life."

"Nevertheless, he stumbled into something very fortuitous, my dear. Perhaps he used your affection for him to ingratiate himself with your father, who, even if he was my brother, might have been an ounce too trusting. We just don't know what went on there all those years ago. And your Ronald could merely be some kind of adventurer—"

"Just like Father," Celia said with a catch in her voice.

"Except that your father made his way and built his fortune, and what has Mr. Winwood to recommend him, my dear? His expertise at managing? Whose word do we have for that? Your father cannot answer for him now, and your aunt Gertrude has never called him to account in all these years. It may be that you won't like what you find if you persist in this foolish plan to go to Ceylon."

Celia had not even thought of these complications, and she did not like Willie's pointing them out with her usual good common sense. But she couldn't think about them now.

"You don't understand. I need to leave London for a while."

Willie's eyes flashed. "Do you, now? Why is that, my dear?"

Celia lifted her chin. How could she put it? Willie must never know the truth—it was too humiliating. "There is an untenable situation which I hope will be resolved by my absence."

"Indeed? What might that be? And why don't I know about it?"

Celia hesitated; in another moment, given her emotions and Aunt Willie's great practical kindness, she might confess everything.

Willie would be shocked and probably annoyed, because this surely was not the outcome she had expected when she had taken Celia to London.

So the best course was to evade the issue.

"There is nothing to know, Aunt Willie. It is just—it is merely—I do not feel comfortable, and it would be so much better if I could take care of two unpleasant events with one decisive action."

Oh, that sounded so good.

And Willie wasn't fooled for an instant.

"Who?"

"Aunt Willie . . ." Celia said pleadingly.

"Is he married?" Willie asked sharply, and Celia could see her mind working like a whirligig, going this way and that, sorting through eligibles and roués, trying to figure it out. "Harville?"

"Aunt Willie!" Celia protested, and then caught herself. Harville was as good as anyone else, given his inordinate attention to her the several times they had been in each other's company.

"The cad," Willie growled. "And a relation too! How could he stoop so low? I'm of a mind to—"

"Please don't," Celia broke in. "But surely now you can see it would make sense for me to travel—and to face up to the obligation of telling Ronald that I cannot be his wife."

Willie's expression was grim. "Perhaps. Perhaps. But I cannot accompany you. I've just received word that my husband may be coming to London, and yet I feel very strongly that this time you should not face these predators by yourself. Can you not wait a month, my dear? In that time we can demand a full accounting from Mr. Winwood and we will have a better idea of just how involved and sincere he is in his wish to marry you."

How reasonable she was, and how much sense her suggestion made. Celia would have given anything to have said yes to her aunt's proposal. To travel to Ceylon with Willie by her side to protect her from adversity and the certain and understandable anger of Ronald Winwood once she broke their engagement—ah, what a luxury that would be!

But it was time for her to take responsibility for herself. Willie had helped her build the foundation; now she must answer for the rest—from the folly of her desire for Grant Hamilton to her childish infatuation with Ronald Winwood.

She shook her head. "I wish I could. But I really must—"

"You don't need to travel out of England. I have many friends who would invite you to . . ."

She should have expected that; her aunt's friends, who would encircle her with love and protection the moment Willie gave the word.

"Aunt Willie, you don't understand. I cannot put Mr. Winwood off any longer. And I cannot stay in London. It is time for me to take control of my destiny. I feel it. It has been foretold. I must return to Ceylon and I must leave soon."

Willie was taken aback by the emotion in her niece's voice. "I see," she said slowly. "Well, then, we must find a chaperone, someone we can trust to—" She broke off because she didn't quite know what to say that would not sound overly melodramatic.

"In any event," she began again, only to have Celia interrupt her.

"I have thought of all that, Aunt Willie. Not a week ago I received a letter from Uncle Theo. He is on his way to London with Anthea and her new husband, and he has committed himself to a year of missionary work in the East—in Ceylon, to honor me and the place from which I came, he says. But I think it's a kind of penance for his guilt over the way Aunt Gertrude treated me. He would be the perfect chaperon. And Anthea will make sure that all proprieties are observed. She is, after all, a Married Lady.''

''I dislike it intensely,'' Willie said feelingly. ''I really do not like this idea at all.''

''Uncle Theo loves me. He would stand behind my decision and make sure that nothing untoward happens.''

''You cannot count on Mr. Winwood's good nature— if he ever had any, and by the evidence of that awful letter, I would think not. Anyway, his good nature will not remain intact for long when he learns you are about to cut the very ground out from beneath him. I'm not sure Theo is good in such critical situations,'' Willie added tartly. ''If you would only—''

''I won't,'' Celia said staunchly.

''Let me send for Grant,'' Willie suggested with a hint of desperation. Surely Grant could talk her out of this folly.

Celia blanched. ''You have saddled him with enough responsibility for me these several months, Aunt Willie. I will not brook his interference in this matter.''

Or yours.

She didn't say it—perhaps she thought it; in any event, Willie understood it, because the worried expression on her face smoothed out and the tone of her voice changed as she said, ''Very well, my dear. I can see that you are determined to do this, and perhaps it might not be bad for you to see how things are firsthand.''

Celia looked at her suspiciously. It wasn't like Willie to back down so quickly. Willie knew that she knew that all her arguments were reasonable and that her request that they take this trip together next month made sense.

''What about your aunt Gertrude?''

The question was so unexpected, Celia had trouble shifting her attention back to her imminent plans.

"According to Uncle Theo, she will not accompany him. You may read the letter if you like; I'm sure that my uncle will be happy to undertake the role of chaperon."

"I have no doubt that he will," Willie said agreeably. "And Emily shall attend you, of course. And there will be Anthea and her husband, and as you said, she is most observant of proprieties, and that is vastly reassuring to me."

The words hung in the air for the briefest moment, and Celia looked closely at her aunt to determine exactly how she had meant them.

But Willie's head was down as if she were thinking, and Celia could not see her face when she spoke again.

"Write your uncle, then, my dear, and I will make all the arrangements. However, I will ask that you agree to one thing."

"Anything, Aunt Willie," Celia said fervently.

"Say that you will welcome my company when at the end of next month I can join you in Ceylon."

"Dearest Aunt Willie," Celia murmured, going to her and kneeling at her feet and into her warm embrace. "Come when you can."

Willie stroked her hair. *Fate,* she thought; *so much of your life, my dear, has been wound up in the notion of fate. But rest assured, I will not let you out of my sight, not for an instant; if I cannot be with you, I will send the one surrogate whom I know I can trust, and all will be well.*

"Rest easy," she murmured out loud, tucking errant strands of Celia's wild, curly hair behind her ear. "I promise you, my dear, I would never let anything or anyone hurt you. And as soon as may be, I will come and make sure of it myself."

* * *

And Uncle Theo, bless his heart, never gave a thought to the oddity of Celia's request to accompany him and welcomed her as if it were planned all along.

Anthea Langbourne Maitland was quite a different story. Celia could not pinpoint just what it was about Anthea, but she seemed more disapproving than ever since her marriage.

She and her husband and Uncle Theo came to dinner at Carlton House Terrace the evening before their departure.

Aunt Willie was cordial and gracious, deferring to Uncle Theo and Mr. Maitland and the gamut of stories they told, all of which had an ecclesiastical flavor.

Anthea did not look happy and Celia drew her aside.

"I have been remiss in offering my congratulations on your marriage."

"Indeed you have," Anthea said crisply. "I had thought we were better friends than that. And please don't plead the excuse of how busy you were. That was tactlessly obvious."

Celia was taken aback. In Aunt Willie's world, no one would dare censure another's behavior to his face, and she was at a loss what to say.

"Believe me, it was not spiteful or intentional, Anthea."

"What could one think after the way you bolted from your aunt's house? She took to her bed with smelling salts for days. It was all your uncle and I could do to keep her from haring off after you and legally challenging your—Mrs. Hamilton's rights under this very suspicious codicil to your father's will. However, your uncle prevailed. He was sure that kind of action would entail a scandal that would reflect badly on your aunt, and she had enough to contend with because of those upstart

Templecombes witnessing that *excruciating* scene you caused.

"Well, that's neither here nor there—now. Your aunt Gertrude has recovered and we left her in renewed spirits. But I miss her dearly. Her understanding and sympathy are everything a newlywed could want, and her counsel is wise. How you could act so disgracefully toward her and embarrass her in that way, I will never understand."

Celia shook herself. Anthea actually felt affection for her aunt! But she would not fall into the trap of defending herself or making any more excuses for ignoring Anthea; they had chosen different courses and that was the sum of it. Why should she have Anthea's needs on her mind, after all?

"I will not discuss it," she said coolly. "However, I am happy to know my aunt has recovered and that Uncle Theo can travel without his heart being burdened by that. Now, tell me all about the wedding."

She had expected this turn of conversation to lighten Anthea's mood, but she was shocked again when Anthea answered dourly, "What is there to tell? Your uncle performed the ceremony; your aunt stood up for me, and our nuptials were celebrated through the kindnesses of your aunt's friends, who joined us for the wedding breakfast.

"As for the rest—" She turned away and shrugged. "It was nothing I had thought it would be. I had prepared for a union in God, but I reckoned without the baser nature of man. Who can know it?"

She gave a short, bitter laugh. "Who would want to? Were it not for that—well, what God has joined . . ."

Again Celia did not know what to say. Anthea's disappointment was off-putting, and she didn't see how she was going to spend weeks of enforced closeness on a steamship and endure her bitterness.

"I'm sorry," she murmured.

"Why should you be? Everything seems to have worked out for you. I would rejoice in that were it not for your treatment of your aunt. But I am happy that you are finally making the right choice and returning to Ceylon to marry Mr. Winwood. We will have that in common at least. Now, do excuse me while I thank your aunt for her hospitality."

She turned away abruptly before Celia could correct her impression, and as she watched her stiffly retreating back, Celia thought that perhaps it was best Anthea did not know of her plans; she had not even told Uncle Theo.

He knew nothing more than that Ronald had written to her and she had decided to return to Ceylon at his behest.

She felt like a fraud as she stood on the steamer dock the following morning with her uncle. She was trading on his love and his good nature to take her to a place where she would choose the next path in her life.

He deserved to know that, especially when he thought she was going home finally to marry Ronald Winwood and had expressed himself as being so very happy for her.

Well, there was time enough to go into the details.

The hard part was leaving Willie.

She hadn't even considered how hard it would be to leave Willie.

"Oh, my dear," Willie murmured, enfolding her comfortingly once again. "The days will fly; I will join you soon. But as you know, there are engagements and business I cannot put aside, not even for you. Soon, my dear, soon. Just stick with your convictions and know that I support you in whatever you wish to do."

Celia felt the tears streaking down her cheeks. "Oh, Aunt Willie, maybe this was not such a good idea—"

Willie hugged her closer. "Oh, I don't know. Perhaps it was. Come, I'll escort you on board."

"It is so big . . ."

"Yes, it certainly is. Now, here are your tickets and your port-of-call boarding passes; don't lose those."

"No, Aunt Willie."

"Make sure you always have a hat or a parasol."

"Yes, Aunt Willie."

"Write to me every day."

"Absolutely, Aunt Willie."

"Do not let anyone deter you from your decision. It is the right one."

"I promise, Aunt Willie."

"Then you are ready to carry on, my dear. And here is your stateroom, side by side with that of your uncle and the Maitlands. Very fortuitous for us, claiming such a late ticket . . ."

"Not in the least," a voice said behind them, and Willie and Celia both froze. "I made them move an obnoxious family of provincials to make room for us. Of course they accommodated the bishop—how could they not?"

Willie and Celia turned simultaneously.

Willie recovered her composure first. "Gertrude."

"Willie—how nice to see you again," Gertrude said, seeming in fine fettle. "Let me commend you on your good offices in finally convincing Celia to end her self-indulgent social whirl and take her rightful place by her fiancé's side. Celia, did you say something?"

Celia pulled herself together. "How are you, Aunt Gertrude?"

"Better than you left me, you ungrateful child. But I have forgiven you. In truth, how could you know better, what with your head being turned by those insufferable Templecombe whelps? And your stepson, Willie—disgraceful, how he talked to me. It's as I have ever known: there are no manners or civilization outside England."

"And yet you are traveling to Ceylon," Willie pointed out with no little sarcasm which, as she could have predicted, Gertrude did not even hear.

"Well, of course. One could not let such an unworldly man as Theo loose among the pagans in the East. Theo needs a firm hand guiding him in his ministrations—no Gypsy woman will get her claws into my husband," she added meaningfully. "I know my Duty and I have always done it. And even Celia cannot say differently. Ah, there is Theo now! Hello-o, my dear—I am here."

Celia wheeled around—just in time to see Uncle Theo's face before he schooled his features into their accustomed expression of resignation.

He had not expected to see her there. He had intended to travel alone.

She felt Willie's hand clutch her arm.

"Celia—"

"It's all right; I can handle her," she whispered.

"I wonder—"

"Me too. I wonder why she changed her mind."

Twenty-four

Egypt! The mysterious, beckoning desert with its sand dunes and great pyramids covering the resting places of ancient kings and queens.

Celia leaned over the rail of the luxurious P&O steamship, watching the silent white wake as the big steamer slid through the narrow Suez Canal.

Except for the running lights of the ship, everything was black as pitch, pierced occasionally by the flickering orange light from a Bedouin campfire on the shore.

It was a hot, still night. Somewhere in the distance a jackal howled at the half-moon that hung suspended in the blue-black sky.

She wished for a breeze; she wished she could divest herself of her sensible clothes because she was far too confiningly gowned for the climate of the East in her high-necked shirtwaist and sensible serge skirt.

She tucked a wisp of hair up off her neck. Even her hair felt heavy, almost as if the humid air were pulling it down from its neat topknot.

She felt sluggish, enervated by the trip and by the energy of having to deal with her aunt and Anthea both. It was like having two Aunt Gertrudes. They were kindred souls—surely she had thought before that Anthea would have been Aunt Gertrude's ideal child.

So she meant to stay topside as long as possible in spite of the heat; it was her only escape from Aunt Gertrude's incessant carping about the accommodations, the company—and everything else.

In the heat of these nights, hundreds of miles away from England, and in the heat of Aunt Gertrude's censure, Celia suddenly felt very unsure of everything.

She should have waited for Aunt Willie. She just did not have the experience to handle Aunt Gertrude's mean-spiritedness. Not even Uncle Theo was enough of a buffer, and he was trying harder than ever to see her side when she and Gertrude had some set-to.

Lord, she had to get out of these clothes. She made her way slowly back to her luxurious stateroom, hoping against hope that everyone was asleep. The only saving grace of this trip was that she occupied her own room, although she felt sure that Anthea would share it at the drop of a hint in order to avoid any intimacy with Mr. Maitland.

Whereas she craved that intimacy—

But what could it be like to kiss someone like Mr. Maitland? She couldn't even begin to imagine.

She rummaged through one of her cabin trunks, looking for something light and filmy to wear, pulling out one handful of perfumed and daring undergarments after another.

Flimsy, feminine underwear a man might buy for a mistress, things that had been bought for her as a proper part of her outfitting as a society belle . . . a Gypsy who would prefer to run barefoot and wear cotton skirts and improper Gypsy blouses . . .

Who was returning to Ceylon, after all?

The woman who shamelessly desired Grant Hamilton?

Or the wild child who had always wanted Ronald Winwood?

Which one was she?

Or was she the child of her mother and fated to have neither?

But she was different—she had changed her fate already by moving successfully and elegantly through a London Season with not a misstep or a mistake.

But had she offended the gods by deliberately seeking to change her destiny?

She slipped her arms out of her high-necked blouse and unbuttoned her skirt and let it slide to the floor.

All these encumbering undergarments, meant solely to repress and constrict and control, surely designed by a man, she thought mordantly as she unhooked her corset—awkwardly without Emily's help—and removed her chemise and drawers.

Now she could feel the air, heavy and hot on her skin.

If she had felt more confident, she might have gone to her bed naked, but she was still a coward about the passion of her body. She found a silk robe and draped it around herself before she settled into bed.

But the heat made it difficult for her to fall asleep, except in fitful snatches, and then her dreams kept crowding in, and she thrashed about, trying desperately to escape the memories . . .

. . . no, her own naive, childish misinterpretations . . . no—

All night the dreams came, as if drawn from the most hidden recesses of her mind by the distant wavering call of a muezzin summoning Allah's faithful to pray.

All he had been trying to do was teach her to flirt—and even to kiss, she recited to herself like a litany as she frantically tried to dislodge the dreams; *nothing different from teaching her to shoot or ride a horse. She*

*had amused him and his friends, that was all. She had
been no more than an amusing diversion . . .*

. . . a doll . . .

. . . a toy—

She jolted awake, awash in perspiration.

She couldn't remember a thing except the hovering
feeling of losing control.

But that was what nightmares were, one's mind spin-
ning out of control and down pathways that made no
sense and had no connection to anything real.

She was sure of it.

It had to be so—or she might lose her mind.

They anchored briefly at Port Said. All the hustle and
bustle there, with the hawkers of supposedly ancient ar-
tifacts swarming all over the ship, spreading out their
wares on the sun-baked decks.

Such heat!

All the ladies had their parasols unfurled to protect
their precious English complexions, and most of them
elected to stay on board the ship.

But Celia wanted to explore the native shops; Uncle
Theo felt obliged to chaperon her, and Anthea decided
that she and George also needed to *experience* the East.

Aunt Gertrude was going to stay on board, but that
did not deter her from accompanying them onto the dock
and issuing admonitions one after the other.

"Be sure to use your parasols; this heat is ghastly—it
will just destroy your complexion, Celia. You're not used
to the sun anymore—you don't want to darken that
lovely pale skin again. Watch out in the bazaars—they're
always looking to cheat you or rob you. Bargain for
everything, and, Theo—use discretion please. You don't
have to buy *everything*."

They left her there, and it seemed as if her voice were

still ringing in their ears when they finally reached the narrow streets of the bazaars.

Anthea and her husband moved gingerly among the stalls and through the crowds, disdainful of the merchandise and the natives both.

But Celia suddenly felt as if she could actually *smell* the East in the many odors that assaulted her senses all at once as she followed them.

And some of the alleyways were so narrow that the ancient walls on either side seemed to close around her, almost suffocating her, while the constant cries of the street vendors and the half-naked children plucking at her skirts took her back in time to pleasurable moments of her childhood.

Finally, Anthea and Mr. Maitland discovered a *British* shop where, Anthea pronounced with relief, they were sure they would not be cheated.

Uncle Theo, mopping his brow, murmured a brief prayer as he sank into a chair and thankfully accepted a glass of cool lemon-barley water. While Anthea and George bargained over linens, lace and other household goods, Celia wandered over to a small, cluttered area overlooking the street and picked through an array of ornate and gaudy jewelry.

A copper-and-gold necklace that might have been designed for the bride of a Pharaoh caught her eye, along with matching and equally ornate earrings that were so long they would touch her shoulders.

Did she dare? She bit her lip. The necklace, which had miniature gold coins overlapping the edges, would drape over her shoulders like a collar and drop to a point between her breasts. The earrings were made of matching overlapping coins and would dance with each movement of her head. What Gypsy woman could resist such a flamboyant treasure?

And didn't she have someone in mind for whom she would wear it?

But even she could not think that far ahead; it was enough that the beautiful jewelry attracted her, enough that she wanted it and had the wherewithal to buy it.

Surely, surely, she needed no other reason than that.

Dry, dusty Aden was their next stop, the last before Colombo. Celia hated Aden. It was nothing but a parched rock jutting out of the Indian Ocean that used to be a prison colony.

And it meant that Ceylon was close—too close—and the hour of reckoning was at hand.

She wished she had waited until Aunt Willie had been able to travel with her. Aunt Willie could have fought off the demons that obsessed her as she lay in her narrow bunk at night.

The memories swarmed over her then, amorphous and hovering like fog, waiting to swallow her up and sap the very life out of her.

And during the day there was Aunt Gertrude with her sharp viper's tongue, waiting at every moment to inflict a sting, a cut, a gash, blindly hoping to make Celia bleed and nursing grudges and secrets to her pious bosom.

"I hope Wilhelmina had the good manners to write to Mr. Winwood to explain the change in your situation. You have no idea, Celia, how embarrassing and awkward this has been for your uncle and me, especially since there have been some offers to buy your estate. Sir Thomas Lipton is—was—very interested. But you were nowhere around to be presented with his proposal. What could one say? That the ungrateful child decamped with her aunt's stepson and we have no way of consulting her?"

Celia flushed; her aunt was going too far. "I'm sorry. I thought there was mail delivery to London from the country. Perhaps you could have thought to forward my mail to me?''

"A properly brought up young lady *always* defers to the man in the family on such weighty matters as the disposal of property," Gertrude said huffily. "But, of course, that flighty Wilhelmina does not abide by the accepted norms; she has been away from England and living among savages far too long. If I had thought she would have taken Theo's advice, I would have written to her at the instant. Nonetheless, the issue will soon be resolved. Once you are married to Mr. Winwood, he can act for you. Uncle Theo has all the particulars.''

But it's my estate, Celia thought resentfully. And she should have had at hand all offers and interest. Yes, Ronald had managed everything for her for a long time, but that did not mitigate the fact that the estate was hers.

It was very strange; she had never been accustomed to thinking of the tea plantation as hers, but now she felt a fierce possessiveness to protect what was hers and not let anyone wrest it away from her.

Aunt Willie would understand. Hopefully, Uncle Theo would as well. But if not . . .

Within a day or two they would be disembarking in Colombo Harbor, and then there would be no question— she would take control of this whole new part of her life that was about to begin.

It was perfectly clear to Grant as he leaned over the split-log railing of the veranda at Monerakande that Willie had consigned him to hell.

Ceylon in summer was hell—mind-numbingly hot and humid, peopled with expatriate upper-crust English who were harvesting their plantations and cultivating their lives by the sweat of the local populace, and therefore were bored and bent on making trouble.

When they could get up the energy to do it.

Hell.

He had told Willie in no uncertain terms that he was finished playing knight-errant to Celia Penmaris.

"Of course you are," Willie had agreed placatingly. "She's matured beautifully. There is nowhere now that she would not feel comfortable. You have done your last signal service by abducting her from Gertrude's clutches."

"Exactly."

"And you've treated her just like a brother, which pleases me enormously."

"Precisely," Grant had said grimly. "And now, *madrastra,* may I be excused to live my own life?"

"Certainly," Willie had promptly replied—and he thought later that he ought to have been warned by the gleam in her eye. "And in any event, Celia is leaving England and planning to return to Ceylon to tell Mr. Winwood she cannot marry him and—"

"*What?*"

"You heard me, Grant. She felt it was time to face Mr. Winwood, and I could not dissuade her."

"Are you crazy?"

"Please, Grant, even I can't combat Gypsy mumbo jumbo about fortune and destiny. And besides, she won't be traveling alone. She planned it very nicely so that she could accompany Theo, who has had some kind of revelation about ministering to the natives."

He almost choked trying to contain his rage. Celia, in the limp hands of Uncle Theo, who couldn't even curtail his own wife. Celia, facing the unknown Winwood to tell him that she would not marry him and to pack his belongings and leave.

The ramifications raced through Grant's mind like wildfire.

"Of course," Willie went on placidly, "Mr. Winwood will not be too happy."

"You have a gift for understatement," Grant growled.

"Yes, well, I *will* be joining her in several weeks—I could not leave now. What can happen in that time, after all?"

"He could murder her."

"Oh, really, Grant, don't be melodramatic. Theo will be there, and Anthea and her new husband."

"Oh, excellent—a young Gertrude who is hell-bent on diminishing Celia, and two men who will snap under pressure like a piece of bamboo. You have lost your mind, *madrastra*."

"My dear, it's done."

"You have to undo it."

"They sail tomorrow."

"Hell . . ."

Willie waited.

"Damn it, I don't want to go."

"Who would?"

Grant's expression turned darker. "What do you know about this Winwood?"

"Very little, actually; this is my brother's doing, fostered by Gertrude after his death. Celia has a picture. He is very blond, very handsome. And he writes nasty, guilt-inducing letters. I don't like him already."

I hate him.

The thought shot out of nowhere and Grant wanted to blast it to oblivion—he wanted to blast Ronald Winwood to oblivion.

And so he had devised an elaborate scheme, shamelessly enlisted the aid of his friends, commandeered a whole plantation to carry out his plot and invented a cover for himself that would probably last no longer than it took the sun to burn off the morning mist.

He had arrived in Ceylon by freighter days before Celia and her party in order to establish his presence and his story, and to mark the actors in the play.

Willie hadn't had to do a thing: he had done it all by himself—volunteered to go, conjured up the plan, got on the freighter—all in a haze of frustrated fury and fear for Celia.

Whom he did not want.

So what *did* he want?

He wanted to protect her.

He wanted to keep her from falling into whatever traps Ronald Winwood might have laid to seduce her into marrying him.

He wanted to make sure she was safe until Willie could come and deal with the matter.

And now, as he looked out over the rolling fields that stretched far into the distance, he cursed Willie's perceptiveness and damned his own gullibility.

She hadn't had to say a word. He had leapt right into the silence and her seemingly complacent acceptance of the thing—and by his complicity, he had given himself away.

Twenty-five

There was a gathering at the Hunt Club.

As were all the clubs in the up-country planting district, this one was for Europeans only, and it was one of the better ones. It offered two tennis courts, a clay-pigeon shooting gallery and a decent clubhouse with a veranda and comfortable lounge chairs. There was a small library and a billiard table as well, thanks to the generosity of Sir Thomas Lipton, who had recently purchased the Monerakande estate to add to his already vast holdings in the area.

Ronald had been reclining in one of the chairs that lined the shaded veranda, sipping his favorite gin and tonic, his eyes half closed, when suddenly he was jerked back to the present by the turn in the general conversation.

McPherson, from Kinross Estate, was talking to Adriana's husband, Eddie Branham, about the latest arrival in the district, the American protégé of Lipton's who was installed at Monerakande and who was supposed to be managing all of Sir Thomas's property in Ceylon from now on.

An American, Ronald thought. What in hell would an

American know about tea planting or how to manage coolies, when his own country had fought a civil war just to free them?

"Probably be bad for discipline—set a bad example everywhere," he muttered, as if everyone were privy to his previous thought.

"Understand he's an honorary member here, thanks to Lipton. Maybe we can put him straight, d'you think?" McPherson went on, ignoring Ronald.

"Maybe. Who knows?" Adriana said languidly as she fanned herself. "What did you say his name was, this American?"

"Hamilton, I think. Good Scottish name. Hear he's Lipton's godson, or something of the sort. Still!"

"Hmmm . . . Hamilton? Do you know what he looks like? Is he old? Is he young? Is he—handsome, this man? And what is the first name, do you know?"

"All I know is he's being taught the ropes by Dougal Drummond—and if Dougal knows anything, he knows about tea. He used to plant in Assam, you know. That's why Lipton brought him over here. Say, maybe there's something more about Hamilton in the membership book."

He snapped his fingers and sent a waiter to tell Kandappu, the stately Sinhalese who ran the club, to bring out the membership book.

"Nothing but the best for Sir Thomas, you know," McPherson continued when Kandappu placed the ornately inscribed membership book before him. "So this—this—" He began leafing through the pages. "Aha! Grant S. Hamilton—that's the name. Well, whoever he is, he must be good or Lipton, who is as canny a businessman as I've ever met, would never have picked him to manage his affairs."

He motioned to Kandappu to remove the book and ordered another whiskey and soda, and so he did not notice that the normally cool and controlled Adriana had suddenly sat upright as she exchanged a speaking look with her husband, who raised one eyebrow quizzically.

Immediately Ronald felt excluded and quite sulky at what seemed to be a kind of conspiracy between them.

"*Grant* Hamilton? Eddie—do you think?—oh, how delicious!" Adriana gave a husky little laugh. Her eyes sparkled. "I have a feeling, my darlings, that the next few months are going to be such fun!" She slanted a gaze up at the impassive Kandappu, who had silently appeared with another round of drinks and a platter of "short eats," hors d'oeuvres.

"Have you met this man, Kandappu? What does he look like? Does he have green eyes that can be as deep as the sea and as hard as emeralds? Is he tall—very tall— and does he have hair that sparks red in the sun?"

"All I know, lady, is that the new master of Moner- akande has the kind of rifle that I have never seen be- fore—and he can shoot better than any of the other masters. Also, which is very strange, I think, he has two belts filled with cartridges that he wears around his waist, with two long-barreled pistols in holsters that he can pull out very fast—and still shoot straight. I saw him come here only once, lady. With the English lordship who has married an American lady. They were all very friendly, and the English lordship could shoot the same way too, only not quite as well."

"What on earth is he talking about?" Ronald asked petulantly, annoyed at being left out. "Look, who are these people you're talking about?"

"Viscount Harville and his rich American wife are vis- iting our district, didn't you know?" Adriana said. "And they are long-standing friends of our new American neighbor, Mr. Hamilton. Ronald, dear! Do try to think! Remember those lurid newspaper cuttings that your men- tor, Lady Gertrude, sent you to advise you that your

mousy little fiancée was being introduced into London
society by her aunt Wilhelmina, the Dowager Duchess of
Millhaven? The lady who is now happily married to a
very rich American rancher who was the widower of a
Spanish heiress? Well, his name is Hamilton. And Viscount Harville is the heir of the current Duke of Millhaven. Now does it start to make sense to you? Why, my
poor sweet, your naive little bride-to-be comes to you
very well protected indeed—and not only by her uncle,
the reverend bishop. I think this is priceless. Isn't it,
Eddie? Just like an opera!''

Adriana's rich laugh cut into Ronald like broken glass,
and he stared at his tormentor with frustrated rage as his
head began to throb alarmingly.

He was being taunted—as usual—but that was Adriana's style. It was just that this afternoon, he felt he
couldn't stand it.

Celia was on her way; he had gotten word only that
morning from Lady Gertrude herself. So the fact she
might know Sir Thomas's protégé was not good news.

''Why don't you let me in on the joke? You actually
know these people you're talking about? And in that
case, I have a right to know, damn it!''

''Ronald! Don't swear at me in public—unless you
want me to punish you in public!'' Adriana murmured
suggestively, then ruffled his hair as if to take away the
sting of her words. ''Of course I know Grant Hamilton—
he's a womanizer *and* a very dangerous man. The dom-
ineering kind, I'm afraid. And if he is here because he is
interested in your little Celia's welfare, it can only be
because he's absolutely devoted to his stepmother.
Maybe he's even a little in love with her. Who knows?
But it is a well-known fact he would do anything for her.
So—I'm sure that your child-bride is as safe and as much
a virgin as you left her, my dear.''

As Adriana leaned back in her chair again, fanning

herself, a slyly sensual smile curving her lips, Ronald felt a stab of rage and jealousy knife through him.

How stupid he had been to confide in her about his hold on Celia. And after he had gone to great pains to keep his secrets and to make sure that Celia would never remember what she had experienced as a child.

After all, his father had known Marianna in every sense, so why should he not have known the daughter?

And anyway, if the damned barefoot brat she had been then had not been so curious and crept up to spy on him and Cora, nothing would have happened.

But as young as she had been then, she had *wanted* it. She had wanted *him*. Even then she would have done anything for him.

And she would again, once he had jogged her memory. Then he would have no trouble from her, or her puritanical uncle, or her rich and highborn relatives.

But if he did, there were always those damning photographs.

All he needed to do was manage to spend some time alone with his little fiancée when she arrived. He would take her for a walk down a little side street in Kandy. He had arranged so many years ago to have her forget, knowing always that he had the key to make her remember.

Suddenly he thought of Adriana and Celia together— Adriana teaching and instructing his naive little wife-to-be—and his cock began to harden.

Why not? Why the hell not?

And perhaps later they could bring Sujatha in to join them—and Eddie, of course. *That* should keep little Celia in line if she ever dared to protest or question anything he did.

Delightful thought.

Unfortunately, Sujatha had not been as understanding as he had hoped, even when he had gone to great pains to explain to her that this was all a matter of convenience and not feeling, his having to marry the little English girl so he could become the real owner of the estate he now managed.

"Once you are married," Sujatha had stormed, "I will take care of her for you! There are many poisonous snakes here—there are charms that can make her wither away, very slowly. She'll never give you any satisfaction in bed anyway, don't you know that? You have lived here too long to be satisfied with a cold, dutiful English wife! And you have lived here too long not to be aware of the power of a Kattadiya who can cast killing spells!"

His head was throbbing unmercifully now. Why must he be caught between three such disparate women, and why must he so desperately need the one he hated the most?

It was too much for any man, too much.

And Celia would be arriving any day now—it was too much pressure too soon.

He levered himself upright explosively.

"Where are you off to, Ronnie, darling?" Adriana queried lazily.

There were times, Ronald thought resentfully, when he could hate Adriana almost as much as he needed her, bitch that she was.

He didn't want to have to answer to her anyway; all he wanted right at this moment was to escape to the bungalow where he hoped Sujatha would be waiting for him with a pipe filled with the special smoke that always soothed his nerves and got rid of his headaches.

She would spread scented oil on those strong, supple hands of hers and she would massage the tension out of every muscle in his body, knowing how the firm, lean touch of her fingers aroused him and got him ready for her.

"Ronnie?" Adriana's voice—amused, insidious, despised. He did—he despised her—and she knew too much and she wouldn't hesitate to use it against him.

"Rest easy, Adriana; you'll have your fun. Celia and her relatives will be arriving any day now, and it would be in my best interests to make sure that Sujatha has moved out."

"She has been rather difficult," Adriana mused. "I'll talk to her if you think it will help. She'll listen to me—we've grown quite friendly. You will let us know if you need—well, any kind of assistance, won't you? Shall Eddie and I come with you to meet your little innocent, do you think?"

She smiled up at him, amused by the thought and his obvious discomfiture.

No wonder he hated her; no wonder. God, he needed Sujatha this evening—she would make him feel like a man and the master that he was.

And then Ceylon. Celia rose at dawn to be among those early risers who crowded the rail to get a first glimpse of the harbor at daybreak.

Nor was she surprised to find Uncle Theo nudging in beside her moments later, when the mists seemed to rise to obscure the mountains and bring into prominence the luxuriant greenery of the palm-fringed shore with its masses of foliage.

"The lost paradise of the Bible," he murmured, his voice tinged with awe, just as one of the ship's officers broke the spell by announcing the points of interest through a bullhorn.

There, on the extreme right, was the Mount Lavinia Hotel, seven miles south of the harbor. There, Galle Face esplanade—three hundred acres devoted to cricket, hockey, football and riding; there, on the starboard bow, to the south where the greensward ended, was the famous Galle Face Hotel, the ultimate in luxury. And, conveniently close to the hotel, in the oval-shaped building, the Colombo Club. And farther on, the towers and spires of the various Christian churches.

Home, Celia thought, a shiver of apprehension coursing down her spine. She was coming home—to nothing familiar at all—as a young woman, her father's heiress, and about to jilt the man to whom she had been promised for most of her life.

She grasped the rail tightly as the ship entered the harbor between the cradling arms of two massive breakwaters to a scene of bustling activity.

They were coming closer and closer, to her past and to her future, and the reflected light of the rising sun seemed to blind her vision as the P&O liner crept slowly toward its allotted berth, its foghorn blaring.

Celia felt a surge of panic when she and Theo were joined on deck by Aunt Gertrude and Anthea and her husband.

"The sun!" Gertrude moaned, shielding her eyes. "The heat! Theo, what *have* you done? Look at those . . . persons in those little boats—they're hardly wearing *anything*—what on earth are they doing? Dear Lord, I feel faint . . ."

"They are trading, my dear," Theo said calmly, handing her a lemon-water-soaked handkerchief.

"I just don't know how I'm going to take this," Gertrude muttered as she wiped her perspiring face with the handkerchief. "Nearly naked people selling baubles and junk to unsuspecting Englishmen . . . it simply numbs the mind. And this sun—it will fry my skin. Celia, I'm pleased to see you dressed sensibly at least. But where is your parasol? Anthea, dear, you are perfect as always. I do believe you have the right of it: white is the best color for this awful tropical heat."

"Oh, but it was Mr. Maitland's good common sense and uncommon knowledge of how things are here that directed my choice of clothes," Anthea murmured self-effacingly, all the while preening at Gertrude's compliment.

It made Celia nauseated, how they fed each other's pious superiority, but her reaction was partly compounded by the fact that she knew she would be facing Ronald in another couple of hours.

She had dressed the part too, and it had nothing to do with Aunt Gertrude's proprieties. She wore a dark serge skirt, high-buttoned, serviceable boots, a ruffled, high-necked blouse and a sola topee she had purchased on their one shore trip in Aden.

She knew she looked like a missionary herself—she *wanted* to look severe and old-maidish so that Ronald Winwood would be so discouraged by her appearance, he would not mind her crying off.

And Uncle Theo—of course he noticed nothing: his eyes were bright with all the new sights and sounds and the thought of all the souls he might save; he hardly seemed to mind the heat and the humidity or Aunt Gertrude's usual complaints.

The sound of a voice barking through the bullhorn to announce that they had docked at Colombo Harbor brought him out of his reverie.

"Now, did we label all of our luggage?" Aunt Gertrude asked briskly, shaking off her despair now that she had something definite to do. "Wasn't the Bishop of Colombo supposed to send someone to see us through customs and all the red tape? My dear, did you even write the letter?"

"Calm yourself," Uncle Theo said. "The bishop has arranged everything. His representative will be here, and he will escort us to Mutwal, where the bishop has arranged for us to stay at a house on the grounds of St. Thomas's College. Now, I've told you all this, and I don't understand why you think all our plans will go awry at the very last moment."

"No, I don't think you do understand," Aunt Gertrude muttered under her breath, while Anthea patted her arm in commiseration.

And then Emily, her piercing voice drowning out whatever else Gertrude wanted to say, embarrassing them all with her candid, naive questions.

"But, miss, how do you tell the men from the wimmen? Is it from those funny combs they wear in their 'air? An' all those others in the funny costumes—is that 'ow they all dress in this part of the world?"

"Come, everyone," Aunt Gertrude said loudly above the deathly silence that greeted these artless questions. "The bishop's man has not arrived and we are next through customs."

Celia followed slowly behind, her emotions in a turmoil. She was home, she thought yet again, but she was home among strangers. Everything looked as odd to her as it did to Emily. Maybe more so.

She had never felt so torn between her two worlds.

And yet she could appreciate the ceremony of going through customs and watching her uncle being greeted respectfully, like the visiting dignitary that he was.

It was even a sop to Aunt Gertrude to be treated so deferentially and to be escorted with so much ceremony to the Grand Oriental Hotel, where they could rest from the long journey, take tea and await the bishop's representative.

The hotel was situated facing the harbor, and the charming Palm Court provided a welcome respite for the tired travelers.

And it was well up to Aunt Gertrude's standards.

She imperiously ordered an English tea, complete with little savory sandwiches cut into tiny triangles, asparagus rolls, scones and petits fours—then pronounced herself astonished that such a complete menu could be provided in such primitive surroundings.

The well-trained Sinhalese waiters, all clad in white with red sashes embroidered with the hotel insignia GOH, served them silently, unobtrusively and with the utmost respect—in spite of Aunt Gertrude's constant demands and fault-finding.

"Well," she said at last when they had finished, "I will say it was surprisingly tolerable."

"You wouldn't think that such an out-of-the-way place would have electricity and fans," Anthea added in a tone of voice calculated to disparage the fact that indeed the hotel did.

You would think she would rather suffer, Celia thought uncharitably; but, of course, that was the nature of her aunt and her protégée—they reveled in the negative, the improper, the anguish of others, and she was wasting more time thinking about them than they warranted.

It was her uncle's distress she should be attending to, because the bishop's representative had not appeared and he was feeling the heat of Aunt Gertrude's disapproval, even though barely two hours had passed since they had finished with customs and settled in for tea.

"Well," Aunt Gertrude said, "I could have predicted this."

"My dear," Uncle Theo protested just as one of the waiters entered the room, paused so that Uncle Theo could see him and acknowledge him, then approached the group with a silver salver in hand. He presented this to Uncle Theo, and waited for him to read the handwritten note which was on it, and to give him direction.

"Well, my dear!" Uncle Theo exclaimed, his voice mildly tinged with triumph—which Aunt Gertrude totally ignored.

Or missed, Celia thought, wiping her lips with her napkin and awaiting his pronouncement; obviously their escort had arrived and all would proceed now as expeditiously as possible.

"Mr. Winwood is here—both to meet our dear Celia and, at the bishop's behest, to escort us to Mutwal."

Celia froze, and her uncle went on with every evidence of delight and as if he were the one who had deliberately arranged it: "Now, what could be better than to continue on our journey with someone we know?"

She wasn't ready, she just wasn't ready, and she wondered as she waited, suspended in that one moment before Ronald Winwood would appear at the door—she wondered how she had thought she would ever be ready when nothing was the way she remembered it—and she was not the same.

But then, Ronald was not the way she remembered him either.

He paused at the entrance to the tearoom, a handsome, awkward stranger. Nothing at all like the dashing young man in the framed photograph she had kept on the table beside her bed.

Nothing like the gallant who had walked beside her in the rose garden and asked her to marry him someday when she was ready—and had begged her to wait for him.

The golden knight of her girlish dreams—her Ronald.

And here he was before her in the present, perspiring in his white drill suit as he held out a bouquet and his hand to . . . Aunt Gertrude!

Celia felt numb and detached as he greeted her aunt, her uncle, and then finally came to stand before her.

"My darling Celia . . ."

She sat rooted, unable to move.

Behind her, she heard Aunt Gertrude. "Well, Celia,

aren't you going to greet your fiancé? After all this time, nothing to say?''

She wet her lips. "Ronald."

He followed the motion of her mouth avidly. "How very English you look. And how very proper you are today."

"Celia! Give him your hand!"

She couldn't move; she was rooted to the spot, overcome with inexplicable feelings of aversion.

"You must excuse her." Aunt Gertrude leapt into the silence. "She was up so early to watch the entrance to the harbor. Although why anyone would want to stare at a bunch of naked natives, I will never understand."

"Of course," Ronald said smoothly, bowing to Gertrude's superior wisdom; Gertrude was his ally. Gertrude would not let his panicked little bird of prey escape. "Of course you're tired. It's such a disgustingly long journey, anyone would be faint with fatigue by now."

He turned to look at all of them. "The first order of business is to extend your invitation to the reception at the Queen's House this evening."

He paused for effect, noticing the calculated pleasure in Gertrude's eyes.

"A very proper welcome indeed," she murmured.

"And I have arranged for a suite in the hotel where you may rest and bathe and have the time to get ready for this evening's festivities. Tomorrow, I will have the pleasure of escorting you to Mutwal, and . . .''

His eyes lit on Emily, who was sitting slightly apart. Wasn't she fetching with her trim little figure, sparkling eyes and elfin, heart-shaped face—quite a pretty picture that offered up tantalizing possibilities next to his fiancée's drab passivity.

Obviously Celia's much vaunted Season in London had proved fruitless; she was the same—buttoned up and colorless, waiting for her master to control her.

He would marry her, and he would have her—for duty's sake—and then he would bring Emily into the fold: mistress and maid . . . a most delectable thought.

He brought his attention forcibly back to the company at hand as Gertrude finally finished fussing with her hat and gloves.

". . . I will leave the details about that until morning."

He looked pointedly at Celia. "Celia?"

She looked up at him, startled like a frightened doe. He liked that. He liked it a lot that he still had the power to frighten her.

"There is time—there is plenty of time, my darling," he said solicitously. "Another day only enhances the anticipation. Take your time. Rest. And then we will talk."

❧ Twenty-six

Celia dropped wearily onto the bed in the luxurious room that had been assigned to her.

She just did not know what was the matter with her. She had longed so much to return home and now that she was there, the reality did not seem to live up to the anticipation.

And Ronald—dear God, Ronald!

Nothing like she remembered him—something about him so slick and forceful and just a little dissolute—how was she going to tell this man, this *stranger*, she could not marry him?

She wandered restlessly to the window and opened it. The sickly-sweet perfume of incense drifted into the room and made her feel stranger still, as if she were about to float outside this rigidly controlled self she had presented to Ronald Winwood and into another, darker self she did not want to face.

As if she were on the verge of remembering something she ought not and must not remember . . . because otherwise she would be hurt and in pain, and frightened . . .

Of what?

She could not shake her feeling of dislocation; it was

as if when she stepped on shore, everything that was vague and threatening had gathered with some kind of supernatural force to frighten her.

What was the matter with her?

It could only be that she was tired and she needed to lie down; the trip had been emotionally exhausting, between Aunt Gertrude's strictures and her own anxiety over Ronald's reaction to her return and her telling him she could not marry him.

And she surely was not over the shock of seeing him sooner than she had anticipated. How had he turned up so conveniently?

When she was feeling less fraught, when she had rested, then she would assess the situation and her feeling that something wasn't right.

All she had to do now was relax; she had a real bed now, and Emily had come at her summons to rub cologne into her temples to soothe her.

As she drifted off, she could hear the ceaseless rising and falling of the sea below her windows, the sound pierced by the night sounds of the crickets and the tree frogs outside.

She had come back—at last—to the illusory beauty of a tropical night, with its blazing stars and a moon that rose like an enormous silver globe from behind the midnight-blue mountains, or out of the phosphorescent waters of a lagoon or river . . .

Larger than life; everything seemed larger than real life here . . .

Hovering between dreams and sleep, she was aware of Emily turning the lampwick down, of her soft footsteps retreating, of the faint click of the door closing, of the cry of an owl, of a faint whistle someplace in her mind, a hissing sound, as if there were a serpent in this Garden of Eden—

She jolted awake suddenly, her braided hair swinging

heavily over one shoulder as she shook her head to clear it.

She had heard something, felt something; something had roused her from that blissful oblivion where, for once, there had been no foreboding nightmares.

She thrust her bare feet into slippers and threw a flimsy cotton-and-lace wrapper over her severe batiste night-gown, and then she pushed open the windows and the heavy shutters to follow the lure of the serpent and the haunting hoot of the owl.

Like a sleepwalker, she maneuvered her way through the darkness of the coconut trees that fringed the narrow stretch of beach licked by wavelets that rose and fell with the tide.

Something pulled her—as if she already knew deep inside herself whom she would find waiting for her under the moon.

The serpent—the devil-owl—he was either the devil himself or her nemesis, and she had never had a choice: she knew it with all the fatalism of her Gypsy instinct. He had called to her and she had to go, and she had to find whatever it was she was meant to discover, because whatever happened tonight was meant to happen . . . meant to be.

He had called to her . . . by his mere presence, she had sensed him waiting, holding back, watching, waiting, wanting—

He hadn't just walked away indifferently.

He was here, in Ceylon, because of her—

As she ran into the moon-drenched night to meet her fate, that secret thought kept humming through her veins and beating in her heart—

Because of her . . .

Her thin wrapper caught in the branches of a thorny shrub and she shrugged out of it; her slippers impeded her headlong flight toward her destiny, so she kicked

them off and ran barefoot out of the shadows of the coconut grove and onto the sands bleached silvery white
by the moon.

He caught her hand impatiently with his work-callused
fingers and pulled her into the moonlight where he could
see her. Her lips parted as she gasped for breath; he had
come when she least expected him, and he looked so
different, with his tropical clothes and weeks' worth of
grizzled beard, and yet so terrifyingly, endearingly the
same.

The moment was magical: the two of them, the
moon, her mystical response to something beyond herself that she could never explain, the sound of the
breeze ruffling the swaying, long-leafed branches of the
coconut trees, the soughing sound of the sea behind
them—they could have been castaways on some de-
serted island, Adam and Eve before the serpent and the
forbidden apple.

Only nothing would be forbidden tonight.

He pulled her against his half-naked body with a
muttered expletive and kissed that Gypsy mouth of hers
before she could protest and thrust his fingers through
that thick, decorous braid that was meant to come undone.

And he damned himself for pushing aside all caution
and every sensibility; he could not keep away—and here,
in the sultry heat of her native country, he could not stop
himself from taking what he wanted as well.

"Gypsy wench," he growled. "Witch . . . don't you
know any better—" He broke off and slanted his mouth
over hers again.

Dear God, she was wearing nothing under that thin
nightgown, and under a *Poya* moon—so bright that her
dark, pointed nipples and the shadowy triangle of hair
between her sleek thighs showed clearly through the
damp, clinging garment.

And she was responding to his kisses like the wild and wanton creature she was, her thick dark hair whipping against his face, her soft breasts and hard nipples pressing tightly against his bare skin.

Oh, Christ! Was she the Gypsy or the lady—which of them was responding to the unbearable swelling ache in his groin? Where was the fine line between pure animal lust and morality?

Why in hell did he suddenly find all lines blurred and disappearing as she writhed against his hardness as if she recognized it for what it was and responded to his hands cupping her taut buttocks to draw her even more tightly against him?

How did she know just which way to move to give him purchase to reach beneath her flimsy nightgown so that he could feel her heated flesh against his nakedness?

She pulled away from his kiss—a breath away. "You're here," she whispered, and it was like a benediction; she could not have lived if he had not come, she knew it; she didn't know what it meant, only that fate had intervened and given her what she most wanted, even if he was resisting it as ferociously as he wanted it.

"Duty—" His mouth settled on hers again, and she gave herself up to the lush exploration of his kiss. "Responsibility—"

He was taunting her, with his words and with his kisses, and she didn't care.

"Teach me," she whispered. "Show me."

He felt as if someone had pummeled the very air out of his lungs.

"You know—"

She was kneading the corded muscles of his arms. "I want . . . ." The words caught in her throat; his skin was hot, pliant, melting against her hands—he couldn't help himself either; he wanted as well—

It was written in the moon . . . tonight . . .

He felt himself giving; her hands left a trail of shimmering sensations against his skin; he had waited all his life for her touch, and now . . .

And now—what of the consequences? He had to think of the consequences. Always the consequences when you were dealing with a Gypsy witch.

Hadn't he been told—*watch your step, do what you must, follow your instincts?* He hadn't forgotten Alzena's prophecy for a moment, and it had all come true.

Except that he was supposed to protect Celia, not seduce her.

And the one thing Alzena hadn't predicted was his molten need and desire for her, or that, because of it, he would follow her halfway around the goddamned world to have her offer herself to him at the very moment he absolutely had to refuse her.

And if he kissed her one more time, it might be the very last.

He groaned and lifted her against him once again.

The very last . . .

His kiss was savage, full of his repressed fury and yearning, and she met it with a need that was every bit as ferocious as his.

He was a breath away from taking her and damning the consequences—one moment, as his hands explored her lush nakedness, as she opened herself willingly to him, encouraging him with the wanton movement of her body and the wild, hot sounds in the back of her throat.

Damn them all—damn them all . . .

He pushed his fingers against her and into her velvet fold. He heard her telling gasp, he felt her body stiffen in opposition to the erotic thrust of them.

And then she settled down tightly against them and began to undulate her hips, and he felt the urgency in her, and in himself, as he took her mouth in a raw and brutal kiss.

This was not meant to be, this was not meant to be— and yet she wanted it as much as he, even more, as she began feeling the pulsating pleasure of his touch and the urgency of her culmination.

Dear God, Celia . . . He groaned as she suddenly and explosively reached her climax, moaning in cadence with the wave of sensation that engulfed her.

Damn, damn, damn and damn . . .

"Ceee-eeelia-a-a-a . . . Ce-e-e-eli-i-i-a-a-a-a . . ."

Suddenly there were voices—and torches moving among the trees.

Grant wrenched his mouth away from hers. "Jesus— Gertrude?"

Celia felt bereft; the magic dissipated instantly, like a plume of smoke. "Didn't you know?"

"No," he said tightly. This was a new wrinkle; Gertrude was determined—and therefore dangerous, more so than she had ever been.

"Get your wrap."

"Grant—"

"I can't—I won't—damn it, Celia!"

"I see," she said coldly. "Just the moon and the flower-scented night, and you got carried away."

"Something like that," he muttered, feeling around for her wrapper as the voices and the lights grew closer and closer.

"And you're going to leave me to deal with them, aren't you?" she concluded numbly. *Fate—Gypsy destiny—*

Stupid nonsense, and she was a gullible fool.

He found her wrapper, a hundred yards away, a minute in advance of the lights. "Take it."

He thrust it at her and melted into the shadows.

She held it tightly to her breast as the lights flared closer still, and finally she slipped it around her shivering body as Gertrude heaved into view.

"For heaven's sake, Celia—!"

That set her hackles up—and her fury at Grant Hamilton's rejection. Why should she back down?

"Aunt Gertrude?"

"It didn't take you an hour to go native, but what could I expect, after all?"

"I'm not sure, Aunt Gertrude, since it is Uncle Theo who is supposed to be my chaperon."

"Yes, and furious he will be as well that you're out on the beach wearing next to nothing—and with the reception only an hour away and your bath having been drawn by Emily and by now cold. Intractable as ever, Celia—but look at how and where you were raised."

She paused as Anthea and George Maitland joined her, holding their torches up high so they could fully see Celia's folly.

Anthea turned white. "George—I can't—"

George immediately led her away.

"And not an instant of remorse. If that isn't just like your mother," Gertrude said in a tone meant to be disapproving but was rife with satisfaction, as though this was something she had always known and now she was proven right and no one could ever disprove her again. "Raised a pagan, always a pagan. You thank your God that Mr. Winwood did not accompany us after Emily raised the alarm. If he ever saw you like this, there would be no betrothal and no marriage, and your godless soul would be lost forever."

Oh, I am damned forever already, Celia thought mordantly as Uncle Theo lumbered into the light.

"Oh, my dear." He sighed heavily. "I don't suppose you realized you might not have been safe out here by yourself with all those natives lurking about . . .'' He offered her the comfort of his arm as he turned her back toward the hotel, and threw a warning glance over his shoulder at the speechless Gertrude.

''Although I'm sure none of them would have dared molest a white woman. But still, it was most unwise of you, dear Celia, and you must promise me that next time you come out for a walk''—his voice trailed off as Gertrude stood rooted to the spot, and Celia resisted the temptation to laugh at Uncle Theo's calm acceptance at finding her nearly naked on the beach—''you will take Emily and make sure you are more suitably dressed.''

''I promise,'' she said solemnly.

''Well, good. Now we can all enjoy ourselves at the reception.''

Except she didn't want to go to any receptions; she didn't want to go anywhere or see anyone.

She felt mortified by Grant's cavalier dismissal of her. She felt numb. And betrayed.

Gypsy prophecy . . . fate . . . destiny . . . utter poppycock . . . how could she ever have believed—how could she ever have put her trust in something so intangible and then offered her most precious gift to a man who did not want her?

The reality of what had happened was stunning; in the heat of the moment, it had seemed as if destiny called.

And now she felt hot with the humiliation of it.

And what was left for someone such as she? Just what Aunt Gertrude had always told her: a man willing to marry her in spite of her history—as opposed to a man who led her on, denied her and never talked of marriage at all.

Perhaps this was her destiny—to travel this long and winding road to the place where she understood that

for all her success and all of her pride, she must still
humble herself to accept that which was offered by the
one who was staunch and loyal and had waited all
these years.

She had come back to Ceylon not to take control but
to submit to some force outside herself.

And so therefore she must forget Grant Hamilton and
give Ronald every chance—*every chance*—to know the
woman she had become, as she must come to know the
man he really was.

With cold hands and a hard heart—and Emily's sym-
pathetic help—Celia began dressing for the evening.

She was late, of course, after her excursion into the
coconut fronds and the near forbidden, and Gertrude,
who couldn't bear waiting, came to make sure she didn't
cry off altogether.

"Your dear fiancé . . . how can you keep treating him
like a stranger?"

Prescient Aunt Gertrude, she thought. "He is a
stranger."

"Oh, nonsense, he can't have changed that much."

"No, he hasn't," Celia murmured, holding up dresses
and waving off Emily's attempts to fuss with her hair. *I
have.*

But she didn't say it. She would go—she had no
choice—and she would give Ronald every chance—
every chance indeed—because there was nothing else.

When she came down to join the others, she was
dressed as decorously as possible in a plain promenade
gown of brown silk with a high neck and bishop sleeves;
it was draped with a collar of ecru lace and enhanced
with a pretty gold brooch at her throat.

She wore her hair twisted into a severe topknot and
unadorned by any decoration or a hat.

She looked slender and fragile and submissive with her
downcast eyes and her subdued demeanor, and not even

Aunt Gertrude could complain about her appearance, which was just how Celia had planned it.

And she clamped down on every thought of Grant Hamilton and the freedom she had felt in his arms.

There were carriages lined up outside the hotel to transport them to the Queen's House; she could not prevent their escorts from seating her next to Aunt Gertrude, who was primly dressed in purple with black lace.

"Well, my dear, at least now you look reputable and not like some native servant on her way to an assignation."

"So do you, Aunt Gertrude," Celia murmured, fighting against her feelings of antagonism. Gertrude's spiteful comments could not matter, should not matter.

Anthea's antipathy was something else; Anthea had been shocked to the core, and it was as if she could not get the picture of Celia out of her mind. She would not look at Celia, preferring to stare out of the carriage window and ignore everyone, including her husband.

The Queen's House was beautiful and large, built in the Colonial style, surrounded by fences and columns and lit up like a Christmas tree. The carriages bowled up the circular driveway to the marble steps, where servants efficiently greeted the guests, helped them out and led them up the steps and into the reception hallway to be announced.

The social elite of Colombo was out in force, dressed to the hilt and dripping with jewels, and as they entered the reception room, Celia could see that, by contrast, she and her party looked like someone's poor relations.

Nevertheless, Gertrude sailed in as if she were the queen, and Uncle Theo meekly followed in her wake.

After their introduction to the governors and officials of the district, Celia began to relax. There was no sign of Ronald, just a sea of smiling faces and the offer of cordial hospitality with no thought at all to appearances.

Yes—this was the way she remembered things had been. Just like this, warm, open, accepting—an atmosphere that had nourished her mother and her younger self.

Of course, her butterfly mother had been content to settle here with her father. These were her people; she felt the sense of their love suffuse her body.

"Ah, there you are, Celia."

She froze. Gertrude. That hated voice, that snide disapproval, as if she were the arbiter of morals even this far away from England.

"My dear, mingling with the officials is quite proper, but going unchaperoned amongst the guests is just . . . well, it just isn't done. Luckily, your fiancé is here to save you from any further faux pas. I know you've been so anxious to see him."

Celia turned slowly, oh so slowly, to face Ronald Winwood's self-satisfied, knowing look.

"Celia."

"Ronald."

She stood as still as a statue, not even offering him her hand. *There was no one else—no one; Ronald is my fate, my destiny.*

"Of course," Gertrude went on, oblivious of the undercurrents, "you two have so much to talk about, although this really isn't the place. But still, here is Celia all grown up, and splendidly too, I think."

And how her aunt could mouth that blatant lie, Celia could not even guess. She wondered if Gertrude would take penance to expiate that little sin.

"You've done an excellent job," Ronald said smoothly. He held out his hand. "Celia?"

"Yes, Ronald?"

"Are you not glad to see me?"

Twenty-seven

She was beautiful! How could Ronald not love her the best? She had just bathed in the stream that ran by her brother's little house, and the bathing cloth—the *diya-redde* of white cotton that she wore for modesty's sake—clung wetly to her body, emphasizing every curve and hollow.

Ronald loved her body—he had told her over and over how he delighted in it and how he could not live without her.

And surely that was true. Nevertheless, she had made certain of it with all her visits to the Kattadiya, paying handsomely for the charms and potions he had given her to bind this Englishman she loved closer and closer to her.

Sujatha studied her image in the mirror that Ronald had given her, and what she saw pleased her. She was fair-complexioned, even for a Kandyan woman—her skin was golden-tinted, complementing her long, silky black hair and light brown eyes.

No Englishwoman could compete with her! They were all so very ugly. And this one would surely be no different. She would be afraid of snakes and centipedes and

even large moths and beetles. Her milky-white face
would turn a mottled red under the sun, and her Euro-
pean-style clothes, so unsuited to this hot climate, would
soon give her prickly heat.

No, she wouldn't want to stay here, even if she lived
long enough for Ronald to go through a formal marriage
ceremony with her.

One way or another, the silly creature would be
gone—and Ronald would be hers again.

The devil-doctor, the Kattadiya, had sworn it, and Sujatha believed him.

However, an incident with the Gypsies—the *ahikun-
takayo*—had left her feeling somewhat uneasy, and she
could not shake off her sense of disquiet.

She had gone to an old Gypsy crone to have her cards
read, just to be certain the stars were in their right aspect
and that Ronald would be hers in the end, and she had
taken a copy of her horoscope, which had been cast at
the time of her birth.

To her dismay, the crone had recast both her horoscope and Ronald's, and then she had gone into a trance
and begun speaking in a dark, snarling voice, like a soul
in torment, that made Sujatha's flesh crawl with fear and
the hairs rise on the back of her neck.

"Be careful, pretty one. It is you who must be careful—you, and your brother. The young Englishwoman is
no threat, I tell you. There is another one, a dark, powerful one protecting her, and she belongs to him, not to
the man you crave. But it is your Englishman who is the
danger, you must be careful, child! The man you say you
love could turn suddenly mad; there is something in him
growing, a poisoned fruit, fed by the *ganja* pipe and a
secret—a terrible, ugly secret—and he could strike like
the *mahasona* himself who stalks in the night in the shape
of a black dog. But you—you must not try to find out

about this secret, or he could kill you too. That is all . . . that is all.''

And what had been even more frightening for Sujatha was that afterward the old woman had remembered nothing of what she had said, whereas Sujatha could not forget it.

She started shivering with a coldness that came from deep within her. She had to get dried off and comb out her hair, and then she would go to the temple and make a *puja* to ward away all evil spirits and thoughts.

Ronald had not yet sent word when he would be arriving, but he had to come soon; the workers were not producing nearly as well for her poor brother as they did for the Periya Dorai who carried a horsewhip and was not slow to use it.

They were afraid of Ronald, and they worked harder because of it.

And that was good—wasn't it?

''You're a fool, Ronnie—a fool!'' Adriana said contemptuously as she watched Ronald slump into a bedroom chair, his eyes bloodshot and his body jittery with need.

''Your little fiancée has arrived and what do you do on her first night here? Instead of invading her bedroom and claiming her, you seek refuge in your pipe and your cocaine. Be careful, my pet, that the drugs do not master you in time.''

Nevertheless, she herself had given him a dose of opium elixir to calm him down. He had a headache that was driving him mad, he had said, but it was more likely he would wake the servants with his incoherent ravings.

He was becoming more and more difficult to control; this night was proof. Who else but a lunatic would come crashing through her bedroom window and expect her to respond with equanimity? And on top of that, he had interrupted her as she was plotting how to arrange a meeting with his stupid little fiancée.

Especially since she had tactfully stayed in the background at the Queen's House reception instead of making trouble while Ronald romanced his English heiress. But obviously nothing had been settled, and she had barely caught a glimpse of the creature's drab dress and tightly knotted black hair.

Ronnie had never even thanked her for her discretion.

But the things Ronnie had told her—the photographs he had shown her of a young, unformed child with the dazed look of innocence even while she posed naked or garlanded with flowers—had struck a chord in her that Adriana did not even know existed.

The child in those photographs reminded her painfully of herself at that age, full of curiosity and so much in love with her handsome, tall papa.

And what had the child in those pictures felt? How had the child in those pictures grown up, and into what kind of young woman?

Ronnie had said Celia would never remember; he had taken her to a caster of spells, a very famous Kattadiya, and the old man had assured him the child would never remember—unless there were some countercharm or some shock to her system.

Ronnie was convinced that so far, Celia remembered nothing of the past, but how could Adriana trust his judgment anymore?

And, of course, there was Grant Hamilton to be taken into consideration.

And now this—Ronald practically unconscious on her chaise longue!

The situation required a letter to her husband, written in Italian—just as a precautionary measure, since neither Ronald nor anyone else she knew was fluent in that language—telling him that she would be staying on for a while in Colombo, renewing old acquaintances. Ronald would probably take the night train to Bandarawela as soon as he was in condition to do so; after all, he needed to get everything in order before his fiancée arrived to inspect her tea estate. And if he didn't realize where his duty lay, Adriana would remind him of it.

There was too much at stake for her to be at the mercy of his mercurial temperament.

So now Celia felt trapped; she should not have come back to Ceylon. The sights, the smells, her strange, uneasy feelings and her precipitate agreement to marry Ronald made her days and nights tense and troubled.

And when she managed to suppress the memory of her night of folly with Grant, she could not hold back the dreams, the nightmares which made her dread going to sleep. There was a dark-shadowed, forbidden place somewhere in her mind and she lived in fear that her strange dreams would lead her there.

So Emily now slept by her bed, with strict instructions to awaken her if she began to toss and turn or call out in her sleep.

During the day it was much easier. She could keep busy with riding, sightseeing or expeditions along the river and she did not have to torture herself with questions about Ronald.

Since they were spending some time in Colombo, she thankfully could put off her decision about a wedding date a while longer.

Which didn't mean Aunt Gertrude didn't push the issue.

"Look at this lovely material. You could have it made up into day dresses. You'll want to look lovely for Ronald any time of the day. I mean, surely you didn't think you would run around in those—sheets—these people wear once you are married. I'm sure Wilhelmina taught you better than that—certainly I did.

"Of course, we'll need time to plan things, and dear Ronald is sooo anxious; come—take some time and let us discuss your dress and whom we should invite . . . although the guest list can't be too long. You know no one and Ronald's acquaintances number only those who belong to the country club . . ."

In another lifetime, Celia might have looked forward to all the preparations. She had loved Ronald. She had *worshipped* him. And the day he had begged her to marry him, she had thought all her dreams had come true.

And now those dreams were tarnished; he was no golden knight—his hair was thinning and not nearly as golden as she remembered it; and he had become a petulant, rather pompous Englishman who was spoiled by the good life in the tropics.

Her hope, her destiny.

"You should be thankful," Aunt Gertrude said again, and Celia utterly lost the thread of the conversation. "Such a decent man . . . even knowing your history . . ."

She was thankful for nothing except the moments when she could escape her dreams and her awful feeling of doom.

They drove out in a hired carriage to the Mount Lavinia Hotel, which was situated on a tall bluff overlooking the sea and the most glorious stretch of yellow sand.

Tiffin, the midday meal, had been prawn curry with yellow rice and an assortment of condiments, some sweet and some spicy-hot enough to burn an unaccustomed palate.

Anthea, with unusual tact even as she made a face, declared that she simply loved this kind of food—and Celia suddenly had a flash of memory that completely disoriented her.

She had been a child, and she had enjoyed squatting

down in the kitchen with the servants, eating curry that
was much hotter than this off a plate with her fingers like
they did . . .

And sometimes she would look across at Cora and
they would giggle together until the cook told them to
stop that silliness.

The memory was like a jab of pain. Cora? Who was
Cora? And why haven't I thought of her in all these years
if she was my friend?

And why did I remember her now?

She turned impulsively to Ronald, who was seated beside her. "Ronald, do you remember? Who was Cora?"

She watched him closely. Was there a startled, almost
frightened look in his eyes for a moment before he
shrugged, touched his mustache deprecatingly and gave
a smile to the others at the table? Then he looked back
at her to say in an amused, I'll-humor-you tone of voice:
"Cora? Oh, yes—I do believe that was the name of your
ayah when you were little. Not that I remember what she
looked like or anything like that. But I think I remember
the name. Unusual for a Sinhalese. Or was she Eur-
asian?"

His voice lowered. "Do you recall?"

She felt out of step with him: she had barely heard a
word he said. She had watched Anthea taste the curry,
had eaten some herself, and suddenly she had felt ten
years old and as if she had been whisked back in time.

The curry . . . the curry had reminded her of Cora.

She shook her head. "No, that's all I remember. It
was the curry—" She stopped, wondering if she should
even reveal that much with Anthea looking on avidly,
just waiting for some gaffe to lecture her about, and Aunt
Gertrude sniffing her usual disapproval, and Ronald's expression guarded and somewhat uneasy.

But she couldn't tell if that was because she had

brought up something unmentionable or because the others were beginning to think she was crazy.

Even Uncle Theo looked a little uncertain.

"My ayah," she said hesitantly, trying desperately to dredge up more from her memory; she couldn't even remember that much . . . just the curry and sitting with the servants.

And the sense that there was something more. "Do you know what happened to her? Could you find out? You're going back to the estate tomorrow, aren't you?"

"Well, yes, although I am loath to leave you. But duty calls. Those coolies need to be kept on their toes to maintain production. And certainly I'll try to find out about your old ayah by the time you come up—how's that?"

He smiled at her benignly and she answered with some hesitancy. Oh, there was a willful streak in his little Celia that would have to be taken care of immediately. He couldn't wait to get her away from her entourage when she finally arrived at the plantation.

The thought aroused him to a point where he was most uncomfortable, but his fantasy gave him great pleasure as he sipped his wine and consumed his dessert and pretended the little bitch hadn't disconcerted the hell out of him.

He would get her alone and finally, after all these years, he would have her at his mercy.

And then—oh, then he would have the pleasure of jogging her memory and subjugating her to his forbidden desires once again.

Adriana always knew, or thought she knew, what she was doing. She had always been different and the subject of gossip. She had also always enjoyed a challenge—she loved seeing how far she could go without getting caught.

And she hated being bored.

Ronnie was beginning to bore her; his sulkiness was

becoming a nuisance, a matter she had easily taken care
of before he'd left, just to teach him some discipline and
self-control.

But lately he had needed a lot of lessons, and lately
she was getting very tired of weak and fawning men.

Or were her thoughts turning in that direction because
she had been out riding more since her stay in Colombo
and she was beginning to fantasize about the European
beachcombers who were the scandal of the city?

They lived among the natives, ate their hot curries and
rice with their fingers, and some of them, moreover, were
shameless enough to wear only a sarong, just as if they
had been Sinhalese themselves—baring their muscular,
tanned torsos and giving a tantalizing glimpse of what
might possibly lie under the tucked-up material.

And, of course, she paid no attention to their low whis-
tles, nor to their comments on her looks or their opinions
about what she might be like to bed down—even if she
could understand the one who had spoken Italian.

Such insolence!

Except that such raw insolence excited her too in some
secret way.

And she knew something that no one else knew: the
newcomer, Grant Hamilton, secretly paraded among
them, and it was he she watched the most when she
looked them over as she rode past.

He was something else altogether; he was strong—
even stronger than she was—and she was not used to
encountering that kind of easy dominance in any man.

She was intrigued, as much by this seemingly secret
life as by her fascination with him, and she wondered
whether there was a hidden part of her nature that desired
to be taken over and dominated by a man like that.

It was a most delicious reverie now that Ronald was
gone; she had seen him off at the station just last night
and had felt an inordinate sense of relief.

Now there was no one with whom she had to share her secrets, her passion or her fantasies.

And she could ruminate on all the possibilities of a man like Grant Hamilton to her heart's content.

She felt the excitement as she lay in her bed late at night, naked, with only her imagination for a lover.

A one like this Hamilton—pretending to be something he was not. There was a mystery here, and one that she would solve—while she was exploring the intricacies of making him bend to her will.

She was so lost in this delectable scenario two nights later that she was hardly conscious of the fact that some-one had entered her room once again, and much more subtly than had Ronald.

An invader . . . she wasn't afraid, even when her con-queror leaned over her prone body and spoke to her in Italian; she felt a shiver of anticipation—the naked beachcomber—and she stopped struggling.

She could see him dimly in the light of the waning moon outside; he was tall and muscular and he held her body pinned to the bed and he was going to take her forcibly.

What a delicious idea!

But then she could hardly believe what he was doing: he was tying her to the bedposts, spread-eagled, with her wrists pinioned up above her head and her legs anchored with coir rope that instantly irritated the delicate skin of her ankles and irritated her irrationally.

She was the one who was used to being in control; and now, as if in answer to her fantasies, on this humid night in the forbidden hours between darkness and dawn, she was suddenly bound and helpless and con-trolled by this wild, savage creature who had appeared out of nowhere in order to ravage her, to take her, to master her . . . yes!

"If you scream, I'll gag you. But then I will have the

pleasure of hearing your moans behind that gag, and you won't look nearly as pretty either with a piece of cloth between those luscious lips of yours."

"No!" she whispered hoarsely, already excited almost beyond measure. "I won't scream, I promise. You didn't have to tie me up; I would have given you what you want willingly. You are quite magnificent, do you know that? I would love to wrap my arms and legs around you and give you as much pleasure as this daring act of yours deserves."

"Hmmm—like a little dagger in the back? No, I'd rather have you this way so I can play with your body that you use to such advantage when it pleases you. Well, now it will please me, and while I take what I want, you, cara mia, will answer all my questions, and in very precise detail, sì? Do we begin to understand each other?"

Dio, she hated him—and she desired him.

"Whatever you want—tell me, do me—"

But he did nothing except deliberately tantalize and tease her body until she was ready to kill him.

And he said nothing; after each torrid caress, after each stinging slap, he waited, watching her body squirming to reach the ultimate moment of release that he so skillfully denied her.

"Whatever you want," she whimpered, writhing in self-disgust. But wasn't this what she had demanded of all her men-slaves? Oh, God! "Tell me what you want—" Let him take anything he wanted, let him do anything he wished with her body—she would love every minute of the whole degrading experience.

And still—he used her willfully and tormentingly, almost without conscience, refusing and resisting her willing surrender until she was sweat-soaked and exhausted by the strength of the passions he had aroused in her and crying out for him to bring her to culmination.

"You beg me, do you?" he growled, pulling her

hair so that he could look directly into her eyes and her hellish soul. "Well, now, *principessa mia,* perhaps we will be able to strike a bargain. You will tell me everything you know about your little friend Ronald Winwood—past and present—*and* everything he has told you about Celia Penmaris and her mother, and then I will think about letting you have your pleasure. And if I were you," he added suddenly in English, "I wouldn't think of holding anything back. It might make me very angry."

She recognized the voice; she knew the man—perhaps subconsciously she had known from the moment he had forced his way into the room, in spite of his shaggy hair, bared bronzed torso and raffish beard—but in that moment, as he held her hair tightly and stared into her eyes and made his demands, she began for the first time to fear him.

And so she told him everything she knew. She was pragmatic to a fault, and she would always support the winning side when or if she could get a toehold.

Ronnie was so damned weak, it was pititful. It was the chit who was the unknown quantity; the child who had posed all too innocently for those photographs that Ronald had shown her was now the same young woman who was the heiress to the estate Ronald had for so long considered almost his own.

And now Grant Hamilton—ruthless son of a bitch that he was—had entered the picture, and was perfectly willing to seduce *her* in order to—what? What was his *real* interest in the creature? Could it be . . . ah, could it possibly be that the bastard was really interested in the child?

What a quaint idea that was, and how full of possibilities . . . none of which occurred to her until that lousebastard had gotten what he wanted—and it was not the pleasure of her orgasm; the son of a bitch had left her hanging there, and sent her servant up to untie her, and she thought she would spit cowrie shells, she was in such a fury.

No man had ever overpowered her and then left her high and dry, and Mr. Grant Hamilton had much to answer for; and so did that Gypsy brat of a Gypsy dam, as Ronald had described her.

But she could wait—she had always been good at that, waiting and anticipating and ferreting out secrets.

And the one secret that enticed her beyond all measure was why the bastard was interested in Ronald's mousy little fiancée. She had seen for herself—what would any man of taste and discrimination want with a creature who looked and dressed like a missionary in high-necked shirtwaists, sensible, dark serge skirts and sturdy boots.

It was a paradox, and an interesting one at that.

What could that English mouse give a man like Grant Hamilton that she, Adriana, couldn't?

She wouldn't rest until she found the answer to that mystery, and since she was planning to return up-country the next day (this coincided with Mr. Hamilton's plans, which she had made it her business to find out), she was looking forward to the excitement of stirring up some trouble to relieve the usual boring routine of the days and nights in the planting districts of the hill country.

Celia was ready to leave Colombo; she wanted to go back home to her estate, which her father had romantically named after Marianna.

Even if Ronald would be waiting for her there.

She could not feel excited at the prospect of marrying him, and several days' distance between them had not made her any more enthusiastic.

This was not taking control of her life, she thought at one point while accompanying her uncle to meet with other Anglican priests and missionaries.

But something was taking control of her—she continued having disturbing little flashes of memory from her childhood.

Once, while removing her boots before entering a temple in the small fishing village of Pandadura, she had felt a shocking sense of déjà vu:

She had gone to the Buddhist temple with Cora.

Cora, her ayah—

No, Cora who Ronald had *said* was her ayah.

The experience only made her want to return to Marianna Plantation that much sooner.

The answers lay with the past, and the past had all to do with what had happened on the plantation.

The thought scared her, but no more so than this feeling of dislocation that came with the nightmares and now with the disquieting flashes of scenes from her past.

She was in control, wasn't she? Ronald would marry her even if Grant Hamilton wouldn't, and he had been loyal and faithful and managed everything for her just as she would have wished.

Oh, surely that was enough to build a life on.

Or enough to make the nightmares stop . . .

But when she was finally ensconced comfortably in a private first-class compartment aboard the train that was taking her to her longed-for destination, Celia felt no excitement or sense of anticipation.

She drew the curtains back from the window and tried to become absorbed by the scenery and the fascinating sights of Sinhalese life, like the smiling, waving, brown-skinned children, wearing next to nothing, who cried out delightedly as the train came chuffing along the tracks.

"Shocking," Aunt Gertrude huffed. "You would think they would know better than to let their children run around like that. This part of our mission is perfectly clear—we must educate these people to dress like decent Christians.''

At every stop they made, hordes of smiling women and children rushed to the train, offering baskets filled with fruit and cut yellow *thambili,* a kind of coconut with a soft inner rind that could be scooped out and eaten.

Celia found that she remembered the names, taste and smells of the different varieties of fruits and native delicacies that were handed up through the windows of their railroad car whenever they stopped to discharge passengers.

And onward they went, with Anthea and George rhapsodizing about the view and the constantly changing scenery as the train gradually climbed its circuitous route toward the mist-shrouded hill country.

With each mile that passed, Emily's eyes grew wider and wider and she was just speechless with excitement as they rolled through the steamy low country with its coconut and rubber trees. This landscape eventually gave way to the wet greenness of terraced rice paddies and then, when the train chugged toward the blue-veiled mountains, to an abundance of hardwood trees and palms of every size and shape.

Anthea began reading aloud to George from her guidebook, with an occasional reproachful glance at Celia, who kept stubbornly silent during the journey along the torturously curving, zigzagging tracks that edged along steep precipices and through black tunnels hewn through rock.

Celia deliberately closed her eyes and turned her head away from Anthea's somewhat droning voice; she felt unbearably weary as they came closer and closer to their destination.

And all that the others could do was discuss the scenery, or whether they should take advantage of the good food provided in the refreshment car or wait until they reached the station at Rambukkana Pass. There they would have a lay-by until another, more powerful engine could be attached to the back of the train to push the cars up the next set of steep inclines.

Suddenly Celia was remembering the taste of curries, the really pepper-hot, mouth-watering kind that she had learned to enjoy as a child. And the roadside vendors who had sold different kinds of gram, or *kadalai,* which was spiced with whole red chilies—some soft and some all crispy.

And most of all, the green, unripe cashews boiled in coconut milk with tumeric and a little salt, then tucked into small cones improvised from leaves.

And the *muscat* too, so sweet and so rich and full of almonds and ghee.

And, of course, hoppers—for breakfast, sometimes with eggs and always with a red-hot *sambol,* or relish, that consisted of either finely chopped raw onions mixed with lime juice, tiny chips of dried maldive fish and ground chilies, or a coconut *sambol* which was lightly sautéed and just as hot to the taste.

She had sat on the floor in the kitchen among the servants and eaten her meals with her fingers, never feeling any different from them—at least not until Aunt Gertrude had arrived with her prying eyes and her biting tongue and her horrified exclamations.

One moment Celia had been staring out the train window through half-closed eyes, and the next . . .

She could not remember, except for fragments of frightening dreams of devil-dancers in masks, and sudden flashing lights that almost blinded her, and the sickly-sweet smell of some kind of incense that seemed to put her to sleep . . .

And with the flashes and acrid smells always came the shapeless man, so big, who moved toward her from be-

hind his black curtain, came to smile at her and give her sweetmeats and praise her for being such a good, sweet little girl . . .

And all of a sudden she had to escape—and she ran and ran . . . and ran and ran—in her bare feet and in her shrunken cotton dress under which she was all bare too.

No! No! She had to escape—all she had to do was open her eyes and she would be safe again, herself again, and not that frightened little girl she did not recognize . . .

"Miss! Miss? I'm sorry 'bout waking you up, but you was thrashing around something awful and I thought you might be sick—Miss Celia! It's me, Em! You been having bad dreams?"

Celia's eyes snapped open; she could feel the swaying motion of the train and hear the incessant clickety-clack of the carriage wheels on the tracks, and for one awful moment she thought that this was the dream and that the fear of the little girl of her dreams was the reality.

She pushed herself into a seated position with an effort. "Emily—oh, Emily . . ." Thank God for dear, practical Emily. "Where are the others?"

"They didn't want to wake you—thought you was probably overtired from the strain of the journey and the excitement and all. But your uncle said if you was to wake up and feel up to it, we could join them in the refreshment car and they'd keep places for us." Emily hesitated and then went determinedly on. "I don't know that it is proper—me, I mean, sitting with all of you when I'm just your maid. I just ain't used to it, miss . . ."

Another fragment of memory blasted through her mind. Or was it merely something she had been told?

Of course, Em was an Englishwoman, a white woman in the East. And as such, she could not possibly be classed with the native ayahs or even allowed to mingle with them.

Forget memories—live in the moment.

Celia smiled reassuringly at Emily. "I did warn you that things were going to be very different here."

"Well, it ain't proper. And I don't know if it's right, me joining you, but I do know you need your face sponged off and your hair redone, and you need somethin' to eat, Miss Celia, and then you'll feel more the thing."

Twenty-eight

The last person she expected to see as she entered the refreshment car was Grant Hamilton, all dressed up as a gentleman again, and with the most stunning auburn-haired woman seated across from him, who seemed to be arguing with him and meeting his habitual stonewall resistance.

The woman was fashionably dressed as well in a traveling gown that could only have been tailored by Worth, and for one pulsating moment Celia felt like a frump as she made her way past his table without acknowledging him or the woman.

But Grant noticed the sudden, imperceptible change in her; he had braced himself for trouble when he saw her scanning the diners and lighting on him—and on the flamboyant Adriana; her eyes seemed to narrow into sparking golden slits when they finally met his, but she did nothing more than lift her chin and sail into the car.

Still, the transformation was there, subtle, a difference in the way she walked, in the way she held herself, in the latent air of sexuality she exuded—as wild and passionate as the tropical storm outside. And she made her entrance at precisely the moment that rain and thunder descended on them. Everything—the conversation, the discreet sound of cutlery against plates, the waiters taking orders—seemed to stop in tandem with her arrival.

"Thank you, I am here to join my friends," she murmured in fluent Sinhalese, which stupefied the obsequious waiter who had hurried to greet her. "I see a place right there next to them."

Too bad her friends had chosen to sit that close to Grant Hamilton and that disgusting woman he was with.

Her coppery eyes frosted over as she finally acknowledged him, but she barely nodded to Adriana, who was introduced as the wife of the Honorable Edward Branham and the former Principessa di Alberti.

Adriana watched in fascinated amusement as the English mouse gave a fairly good imitation of a leopard surveying its prey. Celia looked her up and down before she smiled and murmured that she was overjoyed to meet yet another close friend of her aunt's stepson.

So, she thought as she was seated, he just toys with the likes of me and then seeks the company of a one such as her—damn him. That one was no lady, married or not. Her eyes were far too bold and her delicate fingers seemed to cling tenaciously to whatever they touched.

She was so disgustingly obvious that Celia could not understand how all of them, even Uncle Theo, innocent that he was, could fawn all over such a creature.

Even Aunt Gertrude was captivated by the fact that Adriana had a title, and Adriana was playing up to the lot of them to the hilt—to impress Grant?

No, he looked bored, actually, and just this side of saying something rude.

There was something about this woman—she kept slanting covert glances at Celia, and Celia felt distinctly uncomfortable, as if she were a specimen under observation.

She turned to the waiter who had been waiting to take

her order and gave it in Sinhalese—rice and curry, real curry, fiery hot to singe the taste buds of all but those who were native-born.

The waiter protested; she insisted, and he went off reluctantly to fulfill her request.

When he set it down before her, she inhaled the familiar, delicious smell and her mouth watered. She felt just like digging her fingers into the mound of rice as she arranged the plate with the accompanying condiments.

But Aunt Gertrude was watching, as was everyone else, so she picked up her spoon and fork and proceeded to eat the whole with an unholy, unladylike gusto.

"So ill-mannered," she heard her aunt whisper to Uncle Theo. "My dear, I know we taught her better. A lady simply does not enjoy her food like that. What will the *principessa* think?"

"I daresay she is enjoying her food too," Uncle Theo whispered back and effectively shut his wife up.

Grant, meantime, sipped his single-malt scotch whiskey and studied Celia through half-closed eyes as she attacked her food.

The little baggage—damn, he couldn't keep away from her. The very contrasts and volatility of her nature made him want to explore ever more deeply all the facets of her.

And he could do nothing, damn it, nothing.

I can't—I won't—

Oh, he had said it, and he had meant it.

His duty was clear and proscribed until the damned cavalry arrived, in the form of his wise and wily stepmother. Until then, his hands were tied . . . something others among this crowd hadn't seemed to mind in the least.

It was an odd lot, and even odder still was Adriana accosting him—well planned, he would wager—on the

heels of the abortive night before, and acting as if nothing
had happened and they were now co-conspirators.

It was the first time he had ever found himself at a
loss. What exactly was the etiquette when you had sex-
ually tormented an adversary to get information and
found her on your train-step the following morning, followed in close order by the woman you really wanted,
who sensed the opposition's enmity instantly?

These expatriate colonials made their own rules; and
he would bet they changed on an hourly basis and that
the *principessa* would be his sworn enemy by nightfall.

But Celia didn't play by those kind of rules, and she
knew Adriana for exactly what she was; moreover, she
was furious that her aunt and uncle were ingratiating
themselves with her.

While the others continued to sit over their meal sipping wine and port and engaged in gossipy conversation—with Adriana dropping enough titled names to fill
a British tabloid—Celia looked as if she were caught in
a storm and desperate to find shelter.

But now the thunderstorm had given way to clearing
skies and cascades of water that poured off the surrounding hillsides and into the distant valley below as the train
continued to inch its way upward along the steep gradi-
ent.

Celia pushed away her plate and wine goblet and eyed
her family and the corrosive *principessa* skeptically.

They would be there another hour at least, if not
longer; her aunt, whom she had never seen act this way,
was making a positive fool of herself over Adriana, and
Grant—well, Grant—he looked like any other fool man
who had been caught in the hands of an inamorata.

But it was his right—he could have whomever he
chose—after all, he did not want her.

She felt a sizzling heat course through her body and
stain her cheeks.

Such memories . . .

I can't . . . I won't . . .

I don't want to want you.

That was what it all boiled down to, so why was he traveling on this train with his next flashy mistress . . .

. . . and why was she so horribly upset by it?

She got up abruptly. "If you all will excuse me . . . ?"

If that sounded too curt, too angry; she couldn't help it. It was too much to expect of her—Aunt Gertrude and all her scathing, demoralizing comments, and then Grant Hamilton turning up with that—that whore only days after he had demonstrated every evidence of his need for her—before he had denied her.

It was too much, and the only thing she could think of to do was retreat gracefully and never, ever be in a place where she could possibly see Grant Hamilton again.

She held back her tears, her frustration, her anger even as Aunt Gertrude's voice followed her: ". . . have to learn to be accommodating in this society. I swear, Wilhelmina cannot have taught her any manners at all . . ."

Her compartment was an oasis—suffused with sun and light and the comforting presence of Emily, who then excused herself to get some lemon water and washcloths to cool the flush on her mistress's face.

Oh, God, a moment alone—

How had she come to this? The night on the beach seemed a lifetime ago, and the naive young woman whom her aunt Gertrude had almost refused to let go to London had become another person altogether. She was someone who was still racing toward a future that had been decreed for her long before she had the maturity to make the decision for herself.

And when she had finally made the right decision, it was because she needed to escape from a stupid infatuation that could have no resolution—and where had she gone? Right back to the beginning—to Aunt Gertrude and her unwavering certainty that Ronald was the only man who would ever marry Celia . . . knowing her history—

What history?

—and her own sense of Gypsy destiny leading her right back to the path from which she had willingly detoured almost a year ago.

She could be led anywhere: she would have believed Aunt Gertrude forever that she must honor her commitment to marry Ronald Winwood.

Why? To repay his loyalty, his investment in her inheritance? Because someone else had promised she would?

And then along came Aunt Willie, who taught her that she was not bound by choices that were made without her consent.

And so one man upended her life, and she was so willing to throw herself on the mercy of the other?

How had Ronald known to come to Colombo to meet their ship?

She heard the furious thumping at her door just as that fleeting thought entered her mind. It slipped right out again when she heard Grant's voice.

"Let me in, dammit!"

"Go away." Oh, that sounded strong and imperious.

"Goddamm it, Celia, open up!"

"I don't think so." She wasn't strong enough to face him, really she wasn't.

"I will break down this door."

She drew in a deep, hissing breath. "I'm sure you could."

"Make no mistake, Celia—*I will*."

"I'm not scared." But she was shaking in her kidskin boots.

"Stay away from the door."

She heard him moving away.

"One!" *Thump*—the door gave, just a little.

"Two!" *Thunk*—the door opened a crack, but the jamb held.

She thought in that split second of having to repay the railroad for the damage he could cause and she gave in. "All right—stop—"

She unlocked the door to find him standing there, a tower of fury.

He stalked in, looking as if he wanted to throttle something—someone—her.

"Well, Grant," she murmured. Really, he looked so ferocious she was quaking in her boots, and she wondered how she kept her voice so calm. "Did the *principessa* give you permission to leave her court?"

"Goddammit—"

The sleeping car was too suffocatingly close.

"What do you want, Grant?"

"What do I want—what do I want? You need a keeper—you're dangerous; you have no discretion whatsoever."

That raised her hackles. "I? I? Excuse me, Mr. Hamilton, but who is flaunting that beast of a woman and taking her God knows where for God knows what reason after refusing to—to— Well, it's all of a piece, whether it's the Harville country house or the up-country in the middle of nowhere. You prove yet again, with your excessive bad taste, that indeed it is better for a woman to be indiscreet rather than proper. Believe me, I will take this hard-won lesson to—"

"Shut up," he growled as the train cornered an edge and swooped into the Stygian darkness of an unexpected tunnel.

She caught her breath as they were enveloped by an utter, frightening blackness that felt as if it were one step away from hell, accompanied by the earsplitting wailing whistle of the train as it seemed to speed along a narrow track that surely the engineer could not see.

"Celia—"

She heard his voice; she felt herself caught in an embrace she couldn't—didn't want to?—fight off.

"Don't—" It came out on a breath.

"I will." He trapped her protest with his kiss—no, it was an assault on her senses—harsh, reluctant, overpowering, intensified by the clattering of the wheels, the smell of the coal smoke drifting into the open windows of the carriage, the tightness of the darkness and the urgent thrust of his body.

"You can't—you won't—" she hissed, thrilled to be able to throw his hurtful words in his face at the very moment he wanted her so badly she could feel his body vibrating.

"Gypsy witch," he growled against her pliant lips before he claimed them again with a passion that almost made her swoon.

She was trying to push him away, wasn't she? Her arms were braced against his shoulders; her bones felt like they were melting as he possessed her mouth as fully and intimately as he might have possessed her body.

The endless kiss, winding onward, inward, enveloped in heat and moisture, full of promise, desire, need, explosive passion—

And then—suddenly—light began to filter in through the windows and almost simultaneously her aunt, uncle, Anthea, George and the hateful *principessa* burst through the door.

Grant released Celia so abruptly that she almost fell against the supercilious Adriana, and she grabbed onto Uncle Theo, whose face seemed inordinately flushed, as if he had consumed too much port.

He patted her hand. "There, there, my dear; we saw

the door open and we wanted to make sure you were all right.''

She shot a simmering glance at Grant. ''I'm fine,'' she said tartly, ''just fine. Mr. Hamilton thought he had something important to tell me''—she smiled, her Gypsy cat-smile, her eyes glittering with malice—''but it turned out to be nothing of importance at all.''

Ronald Winwood had decided that it might be more propitious to meet his fiancée and her friends at Peradeniya Junction instead of waiting for them at Kandy station. That way he could appear to show Celia that a separation of only four days had made him eager to see her again.

He had decided the previous night—while Sujatha had massaged his body with her perfumed oils—that he could not afford to waste any more time.

He needed to be married to her immediately so that Marianna Plantation, which he had always considered belonged to him, would finally and legally be his.

And then, wonderful thought, he could finally consider all those wonderful, escalating lucrative offers for the plantation, and he would buy his freedom once and for all.

So he couldn't let Celia stand in his way.

He would not let anyone stand in his way this time— not even his pretty, devoted Sujatha, for whom he had the kind of affection one might have for a faithful bitch who would gladly give her life for her master.

Of course, Sujatha had her uses; her fury over his impending marriage to Celia could be used to his advantage, and he was absolutely sure that she would see to it, with her knowledge of native spells and subtle poisons, that his young wife sickened and died, or met with an unfortunate accident similar to her mother's.

And if that happened, why, then poor Sujatha would

have to take the consequences; and since he was an Englishman and she was nothing more than a native, her highborn status wouldn't matter at all to the magistrates.

So things couldn't be better. If he lost Sujatha, there was always Adriana, and if all his plans came to fruition, he would have a whole world of sophisticated, accomplished women at his feet once he got back to civilization.

He shook off his reverie as he realized the station platform was beginning to fill up—passengers booked on the Matale Line; a few women with squalling brats clinging to their skirts, bound for Nuwara Eliya, no doubt, where the climate was more salubrious. And the usual group of Sinna Dorais and liveried servants waiting for arrivals from Colombo.

And so, of course, the bloody train was late.

He slipped his gold watch into his pocket just as he noticed Dougal Drummond, his curly red hair standing up from his scalp in all different directions, hurrying up the steps to the stationmaster's office.

Ronald tugged on his golden mustache thoughtfully. The man almost never left Monerakande Estate, so something must be in the wind.

Perhaps his own sudden decision to meet Celia at Peradeniya Junction would prove fortunate after all.

The gram vendors, and the sweetmeat vendors had already edged their way to the outskirts of the platform, squatting down cross-legged with their wares ready for sale and brushing away the usual flies.

In the background were the Gypsies—the *ahikuntak-ayo*—with their garish clothes and their strange language which seemed to be a mixture of almost every dialect known to man.

The Gypsies came and went like the seasons. They told fortunes, they beat on their tambourines, they danced their wild dances; they were musicians, snake-charmers and tinkers as well.

Even the Kattadiyas seemed to have a healthy respect and their own particular powers over the elements.

"Winwood." Dougal nodded curtly to him.

"Well, Drummond—Monerakande, is it? Expecting someone on the Colombo train?"

"Aye," Drummond said noncommittally as a sudden gust of wind tore the corner of a notice free from a weathered brick wall nearby.

Automatically he put one hand out to hold the poster back against the wall and simultaneously read the notice.

REWARD POSTED
FOR THE CAPTURE OR KILLING
OF A ROGUE ELEPHANT

A description of the Rogue and its possible whereabouts followed, and both men perused the notice with interest.

"A chap could really test his mettle," Ronald said thoughtfully. "This Rogue looks to be one of the worst."

"Clever—for a beast," Dougal commented. "Haven't been able to trap him yet. And three lives gone already. What a challenge . . ."

"It would be worth it to have a go at him—what do you think, Drummond? I can just see those tusks mounted on either side of the fireplace at the estate."

"There's bound to be others with the same idea," Dougal said dryly. "Sure, I'd like to have a try myself, but I couldn't take the time off. Nor do I own the right gun to bring him down. But I do know someone who does."

Ronald stiffened. Who else could Dougal be talking about but Grant Hamilton? he thought furiously; damn, he was sick and tired of hearing that upstart American's name. Who did he think he was anyhow? Obviously he needed to be put in his place once and for all, and an elephant hunt was just the way to do it.

Ronald had to force himself to be patient—just a short while longer, that was all. First he needed time alone with Celia, without all the bloody chaperons who surrounded her.

Perhaps he would suggest they do some sightseeing—and maybe he could get her alone at the Peradeniya Botanical Gardens. It was easy to get lost there among the meandering paths through the Fernery and the flower and spice gardens, where there were several fine specimens of the coca plant.

Ah, the product of the innocuous-looking coca plant! How it could heighten and intensify one's feelings—and clarify one's thoughts.

It was Eddie Branham and Adriana who always seemed to have a plentiful supply of cocaine, powder and crystals that was mixed with tobacco and smoked through a pipe, but he preferred to inject himself with a hypodermic needle.

God, how strong he felt then—how all-seeing and all-knowing!

He wished he had some now to see him through the inevitable formalities he would have to endure when the damned train finally arrived.

Thank God there would be a little package waiting for him when they got to Peradeniya; that would take care of everything for a few weeks.

He had promised his friend Desmond a go at Sujatha in return—and of course, since a debt was a debt, he would damned well make sure that Sujatha obliged—especially if he was going to be occupied bringing Celia to heel.

Emily followed her mistress out of the curtained shade of the railway car and onto the platform and into the sudden, blinding glare of the sun.

She blinked her eyes against the bright white light that

seemed to reflect off the disheveled red hair of a young man who was standing there and staring at her as if she were some kind of apparition.

She blinked again—and met his solemn blue eyes gazing directly into hers; he seemed to see right into her and she blushed furiously.

It wasn't that he was exceptionally handsome or anything; in spite of his rumpled clothes and that hair, he appeared to be a gentleman, and he had freckles just like she had and the brightest red hair she had ever seen in all her born days.

And there was a pugnacious set to his jaw that spoke of stubbornness, and she wasn't sure how she felt about that, or the fact that suddenly she felt shy and even embarrassed by the intensity of his look.

Her knees felt weak—she who thought she knew everything about men, bastards that they were, and always out to take advantage of a girl if they could with their smiles and their lies and their promises.

The passengers were spilling out onto the station platform now, impatient because they had been delayed in getting to their various destinations, but she just stood there, oblivious of the noise and the crowd, clutching her portmanteau in her hand, and thinking how hot and sweaty and sticky she felt, and wishing he would just take his eyes off her.

Maybe he didn't know she was a lady's maid—and why on earth was he making his way purposefully through the crowd toward her?

She didn't quite know what happened next; maybe it was the heat or the blinding brightness of the sun or the thinner air—but suddenly she was quite dizzy, and she swayed on her feet and was caught by the most gentle pair of hands—

—Mr. Hamilton, whose voice seemed to boom out so close to her ear: "Here, you need to sit down in the shade somewhere. Dougal! Help a damsel in distress. Miss Emily isn't used to the change of climate yet.''

Oh, and didn't she enjoy being treated like a fine piece of china, just like she was a lady; and the man with the mesmerizing blue eyes came to her side so quickly, so solicitiously—oh, she was going to drown in the look of those blue eyes . . . she was, and she had no notion at all of how to deal with it.

Twenty-nine

Ronald Winwood had been in a foul mood to begin with and it worsened when he saw Adriana smiling like a cat lapping cream as she disembarked from the train, clinging to the arm of the staid and proper reverend bishop.

What in hell did she think she was doing?

He walked forward with a forced smile to greet the bishop.

"And where is Celia?"

"She's right behind us, of course, helping Gertrude and seeing to our luggage. Ah, my dear . . ."

She appeared from behind the bishop suddenly and Ronald was struck by how self-possessed she was, for all she was got up like one of her uncle's acolytes; who in their right mind would button themselves up and down in the midst of heat like this?

Damn, but he couldn't wait to strip her bare of her puritanical shirtwaist and heavy skirt and tie her outdoors to a tree until she acquired some color—one way or another.

And if that didn't work, he was sure Sujatha would

enjoy beating her until the little bitch had red welts all over her body.

That would take the starch out of her and her high collars.

And just in case the idea that she was in charge because she was an heiress went to her head, he would be happy to remind her of certain things from her childhood that she surely wouldn't want any of her new society acquaintances to learn about.

But still, he had to make himself pleasant to her uncle and aunt, and it was costing him greatly in terms of his patience and his irritation with the whole scene, for Celia stood by looking haughty and as if she didn't even want to know him.

In fact, she was feeling disoriented once again. The sights and sounds, the smells familiar to her from childhood, were triggering strange and confusing pictures that seemed to race willy-nilly through her mind; she heard nothing anyone said until Anthea's somewhat snappish voice penetrated the thick fog that obscured her memories.

"—you're likely to lose your little maid to that redheaded young man with the smitten expression on his face. Shall I look for a suitable girl to take her place—of course she'll be missionary-trained and -educated. I understand there's a rather good school in the area that trains these village girls in the domestic arts. And, of course, they all speak English . . ."

Anthea paused, noting that Celia was becoming more rude by the moment and looked as if she had caught only the tail end of her observations.

She went on petulantly. "For heaven's sake, Celia! Well, fine, you don't care what happens to Emily, but you might at least acknowledge your fiancé. That Woman looks as if she would like to sink her claws into him, too—

"Celia! Don't you even care? I swear, I find it harder and harder to understand you these days! Is it just coming back to Ceylon that's affecting you or—

"Celia, *do* try to confide in me. George and I are awfully fond of you—and concerned as well. I might be able to help. You just haven't been your usual self of late—don't you feel well?"

Yes, I feel well. I don't understand what I'm feeling—and Ronald—I couldn't bear it if—

But he did—he left Uncle Theo to a crowd of admirers and came up to her and bent to kiss her sweat-damp cheek.

"So here you are at last, my dear. Was the journey unbearable?"

She couldn't even look at him. "Tolerable," she managed as her gaze veered over his shoulder to where Grant stood directing the placement of his long canvas gun cases into one of the carriages that would take him— who knew where?

She turned her attention back to Ronald. "How kind of you to meet us here."

What could she say to him? Once again he was a stranger—and he had left Colombo only four days before.

"Ronnie, dear . . ." Adriana slithered into view and curled her graspy little talons around Ronald's forearm. "We've had the most interesting journey down, your little fiancée's family and I. What a charming lot. You would hardly believe they were persons of the cloth. Your uncle Theo, my dear—what a lovely man!"

Oh, I would wager you think every man is lovely, Celia thought trenchantly. She wasn't going to say one word more than was necessary—she didn't have to; Adriana was intent on doing all the talking for all of them.

"Oh, Ronnie," she was saying reproachfully, "you mean you never, ever told Celia that we're acquainted?

How remiss of you. Of course, I never thought to men-
tion it either. But I'm sure''—she looked pointedly at
Celia—''we will get to know each other very, very well.
Ah, I see my driver. Till we meet again, my dear.''

And she drifted over to where Grant was engaged in
conversation with Dougal Drummond and interrupted
them, her fluty voice carrying through the heat as if it
were being conducted by the air waves.

''Ah, a rogue elephant—such a challenge for the likes
of all of you. I just heard, Mr. Hamilton, about these
unusual firearms you brought with you from America.
From the Wild West we have been reading so much
about,'' she added for the edification of Dougal Drummond, and she swiveled her long-lashed eyes from one
to the other, then threw a darting glance over her shoulder
at Ronald.

She loved the tension she was creating, Celia thought.
She loved intrigue and danger, that woman. And the atmosphere between her and Ronald positively reeked with
murky undercurrents. Celia didn't know whether she
hated it or was relieved.

One thing was clear—Dougal Drummond was thoroughly taken with Emily, just as Anthea had said. Who
would have thought Emily, of all people, would find love
in the least likely of places—a native railroad station in
the hot, humid up-country of Ceylon?

Once again they were to stay overnight before beginning the next phase of their journey; here in Peradeniya,
Ronald was adamant that they should see the botanical
gardens before they continued on to Celia's estate. In
truth, Aunt Gertrude was tired from the trip, which meant
everyone was tired, and therefore, everyone was glad to
have a layover of a day or so.

The next morning, as their carriages bowled along
tree-shaded roads toward the famous gardens, Celia tried

hard to be attentive to Ronald, who sat by her side, but all she could think of was Grant Hamilton and the she-cat *principessa* and whether he was using this break in the journey to make love to her.

Therefore, she barely heard Ronald's instructions—something about meeting alone in the Fernery, and having so many things to talk about.

She felt him grasp her hand tightly beneath her fanned-out skirt and she flinched; his hand was hot and sweaty, and she instantly wanted to pull hers away.

"There's a map, my dear, with directions; be sure to follow them precisely. I couldn't bear it if you got lost."

"I won't get lost," she murmured, trying to make sense out of his request. What could he possibly have to say to her that he couldn't say when they finally reached Marianna Plantation?

But this was Ronald, her childhood idol. Why did she feel uneasy?

"In an hour, my darling. I know you can find a way to slip free of your uncle and aunt for some private time with me."

"I'll try," she said with a noticeable lack of enthusiasm. "But why not right now?" *Why not get it over with?* she wondered.

"I had made an appointment with the assistant curator here to look at a new disease-resistant species of tea," he said smoothly. "It's nearly ready for the planting stage, but I'm so seldom in Peradeniya, I thought I would take the opportunity . . ."

"I understand perfectly," she said. She didn't understand at all, but as he accompanied her back to her entourage, she knew one thing: she was going to make sure that Emily—and perhaps the most attentive Dougal—came with her to the Fernery.

* * *

There was a picturesque little gatehouse at the entrance to the gardens, and the whole party had been thoughtfully provided with maps in case some of them decided to wander off along the pathways that invited closer exploration of the more beautiful features of the gardens that were not visible from the main carriage drives.

And everyone seemed to want to go off in a different direction and study different things. George and Anthea wanted to find out about the edible fruits and vegetables that grew wild in the fertile soil of this island paradise. Ronald went to meet his curator friend. Dougal offered to guide Celia wherever she decided to go, and if it was the Fernery, perhaps she wouldn't mind if he showed Miss Emily the Rose Garden nearby and they would meet her there.

As she turned to follow the path to the Fernery, Celia noticed another carriage draw up—and there was her uncle Theo, making an absolute fool of himself as he handed that *principessa* creature down from the carriage as if she were made of porcelain.

And there was no Aunt Gertrude in sight.

He ought to be wearing garlic around his neck, Celia thought waspishly. *That witch was every bit as blood-thirsty as any vampire.*

She turned away from the nauseating sight of her uncle fawning all over the honey-voweled *principessa,* and made her way along a network of paths alongside of which rivulets of water flowed between banks carpeted with all kinds of ferns and moss.

Lofty trees covered with flowering parasite vines shaded everything, creating a sun-dappled pattern on the pathways; bees and gaily colored butterflies swarmed everywhere. Here and there, blending into the scenery, were a few rustic benches to invite the weary tourist or inveterate sketcher to enjoy the view.

Something about the quiet and the sun-streaked green

haze surrounding her reminded her of her mother, almost as if she had stepped out of time and into the past.

She wondered painfully, for the first time in years, how the beautiful Marianna had felt having been snatched away from the gay, free life she had known to be immured in the isolated loneliness that was the lot of a planter's wife.

For one sentient moment, Celia experienced the awful burden that had descended on the slender, unwitting shoulders of her beautiful mother.

Marianna, Marianna, you are part me and I am of you . . . why do I feel you here, now, so closely?

She shook away her morbid feeling; the dead past could have nothing to do with her living and vital future.

She had only herself to think about from now on, and only one decision to make: whether or not to fulfill her promise to marry Ronald.

Or were her thoughts about her mother some kind of warning?

That notion was too fanciful, too otherworldly, even for her; she was not enjoying the fact it was comparatively cool here, but the rippling sound of running water was almost hypnotic.

How easy it would be to fall asleep here, curled up on one of those inviting wooden benches.

She pulled off her hat impatiently.

When she had been a child, she had worn next to nothing, a single loose garment just like the village girls wore—or a sarong . . . camboy, it was called—topped by a tiny white cotton blouse that bared her midriff . . .

The same as Cora . . .

She felt the chill instantly envelop her body.

Why did the thought of this Cora keep flashing in and out of her consciousness?

She hated these sudden, fragmented shards of memory

that kept stabbing in and out of her mind like lightning so that she could never grasp any details.

There were only black, gaping holes. And things she could almost remember when she was between wakefulness and sleep. But then the fog would descend, and whatever she had been about to remember would dissolve into a shrouding mist.

Oh, Lord, she felt cold and suddenly scared in spite of the soothing scenery that surrounded her.

She felt constricted, hemmed in, as if she were wearing a straitjacket.

Or maybe the sun had made her crazed; she was thinking about floating, like Ophelia, down one of the swiftly running rivulets that flowed back to the Mahaweli River and eventually out to sea.

She wanted Emily. Or even Ronald.

She felt as if she were strangling under the starched lace collar that enclosed her neck from her shoulders to her chin.

If she unfastened just one—two—of the buttons, she might be able to breathe—

And then she felt the embrace of a pair of hard arms encircling her waist and pinioning her back against a body that was equally hard and unyielding.

Not him! Please, God, not him!

She couldn't summon up enough strength to fight him. Maybe it was inevitable. Didn't she believe some things were inevitable, or was that something she had invented to excuse her unforgivable surrender to Grant Hamilton whenever he touched her with his long, sun-browned fingers?

Nor did he have any patience with her clothes; he undid one tiny pearl button and then impatiently ripped the rest of them away to open her blouse to her waist.

But under it, as if to impede him, she wore a thin

camisole which was threaded with pink ribbons, and he swore under his breath in Spanish.

It didn't matter; Grant Hamilton was the master of all the lovemaking arts; all he needed to do was touch her sensitized nipple with one finger—first one and then the other—and she almost swooned from the pure wanton sensation of it.

Just a brush through the sheer lawn of her protective camisole; how did the wretch know exactly how and where to touch her to drive her into a mindless frenzy that made her want only to have him touch her again and again and even more intimately . . . ?

How could a woman ever expect to know . . . ? This was the wanton joy that undermined everything and drove women to subjugation—for this, even she would submit—just to experience the feelings, the rush of exquisite pleasure, that no other man's hand could provoke.

And for once she was not thinking of the duality of her nature. She was herself, Celia, feasting on emotions and feelings she could never have dreamed of—or ever had the weapons to fight either.

She was born for this, she yearned for this—her body knew it and she arched against him in hot demand as he whispered soft, insidious love words in her ear.

Every sensation separated and merged at the same time; she felt the rise and fall of his chest against her back, and the frightening hardness of his masculine arousal against the softness of her bottom.

"Gypsy witch—damn your copper eyes—I can't keep my hands off you . . ."

God, how warm his breath was against her neck, how hot and wet his lips and tongue against her burning cheeks and her too-willing mouth.

He was so experienced in the art of seduction; it was

so easy to lean back against him and give in to the delicious feeling of languor that pervaded her body.

His touch was magic. He knew exactly how to play with her body and her senses. He knew exactly the right words to whisper in her ear, and she didn't care whether they were lies or the truth; they were exactly what she needed to hear at exactly the right moment.

He was a sorcerer, tempting her to surrender everything to his almost overwhelming strength—her will, her body, her self.

He was kissing her as if he wanted to pull the very soul from her body; his tongue explored the virgin recesses of her mouth with a man's hard passion, demanding everything from her, just everything.

She was spellbound by the swirling sensations she felt: the heat, the wet, his hardness, the naked feeling of her breasts as he played with her nipples, the bone-melting nub of feeling that centered in her very vitals, which shimmered with a kind of unknown pleasure.

All of that from the man who couldn't, the man who didn't want to want her.

"I want you."

She heard the words; somewhere in her Gypsy soul she understood that if he kept kissing her and touching her, she would lose control just as she had before. She felt his hardness against her, and a consuming curiosity to understand what it had to do with wanting and desire—

And yet she knew; it throbbed with a life of its own, nudging her and pushing her, as if it too wanted to possess her in tandem with his hands.

And it would fit—she knew this in the rapturous moment when the expansive feeling between her legs exploded into life—it would fit—and she felt as if she were going to fly out of her body as the pleasure of her culmination consumed her, obliterating everything and leaving her open and so vulnerable to the man who did not want to want her.

Dougal Drummond and Emily had been strolling through the flower garden that bordered the Fernery, and Emily had been feeling quite anxious that they find Celia.

It had been too easy to slip into the unaccustomed pleasure of having companionship herself, and she was somewhat worried about the idea that Mr. Winwood had been so insistent on meeting her mistress alone.

So she was not a little relieved when Ronald Winwood suddenly came upon them as they were making their way to the Fernery, his whistle trailing off between his teeth when he glimpsed the two of them.

Dougal immediately moved unobtrusively to block the path.

Ronald's expression instantly darkened into something ugly and threatening.

And he had been in such a good mood up until that moment. Just one hypodermically injected dose of cocaine had made him feel so sure of himself and in charge of the whole world.

He had fully expected to come upon his little missionary fiancée first so that he could have proved to her once and for all who was master and who was servant.

But no, this was ever the way: the servants of the world always made things difficult.

"Well, Drummond," he said curtly. "Have you seen my fiancée?" Why didn't the damned fool move out of the way? He felt like kicking him off the path.

"Hmmm," Dougal said, infusing his speech with a pronounced Scottish burr, "I dinna recollect where or when I last saw the young lady."

Emily looked from one to the other with wary eyes, her nerves starting to jangle. There was something else going on here, something deeper and something neither she nor Miss Celia understood, but she wished Miss Celia had not promised to meet Mr. Winwood in private.

At that moment Grant Hamilton came strolling around a bend in the tree-shaded, meandering path, propelling Celia by the elbow and wrist in a rather possessive grip.

"Well! Everyone is here. Have y'all been waiting long?" Grant drawled deliberately, insinuatingly.

His tone grated on Ronald's already exacerbated nerves, and the look on Celia's face provoked him into an almost mindless rage.

She looked—what? Aware, too aware of the American upstart. And there were two buttons unfastened at the high neckline of her shirtwaist and her hat was missing.

It seemed suspiciously as if something had been going on between the two of them.

Damn it, damn it—Celia was his property, by God, and no other man had the right to lay a hand on her.

Grant raised a quizzical eyebrow at the sight of Ronald's furiously perspiring face and clenched fists.

Intuitively, Dougal stepped out of the way, pulling a stunned Emily with him.

"Damn you, man!" Ronald exploded. "Let go of my fiancée and explain yourself! Let me tell you now that certain behavior is just not tolerated among us here, and I'm perfectly willing to teach you that lesson in manners before you return to America with your tail between your legs like the low-down cur you are!"

Celia choked; Ronald was in a fury and Grant looked utterly unfazed by his histrionics, and she didn't know what she felt.

No, she knew—she felt safe with Grant and scared witless the two of them were going to come to blows.

Before the thought had even formed in her mind, she felt herself shoved roughly and unceremoniously out of the way and into Emily's arms, and Grant's hoarse voice grated in her ears: "Take her back to the carriages, will you? I'll come soon."

But she stood rooted to the spot while everything seemed to stop in the blood-heaving moment as he and Ronald sized each other up.

And then Ronald, maddened with rage, slashed downward with his whip as he rushed at Grant, and Grant, in response, shifted his body slightly to one side as he deflected the blow with one hand and gave Ronald a contemptuous backward shove with the other.

"Look—why don't you cool off in the water for a while? Celia's my ward, and I will decide who she will marry and when. Or if she will marry at all—*comprende?*"

Celia was stunned. His ward? He would decide—if or when? Mr. I can't and I won't—the man who just had?

She froze in horror as Grant suddenly pulled a revolver out from some hidden pocket when Ronald struggled to his feet mouthing threats couched in language not meant for ladies' ears—and fired.

Emily screamed; Dougal flinched, appalled.

And when the smoke cleared, they saw that Winwood was still alive, and at his feet was a venomous cobra, its body still writhing and thrashing in death, its blood spattered all over Ronald's stunned face and khaki shirt.

"He'll no forgive you for that—ever," Dougal said as Ronald remained on his knees in shock beside the dead cobra.

"Get the ladies out of here," Grant said curtly, which Dougal managed to accomplish with a minimum of protest from Celia.

When they were out of sight, he looked down at Winwood, who looked pitiful and weak to him. "You dislodged the son-of-bitch. He would have struck in a minute—"

Winwood looked up at him resentfully, a position he never wanted to find himself in ever again. ''Go to hell, Hamilton. I could have handled it. You're a goddamned peacock, showing off for the ladies, sticking your goddamned nose where it doesn't belong. I won't be beholden to the likes of you, do you hear me? Just get the hell out of here.''

Grant shrugged. ''Your choice, Winwood. I'd much rather go find myself a bottle of good whiskey right now. See you back at the hotel.''

God, he hated that man; what the devil had Celia's father been thinking all those years ago when he handed everything over to that viper?

And how smart had Willie been to send him to make sure things didn't get out of hand.

Maybe, he thought, smarter than she knew.

Something was happening to her; her mind was in tumult because of what had happened between her and Grant—it was impossible not to remember it or to set it aside as a product of the magic of the moment or her fascination with him.

And on top of that the memories—and incessant Aunt Gertrude—going on and on about her wedding and Ronald—

She felt as if she were not herself, not Celia, not the offspring of her mother, not the artless child who had dreamt of returning to Ceylon and claiming the man who had loved her forever.

Who was she? What was she?

Outside her shuttered, darkened hotel room, she could hear the strangely haunting melodies and up-and-down trills that were achingly familiar and somehow separate and apart from everything she had ever known.

She knew and yet she didn't know so many things that

the throbbing drumbeats and flutes were trying to tell her—

Or was it the presence of so many colorfully-costumed Gypsies crowding the streets with their tambourines and discordant pipes that disturbed her?

Or was it the sickly-sweet smell of incense and the loud cries of the street peddlers selling gram and cashews and sweetmeats?

Just the afternoon they had returned from that awful confrontation in the Fernery, she had been accosted by one old and wizened Gypsy woman who had clamored to tell her fortune—Rom to Rom.

The magnificently uniformed porters at the Queen's Hotel had thrust the old woman back into the throng of beggars and peddlers, but Celia had understood what she was saying: even here they were watching over her as one of their own.

Or was it only to insure that she avenged her mother's death?

That curious thought came to her in the midst of a dream—or a nightmare—she was never sure whether it was one or the other as she napped that very afternoon.

"Miss Celia . . ."

Emily's urgent voice intruded, calling her, pulling her from the place where she had been lost and caught up in something she couldn't quite grasp.

She heard the anxiety in Emily's rising voice, and she tried to stir—she had the sense she had cried herself to sleep.

And she smelled incense.

Of course—to drive the mosquitoes away.

She remembered that.

But why did her head feel so heavy? And why did she find it so hard to force herself to wake up—even to move?

Who was she?

Still a child—perhaps six or seven years old, and running barefoot and half-clothed everywhere as she spied on Cora . . . and on the handsome man Cora liked so well. In the end, he had told her it was she that he really loved—and she must only wait until she was old enough for him to claim her and make her his.

What was happening to her?

What was she so afraid of remembering that she had broken out in a cold sweat in spite of the oppressive heat that pressed in against her skin, against the wooden shutters in tandem with flaring lights and the explosion of fireworks, drumbeats and a monotonic chant: *"Sahdu, Sahdu, Sahdu!"*

Déjà vu. She had to have experienced this before.

Young children all clothed in white were chanting and carrying perfumed flowers in shallow baskets held in their hands . . .

Somehow she knew that. She knew as the smell of incense grew stronger and stronger and still more sickly-sweet and she tried to turn her body over and sit up and she felt more and more dizzy as Emily's voice seemed to come from farther and farther away . . .

She was a child, a little girl with a tangled mane of black hair and bare legs and the handsome man was talking to her, cajoling her, while he played with her the same way she had watched him playing with Cora. And he had made her promise that she would wait for him until she was old enough to enjoy everything—*that mysterious and puzzling everything that would make Cora moan and groan and even scream out loud when he rolled on top of her . . .*

He? Why, the handsome man had been Ronald—

How could she have possibly forgotten?

Ronald, her golden knight, carrying her before him, astride his horse with her skirts all up and nothing else to stop his fingers from touching her just the way he had touched Cora before he stabbed himself between her parted legs.

She had been scared of that part of it, and he had promised to wait until she was old enough to do it.

She was remembering, she was remembering suddenly—it was like a flood—a gush of memory spewing out from behind the dam of forgetfulness.

She remembered how she had worshipped him, how she had taken off all her clothes to please him while that fat man with a black cloth over his head told her to be a good girl and do this and do that and to smile nicely before he gave her Kandy jaggery—the sweetmeat she so loved—while Ronald, yes, Ronald—unbuttoned his trousers and brought what she had always thought of as it *out and started stroking it and rubbing it until it got bigger and bigger and then he would jerk his head for her to come close and hold it, too, while it seemed to explode with a thick, white fluid that sometimes got all over her face and neck and made her retch when he put it in her mouth and told her to swallow it . . .*

And then—and then, he had told her that she must forget—she must forget everything until he wanted her to remember again, and he had taken her to this place that smelled of sickly-sweet incense—just like she was smelling now—and it had seemed so much better and so much easier to forget . . .

To forget!

Secrets should never be shared, he had told her—her knight—*and she had promised . . .*

And she had kept her promise—until now.

She reached for the sound of Emily's voice, which seemed to be fading away into a hollow distance.

What was happening?

Why couldn't she seem to move even while she felt her clothes being stripped off her, felt someone wrap her body in a flimsy length of fabric—a sari?—and felt a pair of strong arms pick her up and carry her away.

A different kind of sickly-sweet smell permeated her nostrils and her mind, deadening her senses, pulling her into oblivion.

Was she in a carriage? She was jolting about, feeling nauseated and so sick . . .

And an old man kept asking questions for which a familiar voice kept giving her answers—

Ronald? But where was everyone else if she was going to marry Ronald? Where was Uncle Theo, and where was— But she mustn't even think his name, much less say it aloud, or Ronald would be very angry with her.

And when he was angry, or when she had displeased him, he used to spank her on her bare bottom, and she remembered very clearly how it had stung and hurt for long afterward.

Why was she suddenly remembering all this?

She heard a voice from someplace far away and distanced from anything that was real, and then she had the sense that she was being touched and probed and handled. She squirmed and cried out—and then the voice, suddenly very close by—

"She might actually be a virgin still, although *I* wouldn't have believed it. Well, so much the better. Not that even *he* would have her now—after I've had her— after he's seen the pictures of his innocent little ward when she was a child.

"Don't you remember, my darling Celia—taking off your clothes when I told you to, looking so sweet and angelic for the camera as you posed exactly how I told you to? And how, if you weren't good, I would spank your little bottom, wouldn't I, and make you say how much you loved it? And remember how you promised to wait for me—you little bitch?"

She didn't want to—oh, God, no—she must not, could not, remember any of the horrible, ugly things he was saying—the memories, the memories—she had to be strong—as strong as Marianna—

Oh, God, she was drowning, drowning—who could save her?

Grant—goddamn you—where are you?

⚘ Thirty

They had been down to dinner and were now sitting in the hotel lounge among the palms while the sounds and smells of the Esala Perahera, the famous exhibition of the sacred tooth of Buddha which culminated in a spectacular annual festival, beckoned to them from outside the open doors and crowded verandas.

"I suppose this native pageant does have some cultural benefit," Aunt Gertrude sniffed. "But, of course, we all must wait on Celia."

"It's been ages since Emily went up to rouse her from her nap," Anthea said irritatedly. "You would think she would have rested enough. Perhaps I should go check?"

"Certainly, my dear," Aunt Gertrude agreed. "I mean, she should at least have the consideration not to hold us up. Or perhaps she thinks now that she is back among her people, she owes nothing to her relations."

Anthea rose gracefully, excused herself and went purposefully toward the stairs. Celia's room was on the second floor—not even that far away, which made it seem odd that Emily had not even come down to make Celia's excuses.

And odd that the DO NOT DISTURB sign was hanging askew.

Where was Celia? And Emily?

Anthea knocked on the door authoritatively, feeling more and more righteously angry by the moment.

Wasn't it just like Celia . . . ?

She had every reason to simply barge into that room and demand some explanation for Celia's bad manners—

She turned the knob experimentally, never expecting the door to open, then paused for a moment to examine her conscience before she pushed her way into the room.

The scent of incense that permeated the chamber was overpowering; she felt dizzy and had to clutch at the wall to keep her balance.

And then she heard moans and heavy breathing, and in the dimness of the turned-down lamps she just barely discerned Emily lying outstretched on the floor nearby a rumpled bed with its covers trailing to the floor—and—

Was she seeing right? Was there a large sheet of foolscap with writing scrawled all over it on the pillow—and were those photographs scattered all around it?

Anthea felt a frisson of fear; she could think of nothing else but sorcery and evil spells—everything she had read about native customs seemed to spin around her like a poisonous spider's web.

Where was Celia?

She was fixed to the spot, her breath catching in her throat, her sense that something awful had happened utterly overwhelming her.

She thought she screamed—she couldn't remember afterward—but she remembered shouts and booted footsteps pounding up the stairs, and then being pushed aside and into her husband's strong and steadying arms.

And suddenly Grant Hamilton was there, kicking open windows and shutters—and Dougal Drummond, leaning over Emily and cradling her head while he murmured to her.

Scurrying servants everywhere, and then the bishop—Anthea couldn't remember him coming in. She saw him in the center of the room, studying with a frown of incomprehension the note that had been left on Celia's bed, his mouth working as he then scanned the photographs in the light.

"I just can't believe this—I can't—" His querulous voice broke through the scented silence of the room. "If these were to become public knowledge—poor, poor child—thank God Winwood is willing to marry her in spite of this."

At the sound of the bishop's voice, Grant abruptly turned like a sleeping tiger about to pounce on its prey and snatched the letter and the photographs from the bishop's trembling hands.

By the time you read this, Ronald had written, *Celia and I will have eloped and our marriage will have been consummated. We both have felt, since the moment she stepped off the train, that there were too many obstacles, too many people standing in the way of our happiness. And now Celia is mine, fulfilling the promise made by her beloved father so many years ago.*

We pray you wish us well. We hope you will do all in your power to suppress any gossip, rumors or unpleasant publicity.

In the interests of that, I'm leaving you several old photographs which were willingly posed for by Celia, and even she agrees that neither the bishop nor her aunt Gertrude would want to have these photographs revealed in the wake of their arrival, and the ceremonies attendant to that, and the commencement of this new phase of their lives.

Grant crumpled the letter in his hand with the tension with which he would have broken Ronald Winwood's neck.

He felt like a volcano on the verge of erupting. The unholy son of a bitch, threatening the bishop, threatening Celia—

Threatening *him.*

"I suppose it is too late to prevent the inevitable?" The bishop's voice wavered only a little as he fought an internal battle with himself over Celia's welfare; this was not what he had promised her in the garden that day so long ago, and he felt, all at once, as if he were abandoning her to circumstances over which she had no control. "I mean, as long as they are married—Winwood would never want these disgusting photographs to become a matter of public knowledge . . . I just don't know what else to do or say. Perhaps if we all knelt in prayer . . ."

His voice trailed off as Grant wheeled on him. "Prayer? I don't believe in prayer, Bishop—I believe in retribution and prayers afterward, over the graves of the wicked. But before you pray over that bastard's coffin, I'm going to find Celia—and I'm going to kill that bastard—and I'm going to make sure he dies a slow and painful death. After he repents his sins . . ."

"But"—Anthea's voice now, rising high and cracked with hysteria—"you cannot be talking about *murder?* And it is possible Celia went off with her fiancé of her own accord, no matter how ill-timed and ill-conceived the circumstances. You're talking like a savage!"

"Really, my dear," George Maitland whispered in his wife's ear with some asperity, "surely you're not implying Mr. Hamilton is a savage—nor do you know

anything of the circumstances that have pertained.
You're being judgmental and uncharitable at the very
least—''

Which gentle scolding made Anthea burst into tears
and bury her face against her husband's shoulder, just as
Emily began to stir, muttering words that were slurred
and incoherent.

Dougal helped her sit up and forced a drink of brandy
between her cold lips, and she looked up at him with
terrified eyes.

''Miss Celia—is Miss Celia here?''

''There's no sign of Miss Penmaris,'' Dougal said.

Emily groaned as Dougal shifted to support her comfortingly. ''It was incense—burnin' so strong . . . it made
us so dizzy. And then there was some other scent, and
Mr. Winwood came and just clamped this cloth over
Miss Celia's mouth and nose and she couldn't scream.
And then over my face and I swear, the floor just come
up to meet me. I know I heard him say—I think he said
he would be comin' back for me as soon as he tamed
her—Miss Celia—''

She caught back a sob and looked around at them
with tear-filled eyes. ''Well, why are you all standin'
around and draggin' your feet? We've got to help Miss
Celia, for heaven's sake! She didn't ask for that black-
guard to come after her like that—she was hardly in
her right mind . . .

''Please do something—we've got to rescue Miss Celia!''

Lady Gertrude, of course, had to be told.

And the bishop wondered whether she had suspected
all those years ago, and that had been why she had insisted that Celia must be brought up in a decent Christian
atmosphere.

But then, she had also been the one who had encouraged Ronald Winwood, who had kept in touch and supported his long-distance courtship of Celia.

Had she known something—and then not told him? It was unthinkable—or was it?

Gertrude took the news with such equanimity that even the bishop felt like shaking her.

"Well, what can you expect?" she said, shrugging complacently. "A child runs around almost naked in this pagan atmosphere—any man would be tempted. I have always told her she was lucky that a decent man would want to marry her—especially one who knows her history."

Even Grant was nonplussed by this outrageous statement.

"What exactly do you mean by that?" he asked; his voice was low, calm, and yet there was a thread of a threat running through it to which even Gertrude was not immune.

"I mean her ridiculous Gypsy mother—what did you think I meant?" she said sharply.

"You mean you *taught* her that her mixed blood would taint her and no man could ever want her—except one who cared only about getting legal possession of Marianna Plantation," Grant amplified, putting into words the unthinkable—the evidence of Gertrude's prejudices and schemes. "I wonder what was in it for you," he added almost as an afterthought.

"It's obvious they do not teach manners in that reprehensible country you come from. To accuse me of something like that—to my face—and in *company!*—is outside of enough! It is too much—Theo!"

But even the bishop couldn't rescue her from Grant's fearsome rage.

"I think it has been too little—too little help, understanding, sympathy or love for Celia," Grant interposed acidly. "And the bishop can't possibly have enough time in this lifetime to hear the confession of all the sins on *your* conscience, my lady—although he certainly will want to try. Perhaps you would wish to expiate them by telling us what you know.''

''Theo''—Gertrude was positively livid—''tell this— this upstart colonial that I will never, ever talk to him as long as I live—and I will leave it to you to decide whom you will believe.''

And with that she rose and swept toward the lounge door, her ramrod body shaking with anger and frustration.

Grant looked at the bishop, whose eyes veered from his icy green gaze to his wife's stiff figure exiting the room.

''Mr. Hamilton—'' He had to say something, he just didn't know what.

Grant waved away his conciliatory gestures. ''I see exactly the person we need to speak with to shed light on this situation.''

It was Adriana, purring and looking for trouble. She could sense a tense atmosphere from a hundred feet away, and sure enough, as Grant watched, she walked into the hotel reception room, caught sight of him and the bishop and turned toward the lounge, her glittering gaze bright with anticipation.

He had allowed her to get just a glimpse of him, a cat luring its prey, before he shifted his position so that he would be closer to the door.

As she sauntered in, he seized her arm in a painful grip and she cried out.

''Mr. Hamilton!'' the bishop exclaimed, protesting his rough treatment of a woman with a royal title.

Grant ignored the bishop and wrenched Adriana around without warning to face him.

There was a small cat-lapping smile on her face which

told him just how much she liked this rude and crude behavior.

"Ah, *principessa*—just in time!" He pulled her arm tightly behind her, to the horror of the bishop, and her eyes met his boldly, sending messages he did not want to comprehend.

"Just tell me, you bitch—what has your little man Ronnie done with Celia? Let me assure you, if you don't tell me the truth right now, I will first break your arm, then your back—and maybe, *cara,* just maybe you will die quickly and without too much of the pain you love so well to inflict."

Celia had drifted in and out of consciousness, but she found herself choosing to burrow back into blackness before the memories overwhelmed her.

But she couldn't escape anything—not the memories, not her knowledge, not her awareness of how all the components of her life now fit together.

And all to do with her beautiful mother, Marianna; deep inside she knew even Marianna at the end had become weak and frightened, every bit as much a victim as she in these circumstances.

Only her mother had refused to be a dupe and go meekly to her fate.

What had been her fate? She had died tragically in a carriage accident, an unborn child in her womb, running away from her husband—her daughter, Celia had always guiltily believed.

But now? Now, when all the tangled threads and elusive memories had begun to make some sense?

She had no more illusions about Ronald; perhaps she had never had them. All of her instincts had told her, and she had listened to them and she should have heeded them with respect to her feelings about Grant Hamilton as well.

She needed—she had to somehow give herself that second chance. She had to keep her head—as soon as it cleared—and Grant would come for her to rescue her and to claim her.

"So! You are waking up at last. Have you been enjoying your homecoming so much that you have been dreaming of all kinds of pleasant things?"

The voice was like an assault, high-pitched, insinuating, spiteful, and Celia struggled to open her eyes.

A young woman leaned over her who was fair-skinned and would have been very pretty if her face had not been contorted by the force of her jealousy.

It would have been very easy, Sujatha thought, to strangle this woman. Her fingers itched to encircle the mouse's slender neck as she lay sprawled out against the clean cotton sheets of *her* bed.

She didn't even look like the prim and prissy English miss whom Sujatha had envisioned; she looked, this creature, more like a Gypsy—or even a Rodiya woman, an Untouchable—with her black mane spread out around her head and over her bare arms—

And then her eyes—when she forced open her eyes, Sujatha gasped; she was looking into the eyes of a leopard woman—or a female devil. Was it possible she had cast some kind of destructive spell over poor Ronald?

How fortunate it was that Ronald had so predictably demanded his usual opium with his tea, so that now he was asleep instead of enjoying his new bride.

The thought that the Englishwoman might not want Ronald never entered Sujatha's mind; what woman would not want him in all his golden, masculine glory?

He was the kind of insatiable lover that only a real woman with an insatiable appetite for sex could ever appreciate.

And this one—this one didn't look as if she would

enjoy being mastered and ridden until—until the ultimate moment.

But then—Sujatha must keep in mind always—Ronald had forced himself to marry this evil creature only in order to control Marianna Plantation.

Suddenly the creature's eyes focused, and Sujatha recoiled and instantly reached for the thin gold cylinder she wore suspended around her neck as a protection against the evil eye.

What did she see? What could she know?

What Celia saw was the ferocious hate in this strange young woman's eyes. She had the vague impression she had been offered a cup of tea sometime before by this woman—she felt as if she were rising from a dense fog and things were finally taking shape and making some sense.

Her throat felt parched and dry, and she ached in every limb, and she desperately wanted a cool and cleansing glass of water, but she would die before she asked this creature, who might just put poison in it.

She shifted her eyes away from her captor to look around and try to get her bearings.

She felt a jolt of recognition and shock when she realized where she was: she was on Marianna Plantation, and she knew this room; she had shared it with her mother whenever her father was away on one of his mysterious trips abroad.

Oh, God—the memories swamped her once again, too fast for her still-drowsy mind to comprehend, and so much, she felt as if they would suck her into a drowning-place of unspeakable horror.

She had been subjected to unspeakable things, even as a child—and the bastard had even made her believe that she liked playing his games of make-believe . . .

Don't think about it—don't think about it.

The pain descended, banding from her temples all across her head and behind her eyes, almost blinding her.

She had to keep her wits and concentrate on anything else but the past and Ronald's possible intentions.

It was night—she couldn't tell what time, but she knew from the coolness of the breeze coming through the open window and the soft hooting of an owl somewhere outside.

She could hear drums too, from somewhere in the distance—a monotonous pounding that seemed to keep time with the painful pulsing of the veins in her head.

There were two lamps lit, one on either side of the bed on which she lay, and she could almost envision that the monster fully intended to sacrifice her to the god of lust.

And she noticed too that the hate-filled creature had flinched when she heard the sound of the owl—a bad omen to those like her who were of a superstitious nature.

She struggled into an upright position, keeping her eyes on the wary young woman who was looking at her as if she were some kind of demon.

"Please"—she spoke to her in formal Sinhalese—"I can see that you are not happy at my being here, and I would much rather not be here either. Won't you please help me to leave? I don't care where I go as long as it is away from here. If you could only find me a horse—you could say that I tricked you—anything!"

So—the bitch actually spoke fluent Sinhalese—and what was this she was saying, all with those copper-gold demon eyes fixed on Sujatha's face so she could not look away?

She wanted to leave, did she? In the middle of the night, without any fear of what might await her out there?

"He married you only for the money and the estate, you know," Sujatha said spitefully. "He never loved you except for what you could give him once you were married in the eyes of the English law. Now everything that was yours becomes his. And you don't matter. He loves me—*me*—so why are you here? Why couldn't you have stayed in England and found someone else to bewitch? Don't come close to me or I will kill you—*Rakshashi* or not! I will send for the Gypsy people and *they* will deal with you!''

''Oh, send for them, by all means—or let me go to them, for I am of their blood through my mother. Didn't Ronald tell you? And what is your name? You know mine—it is Celia Marianna. And I have a man of my own whom I want just as much as you seem to want Ronald.''

Oh, yes, the creature wanted Ronald. Celia saw it in her glittering eyes and in her posture. Sujatha was jealous, she was afraid—and she was listening, too. What would convince her, what could she use to bribe her?

Anything, anything. Ronald only wanted the plantation after all, but what if she could convince this woman it could be hers? What a hold she would have over Ronald then.

Maybe it would work. Maybe.

''Hear me—I only want to leave here; I do not care about the estate or anything else. Ronald can have it . . . or *you* can have it—wouldn't that be turning the tables?''

Yes; Celia saw Sujatha lean toward her attentively, and she repressed her feeling of triumph and continued slowly and patiently, ''If you will just find me a horse, or take me to the Gypsy encampment, I'll willingly sign over my title in this estate to you in your name. And then you'll really have Ronald in your pocket. If you still want him after that . . . And hear me—there is a new English law that says a woman may keep her property even after marriage if she owns it before she is married. Think of that—just *think* of what that could mean!''

Celia saw the sudden calculating gleam in Sujatha's feral eyes; Sujatha could be seduced by the thought of owning property—and the icing on the cake would be the fact that she could retain title even if she married Ronald.

And quite obviously her *golden knight* could have known nothing of this new law or he would not have abducted Celia and forced her into some kind of legal ceremony she could hardly remember.

But she could almost see her captor working out the ramifications in her mind of *her* owning the property that Ronald so coveted. And slowly, surely, inevitably, she perceived the flashing moment in which the woman finally started to believe that Celia meant every fervent word she had said.

They started out, Celia wearing an old pair of her father's breeches that had been stored in an old camphor chest, and an oversized pair of his riding boots they had found.

Sujatha still was wary; she had provided Celia with a pen, an inkwell and paper to make sure that there was some document that would legally see her through the crisis, and Celia had painstakingly written it out.

"I can't sign it yet—I will have to do that in front of witnesses. Otherwise, the courts might believe *anyone* had written this piece of paper."

"I understand," Sujatha had said, though she wondered if it could be a trick.

But there was no time to think it through any further than that; she wanted to be rid of this woman and the burden she had become and the risks that she posed.

The sooner she was gone, the better, in spite of all the bad omens. The Gypsies could take care of all of that.

And fortuitously, Sujatha knew someone—her brother, Anil, who lived nearby and who would do anything for her. He would see the devil-woman safely to those she called her people.

It was as dark as pitch as they made their way slowly through the fields of the plantation and backroads that only Sujatha knew.

And it was scary, almost like traveling blind, and Celia was totally dependent on a woman who hated her, was suspicious of her, and only wanted to get rid of her.

So be it; the loss of Marianna Plantation and the excision of Ronald Winwood from her life was worth it.

But as they kept plodding through the black night, Celia began to feel less sure of Sujatha's intentions. The woman could be taking her to Ronald, or she could be plotting her death.

And then she saw a pinprick of light.

"There!" Sujatha said, and they veered their horses toward the light and the small hut that was the home of Sujatha's brother.

It was tiny. There was a table, a bed, a place to cook and to store food and bowls, and very little else.

"Here is the paper," Sujatha said, laying it on the table. "You sign. Anil will witness and we have one part of the bargain sealed."

Celia licked her lips. She hadn't expected that. She looked around at the meager surroundings and the dark shadows on the walls. They would either kill her or save her, and either way the plantation would be lost to her forever.

She signed the paper, and Anil took the pen from her and scratched his name.

"It is done. You stay the night and Anil will show you the way to Peradeniya in the morning," Sujatha said.

She looked at her brother and then she turned, ducked out the door, and was gone.

But before Sujatha got back anywhere near the plantation house, she heard the sound of hard-driving hoofbeats, and immediately she raced for the trees and cover.

From behind the trunk of a particularly large tree, she saw someone furiously galloping down the moonlit road from the estate house, followed by a small, light carriage with swinging lanterns shooting off spears of light in the blackness.

The rider pulled his horse up sharply, with an oath, and simultaneously pulled his gun free of its holster.

If she bolted, Sujatha thought, the man would shoot her. And anyway, she had nothing to hide.

She moved her mount slowly from behind the trees into the lantern light and the man wheeled as she brought her horse to a standstill before lightly slipping off its back.

"Ah! That is my little friend Sujatha," Adriana announced from her perch in the carriage. "Didn't I tell you she would be sensible about all of this? Do not worry, my dear; this angry madman here is just looking for his little friend. He won't hurt you, I promise. You have only to tell him where she is."

So this was the man, Sujatha was thinking, as the black-clad, tall stranger slid off his horse and came toward her purposefully.

"Where is she?"

Sujatha shrank back. He was fearsome and his voice was as deep as an ocean and as angry as a storm. This was not a man to be crossed. This was a man who would take action and never count the consequences.

And if she lied, he would find the truth anyway.

"I did not want Ronald to lie with her," Sujatha said when she finally collected her wits. "I helped her to run away after she told me there was this other man she wanted. And it was true, wasn't it?'' she added with some satisfaction.

True? True? Grant felt so upended he didn't know what was the truth and what was a lie. Not an hour ago, he had been ready to kill that despicable, drug-crazed madman who had abducted Celia. And now he was faced with having to search for her all over again.

''I gave her a horse,'' Sujatha said, almost as if she divined Grant's next question. ''She gave me a piece of paper. We made a bargain. And now she is gone and all will be as it should be.''

''Oh dear,'' Adriana murmured, ''Ronald is not going to like any of this, and you know he will take his rage out on you. Eddie and I will handle him. You had better come with me tonight—''

She was interrupted by a sudden, spine-tingling scream that seemed to come from high above and all around them. It sounded for all the world like a soul in torture—high-pitched and rising and then subsiding into an agonized gurgling that rose again before it faded into silence.

''Dear God—what was *that?*'' Adriana exclaimed. Sujatha flung herself against her hysterically, her whole body shaking convulsively while she cried out as if in answer to that chilling sound.

''Ohhhh—it is the Devil Bird!—the *Bodilima* means death! The death of a man! I never want to hear the like of it again in this life. Ahhh—all the omens were bad tonight. I must go to the temple and do *puja*—I must! Ah, help me—help me! Those two, they are demons, bringing bad luck. Take me away, take me away . . .''

Even Grant felt a tingle run down his spine at the eerie sound; he had never heard anything like it before.

And he did not want to deal with Sujatha's emotional outburst.

"I leave her to you," he said abruptly. "I want Celia." He wheeled his horse around; it reared up as the Devil Bird shrieked again, and in another moment he was gone, melting into the black shadows before Adriana had time to argue the folly of his pursuing Celia this night.

Well, damn him, Adriana thought savagely. And wasn't it just like a man to abandon a woman after he had almost broken her arm and left bruises that would be changing colors for at least two weeks?

And he hadn't even apologized or thanked her for cooperating with him and leading him to his precious little Gypsy.

She cursed under her breath in Italian. She hadn't quite liked the sound of that Devil Bird either.

And then there was Sujatha. She was jabbering incoherently now, and it took a lot of cajoling to convince her that she would be safer with Eddie and Adriana until Ronnie came to his senses; finally the former princess was able to persuade Sujatha to climb into the carriage for the trip back to her bungalow.

Once they had arrived, Eddie knew just what to do. He had drinks on the table, lent a willing ear to the whole sordid story, looked over the papers that Celia had written out deeding the estate to Sujatha, and whistled low under his breath.

"Needs just the signatures of another witness, eh? I'll be happy to oblige. It's poetic justice, I'd say. Just don't let Ronnie talk you into signing anything away to him. Well, well, well—isn't this all very interesting, my love? Quite enlivens our dull existence here, doesn't it?"

He sipped his drink thoughtfully for a moment. "I wonder how it will go when everyone meets to hunt that

Rogue. It's become the event of the season, and they're even taking bets on the outcome at the club. I know *I* wouldn't miss it for the world.''

He took another long drink from the glass and added, ''Of course, it also depends, doesn't it, on which is the Rogue and who will be hunting whom. But I expect it will all be sorted out, won't it, my love?''

He and Adriana smiled at each other, understanding each other completely, as usual.

They packed Sujatha off to bed with a small dose of laudanum, which would soothe her fears and put her to sleep; Eddie had promised as well to send one of the coolies for the local Kattadiya to break whatever evil spell might have been put on her.

And now he and Adriana had what remained of the night to spend together. And there was a new, young kitchen helper they had hired recently—a very pretty girl given to nervous giggling, and perhaps to . . . ?

Ah, Eddie thought fondly. Life with Adriana could never be dull, no matter in what remote part of the world they happened to end up.

Thirty-one

The dreaded Devil Bird!

That cry! It meant death. Celia had heard it only one other time before—the very night that her mother had run away and died.

And she had never told anyone what she had heard because the person would have thought she had the evil eye, and she didn't want to be different . . .

She didn't want to remember.

Why hadn't her mama taken her along when she ran away? She would have if she had really loved her daughter.

And then they could have died together and she would never have had to suffer this pain—

She sat bolt upright in a strange bed—dizzy again, and disoriented, and a strange man had handed her a cup of tea.

She had drunk it—really, she hadn't wanted it—and she had tumbled headlong once again into fitful dreams.

Of her mother—

—the Bodilima—death . . .

No, life—she wanted life—she wanted . . .

She wanted Grant Hamilton—perhaps he had stolen

*her soul with those fierce, searching, demanding kisses
and the gorgeous way he had touched her . . .*

*She wanted peace of mind; she wanted more, more of
his kisses, more of those touches that made her crave
more.*

*She wanted him to make love to her and to be the one
to wipe away forever the taste and feel and memory of
Ronald Winwood from her mind, her soul, her dreams.*

*She wanted—she wanted it again—that pure feeling,
pure lust—those sensations that only he could arouse in
her with all his patient experience.*

Damn him—where was he?—why didn't he know?

Why didn't he know . . . ?

And then it was morning, and Celia awakened to unfamiliar scents and sounds and the one thing that she
remembered after a night of horrible dreams and memories: Aunt Gertrude did not know she did not intend to
marry Ronald.

It was a strange thing to have remained clearly in her
mind when she could never remember anything after
such a night, and she wasn't sure she wanted to examine
the reasons for it.

She propped herself up on her elbow. Anil was cook-
ing, hunched over the fire and shaking pans and pots.

He had given her his bed and gone outside to sleep.
He had fed her some tea, in the throes of her nightmares,
and watched over her for the rest of the night.

He had guarded her against the Devil Bird at the risk
of his life.

Slowly Celia pushed herself to a seated position, and
he turned when he heard her. "There is tea. There is
food."

"I must get to Peradeniya," she said, and she was
shocked at how urgent her voice sounded, even to her.

Why? Why?

To see Grant, of course. To end the thing with Ronald. To tell Aunt Gertrude.

But why? Why now, why Aunt Gertrude?

She didn't know; she felt the answer was lodged in her dreams, in that netherworld where the truth dances around the edges of reality.

Ronald had kidnapped her because the moment he saw her, he knew exactly what her intentions were, and they did not mesh with his. He wanted the plantation, he had never wanted her, and he was going to have the plantation whether she were a willing bride or not.

And Aunt Gertrude had always promoted the marriage, had been righteously certain that Ronald was the only man who, knowing her history, would marry her.

It always came back to that: *knowing her history,* as if it were a stain, a blot, an irredeemable sin of some kind.

Until Willie. Aunt Gertrude must have been furious when Willie stepped in and took over.

But why? That was the question that kept nosing around the edge of her dreams, the question to which she had never had an answer.

She hardly tasted anything that Anil set before her.

"We must leave soon."

"I will keep the bargain."

It was midmorning when she crept into the hotel through a side door. She looked like a beggar in her breeches and boots, with her hair tucked up under a straw hat and her arms burned by the sun.

It felt like a lifetime ago that she had entered this hotel and settled into her room with Emily in attendance, and she had to trust that Aunt Gertrude was comfortable enough in these civilized surroundings that she hadn't wanted to move in the intervening two days that Ronald had held her captive.

She moved cautiously up the stairs, ducking behind pillars and furniture to hide from the odd guest who happened down the hallway, until she reached the suite of rooms which were occupied by Theo, Gertrude, and Anthea and her husband.

There was not a sound anywhere except the violent thudding of her heart.

She knocked on the door.

Footsteps. A hesitation. Aunt Gertrude's voice. "Who is it?"

Celia remained silent, counting on Gertrude's curiosity to compel her to unlock the door.

A moment later, Gertrude unlatched the lock and turned the knob. The door swung open.

"Oh, it's you."

Gertrude stared at her for a moment and then turned away.

Celia could not believe it; she had been missing two days and that was all Gertrude had to say to her?

She closed the door slowly behind her as Gertrude settled herself composedly into a chair by the window. The curtains were drawn, as if her aunt wanted to shut out the reality of the world beyond; only a soft light filtered through, and nothing else.

"Look at you," Gertrude said. "You're a disgrace to this family. You ran off to get married in the most dishonorable way possible. And those disgusting pictures! I washed my hands of you the very moment we found Ronald's note. I told him we never wanted to see you again, even though it distressed your uncle greatly to make that decision."

She was lying. She had to be lying.

Pictures—yes . . . no, she couldn't think about that, about the memories, about Ronald; one more piece of the puzzle, one more piece. He had wanted the plantation all

those years ago. He had planned it from the very begin-
ning, all those years ago.

And then Mother had died and Aunt Gertrude had
come and made her return to England with her and Un-
cle Theo.

But it couldn't have been as simple as that. It couldn't.

"I did not marry Mr. Winwood," Celia said slowly
and deliberately, and watched as Gertrude's expression
changed from sanctimonious to furious before she
charged to her feet.

"Get out of my sight, you—you—" Words failed her.
"You are just like your mother—ever and always like
your trollop of a mother. She destroyed your father, and
now you—now you! Get out of here. GET OUT OF
HERE!"

Celia stood still as stone. She hardly heard Gertrude's
harangue.

Why had Gertrude and Theo taken her?

"Your stupid father, taken in by that Gypsy whore—
and now Ronald; my girl, you have so many sins for
which to repent, your soul will burn forever . . ."

Her aunt's eyes were glazed as she started toward her;
she had seen that expression in someone else's eyes not
two days ago. The same rage, the same jealousy, the
same obsessiveness.

"You loved my father." She said the words, she heard
them, and she saw Gertrude stop in her tracks.

"Nonsense." Gertrude wheeled away from her and toward the door. "Just get out of here."

"You came to Ceylon after my mother died. You were
hoping . . . you wanted—" she couldn't quite link the
surmises together. Gertrude had come with Uncle Theo.
What could she have been hoping?

She thought that if she took Richard's child it would
be a bond to the man she really wanted, and maybe
someday she might have him.

"You wanted my father," she said again.

"You stupid ignorant girl."

"My mother died and you hoped against hope that he would see you as everything she wasn't. You took me to prove it. To bind him to you so you would never lose him. Were you hoping Uncle Theo would die? Were you planning to help him along?"

"I could kill you," Gertrude snarled.

"But then Father died too," Celia went on, feeling her way, gauging Gertrude's reactions, reaching for the truth. "And you still had me—the reminder of his folly in loving my mother and not you. What did you settle for, dear aunt? Selling me to Ronald Winwood?"

That was a crack in the dark. Her aunt's expression changed again.

"Don't be ridiculous. Your father and Ronald planned it for years."

"Ronald paid you to nurture it then, and to make sure that I would feel he was my only possible savior—*given my history*—until the deed was finally done."

"A fairy tale, my dear, made up out of whole cloth." Gertrude had settled herself back in the chair again, her murderous rage somehow contained behind her mask of unctuous piety. "Your mother was a flirt and cheat. After she died, your father was plainly on the road to ruin. It was no place for a child, so Theo and I took you. The story is what it is. There's no dark secret behind it. You have ever been an ungrateful brat, you have grown up just like your mother, and I will wager my soul you will bring Ronald to the same grief—if indeed after this degrading episode he will even want to marry you."

"Nothing will deter him, my dear aunt, as you very well know. He wants the plantation; he has lived for the day he will own it, and he has assumed that I did not keep abreast of anything new that might interfere with his plans—or yours."

"I do not know what you are talking about," Gertrude said.

"Of course not. You've never known anything except how to belittle me. I wish my father had lived to hear me tell him about it. Or maybe it is enough that Aunt Willie understands. Oh, Aunt Willie. You do hate Aunt Willie, don't you? And I know why. Because my father left her all that lovely money for me."

"He gave us *nothing*," Gertrude said through gritted teeth. "Not a shilling more than was necessary, not a visit, not a letter, not a thank-you. For all those years, and all our work, and all that time we took care of you. All that besotted fool could do was mourn that faithless whore of a wife who deserved everything she got— *everything* after what she did. And you're no better than she was, in spite of my best efforts. In spite of all my teachings, blood will tell. Blood will always tell.

"Well, you are not of my blood, Celia Marianna, and it is time for you to leave. You've made your bed, just like your mother, and now you must reap the consequences."

She strode to the door and pulled it open.

"I never want to see you again."

But Celia couldn't move. For the life of her, she could not take the first step forward. She had all the answers but one. She needed only to ask the question, and she wondered if she were brave enough or foolhardy enough to do it.

Did she really want to know?

"What did my mother do?"

There was a long dead silence after she uttered the words. They hung in the air, suffused with a life of their own.

And then Celia understood; the thing she most wanted to know was the secret Gertrude was most eager to tell.

She had only been waiting for the right moment.

She spoke slowly and deliberately so that Celia would not miss one juicy detail. "Your mother and Ronald's father were lovers. And when she discovered she was going to have his baby, she ran away. And she died. As she should have. And your father never forgave her, and he loved her"—and here Gertrude's voice broke with outrage—"for the rest of his life."

When Ronald opened his heavy eyes, it was still dark and he had no idea what time it was or even where he was.

Christ! Was that his assistant calling him? It was damned stuffy in the room, and the shutters were still closed and he felt drowsy and sluggish. Why hadn't Sujatha come to wake him long before this?

He needed something very strong to wake himself up—and that silly sod out there had better stop calling out, or he would pound his head every bit as violently as his own was throbbing.

"Shut up, dammit! Give me a minute to get dressed. And where is that damned sister of yours with my morning tea?"

And where in hell was his blushing little bride? She was supposed to have been given a dose of cantharides to make her more cooperative and ready to receive him— Sujatha had promised to see to it.

And then what had happened? He'd passed out—

Where the devil was Sujatha?

Where was bloody Celia?

He needed to find his syringe and his precious store of cocaine—*that* would clear his mind.

But that bloody fool out there wouldn't give him any peace.

He pulled open the door.

"Mr. Winwood—sir! I cannot find my sister anywhere, and I have begun to worry. Last night, the coolies say they heard the cry of the *Bodilima* and now they are all afraid to leave the lines. Please—I need your help. And my sister—''

''Your sister be damned! Leave me alone until I get dressed and come out there—and stop yelling or I'll shoot your head off, you hear? Now send Kandasamy here to me at once!''

All these bloody Sinhalese were the same, he thought viciously as he rummaged through his bureau drawers until he found what he was looking for.

Bloody superstitious cowards—the lot of them.

At least Kandasamy, his head overseer, was to be counted on in a crisis because he knew on which side his bread was buttered, and he was well rewarded for any extra services he rendered into the bargain.

Ronald would take a tamil over a Sinhalese any time; the blighters were damned loyal servants too—like faithful dogs.

He remembered belatedly that he had sent all the house servants off for the night to celebrate the Buddhist *Poya* because he had intended to initiate his bride-to-be into a lot of fun and games.

And now he couldn't find Sujatha—but she would not have dared to go against his express orders, would she?

His mounting fury seemed to expand until it burst like a red explosion of rage in his head.

His hands shook with anger as he found a vein and drove the needle of the syringe into it. A moment later, he felt the dancing and tingling along his veins and the feeling of clear headed euphoria that always came with this magic potion.

By God! He could beat them all—he could best them all! He would see Sujatha come crawling back to him to lick his feet while he whipped her ripe, round bottom and made her beg for more and more punishment.

He reveled in the thought; the sweat poured off his

body and soaked his freshly donned shirt. His thoughts and plans were making him hot.

He would find those two bitches and he would make them crawl back.

But first, first he was going hunting, wasn't he? For a Rogue—or was it for the rogue male who had humiliated him?

No matter—he had a thirst for blood today, and for bloody vengeance as well, and he knew that now; armed with his potent drugged surety, he was invincible.

Kandasamy, always reliable, was seeing to his guns. And his favorite tracker, Banda, was already outside, squatting on his haunches and chewing on a wad of betel.

He would take two more coolies with him as beaters and gun-bearers; his horses could find their way along any mountain trail and down into the valleys and jungle thickets.

Yes, he was going hunting, all right—for the biggest game of all: *man!*

And it would all be written off as an unfortunate accident afterwards . . .

When he emerged from the house, blinking in the sudden glare of the sun, the last person he wanted to see or be bothered with was Sujatha's bloody brother.

What was the man doing still hanging about with that doleful look on his face and his whining complaints? Why wasn't he out looking for his rebellious sister instead of bothering him?

"Mr. Winwood, I have to talk to you! There is much trouble with some of the coolies—and then, I am sorry, but I have to know where my sister is."

"Oh, you're sorry, are you? Well, I've had enough of you and your bloody incompetence, and I'm going to give you something to be sorry about that will teach you a lesson for the future!"

He lifted his riding crop and slashed downward—

once, twice, and yet again, sending his assistant stagger-
ing back against the wall of the house with his hands
clutched to his bleeding face.

"Now, you bloody wog—get out of my way and stay
away until you learn who is the master and who is the
servant around here—and that applies to that bitch Sujatha as well! When I come back, I want her down on
her hands and knees waiting for me, do you hear? And
you had bloody well better see to it!"

The Sinhalese felt the blood seep through his fingers—
he, Anil, a high-caste Kandyan of princely blood, had
been struck in the face like the lowest of the low and
called a wog—humiliated in front of all the others even
though they had turned their faces away in shame and
horror.

His anger rose like bile in his throat, almost choking
him. This man, who had publicly called his sister a
whore, had done this and he could not—he *would* not—
let this insult go unpunished.

He turned and ran toward his small cottage; it would
no longer be his home, even if he had to live in the jungle
like a wild *veddah* to salve his pride.

He knew whom to go to—and he knew the kind of
killing spell which scared even the bloody upstart, arrogant Britishers, in spite of all their scoffing.

He swore it—for the shame and utter humiliation he
had been made to suffer and in the name of the Lord
Buddha, this Winwood would die for his crimes—and
painfully too.

He wanted to kill himself—no, he wanted first to have
his revenge and to show his sister where her stupid infatuation for this brute of a man had brought them.

He had to see the local *vedarala,* whose oils and potions would soothe and heal his face and prevent the like-
lihood of scars.

And then he had to find Sujatha, because only she had

access to those personal things that a Kattadiya would need to cast a spell.

He *had* to find Sujatha!

Grant looked like hell, and he felt worse. He had been tracking Celia all night, and he hadn't found a trace of her anywhere. He was beginning to feel frantic. Who would have believed he had become such a love-crazed fool with Celia nowhere to be found, and a goddamn rogue elephant to be hunted down.

How Willie would laugh; it was the last thing either she, or Celia's cunning old Gypsy uncle, would have expected.

Hell, he hadn't fulfilled that prophecy either: Ronald Winwood still lived, and he was still in the grip of some Gypsy spell.

He had to take some kind of action, even if it was just to question Sujatha again.

He headed out to Adriana's home only to find when he arrived that Sujatha had decamped, and Adriana had no idea where Celia might be.

"And we know how persistent you can be, darling," she murmured, smiling her cat-lapping smile at him. "What a waste that you've dedicated yourself to that little nun. But men are ever like that. It's the young ones, the innocents, that always capture their imaginations and their souls. Wasn't it so with Ronnie? You couldn't tell the son from the father."

"I thought we were discussing Celia."

"Oh, Celia—bloody boring Celia. Let me tell you about the famous Marianna instead. A much more interesting story that everyone seems to know, except Celia. This is the great secret: Ronnie's father was obsessed with her mother. The stupid man raped her—the wife of his friend. He probably thought that hot Gypsy blood and her reputation were signals to all men to just come and take the wife of a best friend. I tell you—some of these men have no taste and no tact—one has to develop a connoisseur's palate for the nuances of being taken by force, you understand. And Morris Winwood was a great bloody ox.

"So he frightened her with threats that she had better keep it a secret. I suppose it's likely she could have lived with that but—well, every story of this sort must have a moral dilemma, mustn't it? She became with child, and she knew it could not possibly be Richard's.

"Stupidly she told Morris, and that she was going to confess everything to Richard. I think she had decided by that point that she would not only tell him, but she would leave him because of the scandal. She must have intimated something of her plan to Morris because the next we knew, the bridge over the culvert had collapsed under the weight of her buggy.

"And I believe it is not impossible to infer that Morris had had something to do with that. But of course his hands were clean. Nothing was ever proved; no one ever knew—or if anyone did, he did not contest the story. Ronald told it for years in private company, boasting of what a man his father had been, but trust me, the man was a pig and a boor . . ."

And with one violent act, he had set into motion the remorseless treachery of his son and the corruption of the most innocent of them all.

Adriana was right: how stupid some men were, and how greedy. And in the end, they were left with nothing in their hands but dust.

But that story was going to end here, and Celia was never going to suffer any consequences ever again.

Before noon, all the coolies and household servants knew everything that had happened—and even what was fated to happen, for all their European masters had gone hunting for the famous Bintenne Rogue that had already killed.

There had been other hunting expeditions for other Rogues, but this time it would be different, for the cry of the Devil Bird meant death. Even old Sumanasinghe, who would go into a trance and let the devils speak through him as a warning, knew there must be a death, a human sacrifice to appease the angry spirits.

Sujatha sat weeping and rocking back and forth like a woman in mourning. *She* knew—just as she knew that she and her brother were of one blood, and that she would always stand with him.

It was the Devil Bird that had made all these bad things happen, but there was some small solace in the fact that she had the precious deed that made her the owner of the Marianna Plantation. The paper had been duly witnessed and signed by Adriana and Eddie Branham just before they left for the hunt, along with every other European in the district.

She would have at least that much left from all of this, and Anil would share it with her. She hoped it was enough to make up to him for what he had suffered, and enough to save his life.

It was time to hunt the elephant, and every other consideration had to be set aside.

Grant and Dougal Drummond started off cautiously, their tracker leading. And then suddenly they walked into a fusillade of shots, some of them coming too close for comfort.

"That's the damned trouble," Dougal grumbled, "everyone arriving at different times. We should have met at one place before we started out, and then each man would have an appointed place and the beaters and trackers could go about their business. Now look at that thorny underbrush—how can a man tell if he's shooting a damned elephant or another man?''

"I don't like it either," Grant agreed, and then he grabbed Dougal by the arm and pulled him backward just as a bullet went whizzing past his head.

"What the—!"

"Listen to me, Dougal—and for God's sake keep your voice down or we'll both be sitting ducks. I'm the one the bastard is hunting—"

I'm the one who walked head first into this damned trap, he thought disgustedly, *and all because I didn't want to let Dougal down.*

"What? What the hell are you talking about?"

"I'm talking about a mad-dog Englishman who's been too long in the sun. Think, man! Whose idea was this hunt in the first place? And who stole his fiancée right out from under his long, thin, aristocratic nose?"

He saw the comprehension dawn in Dougal's eyes. "Oh, aye. He was thinkin' about it even then?"

"Maybe not. Maybe he just likes blood sport, but now he has an excuse, and I'll be damned if I'll sit still for it. I'm going to do some tracking and trailing of my own. You understand? Celia is missing and I've got to get to him first. You just stay out of the way—and watch out for that damned Rogue when he comes charging out of cover, which he will with all this ruckus going on."

And then Grant seemed to vanish—just slipped away without a sound like an Indian—and Dougal hunched his gun to his shoulder and settled in to wait.

Ronald Winwood had sent his tracker out ahead of him with explicit instructions to first find the bad man who had stolen his wife.

First the man, then the elephant, and there would be a sizeable reward for Banda if he led Ronald to his prey.

And initially it had seemed an easy enough task for the tracker. But in a little while he realized that the quarry they were trailing had suddenly seemed to become the one tracking *them*.

It was uncanny, but this man seemed to be playing with them—with the master.

He heard the sound of dry wood cracking, which would usually invite a shot. And then directly ahead of them, he would hear the crunch of a footstep on pebbles, or the gurgle of a rock thrown into water.

Banda did not like this at all; he could be killed too, and then what would happen to his wife and children?

Even the usually impassive Kandasamy, who carried the master's guns and reloaded for him, had begun to look back over his shoulder nervously.

But the master seemed to get angrier and angrier the more the unseen one taunted him.

Ah, it would be much better for all of them if they went back now!

The master would have none of it.

He was being played with, deliberately played with. By God, it was not to be borne, and he *would* have his kill and Celia as his trophy before this was all over.

He was pouring sweat, his hair was plastered to his skull and he was mentally counting all the shots he had wasted on nothing. He wanted the bloody bastard more than he wanted anything in his life.

And the son of a bitch was a coward, afraid even to show himself!

"Come out where I can see you, damn you! I'm tired of your tricks and games. Come out and face me, you coward—or do you want me to tell the world the ugly truth about *our* Celia? I have the photographs, you know—the ones you saw were copies. There are more where they came from. You shouldn't have taken her from me, you know—I mean to make you sorry you did . . . and her too. Now come out, damn you—*damn you!*"

"The man's gone mad," somebody whispered among the onlookers.

"Quite mad. What's he talking about? The sun must have gotten the poor blighter."

"Better get out of the way—he's starting to shoot at everything now. Yes, quite mad!"

High on a hill above them, Celia watched silently, her arms folded impassively across her chest. She had climbed the hill to find a place of solitude and solace after she had fled from Gertrude. She hadn't realized she would be walking into a valley of death.

Just at that instant the maddened rogue elephant charged, bellowing, out of a stand of tall trees, a split second after Grant, his Winchester hunting rifle cocked and ready, had stepped out from the concealing scrub to face Ronald.

And now he had the choice between the elephant and Ronald—and he watched Ronald's face as Ronald realized the choice was his as well.

And he made it. He fired once, wildly, at his hated adversary before he wheeled around to face the Bintenne Rogue—and by then he had no more chances left.

Celia screamed, her terror echoing through the valley, and the coolies and trackers scattered in all directions as the huge beast picked Ronald Winwood up in its trunk and dashed his body again and again against the rocky ground, trampling him into nothingness.

Everyone froze.

And then, as the great beast raised its trunk to trumpet its defiance, Grant took careful aim and fired—and a 170-grain bottleneck bullet entered the Rogue's ear and penetrated its brain.

* * *

In the aftermath, everyone agreed it had all happened so suddenly, and everyone had a different version of exactly what had transpired.

And then there was Celia: he heard the scream through the roaring in his ears as he downed the elephant, and before it hit ground, he had found a mount and was off up the hill to find her.

That was followed by the interminable questioning of the superintendant of police. And the burial of Ronald Winwood which everyone, save Celia, had dutifully attended.

He had kept his promise to Beltran, he thought grimly as he rode back to Monerkande after the funeral. He had found out the truth about his sister's death. He had fulfilled a Gypsy prophecy—that he would travel long and far and find the one he loved; and he would not have been surprised if his stepmother had been very well aware of what would come of her throwing him and Celia together the way she had.

He felt almost as if it were all ordained by fate.

Celia believed in fate, in destiny, in the Gypsy winds and she had made him a believer too.

God, he was tired—

But not too tired, he thought as he felt himself stirring with excitement as he entered the house at Monerakande. Celia was waiting.

His love, his life, his Gypsy witch.

He wanted to marry her and carry her off with him to New Mexico and keep her at his side forever.

She was standing at the top of the steps waiting for him, her cat-eyes glowing, all doubts and fears erased.

Her nightgown hid nothing, her slender body was outlined as fully as if she had been wearing something much more revealing. Her curling mane of hair flowed to her waist, and her eyes—her cougar eyes—glowed as bright as the firelight.

Her voice was husky as she murmured, "Where were you? I've been waiting for you. I thought you wanted me—"

"Jesus Christ, Celia! *Want* you? *Want* you? I can't goddamned live without you."

And then he saw the sheen of unshed tears in her eyes, making them more glowing and brilliant, and her lips, trembling slightly as she clamped her small, white teeth over her lower lip to control her nervousness.

He couldn't get past the eyes and the mouth and the look of her; he felt as if he had never known her at all and he would never know her unless he spent the rest of his life exploring every inch of her body—and her mind—until she understood that he had been chosen to be her lover from the beginning of time.

Did he want her . . .

He held out his hand. "Come to me, Celia, come . . ."

He waited to see if she would respond, after all that had happened, out of fear or out of trust—and it was the longest moment of his life.

And then she moved toward him and took his hand in a gesture of pure faith and they stood looking at each other for one long moment.

She read the promise in his soft green gaze; he read the need, the fear, the hesitation, the desire in hers.

"Come . . ."

He wanted all of her, he wanted to give all that he was back to her—he wanted her to bear his children . . .

"Come to bed with me, my Gypsy. I'm going to keep you naked and in my bed forever—"

And she was there, suddenly, and his long gentle fingers were undressing her as he kept talking to her and touching and stroking her without even attempting to remove her nightgown.

She tumbled headlong into the promise in his eyes; he knew just how to touch her, just when not to hurry or push or prod her in any way that would make her uncomfortable.

She needed him tonight, and all the wonderful, glorious lessons he was teaching her about her body, about herself—about *him*.

Oh, and the slow, teasing, lingering way he explored her body, lifting her modest gown inch by tantalizing inch to reveal to her the pleasures of the taunting, teasing way he caressed her.

And then, and only when she moaned low in her throat, he lowered himself gently—oh damn!—so very gently at first, and then hard and possessively he thrust himself into her—into the very fastness of her, bypassing the pain—and there was pain, he saw it, he worked with it until she was ready—and then—

Oh, and then, she never could have dreamt of such sensations, such feelings as he took her with him into the realm of ecstasy.

He made her want him so! He made her crave his body, his touch, what he was making her feel.

She heard her own moaning, keening sounds in the back of her throat—such pleasure, such gasping, breaking waves of pleasure, her body out of control and his voice in her ear, whispering in tandem with the pounding pleasure, kissing her wildly, violently, as if he could not get enough of her and he wanted to absorb every sound of her pleasure into his body.

And then his culmination—that one, long, thrusting, reaching climax to their night-long exhaustive lovemaking—and he collapsed on top of her and cradled her in his arms.

"You're still too damned innocent," he murmured, his lips close to her ear. And too much had happened and she had suffered too much, and the only thing he could do was keep her safe at Monerakande and in his arms.

"Not now," she whispered, stretching languidly against him.

"Willie is coming to Peradeniya," he went on, ignoring her wriggling body, and twirling a lock of her hair around his finger and tugging on it. "And my father. We'll straighten out this mess with the estate and then I'm going to take you back to New Mexico—"

She closed her eyes as a rush of sheer pleasure enveloped her.

"As my wife."

She caught her breath, as he maneuvered her underneath him, almost as if he wanted to trap her body—and her answer—irrevocably with his.

"Celia—"

Did he sound just a little uncertain, this man of surety?

"Yes, Grant?"

"You haven't said yes."

"I haven't said no either," she countered, her body quivering as he idly ran his hand down her hip to her buttock and lifted her more tightly against his everpresent erection.

"There's hope then." He parted her legs.

"I definitely think you could convince me." She gasped as he thrust himself deeply inside her.

"Persuasive enough?"

She moaned low in her throat. "You've made—" he moved, and she groaned—"a very strong"—he moved again and she made a sharp hissing sound between her teeth—"point."

He moved again and then again, seeking the deep, hot center of her in which to cradle his love. "Say yes, Celia. My father will give you away when he and Willie arrive in Peradeniya. Your uncle will marry us. Say yes."

She met his every thrust eagerly, treasuring his every word in her heart.

He was The One, the one strong one that the Phuri Dai had told her about. The Dark One.

And whatever he wanted of her—anything—so long as she was the only only one, then she was willing, because she would die without this fierce passion that burned between them.

There was no question what her answer would be.

And when she reached her climax, on a bone-crackling slide of incandescent pleasure, she gave him the answer he wanted to hear.